The Adventures of Flash Jackson

Also by William Kowalski

Eddie's Bastard

Somewhere South of Here

The Adventures of Flash Jackson

A Novel

WILLIAM KOWALSKI

HarperCollins*Publishers*

HarperCollins books may be purchased for educational, business, or sales promotional use. For information please write: Special Markets Department, HarperCollins Publishers Inc., 10 East 53rd Street, New York, NY 10022.

FIRST EDITION

Designed by Lindgren/Fuller Design

Printed on acid-free paper

Library of Congress Cataloging-in-Publication Data

Kowalski, William
    The adventures of Flash Jackson: a novel / by William Kowalski.—1st ed.
      p. cm.
    ISBN 0-06-621136-0 (hardcover)
     1. Teenage girls—Fiction. 2. Leg—Fractures—Fiction.
    3. Female friendship—Fiction. I. Title.
    PS3561.O866 A66 2003
    813'.54—dc21   2002068668

02 03 04 05 06 ❖/RRD 10 9 8 7 6 5 4 3 2 1

ACKNOWLEDGMENTS

For matters pertaining to herbal remedies and their uses, I relied largely on Hanna Kroeger's book, *Heal Your Life with Home Remedies and Herbs*, published by Hay House, Inc., in 1998.

I would like to express my gratitude to my wife, Alexandra, who has made my life so much fuller simply by being in it, and whose critical assistance helped shape this book.

Also, thanks to my agent, Anne Hawkins, and my editor, Marjorie Braman, whose support is, as always, deeply appreciated and impossible to repay.

CONTENTS

PART ONE
Summer

1   Off the Barn • 3

2   The Man Who Wanted to Help People • 29

3   Lifting the Veil • 57

4   Celebration Cake • 81

5   Miz Powell and the CIA • 105

6   Sympathy and Protection • 139

7   Epilogue to Part One • 157

PART TWO
The Mother of the Woods

8   Paying Attention • 169

9   The Mother of the Woods • 195

10   The Tree People • 223

11   The Bad Thing • 243

12   Say Hello to Lilith • 263

13   The Hardest Thing • 281

In memory of W. S. "Jack" Kuniczak,
who taught me how to stand at ease.

PART ONE

Summer

① Off the Barn

On my very last day of being sixteen years old, I fell through the roof of our barn like a stone through ice and broke my leg in three places. Don't ask what I was doing up there to begin with—I couldn't give you a straight answer. It had never entered my head to go up there before. I was just in a roof-climbing kind of mood, I guess—the kind of mood that can overtake a farm girl sometimes on a hot July day, when she's bored out of her mind and thinking that if something wonderful and glamorous and exciting doesn't happen to her *immediately, right that minute,* she's going to go crazy. Like I said, it was my last day of being sixteen, and I guess I was feeling my oats a little. That's the only way I know how to explain it. Even a half-wit like my neighbor Frankie Grunveldt would have known better than to climb that barn. My great-great-grandfather built it about a thousand years ago, and the passage of time had turned it into one of those ancient, leaning weathered things that tourists and Sunday drivers think are so wonderful and quaint, but are really only eyesores and death traps.

I was still in my good clothes. It was one of those rare Sundays when Mother had insisted I go to church with her. She got that particular bug up her butt about three times a year. I fought her hard on it, but she always won. Church was the one and only reason in the world I would wear a skirt. I had to, or Mother got upset. I think she had skirts and salvation kind of mixed up in her mind—you couldn't get one if you weren't wearing the other, at least if you were a girl. I had compromised by wearing my ratty old canvas high-tops, the most comfortable things I owned. I never wore socks. I was always taking off my sneakers, tree climbing being an art best performed barefoot, and socks just had to be balled up and stuffed somewhere. One time I stuck them in my bra and forgot they were there. That got me a lecture, I can tell you—but not the kind you might expect. Mother said, "If you're going to stuff yourself, young lady, at least do it in a way that won't let the whole world *know* you're doing it."

That's Mother for you. I guess she was relieved, thinking maybe I was trying to catch the eye of some slack-mouthed idiot of a farm boy. She had pretty much given up on me becoming a normal girl, but occasionally she was still given to flashes of hope—or random moments of insanity, as I prefer to think of them. Well, she had another think coming, as they say. I wasn't interested in farm boys, with their ropelike arms and their beetle brows. I wasn't interested in *any* boys. I was just interested in being me, whatever that entailed. If that happened to involve a boy, okay. If not, I wasn't going to shed any tears.

Climbing trees is hard work, and according to Mother it's not very ladylike, but neither of those things have ever posed much of an obstacle to me. I like getting a little sweaty, and there isn't a tree within two miles of our place I haven't climbed at least once. None of them seemed as challenging as our barn. Yet once I got up on the lower branches I swung across to the overhanging roof, and that was it. I was up.

I crawled up the roof on all fours until I arrived at the peak, where the weather vane that looked like a bear had kept watch since the barn was erected. I couldn't remember a time when it hadn't been rusted in place. I decided I was going to get that weather vane pointing right again. I worked it around until it creaked free, and I spit into the socket a couple of times until it moved without screeching.

Then, feeling mighty satisfied with myself, I stood up and took a look around.

From that distance I could just see the town of Mannville, founded first as Clare Town sometime in the early 1800s, then renamed after our Great Benefactor, the Almighty William Amos Mann, Hero of the Civil War, a raggedy old bastard we all had to learn about in school. Mannville at that distance was a few rooftops and a church spire. I could also see Lake Erie, a thin blue smudge that hung over the town like smoke. My last conscious preaccident memory is that I'd finally managed to accomplish something interesting and useful in my life by getting up higher in the world than ever before, when damned if the roof didn't give way and I woke up later that afternoon in the hospital.

That's life, my father would've said. You can work and work to get to the top, but you still never know when everything is going to collapse under you.

I don't remember falling, which I guess is probably a good thing. Otherwise, I might have come out of the whole mess with a fear of heights. I'd never been afraid of heights before, you see, so it would have been a real shame if I'd started then. Oh yes: my name is Haley Bombauer, I am now twenty-something years old (not to be rude, but I'm already getting to the age where it's none of your business) and I'm not afraid of a blessed thing on this earth, no man or woman or beast or barn. Well—actually—I do admit snakes make me squeamish, but I have since learned from a certain Miz Elizabeth Powell that fear is a useless emotion, one that will map your life out for you if you let it.

The secret, of course, is not to let it.

It was Frankie Grunveldt who found me, the crazy guy from up the road. I shouldn't call him crazy, but since he was always forthcoming about the fact that he was a schizophrenic I guess there's no harm in me stating it for the record. That's what this is: a record of my seventeenth year, which was when things finally began to happen in my boring life, or maybe it was just when I learned to see through slightly wiser eyes that there was already a lot going on around me. That was the year I learned the answers to some things I'd always wondered about, and forgot about other things that up until then had seemed mighty all-fired important—such as dolls, which are about the only really girly trait I can lay claim to, and kissing movie stars, and shit like that. Seventeen was a big year for me, bigger than for most folks if I may be so bold, so I figured I might as well write it all down. If you're not interested in this sort of thing you better stop reading right now. I'm writing this for myself, thank you very much. It's important. There's a lot to remember, and a lot to get straight; plus, writing is what my friend, Miz Elizabeth Powell, would have called "cathartic." As near as I could figure, cathartic meant like when you rammed a snake through a drain—not a *real* snake, but a plumbing snake, which is a metal coil about forty or fifty feet long that's used to get rid of clogs. Your mental pipes tend to get clogged up after a while too, just like the pipes under your kitchen sink. Writing is something you can use to jostle everything up and get it moving again.

Anyway, Frankie, who was ten years older than me but acted about ten years younger, saw me go through the roof. He ran and got my mother, who called an ambulance. We live so far out in the country, the nearest town being Mannville, New York, that it took them a good long while to get there. No ambulance had ever come to our farm before. But then again, nobody'd ever broken a leg in quite so many places before either. My poor old bone snapped in three. Or I should say seven, because you actually have *two* bones down there in your lower leg, which was something I did not know until I busted mine all to hell. I'm told also that my femur—that's the thigh bone—was sticking out of the skin. Now, *that's* something I regret not seeing. It must have been quite a sight. I imagine my skirt probably flew up over my waist, too, which means Frankie most likely saw parts of me he was not intended to see. I *was* wearing panties, for those of you who are wondering.

Frankie gave most people the creeps, but he never bothered me any, and I'm comfortable with the fact that he saw my underwear. Frankie was not the sort of fellow to take advantage. He had a bad habit of spying on me, but that was nothing personal—he spied on everyone. It was only because he was bored. He wasn't a pervert. I never minded it much before my accident, not even when I happened to see the sunlight glinting off his binoculars, and afterwards I was downright grateful for it. If it hadn't been for him, I might have lain there in the barn for days. My mother never went in there anymore. Nobody did, in fact. I kept my horse, Brother, in a smaller shed that my father built a few years before he died. Brother's shed led into a corral, where he could stretch his legs if he was so inclined. That shed, our house, a little pond, and four acres made up the Bombauer property. It wasn't much, but as my mother was always pointing out, it was a lot more than the poor people in Africa had, and so we ought to be grateful—which I guess, in some ways, I am.

I was doomed to spend the summer in a cast, indoors. It was a cruel blow, I can tell you. I'm a country girl, and I grew up outside—running around with some of the more civil local boys, fishing, swimming, riding Brother. In summer I'm as brown as a nut, and wintertime doesn't slow me down much either. The snow gets deep around here in January and February, sometimes drifting up as high as my head. When that happens I shovel us out, and sometimes I ride Brother out to my grandmother's place and shovel her out too. I like snow, I must say. It has a way of quieting things down, nice and peaceful—not like someone yelling at you to shut up, but like they're whispering that you should sit down and relax for a while. Some of my happiest memories are of those long rides out into the woods with a big wide shovel strapped to my back, the snow three or four feet deep and unmarked except for the tracks of birds and rabbits, and Brother pushing his way through the drifts as though he was part Alaskan husky. You wouldn't see a single car on a day like that, and if an airplane happened to pass overhead it looked so small and far away you could hardly believe there were a couple of hundred people in it, sipping coffee and reading the paper as though they were in their very own living rooms.

That's winter around here, white and perfect. But if I had to pick a favorite season, it would be summer, the time of birds and rumbling thunderstorms. Back then if I felt like stripping down to nothing and taking a dip in the pond, I just did it. Still do, as a matter of fact. Frankie isn't around anymore to spy on me, and my mother has by and large given up on telling me what's ladylike and what isn't. Of course, I'm old enough now to know better. That much about me is different. But summer itself has stayed unchanged.

I was in the hospital almost a week. When I came back I had a cast up to my hip and a metal rack sticking out of it that was so big you could have used it to dry your laundry. The rack was there to hold the pins in place—I forgot to say they pinned my bones together, to keep me from coming unraveled, I guess. The doctor said I'd be in that state for about eight weeks, and then they'd take the pins out and put a shorter cast on, and then when *that* was done there would be some kind of a brace, just to make sure everything stayed straight. All in all, I'd be out of action for months. I'd already decided I was going to get better faster than anyone in medical history, but for now I was about as useful as a doorstop, and the idea of being stuck inside all summer was enough to make me lose my mind.

This accident was so bad it caused Mother and me to have words.

"Maybe this will teach you not to be such a tomboy," she said to me.

"I doubt it," I said. "Will you go buy me a pack of cigarettes?"

She started, putting a hand to her throat. "I will not!" she said. "What on earth's gotten into you?"

"I have to do *something*," I told her. "I can't just sit here and *cogitate* all summer, can I?"

Mother got an annoyed look on her face. She sidled out into the living room, where I could hear her rustling through the dictionary. I shouldn't have teased her like that, I know, since she barely had any real schooling and I was going to be a junior in high school next year, but sometimes I just couldn't help myself. She seemed to know so much, I got a zing sometimes out of springing something on her she *didn't* know. A minute later she came back in.

"A little bit of *cogitating* might do you some good," she said, looking mighty smug. "You could cogitate about why young ladies shouldn't climb trees and barns, especially when they're wearing dresses."

"I'm not a young lady," I said. "My name is Flash Jackson, and I'm a stuntman trapped in a female body."

Mother rolled her eyes and left the room. I could tell I'd upset her, asking for cigarettes—it was only a joke, but I remembered too late that cigarettes had been my father's undoing, and hearing them mentioned always brought a little shimmer to her eye. *Well, screw it,* I thought. That was almost eight years ago now. And *I* was the one who had her leg wrapped in rock-solid plaster. That entitled me to a little orneriness, I guessed. But still I felt bad, so I reached under my bed for my plastic tub of paper, got out a few sheets, and set about making her an origami crane. She had about a hundred of them already, but one more would perk her up a bit. They always did.

Frankie was my first visitor—he came the next day.

"Happy birthday," he said. "I brought you a frog."

"So you did," I said. "Thanks. Set 'im right there next to the bed, wouldja?"

Frankie put a margarine container on my nightstand. It had holes punched in the top to let air in. I looked inside, and there was a tiny little pond frog, along with a few tufts of grass and the lid to a jam jar. The jar lid was filled with water. I guess Frankie thought the frog could take a bath in it.

"I caught him in your pond, so he's already yours," said Frankie. "But I thought he could keep you company while you get better."

"Thanks for saving my life, Frankie," I said.

"You're welcome," he said.

He perched himself on a chair next to my bed, his baseball cap getting a workout in his hands. Frankie was about the most nervous fellow I'd ever met. He couldn't handle talking to most adults, and even other people my age usually scared him off—he didn't know how to take them, nor they him. Frankie had taken a few knocks in his time, on account of being so different, and it had left him a little touchy. But he liked me all right. He'd been allowed to hold me when I was a baby— that was how long we'd known each other—and I was about the only person who never made fun of him. He didn't *look* crazy, but he did look *different*, I guess because it's true what they say about the eyes being a window to the soul. You could tell that his soul was confused and unsure of itself, maybe a little homesick. Frankie had green eyes, and sad. You always got the feeling around him that he didn't quite belong on this planet, in the same way saints didn't fit in, which is why they all got martyred. There are some people who just aren't meant to be here for long, I guess. Frankie's eyes were the most different thing about him—that, and the fact that he acted like a ten-year-old most of the time. He watched as much of the world as he could from his thirdstory bedroom, where he hung out the window all day with a pair of binoculars, staring and staring. He claimed he could see Canada when the sky was clear enough. I asked him once what it looked like over there and he looked at me like *I* was the crazy one.

"Same as here, more or less," he said. "Buildings, trees, ground, sky. Whadja think, they all walk around on their hands or something?"

That was Frankie. You never knew when you asked him something if he was going to answer like his crazy self or his regular self.

Frankie lived with his parents, who were already pretty old when he was born. The unkinder wits in this town used to whisper that his sickness was punishment for them fooling around and having a baby so late in life, but I put that down to small-minded gossips who don't have enough going on in their own lives. There's a lot of *that* in this town—believe me, I know. I've borne the brunt of it more than once, because of my ungirly ways. Pretty soon the Grunveldts were going to sell their house and little bit of property. It was already listed, in fact. They were too old to take care of it anymore, and nobody believed that Frankie could take care of himself—except me and Frankie, that is. I thought he would be just fine, if only everyone would leave him alone. And Frankie believed exactly the same thing.

"So," said Frankie. "You're seventeen now."

"Yup," I said.

"Got any plans for the future?"

I could see pretty easily what mood Frankie was in—he only had about three. This was his Serious Conversation mood.

"None to speak of," I said. "I'm thinking about running away to Europe, soon as my leg is better." This was not true, of course—but the beauty of talking to Frankie was that it didn't matter what you said. None of it made sense to him anyway.

He nodded and pursed his lips. "I see, I see," he said. "That sounds like a fine place, Europe. My father was there in the war. It's a good idea, Haley. A very good idea."

"Thank you," I said.

"I suppose you're going to start dating soon, now that you're seventeen?" he said.

I choked back a laugh. "Not bloody likely," I said. That was a British phrase I'd picked up in a book somewhere and used whenever I could. You could get away with stuff like that with Frankie. He just smiled and nodded, doing his best to act like a normal adult man talking to a woman. It just about broke your heart sometimes. I think he was twenty-seven or twenty-eight that year. You could tell he wanted to hang out with people, that he was hungry for human contact. Only problem was, he had no idea how to talk to folks. Poor guy probably wanted to start dating, too. Not *me*, I mean. Just dating in general. It was lonely being crazy.

"I see," said Frankie. "Not bloody likely, eh?"

"No, Frankie," I said. "Not bloody likely at all."

"Hmm. Very interesting," he said. He looked at his bare wrist as though there was a watch on it—which there was not—and stood up. "Well, it's been a real pleasure chatting with you," he said, with excessive formality. "I've got to get going now."

"Okay, Franks," I said, trying not to smile. "By the way, did you happen to get a look at my underwear while I was passed out in the barn?"

He was so startled that for a minute I was afraid I'd traumatized him. "What?" he asked.

"Oh, never mind," I said. "I just hope it was clean, that's all."

"Hee-hee," Frankie said.

"You did, you little sneak, didn't you," I said.

"Hee-hee," Frankie said.

"Get out of here," I said. "Thanks for the frog."

"Bye, now," said Frankie. "Stay off the barn for a while, hear?"

When a person is trapped indoors for too long, the mind starts playing around with things. Frankie telling me to stay "off the barn" stuck in my head until it started sounding like one of those phrases such as "on the wagon," like people say to mean when they stop drinking. After only a day of sitting inside and watching that miserable little pond frog do nothing but breathe, "off the barn" seemed like a good way to express what it was like to be a lady. "I'm off the barn," I could hear myself saying to people, and they would know I meant that I'd given up my errant ways and settled down to a life of sewing lace doilies and drinking tea. The opposite, of course, was "on the barn," which would mean that I was behaving exactly like my usual self. I would go racing down the road on Brother, my braids flying out behind me, and folks would shake their heads and say, "There goes Haley. Been 'on the barn' for weeks now, and no telling when she's coming off again." It was a good metaphor, and it pleased me that I'd thought of it.

Then my thoughts turned to poor Brother. I didn't know what I was going to do about him. He had to be fed and watered at least twice a day, and there was no way I would be able to carry the hay to his stall—Mother had been doing it since my accident, and she would have to keep on doing it, too. As soon as I was able to get around on crutches, I tried to make my way down to the shed. But the ground there was muddy and soft and covered in manure. My crutches sank into it and made me nearly lose my balance several times, and once I got to his stall all I could do was pet him and give him a little bit of a currying before my leg started to ache something awful.

Riding him was out of the question. He knew something was wrong with me, and he shied away from my cast at first, thinking in his horsey way that I was not the same Haley he'd always known, just because I had this new white thing on my leg. Horses are smart, but not *that* smart, and it took me a little while to talk him out of it.

"It's just a cast, old buddy," I said. "Nothing to be afraid of."

He flattened his ears and stretched out his neck like he was going to bite it.

"Go ahead," I said. "Bite it right off me. Just leave those pins in, or there's no telling what all will happen. I could come apart like a Chinese puzzle."

He didn't bite it, though. He just sniffed it once, like a dog, which I do believe he sometimes thinks he is, and then once he realized it was only me he calmed down.

Brother was a gift from my father, who bought him as a foal from some neighbors of ours, the Shumachers. I named him Brother because a brother was what I wanted most in those days. Really, I think I wanted to *be* a brother, and have a little sister—life as an only child is a curse I wouldn't wish on anyone, especially if you happen to be a girl. Life as a girl is pretty bad, all things considered. Seems like you can't just do what you want—you have to do what other folks want you to do, or they might think ill of you. Those are my mother's words, "think ill." The worst thing that could happen in her world is that someone would think ill of her. God forbid. Myself, I don't give two craps in the woods what anyone thinks of me, whether it's ill or good or whatever.

Brother was mostly chestnut, with white stockings on his front feet and a white blaze on his forehead. I never found out exactly what kind of horse he was, though he looked kind of like a quarter horse. I am very proud of the fact that I broke him with only a little help from my father, and rode him almost every day after that. Brother was used to a lot of attention. But I couldn't take care of him as well I could before, and Mother was afraid of him, just as she was afraid of all large animals.

"Brother," I told him, "we've got tough times ahead. I'm going to be off the barn for a long while. Not by choice, you understand. By necessity."

He swiveled his ears around like radar dishes.

"If we lived in a more civilized world, I'd turn you loose and let you be your own horse," I said. "You could get married and have babies, and you could bring your family back to visit whenever you were in the neighborhood. But as it is, that's out of the question, because the world has not yet attained that level of perfection in which horses can walk around and do as they please. Someone would steal you. Or worse."

Brother whickered at me. I let him rub his soft mouth on my neck, smelling the hay on his breath.

"I'm not sure what we're going to do, old pal," I said. "You understand?"

He understood. He looked depressed and resigned.

"That's right," I said. "No more midnight rides to warn folks the British are coming. No more racing our shadows down the road. Just a long, boring summer. A *very* long summer."

Hickety whickety, said Brother with his lips. And *plibbity slibbet.*

"My sentiments exactly," I told him. Sometimes that horse was downright eloquent.

By then all the blood had rushed down to my leg, and it was pounding like a bass drum in an oompah band. I let Brother out into the corral so he wouldn't have to be cooped up in his stall all day, and

I crutched back on up to the house. Then I collapsed on my bed and squinched my eyes shut tight.

I was mighty near to tears at that moment. I hadn't cried once so far, not even when I woke up in the hospital feeling all scared and confused, nor when the pain became so bad that I wanted to holler. But now, when I realized that I couldn't even so much as go for a ride on my beloved horse, it seemed like almost more than a guy could be expected to take. I snuffled and snorfed as quietly as I could, not wanting Mother to hear me and come in all fluttery and cooing. I hadn't cried in front of her since I was a little kid. Instead I popped a pain pill down my throat, and soon it started to ease the leg, and then, since that stuff makes you drowsy, I fell asleep.

I must have slept the whole afternoon away. When I woke up it was almost dark out, and Mother was standing over me in the gloom like a ghost. She was saying something I couldn't understand. *Your Norse is grout*, she said. *Your course is doubt.*

"What are you talking about?" I grumbled.

"Your horse is out!" she said.

I sat up fast, but I had to lay back down again. I was hot and feverish, and my head was swimming.

"Call Frankie," I said. "He'll know what to do." Frankie and Brother had sort of an understanding, you might say. They had known each other as long as Brother and I had, and Frankie was the one other human that Brother didn't resent. I knew Brother would do what he said.

But Mother said, "There's no need. Somebody already caught him for you."

"Who?"

"A neighbor. Miss Powell."

"I don't know any Miss Powell," I said. My heart was racing, and I knew a fever had spread from my bones through my blood and was working its way up to my brain. Maybe that's not the correct medical explanation, but that's what it felt like—all those breaks had created bad energy in me, and my body was heating up to fight it off. I have a natural understanding of the workings of the human system, you see. It's inherited from my grandmother.

"She's a new neighbor," said Mother. "And she already put him back in the shed for you."

Ordinarily this kind of news would have shocked me outright. Brother didn't hardly listen to anybody. For a total stranger not only to have caught him but to have put him up in his shed without getting her front teeth kicked out was incredible. He was that temperamental. To tell you the truth, it made me a little jealous. But, as low as I was, I took it all in stride.

"Ma," I said. "I don't feel so good."

She reached down and felt my forehead.

"You have a fever," she said.

"I'm sorry for every rotten thing I've ever done and said."

"Oh, my, you *are* sick. I better go for your grandmother," she said.

"I've been a lousy daughter," I said.

"I'll go get her right away."

I must have been as delirious as a drunk on the Fourth of July to say things like that. And I didn't even flinch when she said she was going for the old bag. Normally that news was enough to send me off into the trees until the coast was clear again. Call me crazy, but I had an aversion to old ladies whose faces are hairier than some men's, even if she was my own flesh and blood. Besides, I could barely understood a word my grandmother said, so there wasn't much point in me talking to her. She didn't have any teeth left, and she spoke half in some weird kind of German and half in English. But at that moment I didn't care how scary or ugly she was, because I knew she could make me better. She always did.

"I'll wear a dress every day from now on if you want me to. I'll stop climbing trees. I'll be good," I said.

"You're a good girl, Haley," said Mother. "You're not that bad. You're just *willful*."

"I don't wanna have a broken leg anymore," I said. "It hurts. I hate it."

Mother brought me a glass of water and tried to give me another pill, but I didn't want it. I was confused enough already, what with having lost six or so hours of the day. Even though everything on me hurt now, I wanted to feel it. I wanted to let the fever burn me clean.

"I'll be back in a couple of hours or so," she said. "It'll take her that long to get her things together."

"Can't we just have a regular doctor for once?" I mumbled.

But I didn't really mean it. That was just the "willful" me talking, the me that didn't care who thought ill and who didn't. I knew that when it came right down to it, there was nobody in the world as good at curing illness as my mother's mother, the old lady who everybody thought was a witch, even in this day and age.

Here's the story about my old Grandma. She was a Mennonite, which is a kind of religion, in case you hadn't heard. People tend to get Mennonites confused with the Amish, which I guess is understandable, considering they're both Anabaptists. The Amish are a lot more old-fashioned, though. Somewhere back in time, the Amish and the Mennonites split off from each other—I don't know exactly when, history not being one of my strong points. It seems some folks felt they weren't being hard enough on themselves, so they stuck with the horses and buggies, and got rid of all the electricity, et cetera. I guess they decided that would bring them closer to God. Only thing I've never been able to figure out is, when the Amish separated from the rest of us, electricity hadn't been invented yet, and *everybody* was riding in horses and buggies, because there weren't any cars and wouldn't be for another couple of centuries. Kind of makes you wonder that maybe if the whole thing happened today folks'd be saying, *We're sticking with our old-fashioned VCRs and cassette tapes—none of those newfangled CDs for us!* Anyway, we have the same beginnings, but our kind of Mennonites have less restrictions than the Amish do. We can ride in cars if we feel like it, or have electricity, or any dang old thing we want.

I don't go to church anymore, and never got much out of it when I did, but my grandmother was the opposite of me—she was what you'd call Old Order Mennonite, and was about as religious as a person could get without floating straight up to heaven. She wore long, plain dresses with a shawl, and a kind of starched lace handkerchief on her head, and she lived in a tiny shack in the woods, without electricity or a telephone, or anything that might be considered a distraction from a life of Godly goodness—whatever *that* might consist of.

Now, you may have already realized that my mother and I were *not* Old Order. The reason for that is a long story, and I suppose I'll get around to telling it soon enough, but for now it's enough to say that Mother and I lived at the end of the twentieth century, and Grandma lived somewhere in the middle of the eighteenth. That's considerably bigger than your *average* generation gap, I believe.

And my grandmother was odd even for Old Order. I may not be the churchgoing type, but one thing I do like about Mennonites is that they believe in the importance of a community—everyone sticks together and helps each other out, which is a way of life that a lot of the world has lost now. You don't usually find Mennonites living off by themselves. But my grandmother did, kind of like a lady hermit— a witch, in other words. Now, even though she gave me the creeps, here is one point I get a little touchy on. It's a case of antiwomanism, plain and simple. It's always been fine and dandy with everyone if a *man* wants to take off by himself and live in the woods or something. That seems to make him automatically smarter, or wiser, or more holy, or something—people assume he must know something the rest of us don't, and sooner or later they trek out to his tree or to the top of his mountain or wherever to ask him some deep and important question, such as *What the hell's wrong with the Buffalo Bills these days, anyway?* But when a woman does the same thing, she's suspected of witchcraft. Folks think she's up to no good out there all by herself, cooking up

evil potions and eating any children who might happen to wander
into her strawberry patch. Oh, the world is a stupid place sometimes.
I heard no end of cruel comments from folks about my grandmother,
the same folks who thought old Frankie should be locked up somewhere, the same folks who made fun of me for not acting like a girl.
People love to romanticize small-town life, how folks sit around the
general store and chew tobacco and talk on and on about things,
just taking life easy. They seem to forget that what those folks do
mostly is *gossip*—and there never was a bit of gossip that did anyone
any good.

To fetch my grandmother, Mother had to drive our old pickup
about fifteen miles down County Road, due south, and park next to a
big old birch tree that had been standing there since God was in short
pants. There were no towns for many miles in any direction from that
point—you were smack in the middle of nowhere, and praying you
didn't spring a leak in one of your tires or run out of gas. Then she had
to strike out along a path through the woods. It was a path my mother
knew well, since she'd grown up at the other end of it. After about a
mile, she would come to the little clearing where my grandmother
had her shack. Likely as not she wouldn't be home right then—even
though Grandma was old, she was in pretty good shape, and she spent
a lot of time wandering around in the forest gathering herbs and berries
and roots, and grubs and snakes too, if you believed the stories people
told about her—which I didn't. She used these things in making her
homemade medicines, which could cure just about anything: fever,
ague, flu, the vapors, colds, menstrual cramps, menopause, skin rashes,
snakebite, cross-eyedness, you name it. Grandma lived off what she
grew in her garden, which was considerable in size, and also whatever
supplies my mother or others would bring her every once in a while.
She used her own waste as fertilizer (don't get me going on the specifics
of *that*—it was quite an involved process, and not very pleasant to
talk about, even for me) and got her water from a stream that ran
nearby. In short, she preferred to do things her own way.

You might be wondering to yourself, now, why didn't that foolish girl see what an interesting grandmother she had, and why didn't she go out there and spend more time with her? There are two answers to that. One, it was a god-awful pain in the ass to get to my grandmother's place, and that was the way she liked it. She wasn't crazy about having visitors, not even her own relations. Two, my grandmother and I never did have much to say to each other. She didn't approve of girls who wore shorts, for example. In her opinion, a woman ought to wear a long plain dress, and not let any part of her show except for her hands and face. Ankles were out of the question. So you can imagine her reaction whenever she saw me in cutoffs and a halter top. There are other examples I could give, but you get the picture.

Once in a while, some curious soul would go out there to see if they could strike up an acquaintance with my grandmother. This was usually a graduate student, or some religious type, or somebody like that. I have read a bit of Henry David Thoreau's *Walden*, and I see how folks living a modern life could be interested in someone who was living "deliberately," as Mr. Thoreau said—which I took to mean living like you meant it, doing everything for yourself and not relying on anybody else to help you. Grandma was nothing if not deliberate, and she never wanted anything to do with anybody from the outside world. It was hard enough just to get her to talk to my mother and to me.

She had reason to be careful of outsiders, too. Another thing about my grandmother that I don't mention much, for obvious reasons, is that she had a big old patch of marijuana growing out there in the woods. She'd been using it medicinally for decades. I don't think she even knew it was illegal. She smoked it herself once in a while in an old pipe, but mostly she burned it over her patients, whoever they might happen to be, and chanted the little "spells" that she'd learned when she was a girl—I don't know if they were really spells or not, but they sure sounded like it, and stuff like that didn't help her reputation any.

There was another kind of person who went out to see my grandmother: those who had someone sick at home, and who needed her to

come take care of them. You'd be surprised how many people still have
more faith in the old ways than they do in the new. Grandma didn't
trust many people, but if there was somebody in a bad way somewhere
she'd always agree to go out and see them, after hearing a description
of their symptoms and bringing along the things that sounded right.
Often as not that included a little box full of dope. She'd smoked me
up good a few times before, when I was sick—though I was rarely ill as
a child, except the one winter when I got pneumonia, and the odd cold.

My grandmother, the pothead. I don't know how many plants she
had out there, maybe ten or twelve. The law had never given her any
trouble, but sometimes high school kids snuck out there and tried to
help themselves to her stash. I guess it probably would have been the
kind of thing boys dared each other to do. I know some boys who were
likely to do such a thing, and to tear up her garden besides, just out of
plain meanness. It had happened before.

So I knew what was in store for me when Mother got back with
the old lady. I'd have to drink some nasty brew that made your tongue
want to curl up and die, she'd burn a little of the green stuff, and that
would be that. Strange thing was, it always worked. She'd put her
hands on me to find out exactly where the problem was—not the leg,
for sure, that being the obvious one. No, it was more likely she'd say
there was something out of whack with my liver, or my kidneys, or
my humors weren't in the right balance. She'd have been laughed right
out of every hospital in the western hemisphere, but every time she
put her hands on me I felt better right away. You could feel something coming out of her and into you, and when it stopped it was like
she'd reached into your guts and shifted things around just a little bit,
just enough to set things right again.

I was asleep when they came back. I could hear Grandma mumbling
to herself like she always did, clomping across the floor in her big
black shoes. Ma whispered something to her and dragged a chair over
to my bed. I heard the old lady wheeze as she set herself down in it,

and I got a whiff of her breath, and then of the rest of her. That woke me up, I can tell you. Jesus H. Wilson, but she was rank. I guess bathing is a trial when your only source of water is a creek. Grandma probably washed herself once a year, if that.

I just laid there with my eyes shut. I wasn't faking being asleep—it was dark now, but what little light there was in the room hurt my eyes, and I kind of felt like I was dreaming. I felt her run her hands over me to see where the problem was. That woman wasn't shy, either. She gave my hooters a good squeeze and rummaged around my personal area for a moment or two, probably trying to sense whether or not I was still pure down there and when my monthly visitor was coming, waving his little red flag. That was all part of the cure, and you just had to lay there and take it. Then she kept her hands on my abdomen for a long while, and I could tell she'd found whatever it was she was looking for.

"Blocked," she said to my mother—only she said it in German. I can never remember German words off the top of my head, but when I hear them I know what they mean.

Mother said something back to her, and then they left the bedroom and went out into the kitchen, where they talked a while longer. I guess they were arguing about where she would sleep that night—Grandma would want to go back home, and Ma wouldn't want to drive her until morning, since it was already dark out. Finally they settled it, which means Mother won, and Grandma thumped her way up the stairs to the spare bedroom. Mother came in again to see how I was doing.

"Haley?"

"Yes, Mother."

"How are you?"

"I feel as chipper as a corpse."

"Don't joke about things like that," said Mother.

"Sorry. Did she say what it was?"

"Yes. You're constipated, that's all."

I knew it. Seven times out of ten, there's nothing wrong with you that a good crapola won't cure.

"What'd she say to take?"

"Just eat a big salad. That should get things moving again. All that medication they gave you in the hospital slowed your system down. She said she could smell it coming out of your skin."

I breathed a sigh of relief.

"Thanks for getting her, anyway," I said. I still had my eyes shut.

"A cup of coffee might help, too."

"All righty."

"You want me to fix it for you now?"

"Won't it keep me up?"

"You slept all afternoon, didn't you?"

So I sat up and Mother made me a cup of coffee and brought me a bowl of greens from our garden, and sure enough about an hour later things got moving again. I hobbled my way into the bathroom and just let nature take its course, and almost immediately I could feel the fever lifting as all that poison left my body. God bless Thomas Crapper, who perfected the indoor toilet. I would have hated to be using an outhouse at a time like that, what with the snakes that might be crawling around under there.

Not that I'm afraid of snakes, you understand. You just have to be in a certain kind of mood to appreciate them.

Next morning, early, Mother got up and drove Grandma back out to her place. Soon after that I got up and levered myself into the kitchen, where I made some toast and another cup of coffee. I set the little pond frog out on the back step—"The pond is thataway," I told him, but I figured he already knew that, being an animal. Animals are born knowing what's most important for them, and they don't bother with anything else, which is something about them I've always respected.

I was feeling about ten times better by then, and was even starting to feel like a busted leg didn't necessarily have to mean that my entire life was ruined. It's hard to be gloomy on a morning such as that, with the sky a bright blue and the first rays of the sun poking their way into the kitchen. Our house is a cheerful place, I must say. Ma had it fixed up very nicely, with hand-sewn curtains in all the windows and the whole place always in a dust-free state. A number of my dear departed dad's creations could be found throughout the place, too: furniture, lamps, a clock. Dad was very handy with a set of tools. He'd built the addition on our house, in fact, and also Brother's shed, as well as his own workshop, which used to stand where the pond is now. That workshop was where he came up with his inventions. Most of his gadgets weren't useful for anyone except us, but there were a few things he managed to patent. That was partly how we lived, in fact. Royalties were still coming in from one of his widgets. It wasn't millions, but since we owned the house and land, that and his life insurance was plenty to keep us going, as long as we didn't suddenly develop a taste for designer clothes.

Mother came back around ten. I could see right away she was in one of her snits—something Grandma'd said to her about the way she was raising me, no doubt. The two of them got along like dogs and cats most of the time. I just let her be. She went upstairs to her bedroom and closed the door. I knew sooner or later she'd get worked up enough to the point where she'd have to come down and give me a lecture, and then it would be out of her. It always came down to something I'd done wrong, somehow. In this case it was climbing the barn. All right, I admit that was one of my more boneheaded moves. Every little escapade of mine was like a miniature nuclear explosion: There was always fallout, sometimes lasting months. And this was definitely the biggest bomb yet.

When, oh when, are you going to learn? she'd wail. I tried so hard to turn you into a lady, not a man. If only your poor father were still alive—it's too much for one person to take on by herself, this child-raising business. And I would point out to her that it was mostly Dad's fault I turned out the way I did, if fault was even the right word, which I didn't think it was. He was the one who taught me how to ride, how to climb, how to fish and hunt and swim. If I didn't know better

I'd think Dad would have preferred a boy instead of a girl. Matter of fact, he *would* have been more suited to a son, but we never held our personal shortcomings against each other, and they never slowed us down any. He'd been my best friend up until the day he died—we did everything together. I know he'd been looking forward to having a kid, period. Even if he was disappointed on the day I popped out, he never showed it. He just went ahead and did all the things with me he would have done with a boy, and we had high old times. That was a long time ago, but there wasn't a day that went by when I didn't remember some little thing he'd done or said, or for that matter that I didn't use something he'd made with his own two hands. Poor old Dad. Poor old Mother. Poor old everyone except me. I don't waste time on self-pity, thank you very much. I do what I want. Life is too short to while away sitting around in parlors with your legs pressed neatly together so no one can see your coochie, like some kind of lady-in-waiting, fretting about what's happened to you. There's too much to *do*.

Which reminded me that old Brother would be expecting me about now. I made my way down to his shed again and gave him a good brushing, talking to him all the while.

"Now, what's this I hear about you making a break for it yesterday? What's the matter—you don't think you have it good enough? Free room and board, and all the attention a horse could want. All you have to do is let me ride you once in a while, and hell, you like that. Yes, you do, you old horse. Now, I can understand you being *despondent* over this whole business about my leg. You think it means that's it for us, that our riding days are over. And I know you don't like Mother feeding you and brushing you and traipsing around in your own personal barn. Well, let me tell you something, horse. This is only a minor setback. A dip in the road. That's all it is."

Shobbety shoo, said Brother. *Plbbbbbt.*

"You're just an ingrate, that's all. Soon as things get tough, you want to hit the road. Now, you listen up good—we're in it for the long haul, you and me. If *you* broke *your* leg, I wouldn't just give up on you, now, would I? Some folks would take you out back and give you a bullet in the brain. A hot lead cocktail. Execution, gangland style. Shame on you, you old fleabag. And just where the hell were you going, anyway? Where were you headed when you hopped the fence?"

"I believe he was showing quite an interest in my geraniums," said a voice behind me.

I was so startled I forgot I was only working on one gam, and I spun around too fast for the laws of physics to catch up with me. Plop—down I went, into a nice big pile of Brother's poo. I let loose a streak of words so blue that even I was shocked at myself. A bolt of pain shot up my leg and out the top of my head, or so it felt, and when I managed to get to my feet again I was ready to tear whoever it was a new one. You don't sneak up on Flash Jackson, not if you want all your limbs to stay in their original places.

It was a little old lady wearing a tweed skirt suit and an old-fashioned hat. She couldn't have been more than five feet tall, and she was standing in the doorway of the shed, looking for all the world like some kind of elf.

"My goodness," she said mildly. "I haven't heard those kinds of words since the war, and then it was usually from a man, not a young lady."

That was about all I could take.

"Listen, Broom Hilda," I said, "I don't know who the hell you think you are sneaking up on a guy like that, but you have a few things to learn about manners!"

The old lady pursed her lips and stared at me. She wasn't much to look at in terms of size—I mean, she was a tiny little thing—but those eyes took on a steely glint, and suddenly she seemed to grow about three feet. She took in a big breath of air, and I was expecting her to give back to me as good as she got, but she only let it out again. There was a very long moment of silence that she was the first to break.

" 'Guy'?" she said. "Do young ladies in this part of the world refer to themselves as 'guys' now? My goodness, I have been away a long time, haven't I?"

She had an English accent, or at least what I thought was an English accent. The only English people I'd ever heard talk were on television and movie screens, so she could just as easily have been from Botswana and I wouldn't have known the difference. But everything else about her seemed English too—her clothes, her little hat, even the way she carried herself. I just knew she was the kind of person who drank tea with her pinkie sticking out. And even though she was at least six inches shorter than I was, she didn't *act* short. Her personality was ten feet tall.

"And I do seem to recall there being certain restrictions on the kinds of language one uses in speaking to one's elders, when I was your age. Have those, too, fallen by the wayside?"

This lady spoke like the books I read sometimes, in my quieter moods; she was like a character in one of them. Something about her made me calm down right away, and I began to feel something I hadn't felt in a long time: embarrassment.

"No, ma'am," I said. "They haven't."

"I am *so* relieved to hear it," said the tweedy lady. "You must be Haley. I met your mother yesterday."

"You're—you're the lady who brought Brother back home?"

"Yes, my dear," she said, smiling for the first time. She stepped forward and held out a hand. "My name is Elizabeth Powell, and I've been away for a long time, but I'm home to stay. I do apologize for startling you. I thought you'd hear me come in. And may I say what a great pleasure it is to meet you?"

We shook hands, me making sure first that mine was clean. She was that kind of lady—so well pressed I felt dirty just looking at her, and it didn't help that my hind end was covered in horse shit.

"Put 'er there," I said. "Flash Jackson's the name. Most folks just call me Haley, though."

"Then that's what I shall do, if it's all the same to you," said Elizabeth Powell. "By coincidence, I knew a fellow named Flash many years ago. He was an excellent runner. I'm afraid speaking his name aloud brings up painful memories."

"Why? What happened to him?" I asked.

"He was shot dead by the East Germans," said Elizabeth Powell.

Well, that was about the last thing I'd been expecting to hear. I must have looked like a fish, standing there with my mouth opening and closing while I tried to think of something to say, but she saved me the trouble.

"You are a sight. It's my fault, too," she said. "I'm afraid you look as though you've been *fertilized*, my dear. Shall we take you up to the house and clean you?"

"Yes indeed, we sure shall," I said.

I had only known Miz Powell for two minutes, you see, but already she was rubbing off on me.

2

The Man Who Wanted
to Help People

Miz Powell turned out to be the sister of another neighbor of ours, a neighbor I haven't mentioned yet because she kicked the bucket about a year ago—that was old Emma Powell. Until recently I never even knew Emma's last name, though I knew her all my life. We just called her Emma. That was unusual, considering how big folks around here are on Mister and Missus and other terms of respect-for-your-elders. Emma was kind of a recluse. Although she'd lived just up the road, I only met her a handful of times. Mother was always sending me up there with a few ears of corn or some raspberries from the garden, or whatever else we had too much of. Usually I just rang the bell and left them on her porch, because I'd learned from experience that Emma didn't like to answer the door. I shoveled her out a few times in the winter, too, but I never stuck around to ask her for any money—you didn't do that with neighbors, and besides I knew she probably didn't have any money to speak of. Nobody around here does. It's what you might call a depressed economy.

There hasn't been any money in farming for a very long time, as anyone can tell you who's tried it, unless you happen to be a big farmer with hundreds of acres—and then you usually rely on government subsidies to get you through the rough spots. We don't have any big farmers around here anyway. The Shumachers have a decent-sized dairy herd, but even that wouldn't have been enough to support all the people living in that house. It would be hard enough to support just *two* people with dairy money, and at one time there had been as many as twelve or fifteen Shumachers, though some of them were only temporary— foster children, you see. The remaining Shumacher boys mostly had jobs in town, and the girls made quilts to sell to tourists. Most folks around here have about three different things going at once, just to make ends meet—they might sell vegetables and eggs at roadside stands, or deliver the newspaper, or whatever you can think of. Small wonder most young people hit the road once they leave high school and head for more exciting places, like Erie or Buffalo or Pittsburgh. I was getting to the age where I might start thinking about leaving myself, since I'd be graduating in another couple of years. But bored as I was, I couldn't see myself leaving town for good. Sure, I might wander around the world for a year or two just to see how things were done in other countries, but Mannville was home, and home reminded me of Dad…and as much as I hated to admit it, I was pretty attached to Mother, too, God bless her incompetent ways. If I left, there was no telling what would happen to this place, or to her.

Anyway, old Emma never did thank me for anything I did. From time to time I'd see her peeping at me from behind her curtains, and she'd wave and I'd wave back, but that was the extent of it. She never married, which in my opinion shows that she had more going on upstairs than most folks, and as far as anyone knew she didn't have any relations—until the day Miz Powell showed up.

The story, as she told it, goes like this. Way back in the dark days of World War II, Elizabeth joined the WACs and went away to England to do some work for the war effort—that's the Women's Army Corps, you know. She liked England so much that after the war was over she decided to stay, and there she'd been all these years, until her English husband died almost at the same time as her sister back home did. Then she decided to come on back to New York State to revisit her old girl-hood stomping grounds, and to take care of business—Emma having left behind an old farmhouse, and an acre of two of land that would need to be disposed of.

Of course, Miz Powell would never have used a phrase like *stomping* grounds herself. It was too ungenteel.

After I got myself cleaned off and had put on a fresh skirt—ironically, I was going to be wearing skirts for a long while, at least until the cast came off—I listened as she rattled off her story. We sat in the parlor chatting, me with my leg propped up on an ottoman. I hate chatting—I even hate the *word* "chatting"—but I felt like I could afford to lower myself a bit if it meant I could learn more about her. A person like Miz Powell did not come along every day, after all. She was fascinating, like a walking, talking museum exhibit plopped down in our very own living room. And things were going along just fine until Mother heard us talking and had to get in on the action herself. She made us some tea and broke out the sweets, and just like that I was trapped in the middle of a regular old hen party.

Now, this was not what I'd intended. Under normal circumstances, I would've busted out of there faster than you could say Nat King Cole. I'd rather sit in a bathtub of acid than hang around with a couple of yappy old broads. But being in the condition I was in, I was forced to sit there and take it.

"What an *interesting* life you must have led!" Mother kept saying, in a voice so high and sweet and full of fake politeness it just about made me ill. It was the same voice she used with the minister. She was a great one for laying it on thick, especially if she was talking to someone who acted like they were better than the rest of us—which I must say I thought Miz Powell was doing. I guess it was the English accent. If she was born here, which she was, then she would have talked like a regular person, now, wouldn't she? But there she was, ripping out one "rawthah" after another, saying things like "jolly good" and "brilliant show," which try as hard as I might, I couldn't imagine anyone actually saying outside of a book—and all of it in this strange kind of pronunciation. She was practically talking through her nose, and you had to watch close if you wanted to see her lower jaw move, because it seemed like the object was to hold it as still as possible. The worst part was that Mother started trying to imitate her, in her own pathetic way. "*Do* have anothah cookie," she kept saying. I wanted to smack her. Even I knew that English people didn't say "cookie." They say "biscuit."

But Miz Powell just went along with it. I'm not sure she even noticed Mother's cheeseball attempts to sound English herself. "*Thenk* you," she said. "De*light*ful." She took a tiny, mouse-sized nibble of a Nabisco vanilla wafer that I knew for a fact was about six thousand years old. Then she took a sip of tea, and damned if that pinkie didn't come flying out. I knew that for the rest of her life Mother would hold her pinkie exactly that way whenever she drank anything, even water.

"Whatever happened to your leg, Haley?" Miz Powell asked me.

"Oh, well," I said, "that's a funny story. I was just—"

"She fell down the stairs," Mother interrupted me. "Just slipped and fell. A *dreadful* accident."

"Oh, dear," said Miz Powell. "Did it hurt very badly?"

"It hurt like a thundering bitch," I said, fuming. Oh, Lord, I was about ready to blow a gasket. First of all, I hate being interrupted. And second, I knew why Mother was lying: because climbing barns was unladylike, and above all she wanted us both to appear like a couple of proper misses in front of this fancified, stuffed old specimen.

But I learned long ago how to fight my battles with Mother. It didn't work to attack in the open, like an army would, because she just started sniffling and crying and then she would run upstairs and slam her door, and if that happened in front of the Queen here, we'd both look like a couple of idiots. I would use guerrilla tactics instead. I'd take potshots at her from behind bushes and trees, when she was least expecting it. That was how I would get my revenge. Later.

The two of them went on nattering at each other for a while longer, and I learned more of Miz Powell's story, which as much as I hated to admit it to myself sounded kind of interesting. She had all kinds of tales about bombs falling on her, or near her at any rate, in London during the war, and others about how tough the English folks had it with rationing, much worse than it had been here in the States. Even years after the war was over, she told us, an English person couldn't get a bag of sugar or some butter without having to move heaven and earth. Mother made sympathetic little noises at that, because she was old enough to remember those days. I myself was underwhelmed. Like I said, history is not one of my strong points, and neither is cooking—though I did like the stories about the bombs.

Miz Powell didn't have any children. She and her husband, who she called the Captain, seemed to have traveled a lot. She mentioned about six countries in one breath. Though I wanted like crazy to hate her for being a show-off and a priss, the fact was I couldn't. She was too damn interesting. For one thing, Brother had trusted her enough to let her lead him back into his stall. Now, *that* was something. It told me she must have been all right, because Brother was an excellent judge of character. For another thing, she'd been everywhere. She'd gone to places I hadn't even heard of before—where the hell was Kuala Lumpur? Where was Singapore?—but she didn't talk about them like a regular tourist would. She just *mentioned* them, as casual as if she was talking about going to Buffalo. And I couldn't forget that fellow she'd talked about earlier, the one she'd called Flash, who ended up getting shot by the East Germans. Now, how on earth did she even know someone who would find themselves in that kind of predicament? I barely knew what an East German was. I knew that once upon a time there'd been a wall dividing Germany down the middle—the good ones lived on one side and the bad ones on the other, or so I heard it, and the wall ran the length of the country. I figured they had to put it up after Hitler came along, to keep all the Nazis in line. They'd taken it down since, though. If I thought about it, I could recall hearing stories about people trying to escape from the bad side onto the good side, and sometimes getting shot at. I wondered if this Flash fellow had been an East German himself and was trying to make it over to the West. I made up my mind to ask her later, when Mother wasn't around. Mother had a way of taking a conversation over and making it sound stupid, no matter what it was about.

After about eighty years of us sitting around and making nicey-nice with each other, Miz Powell said she had to be getting along home. I hopped up on my crutches and said I would walk her out the door. I said it fast because I didn't want Mother coming along.

"Rawthah de*light*ed to meet you, Ms. Powell," said Mother. "Do come by again."

Oh, Lord, just shoot me now, I thought.

But Miz Powell nodded and smiled. If she'd picked up on what a fruitcake my mother was, she didn't let on. "I shall, my dear Mrs. Bombauer," she murmured. "I shall."

"Let's skedaddle," I said, and I headed through the screen door and down the steps as fast as I could.

"Thank you, dear," said Miz Powell, when we were outside. "It's not necessary for you to walk with me, though. Your leg must be quite painful."

"It ain't that bad," I said.

I usually never said ain't. I prided myself on speaking better than most of the yahoos in this pisswater burg, because of all the reading I'd done. But Ms. Powell's speech and accent and everything else about her were so dandified and high-toned that it kind of brought out the worst in me. "I didn't fall down no stairs, neither," I said.

"You didn't?"

"No, ma'am." I picked my way down the porch steps and crutched along the driveway to the road, Miz Powell walking beside me. "I fell through the roof of that there barn."

"You fell through the—" She cut herself off as she looked at the barn. "Why did your mother tell me you fell down the stairs?"

"She gets kind of embarrassed at me," I said. "I'm too boyish for her liking, I guess. Doesn't want to admit she has a daughter who likes climbing things."

"Why, it must be fifty feet high!"

"At least," I said. I dropped my local-yokel act. It wasn't lost on her, but suddenly I felt pretty stupid.

"What were you *doing* up there?"

"Just looking around," I said. "I was bored."

"Ah, yes. I see."

"You see what?"

"I mean, I understand how easily one grows bored around here. Don't forget, I grew up here myself... although that *was* a very long time ago."

Miz Powell was starting to sound less foreign and more normal, though maybe that was just me getting used to her. She took a moment to look around the countryside. From our house, you could see three other houses—the Grunveldt place, Emma's house up on a slight rise maybe half a mile away, and then in the other direction the Shumacher farm, which at that distance was just a dark cluster of buildings on a hillside. That was it. It was all pastureland and cornfields around here, with a couple of vegetable patches thrown in for variety. If you stopped and listened, you wouldn't hear a blessed thing. Maybe a tractor belching somewhere, or a cow fart.

"When I was your age," she said, "there were times I thought I would go absolutely mad if something exciting didn't happen to me."

"Yes, indeed!" I said. "Lord a'mighty! I know exactly what you're saying."

"The country is peaceful enough," she said. "Heaven knows there have been times in my life when I missed it terribly. But if it's all you've ever seen, it just seems like..."

"Slow death by roasting?" I suggested. "About as much fun as a mouthful of pins?"

Miz Powell laughed. Not a prim, proper laugh with a handkerchief pressed to her mouth, but a good, open hearty chuckle.

"You do have a way of saying what's on your mind, don't you, Haley?" she said.

"Yes, ma'am," I said.

"I think we understand each other perfectly," she said.

By now we'd only just passed Frankie's house, but my hands were already getting sore. I still wasn't used to walking on those crutches.

"I don't mean to be rude, but I think I'm going to stop here and turn around," I said. "This is about as far as I've gone on these things, and I don't want to overdo it."

"I understand, dear," she said. "I'll be fine from here." She stopped. "What on earth is that young man doing hanging out of that window?" she asked.

"Oh, that's just Frankie," I said. I lifted up one crutch and waved it at him, but he was too busy staring at us to wave back. "He's a little touched in the head. He spends all his time spying on people. He doesn't mean any harm, though. He saved my life, actually."

"Indeed," said Miz Powell. "I wonder what kind of binoculars he's using."

That was a curious statement. *What on earth would she know about binoculars?* I wondered.

"Anyhow, thank you for tea, Haley, and I'm sure I'll be seeing you soon," said Miz Powell. "Do stop by sometime, when you're more able to get around."

"You're welcome, ma'am," I said. "I sure will."

"And you can stop calling me ma'am," she said. "My name is Elizabeth."

"All righty," I said. "Elizabeth. Can I ask you something?"

"*May* I ask you something."

"May I...ask you a question?" I felt shy, suddenly. I was so surprised at myself I forgot to get mad at her for correcting me.

"Yes, you may."

"How come you talk with an accent?"

"Do I, dear?" She seemed surprised. "Oh, no. I tried so hard to stifle it. I didn't want anyone to think I was..." She trailed off for a minute. "I've been gone a long time, that's all," she said. "A very long time. My friends in England always teased me because of how American I sounded, but I suppose after almost fifty years...oh dear. I'll have to work on that, now, won't I?"

"That's all right," I said. "I like it, actually." I realized, as I said that, that it was true—I *did* like it. "I just wondered, because you said you were born here and everything, but you sounded so—"

"People can be changed by places, Haley," she said with a twinkle in her eye. "That was the reason I left home in the first place—to be changed. I was looking for adventure, you see, and the war came along at just the right time."

"Yes, ma'am," I said. "I mean, Elizabeth."

"Someday I'll tell you some more of the story," she said. "I think you're the kind of woman who would appreciate it. You'll come by for tea this week, yes?"

"All righty," I said, though two tea parties in one week was about twice as many as I thought I could handle.

"See you then, dear," she said, "and by the way."

"Yeah?"

"Come alone, if you don't mind." She winked at me. I smiled.

"I don't mind one bit, Elizabeth," I said. I guess Mother had gotten on her nerves after all. Well, she'd certainly done a good job of hiding it.

Elizabeth turned and marched on up the road like marching was what she'd been doing all her life. I had completely forgotten to ask her about Flash—the other Flash, I mean. That could wait until I saw her again. As far as I was concerned, I was the original: Flash Jackson, stuntman extraordinaire, who on top of having to suffer the indignity of living in a girl's body was now confined to crutches, and to having a twenty-pound deadweight attached to his leg.

You're probably wondering by now whether I wasn't just as crazy as poor Frankie, what with my carrying on about this invisible person inside me. Did she really believe there was a man trapped inside her? you may be asking yourself. Was she plumb loco? Did she have a screw loose? Well, that's actually a separate question. Living out in the country will make anyone crazy, if that's not what they're cut out for. And just because you're born in a place doesn't mean you're cut out for living there. I didn't mind it much, to be honest, apart from the occasional bout of mind-numbing boredom, but I certainly had to come up with my own ways of entertaining myself, and pretending I was Flash Jackson was one of them.

It was actually my old Dad who came up with that name, not me. We used to play games together when I was little—hide-and-seek, cowboys and Indians, cops and robbers, and my particular favorite, stuntman. Stuntman involved doing all kinds of things that seemed awful exciting, such as swinging out of trees on a rope, or locking myself in a trunk and then making my daring escape. Of course, the branch I swung from was only about three feet high, and the trunk was never locked at all. My dad was always standing right there in case anything went wrong. But it was his imagination that made it all seem so dangerous and exciting—that, and the fact that I was about seven years old.

We both had stuntman names. Mine was Flash Jackson, and his was Fireball McGinty. Fireball McGinty's specialty was jumping a bicycle off a ramp and over a row of my dolls. I wasn't allowed to do that one, because it really was dangerous—I mean, it wasn't life threatening, but there was always the chance that I would fall over and crack a tooth or something when I landed. We would drag a piece of plywood out from the storage area under the house and prop it up on cinder blocks. Then Dad, who had a bit of a wild streak in him, would start off on his bicycle at the far end of the driveway. He'd race down as fast as he could, shouting at the top of his lungs, and then launch himself over. The ramp was only about a foot high, if that. It was hardly death defying. But it seemed to me at the time that it was.

Poor old Fireball. As it turned out, his stunt name was sort of a prediction of how he would die. I wasn't home when it happened—I was in school. The principal came and got me out of my classroom, which was nothing new. I figured I was in trouble again. In fact, I'd been in a fight that very afternoon, my fortieth or forty-first of my career—I was a great brawler in my younger days, but that's going back to first grade now—and I just assumed I was going to be hauled in and lectured one more time about the evils of violent behavior and the need for "self-control," which is *still* a phrase that raises the hair on the back of my neck.

That never happened, though. Instead the principal gave me a lollipop, put me in his car, and drove me home. The first thing I noticed when we got there was that Dad's workshop was gone. In its place was a great gaping crater, with a couple of chunks of smoldering wood lying here and there.

That's how cigarettes killed my Dad. It wasn't lung cancer, which is how they usually get you. It was that he was smoking too close to his stash of nitroglycerin, which he'd bought from a friend of his who owned a construction company and which he was planning on using in one of his experiments. God only knows what he was going to do with it. Not being licensed to handle such stuff, he didn't know just how volatile it was, and I guess he thought his cigarette was safe enough. Nobody knows exactly how it happened, of course, but since he was a smoker, that was the likeliest explanation. That's what the fire chief said, anyway.

You can laugh if you want to. I've had a giggle or two over it myself, after enough time had passed that it didn't hurt quite so much to think about him. I mean, it was a fitting end, though it was way too soon for him to go. And dramatic, too. People still talk about that day. You could hear the explosion way off in Mannville, and folks felt it for miles around. His workshop was obliterated—I mean, just *gone*. It was a huge blast. Luckily, the shed was far enough from the house so it didn't blow up too. It knocked out all our windows, though, and for a while there wasn't a cow in this neck of the woods that would give milk. Mr. Shumacher lost a whole week's worth of dairy money, though he never complained about it. And there was just this big hole in the ground where Dad's shop used to be. As chance would have it, there turned out to be a natural spring running just under the surface there— there's aquifers like that all over the place—and within a few days, the hole was filled with water.

That's where the pond came from. After a while, it looked like it had always been there. Reeds and other water plants grew around the edges, and soon ducks and geese included it in their yearly flight plans. I even got the bright idea of putting some goldfish in it, and they've been living there happily ever after, growing and reproducing. It's only a tiny little thing, as far as ponds go—maybe ten feet deep and fifty feet across. But what I like about it is that it's *alive*. There wasn't enough left of my father to bury, as you might imagine. I was too young to be told such things, but I heard later that they were finding little bits of him for weeks, in the most unlikely places. You can understand if I prefer not to go into that.

There's a headstone for old Fireball in the cemetery, but there's nothing under it. This pond, though—now that's the kind of memorial I want when it's time for me to take the Big Sleep. It's a living, breathing ecosystem, and by now a whole generation or maybe even two generations of fish have grown up there and called it home. Mother won't go near it because it reminds her of him, but I love to spend time at it, or sometimes *in* it, with my snorkeling mask on—just looking at all the bugs and plants and little fish in there, and thinking about old Fireball McGinty and the good times we used to have.

Anyway, that's how I got the name of Flash Jackson. After he died,

I got pretty attached to thinking of myself that way, because it was his name for me. I guess by now it's more than a habit. It's become the real me.

I had gotten kind of lost in the clouds for a minute there watching Elizabeth head down the road, so I roused myself and headed back for home. But then I remembered Frankie, who was still hanging out of his window. I waved at him to come on down. He just stared at me through those stupid lenses of his until I shook my fist at him and pointed to the ground in a threatening manner, meaning if he didn't get down here right now I was going to knock his block off. He came running downstairs and across his yard to the road.

"What?" he said.

"Haven't you got any manners?" I said. "That lady was Miz Elizabeth Powell, and I think there are nicer ways for you to welcome her to the neighborhood than to ogle her like she was an exhibit in a museum."

"What lady?" he said.

"You numbskull," I said, pointing down the road at Miz Powell's rapidly retreating back, "*that* lady."

"I wasn't looking at her," said Frankie. "I was looking for a car."

"What car?"

"I don't know what it *looks* like," he said. "Not yet. But I'll know when I see it."

I noticed then that old Franks seemed pretty nervous about something. He was wringing his baseball cap in his hands again. He only did that in two situations: when he was sitting and talking, or when he was worried. "They're coming today," he said.

"Who's coming?"

"Some people. Some buyers."

"Oh," I said. I understood everything then. "You mean, buyers for the house?"

He nodded. He looked so miserable I thought he was going to cry, so I stretched out my arms and gave him a big hug. Franks was not the greatest hugger in the world—I don't think he really understood what it was all about. He kind of leaned forward at the waist and let me put my arms around his shoulders for a minute, but that was as into it as he would get. Ordinarily I *never* hugged him, but he looked so upset I couldn't help myself.

"Don't worry about it, Frankie," I said. "Let's go pet Brother. Shall we?"

"Pet Brother?"

"Yes. Take your mind off of things."

"I don't know if that's a wise idea," he said. He was dancing around, wanting to get back to his window. "They might come while I'm gone."

"Who cares?" I said. "It's not healthy for you to get so worked up. Besides, you can see the road from my house just as easily. Come on, let's go."

"Not a wise idea, Haley. Not a wise idea."

"Let's *go*."

"Oh, all right," he said; because when it came down to it, Frankie was more like the brother I'd always wanted than anything else, and he always ended up doing what I told him.

We headed back to my house, Frankie trailing behind me. My leg was aching by then and I would have liked nothing better than to go prop it up somewhere for a while, but I didn't like the idea of old Franks sitting up there in his room all day, fretting himself to pieces. I had a soft spot for the old fruitcake. Brother liked him too, and I knew Franks would calm down if he had something to do, so I let him brush the old horse all over again and then saddle him up and take him for a jog around the corral. Brother needed a good run anyway.

Franks was a good rider, his insanity notwithstanding. There were some things he did just like anybody else would do them—most things, in fact. You only knew he was nuts when you started talking to him, or when he forgot to take his medication. I didn't know what kind of pills he was on, but I did know that if he didn't take them he started hearing voices in his head, telling him to do things.

It wasn't like the voices told him to kill people or anything. I asked him about it once, but Franks wouldn't tell me what they talked about. He said they just flat out bothered him, the worst thing about it being that they wouldn't shut up. When the voices were on, he felt like there wasn't a safe place in his entire head for him to go.

"Like, I can plug my ears, but I still hear them," he said. "Sometimes I try to drown them out with noise, but that doesn't work either."

"That sounds terrible," I'd said.

"It *is* terrible," he said. "Mostly. You ever read the Bible, Haley?"

"I guess," I said warily. I tend pretty quick to drop out of conversations that involve religion. But it was usually my grandmother who was starting them up, not Franks.

"You know after Cain killed Abel, and God said his blood was crying out from the ground?"

"I know that story," I said.

"I think Cain must have heard voices too," he said. "He was trying to pretend he didn't do anything wrong, and he was hiding from God's voice. But no matter what he did, he could still hear him."

I didn't say anything. I'd never heard Frankie talk about the Bible before. I hadn't even known he could read, to be honest. I mean, I figured he *could*, but I didn't know he actually *did*. I stayed quiet, just listening to him.

"Sometimes I feel like Cain," he said. He had a sad look on his face, sadder than I'd ever seen before. "I run and run from these voices, but they always find me. Only thing is, I didn't do anything *wrong*. Did I, Haley?"

"No, Frankles," I said. "You didn't do anything wrong."

"All I did," he said, "was be born. And I couldn't help that."

I don't mind admitting I got a bit choked up then. Even at the best of times Frankie seemed confused by the world, kind of like if he had his druthers he'd hop on the next spaceship off this rock and go where people understood him. I never realized until that moment what a trial those voices were, how they hounded him, like a criminal. They mocked him, they poked fun at him, but worst of all they stole his peace of mind. And when that kind of thing is coming from inside you, well, what can you do about *that*?

But the other thing the voices did was to give him ideas. I'd seen Franks during one of what they called his episodes, which happened sometimes even when he did remember to take his pills. He was a different man then—wild-eyed, talking a mile a minute. The big one was about a year ago.

I'd noticed him from the house, walking up and down the road, waving his arms and jabbering on and on. Sometimes he would stop and point at something that wasn't there, or at least nothing that I could see, or he would throw his arms out at the fields like he was welcoming crowds of people. Mother told me to leave him alone, but I went out and talked to him anyway. I think she was a little afraid of him when he was like that, just like she was afraid of everything. But me—well, you'd have to do worse than act crazy to scare me off.

"Hi, Frankie," I said. "What are you doing?"

He stopped in midsentence and stared at me, his mouth hanging open.

"Franks!" I said. "It's just me, Haley. You know me. Remember?"

"Yes," he said. "Of course I remember you."

"What are you doing?"

"Making plans," he said.

"Plans, huh?"

"Yes. Plans."

"For what?"

"I can't talk about it," he said. He started shuffling around in the dust of the road, muttering to himself and kicking up big clouds. "This one can go *here*," he said, "and this one can go *here*, and this one can go *here*...."

"Don't you trust me, Frankie?" I said. "Don't you want to tell me what you're planning?"

"No."

"C'mon. Please? *Please?*" I didn't mean to bug him, you see—I just was a little worried about him, and I thought it might be a good idea for him to talk through whatever was on his mind.

"All right!" he yelled, throwing his arms up in the air. "All right, all right, all right! Just shut up!"

"Sorry," I said.

"Not *you*," he said. *"Them."*

"Who?" I asked, though I knew who he meant—the voices.

"My head hurts," he said. "Okay? It hurts, so don't be loud."

I stayed quiet.

"The pillars can go right here, along the road," he said, pointing to where he'd been shuffling around in the dirt. I looked. He'd marked out a big X with his feet. "One here, and one over there, and one down there, and so on. Got it?"

I followed where he was pointing and saw that he'd made a whole line of big X's in the road, about fifty feet apart.

"And the front doors will go over there," he went on. "The stage can be where that field is—we'll have to level it out, but I think it will work. And the dressing rooms will have to be on the second floor, or maybe in the basement. If we even have a basement. I'm not sure if we can, because it depends on whether I can get John Fitzgerald to loan me his backhoe. But it's going to be a big one, see? A really big one."

"A big what?" I asked, thinking meanwhile, *Note to self: Call John Fitzgerald and tell him to keep an eye on his backhoe.*

He sighed. "A theater, Haley," he said. "That's what I've been trying to tell people, but nobody listens. A theater of the human spirit."

I was impressed, though I had no idea what he was talking about. Whatever he had in that unraveling little mind of his, it certainly *sounded* grand.

"Who's this theater for?" I asked.

"Anyone who's human qualifies as a performer," he said. "It's automatic. You can get up onstage and do whatever you want. But first, I want it to be for the Indians. They get first shot at it."

I had to pause a minute to be sure I heard him right.

"You're building a theater for Indians?" I said. "Here, in Mannville?"

"It's not just for them," he said. "It's for *everyone*. But they should have the first chance, because they haven't been allowed to tell their story yet. This will be a place where people can come and tell their stories. They've been *silenced*, Haley. It's not right. Someone has to help them get their voice back, and I'm going to do it."

"My goodness," I said.

"You think I'm crazy," he said.

"No, I don't."

"Yes, you do."

"Frankie..."

"Look," he said. He jammed his cap on his head and looked at me. His expression was wild and haunted. There was a kind of desperation in his eyes, and that look he normally had—the look of being homesick, soulsick—seemed to have spilled over his whole being. "I know how to raise money for it and everything," he said. "*You* don't have to help. I don't need *you*. I can do it alone. It's important, Haley. Someone has to give them their voice back, or I don't know what will happen. But it'll be bad. It's already bad. And it's going to get worse."

"What's going to get worse?"

"The state of communication," he said. He looked up at the sky and licked his lips. Then he took his hat off again and started twisting it. "The state of communication in the world today," he said, "is very, very bad."

"How are you going to raise the money?" I asked him.

"I can't tell you that," he said. "It's classified. But when I get it, I'll build the theater and they can come from all over. People from the whole world can come right here, and they can get onstage and tell everyone their story, and then things will be okay again. People will understand each other."

Well, you can't have a proper conversation with someone when they're rambling on like that, but all the same there was something to what old Frankie was saying. I don't know how he got this idea about Indians, or about people in general—I mean, what is a theater of the human spirit? Don't ask me, though I liked the sound of it. As far as I knew, Franks didn't know any Indians, and I couldn't imagine he knew much about their history either. I wasn't even sure whether Frankie had ever been to school. I knew a fair bit about the whole story myself, about relocation and reservations and the way Indians had been outright hunted—and he was right. They *had* been silenced. I'd never thought of it that way, but that was what it was.

There were a few Natives left around this area. Seneca, mostly. I imagine that once upon a time they had whole villages with lots of people, but now they just ran a few souvenir-and-discount-cigarette stores and held referendums every year on whether or not they should build a casino. They kept to themselves, pretty much. If you didn't deliberately go out and look for a Seneca, you'd never see one. That was the way it had been ever since I could remember, and certainly it had been that way since my mother's time—probably not even my grandmother remembered a time when there were still Seneca villages. It had been at least a couple hundred years since they'd lived according to the old ways around here. Probably more.

But there was something, some kernel in Frankie's idea, that made sense. Not on an everyday kind of level, but a more...I don't know, a spiritual level, I guess. I don't usually think along those lines. I'm a practical, down-to-earth sort of guy—I mean, woman.

But that was how it was talking to Frankie. Just when you thought he'd finally gone off the deep end, he'd say something that rang true somewhere inside of you, and you had to rethink the whole question of whether or not he was as crazy as he sounded. Who was crazier, anyway—a man who wanted to help people, or a society that didn't care much one way or the other?

Frankie never remembered his episodes once they were over, but all that business about a theater had stuck somewhere in the back of my mind, and though I hadn't thought about it in a while I mused it over again as I watched him ride Brother around and around the corral. Frankie hadn't mentioned his theater idea since that day. Fact is, he disappeared for a week or so after that, and when he came back he was acting normal again, or at least as normal as it was possible for him to be. I don't know where he was taken or what they did to him there, but now that I thought about it, it seemed a little spooky. Where did they keep people who weren't making sense to the rest of the world? And what did they do to them to get them to act right again?

I'd have to find out, I decided, if only to satisfy my own inquiring mind. I wouldn't be able to ask Frankie, though. I'd have to ask someone else.

Then I passed from this subject to Miz Powell. All kinds of questions about her began to pop up. For example, why did she still have her maiden name, if she'd been married for so long? Had she gone back to it after her husband died? And why was she interested in what kind of binoculars Franks used? And why was Flash killed by the East Germans? And why did someone as dramatic and exciting as her want to be friends with me?

It was times like that I wished I had someone my own age to talk to about things. I felt some kind of excitement surging up in me from somewhere I couldn't name, the same feeling that had made me climb the barn. It was killing me to have that broken leg; sometimes, back when I was seventeen, I felt like I could run around the whole world twice just to burn off extra energy. And I wanted someone to share that energy with. But one thing about where I lived was that there was a great shortage of people to talk to. I had a few friends from school, but most of them were boys, and during the summer they all had jobs and couldn't be bothered to come visit poor old gimpy me. I didn't have one female friend that I could think of, not any good ones, anyway. Most of the girls at Mannville Junior-Senior High School thought I was weird, which I guess compared to them I was—but I took that as a compliment, considering who it was coming from. They were the lipstick set, the hair curlers and makeup wearers who thought the main purpose of their existence was to attract attention to themselves. Lord knows I'd tried, when I was younger, to be more like them, but it never felt right.

Before my accident I'd never missed having friends much. There was always Brother, who I rode all over God's green earth whenever I'd a mind to. We went exploring everywhere, through the woods and across fields and way out into Amish country—now, those folks were *really* isolated. It seemed like you passed through some kind of invisible barrier whenever you entered their territory, and you went back a hundred years or so. They kept to themselves most of the time, which was what I liked about them. I could go a whole day without exchanging a word with another human being, and considered myself richer for it, not poorer. But now that I was stuck leaning against the corral fence, watching and wishing, I started kind of taking stock of things. My life was flat-out dull, I realized. Something would have to be done about that.

Maybe I would give old Roberta Ellsworth a call. She and I used to be good friends when we were little, I mean *years* ago. But we had kind of gone different ways as we got older, if you know what I mean. Sometimes that just happens, for no particular reason. Sometimes I felt bad about not spending any more time with her, since it had been me that drifted away from her, not the other way around. Roberta had become a wallflower—but if she wasn't interesting, she was at least nice, and she'd be someone to talk to. Someone besides my mother and poor old Franks and my horse.

Old Roberta didn't have many friends either. She wasn't pretty enough, which if you're a girl means basically it's all over for you. That's not what *I* think, but it's the rule most people seem to live by, at least in high school. Roberta had a tendency to pick her nose in public ever since we were in kindergarten, and she always sounded like she needed to blow her nose. Not exactly Miss Popularity material. But when you have a broken leg, and you're stuck inside all summer...hell, at least we could talk about something different for a change, and I could tell her all about Miz Elizabeth Powell from London, England. It might be good to catch up with her, and see what all had taken place in *her* life in the last six or seven years. Just for a change of pace.

I'm no raving beauty myself, you know. I haven't mentioned much about what I looked like back then, but the fact is I was pretty over-weight—so is Mother, so it's genetic—and my hair has always been kind of stringy and thin, and my hips are almost as wide as my shoulders. I wasn't getting a lot of attention from the fellows on the football team. Which was fine with me, of course. The people I care about don't mind what I look like. But it's not pleasant being one of the plainer girls in school. Even if you don't put much stock in how much attention people pay to you, it's still kind of hard to get ignored all the time. It wears on you after a while.

Out in our neck of the woods you can hear a car coming when it's still pretty far off. I think Brother heard it first, because his ears kind of pricked back and he looked around as he was running. Then Frankie heard it, and then finally me. I turned and watched the road that came from the highway, which was about a ten-minute drive from our place. Sure enough, there was one of those ridiculous new minivans that look like some kind of moon unit, raising up a cloud of dust. Franks stopped Brother and we both stood there watching. Soon the minivan was close, and then it slowed down and stopped in the road. The driver's window rolled down and a preppy-looking guy with his collar turned up stuck his head out.

"'Scuse me!" he called. "Looking for the Grunveldt farm?"

"Right next door," I said, pointing.

"Thanks," he said. He rolled up his window—*probably didn't want to waste his air-conditioning*, I thought—and went up another hundred yards to the Grunveldt's driveway.

"Haley, don't!" screamed Frankie. "What did you tell him for?"

"Jeez, Franks," I said. "He would have figured it out anyway."

"I'm not going!" he shouted.

"Not going where?"

"I'm not going back to Gowanda!" he said.

And with that, he spurred Brother into a graceful leap over the fence and took off across a pasture, heading for God-knows-where. I was so surprised by this that it was several moments before I could remember that I ought to be saying something about it.

"Frankie, come back here!" I yelled. "Where are you going on my horse? Damn it! Frankie!" But he was already too far away. Brother was in a dead run, his long neck stretched out in front of him and his legs working like four pinwheels, almost like a cartoon horse. Brother could really fly when he put his mind to it. It was like he'd thought things over and decided he was on Frankie's side. I hadn't seen him run like that since he was a colt.

"Oh, shit," I said.

I went up to the house in a series of miniature pole vaults. I bumped my foot up against a rock once, and it hurt so bad that for a moment I could only see the color red, nothing else. Never mind what it felt like—those words haven't been invented yet. Suffice it to say I had to stick my fist in my mouth to keep from screaming. It was way too soon for me to be up and around as much as I had been. I was going to need a whole fistful of those little white pills when this day was over.

I went inside and called Mother. She came out of the kitchen, wiping her hands on a rag.

"Franks took off on Brother," I said, tears of pain streaming down my face. "I guess some folks are here to see about buying his house, and he got upset."

"You let him ride Brother?" she said. "Haley, that was very irresponsible."

"Oh, blow it out," I said. "What are you talking about? He rides him all the time!"

Mother reddened. "I beg your pardon?" she said, her voice all ice. "What makes you think you can speak to me that way?"

"What makes you think it's my fault?" I said. "Besides, there's no time for this. We gotta tell his parents. Ma, he ran away. Okay? He ran away on my horse. He was saying something about Gowanda, too."

Mother was mad as hell, but she could see there were bigger problems to worry about. She went to the phone and called up Frankie's parents. I could hear her talking in a low voice while I went to the window and looked off in the direction Frankie had gone. I didn't expect to see him, and I was right. He'd vanished.

Here's what Gowanda is: It's kind of a loony bin, a mental facility. All the crazy-people jokes around here are about Gowanda, just like in New York City they talk about Bellevue, which I also know from reading. It didn't take me longer than two seconds to figure out that Franks was afraid he was going to be sent there if his folks sold the house. Of course, it never occurred to him that wherever they were going, they would take him with them. It's not like they would have had him locked up just because they were moving, for Chrissakes. But sometimes Franks jumped to conclusions. I guess that was how bad he didn't want to leave home. He'd rather run away than see the house get sold. Jeez, what a nut.

Maybe, I thought, *Gowanda was where they sent him that time he was raving about the theater.*

"Haley," said Mother, "I want you to stay here. I'm going over to the Grunveldts."

"They have company," I said.

"I know. Just stay here in case he comes back."

"He's not coming back. Not on his own, anyway."

"Promise me you'll stay put?"

"Where the hell would I go, Ma?"

She snapped her mouth shut and walked out the door. I guess she wanted to sit and fret with Mrs. Grunveldt—Mother never passed up a chance to sit and fret with someone, not if she could help it. I got a little panicked when I realized there was a good chance they would call the police. The cops in this part of the world are not exactly what you'd call sensitive types. Being in a rural area, we didn't have a proper police force—we had a sheriff, and some part-time deputies who loved an excuse to strap on their guns and rampage around in the name of law and order. If they got called out to go look for Frankie, there was no telling how *that* would end up. But I felt pretty safe in guessing it wouldn't be pretty. I could just see them hauling him out by his T-shirt from wherever he was hiding, kicking and screaming, and if he happened to kick one of *them* accidentally, they might get a little too rough with the poor boy in retaliation. They were great ones for retaliation, those deputies. It was how things were kept peaceable.

"Lord," I prayed, half serious and half surprised at myself, "please don't let those screwy old biddies call the sheriff. Let Frankie be safe, and let him come to his senses and realize he's making a mountain of a molehill. And let Brother come home, with or without him, as You see fit, because if anything happens to my horse I'm going to bust someone's head open, and that's a promise. Amen."

I wish my grandmother could have been there to see me, her wayward brazen hussy of a granddaughter communing with the powers that be, because the very next thing that happened was that Brother came trotting back over the hill, riderless, acting as though he'd just been out for a pleasant little jaunt. I could see him out the kitchen window. It gave me a start, I can tell you. I was glad to see him, but I couldn't help wondering if maybe it was a reminder that I should have been going to church right along, if something as simple as a prayer was all that was needed to get things done.

My leg was about ready to fall off by this time, but I crutched on out to the corral again, where Brother was waiting patiently for me to let him in. He stood there nibbling grass, just as calm as could be.

"Now, where did Frankie get to, Brother?" I asked him. "Where'd you drop him off, old boy?"

But Brother just pushed me with his nose, telling me *Hurry up, let me in and give me some sugar. I'm a good horse.* So I did just that. I keep some sugar cubes in a bag in the stable, and I gave him a whole handful, because even though he hadn't been gone ten minutes I'd been afraid I was never going to see him again. I scanned around for some sign of Frankie, thinking maybe Brother had thrown him and he would come limping along behind, but he was nowhere to be seen. Besides, I didn't think Brother would throw Frankie. He knew there was something not quite right about him, that he had to be taken care of. Animals are good that way—much better than most people.

I went back into the house and dialed the Grunveldts. My mother answered.

"Hello?" she said. Her voice was stretched as thin as a guitar string. I imagined the two of them up there along with Mr. Grunveldt, working each other up to fever pitches of worry and excitement.

"Keep your shirt on, honey," I told her. "Brother's back, so Frankie hasn't gone too far off. He's probably hiding somewhere. Try down at the creek."

"You think he might be at the creek?" she said. Over her shoulder she said, "Haley thinks he's down at the creek!"

"Don't be dragging those old mummies around with you," I told her, meaning the Grunveldts. "If they fall down, they'll snap in half."

"Well, there's no reason for *that* kind of tone," said Mother.

"Just head on down there and take a peek around," I said. "I'd go myself, but if I don't lay down soon this leg is never going to get better." I hung up then.

Of course, I didn't think Frankie was down at the creek at all. He was scared to death of water. The creek wasn't much of a creek at all, just a little trickle of water about a foot across and maybe three inches deep, but it led into a kind of swimming hole just like you might have read about in *The Adventures of Tom Sawyer*, if you're the literate type. The swimming hole wasn't very big either, but it was good for cooling off in on a hot day. There were a few fish in there, and some turtles. But Frankie was genuinely terrified of water, and the one time he and I went down there together and I took a jump in the water he started to holler and scream, telling me to get out of there before I drowned. He had a god-awful fear of drowning, that boy. So of all the places he could have gone, I knew for sure the creek wasn't one of them.

I guess, all things considered, I didn't want anyone to find Frankie. I knew as well as anyone else how sometimes a person just needs to run off for a while, when things get to be too much. I still thought Frankie was making something out of nothing, but in his world there was no telling what was going to upset him; if he thought this house-selling business was the end of the world, why then as far as he was concerned it *was*, and nobody would be able to talk him out of it. *Let him be*, I thought. *Just let the poor old fruitcake alone. He'll come home when he's hungry enough.*

Then I felt bad for thinking of him as a fruitcake. He *wasn't* a fruitcake. He was childish, but he wasn't stupid, that boy. And right now he was scared, and alone. I thought about praying for him too, but I didn't want to overdo it. One miracle was enough for that day. *Frankie would be all right*, I thought. *God watches out for fools and children, and he was certainly a little bit of both.*

I laid down on my bed then and helped myself to one of those little white pills, and before I knew it I was asleep.

③
Lifting the Veil

Three days went by and Frankie didn't show up. I probably don't even need to mention that the Grunveldts were worried sick, and that everyone on two legs was out looking for him. That let *me* out, of course. I just stayed in bed.

But let me backtrack for a minute. Only a few hours after Frankie took off, and once the Grunveldts realized he wasn't coming back, the sheriff was called. And *that* was just like I thought it would be. Ed Barnabas—that's the sheriff—came out with his deputies and a bunch of dogs, and for two or three days they tore up the whole countryside, whooping and baying and knocking on doors and sniffing around creeks and woods and barns and what have you. But they never turned him up. I had to tell the whole story of how he'd taken off and how Brother had come back without him about forty thousand times. Even then, old Sheriff Ed acted like he didn't quite believe me. He told me if I knew something more I should come clean, unless I wanted to get charged with obstructing justice or some such nonsense. He knew me and Frankie were pals, I guess, and he must have thought I was holding out on him. I told him right back that he wouldn't get anywhere trying to push *me* around, broken leg or no, because I wasn't afraid of anyone or anything nonsnakelike on this earth; and besides, I *was* telling the truth. I even told them I knew he couldn't have gone far, because Brother hadn't been gone long at all. Had to be somewhere in the neighborhood, I said. Maybe they just weren't looking in the right place.

But after three days, Frankie would have had enough time to go around the world if he'd wanted. I still didn't think he'd gone more than a mile or two, but he'd hidden himself good, that boy. Whatever he thought he was on the lam from, it had him scared to death. Finally, old Sherlock Holmes called off the search, and Frankie went on the books as "missing." I figured it would only be a matter of time before his face started showing up on the backs of milk cartons.

His parents were brokenhearted. If Frankleton's whole idea had been to prevent them from selling the house, it paid off. All their plans were put on hold, and the preppy guy in the minivan went back to the suburbs of Buffalo, houseless. I wasn't sad about that, either. He didn't look like he'd be much of a neighbor.

I had to hand it to old Franks. I wouldn't have believed he had it in him to run away. I mean, that takes a certain kind of *self-sufficiency*, to use another one of Miz Powell's favorite phrases. You have to know where you're going and have the wherewithal to get there, and you have to be smart enough to stay hidden and resourceful enough to feed yourself. In fact, the more I thought about it, the more unlike Frankie it seemed. I wondered if he was getting help from someone, and if so, who that someone was.

Meantime, I stayed home, letting my leg knit up and just taking it easy. There wasn't anything I could have done anyway. I thought about gimping up to Miz Powell's place for tea, but I was feeling kind of shy. I guess didn't want to make a pest of myself—if you act *too* hungry for friends, you might find yourself without any at all. Besides, my leg was still killing me. I didn't feel like I was up for another adventure, even one only just down the road.

Instead, I gave old Roberta Ellsworth a call, after picking up the phone and putting it down about a hundred times. The problem was,

I didn't really have anything to talk to her *about*. I just wanted to talk to someone. Anyone. And finally I gave in.

They say you should never pet a stray dog, because he'll follow you home and you won't be able to get rid of him—he's that starved for affection. Roberta was pretty much a stray dog herself. She acted so surprised when I called her I thought she was going to bust out crying tears of joy. I think I might very well have been the first person ever to phone her on the spur of the moment.

"Haley *Bombauer?*" she kept saying. "*Haley* Bombauer?"

"That's me," I said. Talking to her for five seconds had already made me tired, and I thought about pretending I'd dialed the wrong number and just hanging up. But I couldn't do that to poor old Roberta. The dog had been petted, and now I was going to have to feed it.

"How you doig, Haley?" said Roberta, her nose all plugged up—with her finger, most likely. "I heard you broge your leg!"

"Sure did, Robs," I said. "Got a big old cast on, and everything."

"Oh, by goodness!" she said. "Dat must hab *hurd!*"

"Yup, it hurt," I said.

"How *buch* did it hurd?" she said. "I bead, did id hurd a whole *lod?*"

I was already remembering why me and old Roberta had stopped being friends, and why she hadn't managed to make any *new* friends—because she was about the most boring conversationalist this side of the Mississippi.

"It hurt a whole fuckload, Robertums," I said. "A whole big honking bunch of hurt."

I heard a little gasp on the other end, and then a shocked laugh. Most girls around here didn't say "fuck." In the Greater Mannville Metropolitan Area, that kind of talk qualified as downright scandalous.

"Haley, how cub you're callig me?" said Roberta.

I felt kind of awkward then. I hadn't expected her to get right to the point like that. "Just calling to say hi, Roberta," I said. "See how your summer's going, and all that."

"Oh. 'Cause...you know, we habn't talked buch ladely. Nod in a log time."

"I know, Robs, I know," I said. "I'm, uh...sorry about that. Just been busy, I guess." *Like for the last ten years*, I thought.

"Do you...ubb...want to ged togedder or anythig?"

"Well, tell you the truth, Robs, it's kind of hard for me to get around," I said. "I was really only calling to—"

"I could cub ub dere!" she said, excited. "You wad me do? We could hag out!"

"I've got all kinds of IV tubes in me, and machines and everything," I said. "You know those screens that show your heartbeat and your brainwaves and all? It's not pretty, Robs. They had to shave my head."

"You're kiddig!" she said. "Why did they do *thad*?"

"Brain problems," I said shortly, thinking *I must have BIG brain problems to be calling this character. What the hell was I thinking?* "I'm not really ready for visitors yet, Robs. Won't be for a few weeks. I was just calling to sort of...I don't know, keep in touch with people."

"Well, baby wed you're *bedder* we could hag out," she said. "Ogay?"

"Okay," I said. "I'll give you a call when I'm up and around again. Sound good?"

"Thad souds *real* good," she said. "Ged well sood, Haley."

"Thanks, Robmaster," I said. "Don't take any wooden nickels."

She laughed like that was the funniest thing she'd ever heard.

"Bye," I said, and I hung up, feeling like I'd just dodged a bullet, as they say.

Then I heard the screen door screech open and slam shut, and I knew my mother figure was home again. She'd been up sitting with Mrs. Grunveldt these last few days, just generally holding her hand and trying to calm her down. That was kind of like asking the fattest man in the world to teach aerobics—I mean, in order to make people feel calm, you have to be kind of on an even keel yourself, and old Mom was anything but, even on a good day. I hadn't seen her much since Frankie hopped the fence. She just came home to sleep and change clothes, and the rest of the time they kept up their vigil at the Grunveldt's, hoping Frankie would show up. Or barring that, that there would be a call from the cops, saying *We found him, looks like the coons been nibbling on 'im for a couple of days. You want to come down here and identify the poor slob?*

I don't mean to sound too disrespectful. Fact was, I couldn't manage to get myself as worked up over it all as everyone else. That was because I just had a good feeling about Frankie. I don't know why, exactly. I just had the sense that he was okay, that he was in a safe place and there was somebody taking care of him. I mentioned before that I inherited a kind of what you might call natural instinct for telling things about people's health, mostly my own but sometimes other people's too, which I have every reason to believe was passed on to me from my grandmother. You don't have to believe it yourself, but you have to believe that *I* believed it. I do think a person can be born knowing certain things, almost like they get passed on in your genes. But I think there were other things I'd gotten from the old forest lady too, other "abilities," you could say, that hadn't begun to flower yet but which were coming up in me as of late. By this I mean that sometimes I knew other things I didn't have any reason to know.

My grandmother wasn't known only as a healer. She was sometimes asked to answer questions that nobody else could answer, such as Will I have children, or Is there water on my land and if so where, or What will the price of corn be in three years. She wasn't too good at questions like that last one, to be honest, but that didn't stop people from asking her. It's amazing the kind of hocus-pocus people will lower themselves to if they get desperate enough. She even had a method for finding out the answers to these questions, a little ritual to peek through what she called the Veil—I'd seen her do it once, but there are some things it's better not to report on. People don't need to know *everything* about my family. Just the public parts.

Anyway, I had reason to believe that looking through the Veil was something a person could be born with, just like black hair or a big nose. And I was getting pretty sure as of late that I'd been born with it. I didn't see visions of the Four Horsemen or anything like that, but sometimes I did know well in advance when it was going to rain—*before* the clouds came in, I mean—and other times I could tell who was on the other end when the phone started ringing—little things like that. It was really only a curiosity, nothing more. But I thought it was the kind of thing I could get better at, if I concentrated. And it was that part of me that told me Frankie was probably okay, wherever he was. I just had a feeling. I didn't know where he was hiding, but I knew he was close—and *that* was plain old deductive reasoning, as they say in science class. He didn't have it in him to go traipsing off all over creation. He was a homebody, just like me. He loved home so much it was the reason he ran away from it in the first place, because he couldn't stand to see it sold out from under him. That, and he was afraid to go to Gowanda again.

Mother went upstairs and spent a good long time stomping around up there. I could tell by the noises she was making that she was getting dressed up for something. I heard the medicine cabinet open and close a bunch of times—that was where she kept her makeup, which she only wore for special occasions. I could hear her dresser drawers slide in and out, too, which meant she was putting on her better undergarments. After a while I heard a new noise: clack, clack. *That* meant she was wearing heels. *Oh, Lord,* I thought—*the poor dear is off to a fashion show.*

But of course she wasn't going to any fashion show. She was going to church.

You have to understand the history between old Mummy Dearest and the good Lord if you *really* want to understand my family, or what there was left of it. Mother wasn't always the kind of person she was now—by which I mean, she wasn't always scared of her own shadow. Something in her kind of changed when Dad died. I guess that was when the real trouble started around here. We were like a house that rests on two strong pillars, and then one of them got knocked away without warning. Ever since then we'd been leaning at a crazy angle, like one of those places you see on the news in California after a mudslide—one end hanging off into space, and below is the ocean, waiting patiently to swallow the house up. We'd been teetering like that for years now, trying not to move around too much lest we go careening off into the sea.

Mother had made some big leaps when she married Dad. She came from what was probably the second-strictest religious order in the whole country, the first being the aforementioned Amish. She was raised Old Order Mennonite by my grandmother way out there in the woods, and I don't know how she managed to get away long enough to meet my old man, but she did. Fact is, I never did hear the story of how my parents met. I did know this much, though: Henry—that's my dad—wasn't a Mennonite. He was a Lutheran, but not a serious Lutheran. He didn't have much time for church, and in fact he didn't have much time for anything that didn't directly involve what was going on right in front of his nose. Old Dad didn't have much of a religious side at all. Now, I myself would never hold this against anybody. If you choose not to believe that there's some white-haired old man floating around on a cloud up there in the Wild Blue Yonder, pointing fingers down at us poor little ants here on earth and saying Thou Shalt Do This and Thou Shalt Never Under Any Circumstances Do That, why then it seems to me you're just a realist more than anything else. But of course, some people take a lot grimmer view of it than that, and my grandmother, as you could guess with not much brainpower, was one of those people.

She did not like it one little bit that her daughter married a man from outside, one who lived in the world and even seemed to enjoy it, with no apparent side effects. Well, not quite—I guess you *could* argue that him getting blown up was sort of a side effect of not believing in God. I know my grandmother told my mother once that old Fireball McGinty's argument with a bottle of nitroglycerine was punishment of the biblical kind—punishment on him for not obeying God's law, and punishment on her, my mother, for disobeying her own mother. You have to admit that getting yourself exploded to death *does* seem kind of biblical, just like getting hit by lightning, or any other sudden kind of departure. But folks will always look for a divine cause for things when the real reason is right in front of their noses and they just don't want to accept it. And that whole punishment idea didn't sit well with Mother. She and Grandma didn't talk for a long time after that, and she stopped going to church on a regular basis. It was like Grandma's words had hit home with her, only in a different way than Grandma had meant them to. Maybe my mother really *did* believe God was punishing her for leaving the Old Order. And maybe she held it against Him.

But she still went to church, when she had a special reason to go. I guess Frankie's disappearance qualified as a special reason. They were going to pray that he come home safe and sound, with a minimum of mosquito bites.

"It'd be nice if you would come, Haley," she said.

"Church?" I said. "No, thanks."

I knew she would ask me to go, and she knew I would say no. There was no surprise there. But I was surprised at what she did next: She sat down on the foot of my bed and sighed, like she was tired. More than tired—sad.

"What's up, mutton chop?" I asked her. "Why so glum?"

"There was a time I went to church a lot, you know," she said. "Before you were born."

"I know," I said.

"Before I met your father," she said.

I didn't say anything then. It was unusual for her to talk about my dad. I had the feeling something big was coming, so I stayed quiet. She had a faraway look in her eyes.

"Haley," she said, "I've told you a little about how it was for me growing up, haven't I?"

"Yes," I said.

"Did you know I'd never even ridden in a car before I met your father?"

When Mother was raised in that little house out in the woods, believe me it wasn't any more modern then than it is now. No electricity, no running water, no nothing. Cars were against the rules, too. I'd always known that, but I'd never really thought about it before.

"Never? Never *ever*?" I said. "What was it like? How old were you?"

"I was only a little older than you are now," she said.

"Did you go fast, that first time?" I asked.

But she didn't hear me.

"So many things changed when I met him," she murmured. "My whole world became different then."

"Was Grandma mad when you rode in Dad's car?"

She heard *that*, all right. Her whole face changed and she set her lips tight.

"I didn't tell her," she said. "But she knew anyway. She looked at me different—like I'd been polluted or something. She could tell."

"Just from you sitting in a car?"

"Not just that," she said. "From . . . all kinds of things."

I started getting a little red then, because I thought I knew what she was talking about.

She'd been in love, y'see. She was crazy about my dad, and he was crazy about her. I remember them laughing all the time when I was little. He was a silly, fun-loving, fast-car-driving, dancing fool, and he must have swept her off her feet faster than a tornado goes through a trailer park, because my mother put down everything that was Mennonite and came out here to live with my dad, in the house his grandfather had built.

I remember my mother as two people. One was before Dad died, and the other was after. After, she was kind of like walking dead. Her eyes were hollow, she didn't smile anymore, and everything seemed to startle her. And she never did fully recover from that whole incident, not like I did. I was only little, and children are pretty bouncy—I mean, *resilient.*

"I was afraid, at first," she said. "There were so many new things to understand when I came to live here. I didn't know the simplest things—how to use a dishwasher, or a stove, or a radio. He had to teach me everything."

"Kind of like being taken up to a futuristic alien planet?" I said.

She almost smiled at that, old Mums did. Not quite, but almost.

"He was patient," she said. "He knew everything. He even knew how to *build* some of these things. I think that was what amazed me about him most of all—that he understood *machines.*"

"He sure did," I said.

"I would never have made it in this world if it wasn't for him," she said. "You'll never know what it's like to grow up like I did, Haley, and I think sometimes I feel bad about that."

Aha, I thought. *I knew she was feeling bad about something.*

"Why?" I asked.

"Because," she said. "You understand more about life when you grow up simple."

That didn't mean what it sounded like—growing up simple. In Mother's vocabulary, simple didn't mean dumb. What she meant was, growing up *uncomplicated.* I knew Mother thought the modern world was way too complicated. There was just too much to keep track of. I guess for her it must have been kind of like fast-forwarding a hundred years into the future to come live in this house.

"You just notice more," she said. "You know, when I was a young girl, I knew every wild animal that lived within a mile of our place, just like we know our neighbors now. I talked to them like they were people. And I knew the plants, too. I knew where everything grew, and when it would bloom or seed. I could tell what the weather would be just by looking at the moon."

That kind of impressed me. There was something spooky about it—something powerful. I guess there are things we take for granted about our parents. For example, I'd always known my mother preferred to tell time by looking at the shadows on the lawn rather than at a clock. And she would spend a long time looking at the sky to figure out when the next rain was coming, when she could have just snapped on the radio. It was something she'd always done, and I never thought anything of it. But suddenly it hit me that that was *not* the way things were done anymore in this world, not by most people, anyway, and that made my mother unusual—in a good way.

"But life got easier for you too, right?" I said. "Didn't it? In some ways?"

"In *some* ways," she said. "It doesn't take me all day to do laundry anymore, for example."

"And that's good, right?" I said.

She looked down at her feet, at her nice shoes, as though she was seeing them for the first time.

"I guess so," she said. "It's easier, but..."

I waited.

"It's less, somehow," she said.

"Less of what?" I asked.

She stood up then, and our little moment was over. She was back to herself again.

"Oh, I don't know," she said. "I don't remember what I was talking about. I'm going to drive the Grunveldts to church. I'll be back in a few hours."

"How come you're going to church, anyway?" I asked

"They want to pray for Frankie."

"No, I mean how come *you're* going?"

"Because I'm worried about him."

"Are *you* going to pray for him too? In the Lutheran church? Won't God think you're changing teams?"

She looked at me with that same sad look again. I didn't really think there was anything wrong with it—I was just egging her on.

"I've been praying for him right along," she said. "Have you?"

I thought about telling her about how I prayed for Brother to come home, and how in the next split second he did. But I didn't think she'd like hearing about it. Mother may have quit church, mostly, but she still had strong ideas about religion, and I was pretty sure you weren't supposed to pray for horses. It wouldn't be considered a real prayer—it would be a waste of good praying time. Besides, the whole thing was probably just a big coincidence. I didn't fool myself about the chances of God actually listening to me.

"Sorta," I said.

She sighed. "Anyone calls, take a message," she said.

"I *know*," I said.

"Don't leave the stove on if you go out," she said.

"Mother."

"And be sure not to—"

"*Mom.*"

She stopped then—she just stopped. She clacked out of there and got into the pickup truck, and then she was gone in a screech of tires and a whirlwind of gravel. That's old Moms—she would always drive like someone who'd never seen a motor vehicle before in their lives.

One thing about a broken leg is that it certainly seems to slow life down. I laid there for a while after she left, just kind of twiddling my thumbs. I thought about watching television, but our set was buried under a pile of fabric swatches—fabric swatches were a fact of life when you lived with my mother. She was always re-covering an old chair, or sewing curtains. Besides, there was nothing on. You drive around out here, you see a satellite dish in everyone's yard, just about—but not ours. We didn't even have cable. That was all right with me, before I went all gimpy. I preferred to spend my spare time outside. But now that I was an invalid, suddenly a hundred and forty channels didn't sound so bad. *Maybe I could learn to speak French on one of those educational stations*, I thought. *Maybe I could become addicted to soap operas.*

Old Frankie. I could feel him—he was close, that little runt. But I couldn't imagine where he would be. I wondered why Mother didn't take the Grunveldts to Grandma's place instead of church. She could do her hocus-pocus for them. Maybe they'd get some real answers then.

And then I thought, *why not try it myself?*

It was one of those ideas that seems so crazy you almost toss it out the window right away, but you stop at the last minute and kind of examine it like a weird fossil or something, because it's too damn interesting to get rid of. Try it myself? Well, maybe I could. I'd seen her do it—Grandma, that is. I thought I knew what to do. There were lots of little steps involved, and I wasn't sure I remembered all of them, but the important part was having the feeling, or the seeing, or the knowing—being able to look behind the Veil. And *that* I was pretty sure I had.

The Veil, in case you don't know, means the covering that lies over everything we don't know or understand, everything that isn't right in front of our noses. There were probably a bunch of different ways to lift it, but I'd only seen it done one way before, and that was Grandma's way. Before I knew what I was doing, I was out of bed and poling along into the kitchen, where I got a pot out from under the sink and filled it most of the way with water. I set it on the table and pulled the curtains shut. Then I took a little hand mirror out of the bathroom and propped it up against some books in front of the pot, so that when I looked into the mirror I could see the reflection of the water. That was the real secret—you had to have *two* doors into the other dimension, one opening right into the other. I remembered Grandma saying something about that, a long time ago. Or at least I *thought* I remembered it. I didn't have any dope to burn, but my first time out I wouldn't worry about that. I wasn't seriously expecting it to work anyway. I mean, I had a feeling that it *could* work, but I didn't assume it *would*.

It was good and dim in the kitchen now. I lit a candle and set it next to the mirror, so it kind of made everything glow. Then I set myself down in a chair and leaned over it, positioning myself just right so I could see the glare of the candle of the water, and I asked myself: *Where is Frankie?*

All this was just stuff I'd seen my grandmother do before, but that was the outside stuff. What I didn't know was what to do inside—what to think about. I had to wing it. So I just cleared my mind and tried not to think about anything, which is a lot harder than it sounds. Everything distracted me—the ruffles my breath made on the water, the throbbing in my leg, some damn bird chirping his head off right outside the window. But after a few minutes I kind of got into it, and next thing I knew the world around me went black and all I could see was the water like it was a screen, and there on the water was an image: a bunch of sunflowers.

For about a second it was as plain as a hog in a dress, and then it was gone. I sat bolt upright, feeling mighty shocked. *Sunflowers?* I thought. *What the hell is that all about? What did that have to do with Frankie?*

Nothing, I thought—*a misfire. Just a bunch of stupid flowers.*

But then I started feeling a little warm glow, because I'd *done it*—I'd seen something. It wasn't much, maybe not even accurate, but it was something. And it seemed like it happened right away, too. I couldn't have been sitting there longer than ten minutes. *That* was pretty good.

Call me an optimist, I guess.

I kept staring into the water. *Right,* I thought. *Think. Sunflowers. What do those mean?*

Suddenly I heard the pickup truck come crunching into the driveway, and Mother came up the back steps and into the kitchen. I didn't have time to move, I was so surprised.

She was surprised, too—more than a little. She came in the door and stopped and stared at me like I'd sprouted horns.

"Forget something?" I asked.

"Haley Bombauer, what are you doing?" she whispered.

Well, there was no need to answer that, so I just didn't.

"How come you're home so soon?" I asked.

"What are you talking about?" she said. "I've been gone for three hours!"

Well, I got a bit of a chill then, I don't mind telling you. Mother went to the curtains and threw them back, and sure enough it was dusk. When I sat down it had been broad daylight. I looked at the candle, and it was out. Just a smoking little stump.

"Oh, my," I said.

"Haley," said Mother. "*What are you doing?*"

"Looking for Frankie," I said.

We stayed like that, staring at each other for the longest time. It was like I had been sharpened, and I could see more now—I mean more of *her*. I looked into her eyes and read things I hadn't seen before. I could read her feelings, but more than her feelings—like her thoughts were words in my head. And I knew she couldn't add it all up, poor old Mudder Dearest. It just didn't make sense. Here was me, likely as not the most outrageous undaughterly daughter our family had seen in five hundred years, or even five thousand, and yet I was taking right along after my grandmother, and doing it in secret so nobody would know. She just didn't know what to make of it.

Finally she said, "What did you see?"

No harm in telling her, I thought.

"Sunflowers," I said.

"That's it?"

I nodded.

"Put that stuff away," she said.

"Excuse me," I said, "but I seem to have a broken leg. How 'bout a little help, here?"

But Mother wouldn't budge.

"It's the rules," she said. "You have to put the things away yourself. Nobody else is allowed to touch them until after. It breaks the..." She didn't finish that.

"Breaks the what?" I said.

She didn't say anything.

"Breaks the *what?*" I repeated.

"The spell," she said.

We sat there for a while longer. That strange, old-fashioned word floated between us, echoing. Spell.

"I think you did that when you walked in the door," I said.

"Put it *away*," she said. *"Now."*

I hadn't heard that tone from her in a long time, and suddenly I remembered: She was the one who used to swat me on the bum when I was ornery, and that was the voice she used when she did it. Dad never could bring himself to spank me. So I hopped up and put everything away, and she just stood there and watched me, and when I was done she said, "You knew what you were doing?"

"Not really," I said. "I just kind of figured it out."

"Did your grandmother teach you any of that?"

"No," I said.

"Then how did you know what to do?"

"I was born with it," I said. "I'm a natural."

"How do *you* know what you were born with?" she said. "That's not for you to say. That's for others older than you to—"

"Who else," I said, feeling a little hot under the collar, "could possibly know what I was born with except me?"

"I'm just a little surprised, Haley," she said. "Surprised...and scared."

"Scared of what?" I asked. "There's nothing to be scared of."

"Haley, you have to know what you're doing," she said. "You can't just sail into this like you do everything else, acting so damned arrogant and thinking you know everything when you *don't*. You're still a *child*, Haley."

"How do you know so much about it?" I asked.

She looked at me like I was an idiot. "Haley," she said. "You believe you got this from your grandmother, right?"

"Yes," I said.

"Well, you didn't," she said.

"Whaddaya mean?"

"Think about it," she said. "It had to pass through me to get to you."

"Come again?" I said.

"Haley," she said, "you got it from *me.*"

Well, I have to admit *that* had never occurred to me.

"You mean you know how to do it too?" I said. "Just the same way, with the water and candle and everything?"

"You have to be taught," she said, not answering me. "It's like trying to... I don't know, like trying to fly a jet plane when you've only ever been a passenger. And almost as dangerous. You have to be trained in this."

"Then train me," I said.

"No."

"Why not?"

"Because you're not ready!" she said.

"Well, obviously I am," I said. "If I'm doing it on my own."

"And because I don't do it!" she said. "I don't want anything to do with it, and I never want to. Ever. So don't ask me."

"You *used* to have something to do with it," I said. "Didn't you?"

I could tell she didn't want to answer that question. She looked away.

"Mother?"

"What?"

"You used to have something to do with it."

Silence.

"Yes or no?"

More silence.

"Tell me!" I said.

"All right," she said. "Yes."

I knew it. "So when did you stop?"

She got pale then.

"You want to know when I stopped?" she said. "All right, if you're so grown-up and smart I'll tell you. I stopped when I saw your father die," she said. "I saw it in the water, weeks before it happened. And I wish I never had, because it was *terrible!*"

This word came out as more of a scream. I jumped, and she started to cry. I wanted to hug her suddenly, but I was rooted to where I stood. Her words had seared me, frightened me to death. Suddenly the fiery image of the shed going up in smoke was in my mind, and that was an image that never failed to undo me. Even many years later, it was the worst thing I could think of—it would *always* be the worst thing. And Mother had her arms wrapped around herself, encased in her own sadness, like an unborn baby in its sac of fluids.

"You're not ready to handle what you might see, Haley." Her voice was low through her tears—her voice got deeper when she cried. "You're not ready yet. And you're *never* ready to see something like that."

"It was only *sunflowers!*" I shouted. "That's all it was!"

I started crutching myself out of there. She had me really spooked now. I wanted to go outside, but I had to get past her to get to the door, and she put her hand on my shoulder to stop me.

"This time it was only sunflowers," she said.

Well, she didn't need to finish that statement. Today sunflowers, tomorrow something else—fire, maybe? Blood and guts? Death? I shook her off and went out the door to the corral. Brother was standing in his stall, asleep on his feet. He woke up when I came in and whickered at me. I was shaking pretty hard. I let myself into his stall and put my head on his neck.

"Oh, my, horse," I whispered. "Oh, glory. Things are getting curiouser and curiouser."

Whibbety whicket, he said.

I put my nose into him and smelled his horsiness. It was a smell that always calmed me down.

I stayed out there for a while, not wanting to go back inside. I made myself comfy on a bale of hay and just sat there, thinking things over. I hadn't known for sure I could do it. I just thought I could. Now I felt like something in me had changed, just a little bit. I had looked through the Veil.

But what Mother said about seeing Dad's death had busted me up inside more than a little bit. I'd never known she could look through the Veil too, but it made sense. Just her and Grandma out there alone in the woods all those years, until my Dad came along. There would have been plenty of time for her to learn Grandma's tricks. So she'd taken more than a sense of churchiness with her when she went to live with Dad. She'd taken this gift with her, too—and she'd kept using it. She'd been doing it all the while I was a little girl, without me knowing. I wondered if old Fireball had known about it or if she kept it from him, too. It didn't seem like the kind of thing he'd put any stock in. He probably just thought it was one of her Mennonite things.

Of course, it wasn't a Mennonite thing. I would hate to give people the impression that Mennonites spend all their time staring into pots of water and predicting the future, because that's not the way it is. I think Grandma would have been a Veil Lifter no matter what religion she was, Mennonite or Buddhist or Jew. It was just in her. And it was an *old* thing, older than her, even, older than all three of us put together. I wondered just how long the women in our family had been parting the Veil and looking into the other side—probably a lot longer than we'd been Mennonites, that's for sure.

I didn't believe for a moment that Mother would have told Dad she saw his death ahead of time. But it would have been hard for her to keep that secret locked up inside her, especially if she didn't completely understand what she saw. Maybe she just saw fire. Maybe just an explosion. But she would have known it was him, and that he was leaving us. It would just about have killed me to have to keep a secret like that from the person I loved most in the world.

By then the sun was completely down. I went back out into the yard. All the windows in our house were dark, even my mother's bedroom window. *She was probably locked in there again*, I thought, *crying her eyes out*.

I headed out to the road, slow, just feeling my way with my crutches. I wasn't really going anywhere—just moving for the sake of it. The night air was cool and moist on my face, and I was getting better at those crutches. My hands were toughening up. Once I got on the road I turned left and kept going, past the Grunveldt house—all their windows were dark too. Folks around here go to bed with the chickens, as they say, and get up with the roosters.

Up ahead, at the top of the rise, I could see the Powell house. There were a couple of lights on. Miz Powell was still awake. It wasn't too far—I mean, it would take me a while, but I could do it. By that time my muscles were crying out for some kind of exercise after all that time cooped up inside. I got into the rhythm of it: step, vault, swing the arms forward. It wasn't all that hard. It was trickier on the uphill part, but I just went slower and tried not to overbalance. *What the hell*, I thought. I would pay Miz Elizabeth Powell a visit. It was a little late for callers, but I would knock light. If she didn't hear me, she was in bed. And in that case I would just go home again and get in my own.

I made more noise than I wanted to climbing up to her porch—I still didn't have much practice on steps, and I thumped around like a drunken stiltwalker. Once I got up I could see the living room lamp on through the white lace curtains.

There was a figure sitting in a chair. I gave a little tap on the door, and the figure got up and opened it. It was her, wearing some kind of Chinese-looking robe, and a pair of bifocals perched on her nose.

"Why, Haley!" said Miz Powell. "I was wondering when you'd be dropping by."

She slipped something into her bathrobe pocket. I couldn't quite see what it was, but I caught the gleam of metal.

"Not too late, is it?" I said. "I was just out and about. Your lights were on."

"Not a bit of it, dear," she said, as though poor wandering crip-
pled girls were a normal nocturnal occurrence in this neighborhood.
"Come in, do come in. Tea?"

"Nothing too strong," I said. She closed the door behind me. "No
caffeine."

"Some mint, then," she said. "My sister had lovely mint growing
in the garden."

She put on some water and I set myself down on her sofa like a
fainting elephant, too tired even to look around. It was the first time
I'd ever been in that house. It smelled like perfume and spices. In a
few minutes she came out of the kitchen, and we had a pot of tea
between us. I eyed the outline of the thing in her pocket. Whatever it
was, it hung low and heavy.

"Set your crutches down here, if you like," she said. "They'll be
out of the way."

"Those things will be the death of me," I said.

"Oh, I doubt that very much," she said. "You're durable, Haley.
Rugged. I knew that about you the moment I met you."

"Why, thank you," I said.

"You're quite welcome."

"Mind if I ask you something, Elizabeth?"

"Not at all, dear."

"You packing heat?"

She lifted her eyebrows. "I beg your pardon?"

"Your pocket, there," I said, pointing. "Is that a...a gun?"

"Oh, my goodness, you are observant, aren't you?" she said sweetly.
"That's a quality I respect." She reached into her pocket and sure
enough took out an old-looking pistol. In two shakes she'd popped
the magazine out, taken a round out of the chamber, and handed it to
me butt first. I didn't know much about guns, but she sure did. She
handled that thing like an expert.

"Go on and look at it, love," she said. "It's a souvenir from the war,
an old German piece, but it still works quite well. It's called a Luger.

I suppose I don't need it out here in the country. One does get certain habits after a time, though. And the older you get, the harder they are to break."

I hefted the gun in my hand—it was heavy and cold. With a shudder, I noticed there was a little swastika imprinted on it. I handed it back to her.

"You lived in a bad neighborhood in London, I guess," I said.

"Something like that," she said. "I hope it doesn't frighten you."

"No, ma'am."

"Good," she said firmly. "Fear is a useless quality, my dear. Absolutely useless, and I would beg of you to remember that."

We locked eyes for a minute. I didn't completely understand what she was talking about, but she had a firm way of saying it. I had the feeling there weren't a lot of people in the world who could get away with messing around with Miz Elizabeth Powell. I looked away first. I had to.

"Your tea is getting cold, dear," she said.

She slipped the pistol into the drawer of a nearby end table, and I could tell that was the end of the conversation about the gun. Feeling a little overwhelmed, I took a sip of tea. It was strong, sweet, and almost peppery smelling, dark amber in the cup.

"I don't believe I've ever had mint quite this good before," I said. It sounded like a ridiculous thing to say after the gun, but I guess anything would have. And I was trying my best to be chatty.

"Oh, my sister grew all sorts of things in her garden," she said. "She had champion roses, did you know that?"

"No, ma'am."

"All sorts of amazing flowers, in fact. I was quite astonished when I saw them. Wait just one moment, Haley. I want to show you something."

She went out into the kitchen. I could hear her rustling around out there, and a moment later she came back in with a huge bundle of sunflowers in her arms.

"What do you think of these?" she asked. "I decided to try something new, and cut them like they were regular flowers. Of course they're huge, but they might look interesting standing in a corner, don't you think? Like that?"

She set them down against the wall and stepped back. There were about ten of them, and even with their stalks trimmed they were taller than I was. Ms. Powell looked at me, waiting for me to say something, but I couldn't speak. My throat closed up on me and my breath was coming short.

"Haley?" she said. "Are you unwell?"

I tried to answer her, but I couldn't say anything. Then I heard footsteps on the stairs then, and someone came into the living room. I turned, feeling like I was dreaming, to see who it was.

"Oh, hi, Haley," said Frankie, as casually as though we'd last seen each other five minutes earlier. "What are *you* doing here?"

4

Celebration Cake

What are you doing here indeed—it was just like Franks to be acting casual when he was the subject of a manhunt. Seeing him in Miz Powell's house was so strange and unexpected that I was having a hard time figuring out whether the world was still humming along okay or whether things had gone screwy and the clouds were about to come crashing down around my ears. So I took my cue from Frankie himself, who in spite of his craziness was always the best indicator of whether anything was *really* wrong. You know how they say animals can tell an earthquake is coming long before people can? Well, Frankie was the same way. He always seemed to know ahead of time if something really big was going to go wrong—not earthquakes, I mean, but other things—and if you weren't sure what was happening, all you had to do was look at him to check it out. He was like a human seismograph. And what did Frankie do now but sit down on the couch next to Miz Elizabeth Powell and lean against her like they were the oldest friends in the world, as if he was a little kid and not a hundred-and-eighty-pound man. Elizabeth nearly toppled over from the weight of him, but she righted herself and smiled, patting him on the head like you would a large dog. So I knew things were all right, for the time being.

"Sit up straight, Frankie," said Miz Powell. "We have company."

"It's not company," he said. "It's only Haley."

"Well, thanks a lot, beanbrain," I said. "Nice to see you too. You know the whole town is out looking for you right now?"

"I know," he said. "I saw myself on TV. Elizabeth, can I have a Popsicle?"

"Help yourself, dear," she said.

Frankie got up and went into the kitchen. He came out with not one but two Popsicles, one chocolate and one green. I thought he was going to give one to me, but instead he sat down again and began licking both of them, switching to one when he got tired of the other. Elizabeth looked at him fondly, like a favorite grandchild.

"Well, my dear, I imagine you're wondering what's going on here," she said to me.

"Not just a little, either," I said. "How do you know Frankie?"

"Our acquaintance is the result of a fortuitous encounter," she said. "We met in the garden just the other day, didn't we, Frankie?"

"I was hiding in the roses," Frankie told me, as if he was proud of himself for doing it. He held out an arm, the green popsicle still clamped firmly in his hand, and said, "Look. I got scratched."

"You can't do this," I told Miz Powell. My brain had been whirling around, trying to figure out what she was up to, and I hadn't come up with anything. So I decided to be blunt. "What, are you hiding him or something? His parents are losing their minds."

"They'll be told very soon that Frankie is safe," said Miz Powell. "Don't worry, Haley. I do understand how upset they must be."

"But?"

"Well, we do have *Frankie* to consider, too, you know," she said. "One must ask the question of what *Frankie* wants. He *is* nearly thirty years old."

"I'm twenty-eight and a half," said Frankie.

"Which means he is an adult," Miz Powell went on. "If he chooses not to go home, then it's really up to him, is it not? Nobody has the right to force him to do anything he doesn't wish to do."

"He's not like most adults," I pointed out, needlessly—nobody would ever confuse Frankie, who now had a chocolate mustache and a lime green goatee, with a regular adult.

"I know that, dear," said Miz Powell.

"I'm a very special kind of guy," said Frankie.

"Yes, you are," said Miz Powell.

"But," he said, his face darkening, "I don't want to go away from home."

"You're away from home now," I observed.

"I mean Gowanda!" said Frankie. He stood up on the sofa, still clutching his now-melting Popsicles, waving his arms in the air so that little brown and green drops spattered all around. "I'm not going back to Gowanda! I'm not going back to Gowanda!" He started jumping up and down on the couch, and tears began running down his face. "I'm not going!" he screamed at me.

"All right, all right, Frank," I said, in my most soothing voice. I'd never seen him lose it quite like *this* before. To tell the truth, it was a little scary. He might have had a child's mind, but he had a man's body, and if he was going to hurt somebody—even accidentally—we would have had a hard time stopping him. "You're not going to Gowanda. Nobody's going to send you there."

"That's right, Frankie," said Miz Powell. "Listen to Haley. Nobody's sending you anywhere."

Frankie sat down again, but now he'd managed to discombobulate himself. He tried to cross his arms and ended up jamming the Popsicles into his armpits. He was wearing a light T-shirt, and now he had one green circle under one arm and one brown circle under the other.

"Oh, look what I did," he said distractedly, all traces of anger gone. "Honestly, will I never learn?"

That was what his mother said to him sometimes—*Honestly, will you never learn?* Miz Powell looked at me sideways, her eyebrows arched. I could tell she was trying not to laugh.

"Go clean yourself up, Frankie," I said. "I want to talk to Miz Powell here for a minute."

"I want to listen," he said.

"No. You can't."

"Are you going to talk about *me?*"

"Yes, we are," I said, "and I don't want you around to hear it. Now get your butt out of here before I twist your arms off."

"Sheesh," said Frankie. He stood up and stalked off into the kitchen, where I heard him throw the Popsicles in the trash and run water over his hands. Then he came through the living room again and stomped up the stairs. "You're not my mother," he told me pointedly.

"Thank God for small favors," I said.

He went into some room or other up there and slammed the door. Miz Powell looked at me again, this time in astonishment.

"The only reason he listens to me is because he thinks I'm bigger than him," I explained. "I've known him all my life. We're friends, as much as you can be friends with someone who's about three hearts short of a flush."

"He's told me all about your friendship," said Miz Powell. "He has quite a high regard for you, Haley. But how did you know he was here in my house?"

"I didn't," I said. I wondered whether I should tell her about the sunflowers, but I didn't know yet whether Elizabeth Powell was the kind of person who believed in things like that or not. It was no good telling people about mysterious visions from other dimensions unless you were sure they would understand. So I said, "I was really only out walking around, or crutching around, I should say."

"At this hour?"

"My mother and I had an argument," I said. "I was blowing off some steam."

Miz Powell was way too well-mannered to ask what Mother and I fought about. *Chalk one up for her,* I thought. Most of the old broads around here would have perked up at the first mention of an argument—*anybody's* argument, didn't matter who, as long as it was a good one—and tried to figure out who was right and who was wrong, and just about talked it to death. That's life in the country. You know that song "There's No Business Like Show Business"? Around here they oughta sing "There's No Business Like Other People's Business."

But Miz Powell just leaned back against the sofa, and said, "Well, I don't mind saying that young man nearly frightened me to death when I found him in the garden. Your horse was nearby, of course, and I recognized *him*—what is his name again?"

"Brother."

"Oh, yes. Curious name for a horse."

"Thank you," I said.

"Frankie was *very* upset," she went on. "At first I thought someone had been chasing him. I brought him inside and gave him some tea—tea works wonders on the nerves, don't you find? May I refill your cup?"

"Yes, please," I said.

"And he related to me in great detail what he was running from." She poured us two more cupfuls as carefully as if we were a couple of Japanese dames having ourselves one of those tea ceremonies.

"What did he tell you?" I asked.

"That some bad people had come to the house, that they were going to throw him out and send him away to an institution. Ordinarily, in such circumstances I should have telephoned the police at once. Before I'd spoken to him, that is. Imagine finding a fugitive in the garden! Really. But there was something about him that was so...plaintive. So wounded. After I heard him out I couldn't turn him away. I wouldn't have dreamed of it."

"Even if it got you into some hot water yourself?" I asked her. "Because if anyone finds out you've got him up here, you're going to be in the bullpucky up to your knees. Maybe even your elbows. Pardon my French."

It occurred to me then that sometimes Elizabeth Powell must have had as much trouble understanding me as I did her. She sat there looking at me like I'd been spouting off in Greek, and I could see her mind working as she tried to piece together what I'd just said.

"I mean, you're going to be in trouble," I said.

"Oh," said Miz Powell. "I *thought* that was what you meant. You do have some colorful ways of expressing yourself, Haley."

"Thank you," I said.

"I shan't worry about trouble," she said. "I have great respect for the laws of the state, but sometimes I have more respect for the laws of decency and kindness. Since Frankie is too scared to go home, and since he long ago attained his majority, then he's more than welcome to stay here. At least until I have a better idea of what the consequences are of returning him. Which is where you might be of some help, Haley. I heard the story from him, but I have no way of knowing how much is true. What exactly is he running from?"

I thought about the best way to put it.

"His parents are about sixty thousand years old apiece, and they're selling their house and farm because they're too rickety to take care of it anymore," I told her. "So Frankie, who really doesn't follow everything with *complete* accuracy, thinks that means he's going to get locked up again while his parents go live in an old folks' home."

"Is that in fact what's going to happen?"

"Hell, no," I said. "They're moving to an apartment over in Angola and Frankie is going with them. That's all."

"I am so relieved to hear it," said Miz Powell. But she frowned and tapped one spindly finger on her knee. "But he has been to an institution before, hasn't he?"

"I think so. I'm pretty sure."

"Do you have any idea what that experience was like for him?"

"Pretty bad, I'll wager," I said.

"I think so too," she said. "He's alluded to it constantly. Isolation, uncleanliness, overdosing him on mind-altering drugs. I think they weren't very kind to him there. I haven't known Frankie very long, but he seems the sensitive type."

"That's putting it mildly," I said.

"And there is the matter of his...behavior," she said. "I'm not an expert, but I don't believe it's really common schizophrenic behavior, Haley."

"No," I said. "I think he's got more than one thing wrong with him, though. I'm told he was a normal enough kid, but he started taking some kind of pills when he was around ten or eleven that stopped his development upstairs. I think it was a mistake—it wasn't supposed to happen that way. And they ended up taking those pills off the market a little later, because they had side effects. But it was too late for him."

You might remember the big Fanex scandal in the news a long time ago—I didn't remember it myself, since it happened when I was real little, but I heard all about it from Mother. Fanex was some kind of drug they used to give to kids with behavior problems, meaning kids that acted up more than normal, I guess. Frankie, of course, was one of those kids. He was having problems even before they knew he was schizophrenic—the deck was stacked against the poor guy from the start. The drug worked pretty well, but this was before they had as many testing rules as they do now, and nobody had bothered to fig-ure out the long-term effects of Fanex on children before they started giving it to them. I guess they probably only tested it on rats, or some-thing like that. Anyway, turned out that Fanex caused a lot more problems than it fixed, namely that it stopped these kids' brains from growing the way they were supposed to. I don't know the details of it, but I did know that all across America there were maybe five or ten thousand people Frankie's age who acted like they were still what-ever age they were when they started taking the drug. It was a national tragedy. Most of them were boys, too. There were lots of lawsuits, and the makers of Fanex were of course up shit creek after that, and they had to stop making it—but no amount of money would ever fix what was wrong with those kids, not even millions and millions. That was the real reason Frankie acted like he did—not schizophrenia but Fanex. And the worst part about it was that the Fanex people got out of the whole mess somehow without having to pay anyone a dime. I guess they must have dove headfirst through the first legal loophole that presented itself.

One of the stronger side effects of Fanex was that it stopped these kids from dreaming. Now, everyone knows dreams are important. I don't mean goals and ambitions but the actual dreams we have every night. Even dogs have to dream about rabbits and whatnot. Even Brother dreams—I'm sure of it. I've heard him talking to himself in his sleep. And if your dreams are gone, that means they've reached into your head and stolen something no person should ever lose. As if poor Franks didn't have enough working against him already.

"Just imagine," murmured Miz Powell.

"Oh, I've imagined many a time what it must be like to be Frankie," I said. "And it's never any fun at all."

I flashed back then to Frankie telling me about his theater. I don't know why I thought of it then—it just came to me. It'd been one of those many moments when it seemed like Frankie was tuned into a different channel than the rest of us, one that broadcast ideas only he could understand. I'd never been able to forget the day he drew those plans in the dirt, because I'd never been able to explain it. On the spur of the moment, I told Elizabeth all about it—his idea for a "theater of the human spirit," and how even though he'd never mentioned it again, at the time it had seemed like the most important thing in the world.

She listened with a sort of faint half smile of fascination, and when I was done, she said, "The Oracle at Mannville."

"Beg pardon?"

"I was thinking of the Oracle at Delphi," she said. "Have you ever heard of that?"

"No, ma'am."

"The ancient ones all had their oracles, and for the Greeks it was Delphi," she said. "It was where they went when they had questions about the future. Some say the Oracle was a schizophrenic personality, someone who spoke in riddles which people would then try to piece together. Nowadays we take our oracles to the hospital, but back then they were valued as seers. Delphi was dedicated to Apollo, if I remember correctly. And a very important part of Greek culture oracles were, too. Some say the temple was a holy site even before the Greeks came— part of an even older culture, one that the Greeks themselves had taken over. Possibly the Etruscans."

"I see," I said, though I didn't really see at all.

"If Frankie had been born in Greece three thousand years ago, that's where he would have ended up," said Elizabeth. "People would have come from miles around to ask him questions, and he would have gone into a trance and answered them."

"A *trance?*"

"What they call now an episode," she said. "That's a very interesting story, Haley. Thank you for sharing it with me."

This comment had a kind of air of finality about it, and I looked up at an old clock on the mantelpiece to see that it was nearly ten. I hadn't realized it was so late—time had been getting away from me all day. I reached for my crutches and stood up.

"I better get going," I said. "Thanks for the tea, and the conversation."

"You're most welcome, Haley," said Elizabeth. "You're a very mature young lady, you know. I have enjoyed speaking with you. Are you going to tell anyone where Frankie is?"

I liked that—she wasn't *telling* me not to tell anyone, she was *asking* what I was going to do.

"Not yet," I said. "You're right. It is up to him. But his parents are near the breaking point, so I think the sooner they know he's all right the better."

"I understand completely," said Elizabeth. "We'll have a talk in the morning, he and I, and we'll decide what to do."

She let me out onto the porch and helped me down the stairs, watching as I headed across the dewy lawn toward the road. There was a half-moon up, casting a gauzy white light over everything like a thin film of spiderweb. I love moonlight on a clear night such as that. You can almost feel it in your hair, like wind.

"Safe home, Haley," she called after me.

"Thanks, Miz Powell," I said.

I thought about the Oracle at Delphi as I headed back toward the old Bombauer domicile. What Elizabeth didn't know was that I came from a long line of oracles myself—not the schizo kind but the witchy kind. I was still tingling with weird energy from my little experiment at the kitchen table that afternoon. I wondered what she would make of *that*.

I had completely forgotten to ask her about the old Flash, the one the East Germans got—and now on top of that little mystery there was the matter of that old Nazi pistol in her bathrobe pocket. She was a curious one, she was. I made up my mind to get back there as soon as decency and good manners would allow, maybe after all this business about Frankie was resolved, and then I would ask her some more questions. She would be a wealth of good stories, old Elizabeth Powell. I just knew it.

Next morning around ten, Mother came home from the Grunveldts with her face all flushed with excitement. "He's home," she announced. "Frankie's home!"

"Is he?" I said. I tried to act surprised. "Where's he been?"

"He won't say," she answered. "The police are talking to him, but he won't tell them anything. But the important thing is that he's safe and sound." She kicked off her shoes, and then she stopped and looked at me. "The poor dear thought he was going to be sent away to Gowanda," she said. "That was why he ran away."

"Imagine that," I said.

"I don't know why on earth Frankie would think he was going to

Gowanda, unless someone had *told* him he was going to Gowanda," she said, looking hard at me. "Someone who was trying to tease him, and ended up scaring the life out of him."

"Don't even start with me," I said. "*I* wouldn't tease Frankie like that. I know how sensitive he is."

"Hmm."

"Hmm what?" I said.

"You're sure you don't know where he was?" she asked.

"Sure I'm sure," I said.

"You would have said something, right?"

"'Course I would," I said.

"All right, then," she said. She was so relieved at the whole business being over that she just let it drop right there. "I think I'm going to bake a celebration cake."

I was glad she didn't push me anymore, because lying like that leaves a bad taste in my mouth, and I can only keep it up for so long before I start to fold. And her mention of a celebration cake made my stomach gurgle and shrink at the same time. Even at the tender age of seventeen, I'd already conditioned myself to stay off the sweet stuff— seems it went straight to my rear end without even stopping off in my gut first to say how-de-do. And now that I was leading a "sedentary lifestyle," as they say in those magazine fitness ads, I was porking up a little more than I was happy with. But I never could resist Mother's celebration cake. And she hadn't made one in a long time, not since I was little—because we hadn't had much to celebrate, you see.

I sat with my leg propped up and watched as she took out the flour and baking soda and sugar and got down her favorite mixing bowl, an old piece that had belonged to my father's mother—my other grandmother, who I never knew. She and my grandpop on my dad's side both passed away before I was born, her of cancer and him of a heart attack. That's what country living will do for you—not the clean air, mind you, but the food. Us small-town folks have never been noted for their dietary smarts. Eggs fried in bacon grease for breakfast, and in some families red meat for dinner five nights a week, which you can't help because there's so damn much fresh beef around here. And when you go out for dinner, it's pizza or fried chicken or cheeseburgers. Trucker food, mostly—and I have never in my life seen a healthy-looking trucker.

Mother popped out to the henhouse and swiped herself a couple of eggs, which she proceeded to break into the bowl. Then she stopped herself, and said, "Chocolate or vanilla?"

"Oh, mercy," I said. "That's like the Devil asking Eve if she wants an apple or an orange."

"Very funny," she said. "I think chocolate." She melted up a few squares of the unsweetened kind of chocolate, and added some more sugar to the mixture.

"Mom?" I asked.

"Yes?"

"What about what happened yesterday?"

She put some butter on her fingers and started greasing up a pan.

"What about it?" she asked.

"Don't you want to talk about it some more?"

"Was there something more you wanted to say?"

She wiped her hands on her apron, leaving a big streak of butter and flour. A little wisp of hair was hanging down over her forehead. She was going gray, I realized. I mean, grayer. Seems like she'd always had at least a little gray up top ever since I could remember. But for a moment there she looked more like her own mother than she did like herself, and I got a little twinge, thinking that someday she was going to be an old lady too, and that day was not as far off as it used to seem.

"I guess I just wanted to know more about it," I said. "Like, when Grandma taught you how to do it. What was that like?"

She sort of smiled, not looking at me, but I could tell it wasn't a happy smile. It was the kind of smile someone trains themself to show when what they really feel like doing is crying. My mother would always smile, even with an arrow in the gut. I guess it's a generational thing. Me, I would always let the world know what was going on inside me, even if it wasn't all sugar and spice. Tell you the truth, I think I must have gotten into the line for puppy dog tails and pails of snails instead, or however the hell that stupid song goes.

"What makes you think she taught me?" she said.

I was surprised. "Well, you were acting like—"

"I learned the way you learned, Haley," she said, "which is why I've decided not to be mad at you anymore. I didn't really have any right to be mad in the first place."

"You didn't?" I asked, thinking, *Now, this is progress!*

"I've been thinking it over. I remembered the first time I tried it on my own. My mother found me doing it, just like I found you."

"Was she mad?"

Mother kind of winced. She never told me too much about how it was growing up, other than that they didn't have electricity and running water and all that, and I wondered sometimes if it had been rough on her in more ways than one. Grandma was pretty old now, but she was still tough, which of course would lead one to believe that when she was younger she was even tougher. Stronger. And out there in the woods like that, people get to making their own rules. I wondered what kind of punishment a religious fanatic—hate to say it, but that's pretty much what my grandmother was—would use on her own daughter, out there in the middle of nowhere. She could have been doing just about anything to her. And the fact that Mother didn't talk about it made me think that maybe sometimes some bad things did happen.

"I don't know," she said. "I couldn't tell if she was mad or not."

"What'd she do?"

She stopped pouring the batter into the pan and just stood there, holding a spatula.

"I always swore I'd never do things like that to my children," she said. Her voice had gone soft now, so I could barely hear it. I stayed quiet and listened. "She sent me away," she said.

"Away where?"

"Out. Into the forest."

"You mean by yourself?"

She nodded.

"For how long?" I asked.

"A whole day," she said. "Sometimes two. She thought it would make me stronger. She really didn't do it to hurt me, Haley. I believe that. It wasn't punishment. It was supposed to be a teaching. But...I wasn't allowed to bring any food or water."

"Two days with no food or water? Was she trying to kill you?"

Mother was still staring at the cake batter.

"Yes," she said. "In a way, I think she was. She said if I was still alive when she came back that it would be a sign."

I felt shock settling over me like a cold, wet blanket. My mother, abandoned in the forest as a girl? By her own mother? I felt a kind of protective rage, almost. Like she was my daughter and not the other way around.

"A sign of *what*, for crying out loud?" I asked.

"Of my...connection," she said. "A sign of whether I was fit to carry on her work. She must have gone through the same thing herself, when she was a girl. We all did."

"Who all?" I asked.

"My mother, and her mother, and her mother," said my mother. "It's old, Haley. It's ancient. You come from a long line of very gifted women."

Well, I guess that *makes everything all right then*, I thought. Child abuse wasn't child abuse if it was a family tradition.

"You have to be tested, after all," said Mother. "And you have to be found worthy."

"Those are the rules, huh?" I asked sarcastically.

"Yes, Haley," she said. "Those are the rules. And they're very old rules. We might not like them, but we have to follow them."

"Who's we?"

"Us. The women who decide to take this path."

"What path?"

"The path you started on yesterday," she said, calmly.

Well, that gave me a case of the jumps. If I'd known I was letting myself in to be practically murdered, I certainly wouldn't have gone ahead with my little whatever-you-want-to-call-it.

"Couldn't you find your own food and water?" I asked. "I thought you said you knew the forest pretty well."

"No," she said. "I couldn't."

"Why not?"

"I didn't have it," she said. "I just didn't have what it took."

"What do you mean? To survive?"

She nodded. "I just sat there and cried," she said. "She told me later she found me exactly where she'd left me. I hadn't moved. Not an inch."

"Well, no wonder," I said. "A little kid out there—how old were you?"

"About six, I guess."

"Six! And she left you on your own in the forest!"

"You have to understand," said Mother. "She was testing me. Even children want to fight for survival. It's an instinct."

"But you didn't?"

"But I didn't," she said. "It was as if I didn't care. Like I was waiting for someone to come along and save me. That's just the way I am, I guess. Not like you."

"What do you mean?"

"You're a fighter, Haley," said Mother. She was looking at me now. "You'd survive. You know something? You're a lot stronger than I am."

For a moment I couldn't speak. Mother had never paid me an outright compliment before, not that I could remember. I hardly knew how to react.

"Well," I said. "Thank you."

"Don't be upset at her, Haley," said my mother. "In the end, I survived."

"It *does* make me upset," I said. I was starting to feel hot in the cheeks and moist around the eyes, but I held it back. "Did they come?"

"Did who come?"

"The spirits of the forest," I said.

Mother finished spooning the batter into the pan and began to smooth off the top with the spatula.

"That's a whole other story," she said. "And it's not the right time to tell it yet. It wouldn't make sense, really. You'd have to have some experiences of your own before we could talk about that."

"What kind of experiences?" I asked. "Forest experiences?"

"Nothing I care to push you into," she told me.

"You mean you don't want to tie me up in the forest for two days? Well, I appreciate that."

"It's not funny," she said. "Don't make a joke out of it."

"I wasn't. I just meant—well, what kind of experiences?"

"The kind you have when you're on your own in the woods for a long time," she said. "It's hard, Haley. You get cold and scared, and you really do start dying. You can only go without water for so long. Not very long at all, really. And you start seeing things."

"You mean hallucinating?" I asked. "This is starting to sound like Indian stuff."

"What do you think the Indians knew that we didn't know?" she asked me. "Do you think you have to be an Indian to know about the way nature works?"

"I don't know. Seems like they know an awful lot about it, though."

"Not just because they're Indians. Because of the way they lived."

"Well, how did they live?"

"Close to nature," she said. "Close to everything. Not like us. We live far apart."

I knew what that meant—far apart from the real world, safe in our houses with our appliances and our televisions and our central heating. This wasn't the first time Mother had brought *that* up. She'd lived on both sides of the fence, as it were, and she was more aware of the differences between the two worlds than most people. Living in the modern world made you soft—you relied on things outside of you to help you survive rather than things inside you. That meant you didn't know yourself as well. But living in the old-fashioned way was a lot harder, and a lot... well, *dirtier*, I guess. It isn't easy to stay clean when you don't have running water, plus you're bone-tired all the time from the sheer amount of work involved in keeping yourself going. That much I knew. If Mother had been that sold on living in the woods, then believe me the woods is where we would have lived. So obviously the modern world wasn't all that bad in her eyes. But she would never be completely at home in it, either. She'd always be like a tourist on an extended visa rather than a citizen.

"I don't want to do it," I said. "If that's what it's like, I'm sorry I ever started."

"That's okay with me, Haley," said Mother. "I realized yesterday it's your decision, not mine. That's my gift to you. I won't push you into it. Not like she did to me."

I was quiet for a while, just thinking.

"Mom?"

"Yes."

"Are you ever mad at Grandma for pushing you into it?" I asked.

Mother finished smoothing out the batter and put the pan in the oven. Then she took off her apron, hung it up, and washed her hands in the sink.

"What good would that do?" she asked me over the sound of the running water.

I could see steam rising up around her shoulders, and I wondered just how hot that water was. But she kept her hands in it, even though it would have burned the skin right off a normal person. My mother could lift cake pans out of a hot oven without mitts on—I'd seen her do it. Her skin was part asbestos, seemed like. Or maybe she'd just trained herself not to feel it anymore.

"What good in the world would that do at all?" she asked.

.   .   .

It was getting on towards the Fourth of July by then. Really it was still only June, but out here in the Greater Mannville Metropolitan Area, we take our holidays very seriously, and the Fourth most seriously of all. Us Mannvillians are a very patriotic bunch. On most holidays, like Christmas and Thanksgiving, you have your cousins and uncles and aunts and whatnot coming in from all over the place to sit down to a big dinner—a real family affair. But around here the Fourth was the time when one family in particular had a huge picnic, and every-one else could just drop in whenever they liked, as long as they chipped in with whatever they had to make it a party.

Some years ago, the Shumachers had started throwing a bash that anyone and his dog could come to—didn't even matter if they were American, even though it's supposed to be the day we celebrate our independence from that nasty old King George we learned about in school. It was kind of funny that the Schumachers would be the ones to do it, considering that both the Mr. and Mrs. were from some-where else, or at least *talked* like they were—but then, some folks that had been here for generations *still* had accents, so there you go. Any-way, Mr. Shumacher usually slaughtered a cow and a pig, and they bar-becued it up over a pit big enough to park a truck in and let people eat until they busted. All you had to do was bring the potato salad, or the Jell-O mold with marshmallows floating in it, or whatever you made best. Last year there were almost a hundred people at their party, and this year there would probably be more than that—folks were gear-ing up in advance, planning what they were going to bring and maybe cooking it and freezing it up so that on the actual day of the party they wouldn't have to waste valuable time.

As far as holidays went, Christmas was the one where you could tell what kind of year it had been by how many presents were under people's trees—lots of presents in a good year, and just one or two in a bad. But the Fourth was a holiday you could rely on, when everyone went all out no matter what kind of financial condition they were in, and when everyone was in a good mood, even if things weren't going all that well.

The Schumachers threw the best parties in the history of the world. If they'd been in charge of the Last Supper, there would have been a lot more than thirteen guests, let me tell you—and the course of history would be completely different. Jesus would have turned the water into Schlitz, and Judas would have passed out, drunk and stuffed full of barbecued ribs, by about nine-thirty. Most likely the Romans would have been invited too—and they would have come, since nobody turns down a chance to go to a Shumacher party. It was the kind of event I could see being carried on a thousand years from now. It could become the sort of tradition that everyone keeps up without even remembering why, like that crazy running of the bulls in Spain that you read about in *National Geographic.*

It was also the kind of deal where young folks, who were usually busy working on their parent's farms or at their town jobs, could get together and cut up a little, and check each other out—and maybe sneak off into the barn for a while, if you get my drift. It was a big old barn, and it could hold many a couple without them having to give up too much in the way of privacy. I knew that for a fact: Last year, during a moment of weakness, myself and Adam Shumacher sort of got lost among the hay bales for a brief time, even though I have never considered myself to have much interest in members of the opposite sex—the whole business just seems too messy, if you want to know the truth. I am not opposed to men in general, lest you get the wrong idea, but I had heard enough football players sniggering to each other in school about their various so-called "conquests," which if you ask me were mostly made up anyway, to allow myself to fall victim to their raging hormones. The most dangerous thing in the world is a randy male. Adam himself wasn't a bad sort—he was nicer than most, always polite not only to me but also to Mother, even after our little tryst. To give him credit, I don't think he ever told anybody about it. But I chalk the whole thing up to temporary insanity on my part. I had been sneaking sips of beer all afternoon, and the alcohol had worn away my defenses until, to my eternal mortification, I fell for his stupid ploy of going to look at the old dates carved on the rafters of the barn.

But before this year's party, I had to go back into the hospital and get that big old stabilizing rack taken off my leg, the pins inside me having settled well enough by now so that they could stay put on their own. This meant another operation, which meant they had to knock me out again, which meant that I was laid up in bed once more, getting addle-headed and clogged up from all that medication. But things went a little smoother all in all, since this time around I knew what to expect. Even so, I spent the next couple of weeks just taking it easy. The doctor told me I'd done too much moving around, and that I should just lay low for a while and let nature take its course. So I didn't see anything of either Frankie or Miz Elizabeth Powell until the Shumacher's party.

The Shumachers were the kind of typical farming family that used to be more common than it is now, by which I mean I don't think even the Shumachers themselves knew for sure how many kids they had. Most of them had grown up and started families of their own by now. Amos Junior was the oldest. He married and bought a small farm about ten miles away, where he'd begun reproducing himself as fast as possible, in true Shumacher tradition. He had a number of younger brothers and sisters, most of who were married, and one—Marky, I think—was in agricultural school somewhere. There were twin girls, one married and the other not, but I forget which was which. Adam was the youngest, and strictly speaking he wasn't a Shumacher—he was one of the temporaries, a foster kid from a troubled home. Some folks take in dogs, some take in cats—well, once upon a time the Shumachers used to take in every stray kid that came along, and keep them safe and warm until they'd plucked up the courage to head out into the world again. That farm used to look like Kidville, U.S.A., population ten thousand. They didn't do it anymore, I guess because it wore them out. But Adam never left, so they must have adopted him somewhere along the line.

I remember when Adam first showed up—he was a year or two older than me, but I can still see him as a little kid. Back then he hardly talked at all, and when he did his voice was all ratchety and squeaky. I'd heard it was because his real father had done something to him to make him talk like that—something terrible. His voice had repaired itself now, but Adam was still the shy and quiet sort, which I guess was why I liked him. I never have cared much for your louder, more crude boys, which excuse me for saying so is what most boys are like anyway. Not Adam, though. He was a lot smaller when he was little— well, that sounds stupid, I mean *of course* he was smaller, but he'd been small even for a kid. But all these years of Shumacher cooking and farm work had turned him into a dead-on Shumacher look-alike, meaning he was tall and beefy and as strong as a mule. The only real difference between Adam and the rest of the whole clan was his hair, which was a kind of whitish blond; his eyes, which were deep blue; and his skin, which tanned like mine did. The others in the family were more on the pink side, with darker hair.

On July the second, I was just feeling like getting up and around again, hoping I might make it to this year's party and wondering if Adam would talk to me. Not that I *cared*, mind you—I just wondered, is all. That morning Frankie, who I hadn't seen in a couple of weeks, paid me a little visit. He was carrying something behind his back.

"Hi, Haley," he said.

"What's up, Frankie?" I asked. "Close the door, would you?"

Frankie closed the door, which I asked him to do so Mother wouldn't overhear us.

"Does anyone know where you were?" I asked.

Frankie giggled. "Uh-uh," he said. "It's still a secret."

"Good for you," I said. "What's that behind your back?"

Frankie showed me another margarine container.

"Another frog?" I said.

"Snake," he said, opening it up.

"Jesus Baines Johnson!" I shouted, and before I knew what I was doing I whacked it out of his hand and sent it sailing across the room. I didn't mean to react like that—I just couldn't help it. The margarine container hit the wall with a big *thwap!* and the snake fell out of it and disappeared in an instant.

"Haley!" Frankie yelled. He got down on his hands and knees and began hunting around the floor. "Why did you do that?"

"Frankie Grunveldt, you know I hate snakes more than anything!" I said, breathing hard. My instinct in such situations is to draw my legs up under me, but I forgot that one of them was in a cast and wasn't ready for moving, and pain shot through me like a million volts of pure, unadulterated electricity. For a minute or two I could only lay there whimpering, it hurt so bad.

"He's gone," said Frankie. "You probably killed him. Are you happy now?"

I still couldn't say anything.

"Jeez LOUISE!" he yelled. "How could you hit a little snake like that?"

"I'm sorry," I whispered. "Can I have a pill, please?"

"A what?"

I pointed to the bottle of pills on the nightstand. I had hoped to sort of avoid them altogether, not wanting to end up a graduate of the Betty Ford Clinic, but I felt the occasion merited a little painkilling. Frankie handed them to me and I took one. It wouldn't kick in for a while, but just knowing it was working in me made me feel a little better.

"Well, he's loose now," said Frankie. "Probably somewhere under your bed."

"Find him."

"How? He's scared. He's probably under the floorboards."

"Frankie, you find that thing and get it out of here. I don't care if it means you have to rip up the floor. You do it. Hear?"

Frankie looked from me to the floor and back to me. Then he looked at the floor again. Then he looked at me, and a devilish grin crossed his face.

"No," he said. "I won't."

It was a Mexican standoff. The two of us just stared at each other, me wanting to jump out of bed and wring his neck, and him smug and secure knowing I couldn't do it. He stood there with his arms crossed and stuck his tongue out at me.

"I will kill you," I said calmly. "If you don't get that snake, I will wait until I'm better and I will cut your throat like a pirate. And there's nowhere you can hide."

"It serves you right," said Frankie. "First off, you shouldn't hurt animals."

"A snake is not an animal," I said. "A horse is an animal. A snake is a snake."

"Second of all, it'll teach you not to be so mean to me," said Frankie.

"I'm not mean to you, you shitbird," I said. "I'm the only friend you've got, and if you don't find that snake and relocate him fast, you won't have any friends at all. *Comprende?*"

Frankie colored red and crossed his arms. "That's not true," he said. "Elizabeth is my friend too."

"No, she isn't," I said.

"Yes, she is!"

"You scared her in her garden," I said. I really *was* being mean now, but I was so mad at him for bringing that snake in I didn't care what I said. "She told me she didn't like that. She was scared of you."

"Shut up," said Frankie. "She knows I didn't mean to."

"She only felt sorry for you," I said. "That's the only reason she let you in. She doesn't really like you."

Frankie's lower lip started to tremble and his eyes filled up. He picked up the empty margarine container and backed toward the door. I could see I had gone too far.

"Frankus, no," I said. "I was only kidding."

"No, you weren't," he said.

"I was too."

"It sounded real."

"It wasn't. I'm sorry."

"I don't believe you," he said. And he turned and ran. I could hear his size thirteens clomping on the floorboards as he ran down the hall and through the kitchen, and then the screen door as it squeaked open and slammed shut, and my mother's faint voice, saying, "Bye, Frankie, nice to see you."

"Oh, shit," I said.

I sat up in bed and swung my legs over the edge, resting the bad one on a chair. I'd have to find that snake myself, because Mother sure as hell wouldn't want anything to do with it, and I would not be able to think of anything else for the rest of my life until it was gone. I scanned around the floor until I saw something move underneath the window, just a little flicker of a tail. Then I saw it in plain sight, lying tucked in the crack between the wall and the floor. My stomach did about three flips, but I stayed in control of myself. I reached over with my crutches and prodded it once. It didn't move. Frankie was right— I had killed it. That little movement I'd seen must have been its death shudder.

"Lord, you and I both know this snake deserved to die, but please don't let Frankie know I really did kill it," I said. "And let him know I was only kidding, because I shouldn't have said what I said to him, amen."

"Are you talking to yourself in there?" Mother hollered from the living room.

"Yes, I am, thank you very much!" I hollered back. And I went and hunted up an old pair of gloves and some tongs, ignoring the pain in my leg so I could safely get that abomination of nature out of my room.

5

Miz Powell and the CIA

Mother asked me if I wanted Grandma to come out again and check me over while I was recuperating from my latest visit to the hospital, but I said I didn't care to see her anytime soon, not after the stories she'd been telling me about being abandoned in the forest. I went so far as to say that as a matter of plain fact I didn't think I wanted to see that whiskery old sorceress ever again, but Mother said I shouldn't take it that way. If anybody should have been mad about it, it was her, she said, not me. And she wasn't mad about it, not anymore. She'd gotten over it a long time ago.

"You could learn a lot from your grandmother, you know," she told me.

"Like what?" I asked.

"Like all that information she's got stored in her head, all about herbs and healing and stuff like that. Things that might get forgotten otherwise. I think she's waiting for you to come ask her about it."

"What makes you think that?"

"A feeling," she said. "You're old enough now, after all."

"You change your mind or something?" I asked. "Seems to me just a few days ago you were ready to burn me at the stake for looking into that pot."

"Don't make jokes about being burned at the stake," she said. "That really used to happen to us, you know."

"*Really?*" I asked. "To *us?* Our family? Cool!"

"No, it was not cool," she said. "I could tell you stories that would curl your hair."

"Do tell," I said.

But Mother shook her head. "Not until you can hear them without poking fun," she said. "Maybe you're not ready after all."

"Please," I said. "What good is all that stuff, anyway?"

Mother looked at me for a long minute. "You know the answer to that," she said. "You were born knowing what good it is."

"Well, she's going to be waiting a long while," I said.

I knew that upset Mother, but for some reason she didn't say so. That was pretty unusual, because ordinarily she never held back when she was upset about something. She must have been turning all this over in her mind, thinking about whether or not she wanted me to learn Grandma's secrets, thinking about what kind of person it would turn me into. And she must have realized that she did want me to do it after all. In fact, I began to think that she wanted me to do it so much she was afraid to push me into it, for fear I'd push back even harder. *What gives with the sudden urge?* I wondered. She'd left Grandma long ago—maybe even before she'd had a chance to learn much from her. Maybe she was sorry now that she did it. Maybe she wanted me to make up for her own mistakes. *Well, fat chance of that happening*, I thought. *I don't live other people's lives for them. That's not why I'm here.*

Mother bit her lip, and said, "I know she'd like to get to know you better, Haley. Every time I see her she asks why you don't come visit more."

"That," I said, "is a riot. Last time I went out there she smacked me on the ass because I was wearing shorts. On the ass. You do not slap Flash Jackson on the ass or anywhere else. Got it? You just don't do it."

"Shorts are unladylike, in her mind," said Mother. "That's why she did it."

"Flash Jackson doesn't give a flying fart what's ladylike and what isn't."

Mother rolled her eyes. "I see we're back on the Flash Jackson kick now," she said.

"It's not a kick," I said. "It's reality."

"Haley," she said, "she's the only grandmother you have."

Regardless of my grandmother shortage, I was done with all that oracle-witchery-healing stuff. If learning how to Lift the Veil meant I was going to have to be left out in the woods for days, or something else just as horrible, I wanted nothing to do with it. I'd be content never to have another vision as long as I lived.

And what Mother didn't seem to understand was that Flash Jackson wasn't a joke. He was a way of life, and one I intended to continue living to the fullest, just as soon as I was perambulatory again. Flash Jackson wasn't really any more of a person than Bugs Bunny—I knew that full well. He was a state of mind, a way of looking at the world, a costume I could put on that kept me from getting shunted in with all the other simpering little hussies in Home Ec or the Future House-wives of America Club—believe it or not, there really *was* such a club at Mannville Junior-Senior High School, even though it had been phased out of every other school in the country thirty years earlier. Yes, old Flash Jackson was my religion and my drug, my Jesus of Nazareth and my little white painkilling pills. He was all my imaginary lovers that came at night and did things with me that I can't even bring myself to put on paper. He was the feeling I got when I was soaring bare-assed naked from the topmost branches of a sycamore into the depths of the swimming hole. Nothing I knew about God came close to comparing with what I knew about Flash Jackson. And nobody

in the world was even worth explaining Flash Jackson to, or so I
thought—until I got to know Miz Elizabeth Powell better. *She* was the
one who taught me that Flash Jackson had been around even longer
than I had, that he'd had other names in other lifetimes—and he'd been
known to other people besides me. I hadn't discovered him at all. *He*
discovered *me.*

But before I get into that any further I should probably back up a
few steps, to when Frankie ran out of my room all upset and teary
eyed because of the snake incident.

It was the same old story: me lying around after my latest operation,
with too much time on my hands and only my own poor brain to amuse
me. It was just like when I'd broken my leg in the first place—things
started spinning around and around in my head, only this time instead
of word games all I could think of was Frankie's face. He was so
upset about what I'd said that I got to thinking maybe he was going
to run away again, and that it would be all my fault this time. I'm the
first to admit it—sometimes I just don't know when to let up on a soul.
I don't know why I have this mean streak in me, and why it always
seems to hurt the people I care about most. It hasn't always been there.
In fact, I don't remember ever feeling that way until after old Fireball
McGinty passed on to the other side. I guess it has something to do
with how hard it was on me to lose him. And part of me, a small and
hidden part, was afraid that one of these days I was going to push
someone so far away from me they'd never come back.

Which wouldn't do at all, of course. I didn't want to end up a
lonely old lady with no friends and a herd of cats winding around her
ankles. You saw plenty of that around here, if you kept your eyes
open—there were as many abandoned people around Mannville as
there were abandoned cars in the woods, old people whose children
were sacrificed in war or else grown up and gone away to the cities.
You ever get to feeling sorry for yourself and need a reminder of how
good you actually got it, head over to the old folks' home by the high

school and spend an hour talking to the people there. The school choir used to go there at Christmas to sing carols, and I never went in but that I came out as depressed as a turkey on the last Wednesday in November. No, there was nothing for it but that I'd have to mend my ways. For the ten thousandth time in my life, I resolved to be *good*.

And for the ten-thousand-and-first time, I wondered how long it would stick.

I got to feeling so miserable I had to talk to someone. For obvious reasons that someone was not going to be my mother—she didn't know Elizabeth had been harboring him, and if I had anything to say about it she never would. I felt sure that was going to come out if I unloaded myself on anyone but the right person. So what did I do but call Elizabeth Powell herself and ask her to come over—because when two people have a secret, it's most natural for them to confide in each other about everything else.

"I'd come up to your place, but I'm still kind of laid up," I said. "Just had another operation."

"Shall we have tea?" said Miz Powell. "I've just had some Darjeeling mailed to me by a friend in India."

"Sure," I said, thinking *Who the hell has friends in India?* "But this has got to be a kind of personal conversation between you and me. Not Mother." In a whisper I said, "It's about Frankie."

"I see," said Elizabeth. Her tone didn't change a bit. She didn't even sound worried that someone might have discovered her part in the whole mess. She was as cool as ice. *Man*, but she had style. She had Flash Jackson written all over her. "Shall we say in one hour?" she said.

"See you then."

An hour later on the nose there was a knock at the door. I heard Mother exclaim "Why, Miss Powell! How nice!" and the two of them yipped and yapped at each other until Mother walked her back to my room, and said, "Haley, isn't this a nice treat? You have a guest!"

"How frightfully charming!" I said, trying to sound surprised.

"I thought I'd stop by and bring you this tea," said Elizabeth, setting down a tin box on my nightstand. I guessed it was the Darjeeling from India. I opened it up and took a whiff of it. Your sense of smell can carry you instantly across miles and years, you know, and for a moment I was somewhere I'd never been: a tent in a high, foreign desert, the scent of nearby elephants competing with the odor of something delicious cooking in an iron pot, over a fire of fragrant wood.

"This for me?" I asked, returning to the here and now. "Wow."

"It is, Haley," she said. "For both of you," she said, nodding at Mother, who practically curtseyed with gratitude.

Nobody had ever brought me anything from India before. I held the box close to me like it was some kind of religious relic. Elizabeth looked like she was trying to hide a smile. I guess around me she must have felt like Christopher Columbus, handing out mirrors and baubles to the natives.

"I can't stay long," she said. "I have an appointment in town."

"You look nice," I told her.

"Yes, I *love* your outfit," Mother said.

Elizabeth looked the very model of an English lady, in fact. She wore a tweed skirt and jacket and a little hat pinned to her iron-colored curls, and a pair of white gloves. I could see Mother eyeing up those gloves, all right—it might have been the first time a woman was seen dressed like that around here. I wondered how long it would be before a pair of the same gloves found their way into Mother's Sunday church getup. And yet you could tell that Elizabeth wasn't *trying* to be fancy. She wore those clothes like they were everyday things, like housecleaning togs.

"You want to sit down?" I asked.

"Certainly," she said.

"I'll leave you two alone," said Mother, not without a touch of envy—she wanted to be part of whatever we would talk about, but she could tell that Elizabeth had come there to see me, not her, and thank goodness she had the sense not to intrude. She stepped out into the hallway and went back into the living room. Elizabeth sat down next to the bed and folded her hands on her lap.

"Now," she said, "what's all this about Frankie?"

"I've really gone and done it," I said. I told her about the snake, and the kinds of things I'd said to him, and how awful I felt about it.

"And I'm worried about him again," I said. "It looks like his parents have decided not to move for now. But honestly, Elizabeth, they can't live forever. They're both heading into their eighties. What's he going to do when they're gone?"

Elizabeth settled back in her chair, took a deep breath and held it for a minute, like she was displeased.

"Is he *really* so incapable of taking care of himself?" she said, letting her breath out slowly. It wasn't really a question—it was more of an out-loud thought. "Is he so *helpless?*"

"That's what he acts like," I said. "Because of that Fanex and everything."

"But has he ever been encouraged to get beyond that? Or has he always been treated like he's never going to grow older, and so he simply *doesn't* grow older?"

"I don't know," I said. "He's been the same way ever since I've known him, which is practically forever. He's not faking it."

"I know that, Haley, dear," said Elizabeth with a touch of impatience. "All I'm saying is, if Frankie were to be put in a situation where he had to rely on himself more, I think he might be equal to it—as long as he had friends to rely on in turn. Friends like you, for example."

"Like me?"

"You would help him, wouldn't you? If he was in trouble?"

"'Course I would," I said.

"Even if it was something simple, like showing him how to cook, or something like that?"

An image of Frankie alone in the kitchen came to me, and I shuddered with dread. Frankie on his own wouldn't need a friend—he wouldn't even need parents. He would need four full-time maids.

"I suppose I could show him a thing or two," I said.

"And do you think he knows you would do that?"

"Sure he does," I said. "We're always helping each other out. He saved my life when I fell through the barn roof, after all. I'll always owe him for that one."

"I haven't known Frankie for very long," said Miz Powell. "Yet he seems like one of those rare, trusting souls."

"You're right," I said. "He does get worked up about things sometimes, but he's not the type to stay mad. He's like a little kid that way."

"Of course, children are easily frightened," said Miz Powell. "They often believe everything they're told. Isn't that true?"

Suddenly I felt like the biggest cad in the world. "Yes," I said.

"So if you told Frankie something that upset him, yet you knew not to be true…"

"…but he didn't," I finished for her. I was feeling pretty sheepish by now.

"Maybe you ought to tell him you're sorry," said Miz Powell. "That you didn't mean what you said."

"Yes, ma'am," I said quietly. "You're right. I will."

"We have to take extra care with the Frankies of the world," said Miz Powell. "Some may see them as burdensome, but the fact is they're rare as white bulls."

I didn't say anything. Her point was well taken.

"Do perk up, Haley, dear," said Miz Powell. "We all say things we're sorry for later."

I did my best to smile at her. She smiled back. Then she checked her watch.

"Do you have to go just yet?" I asked.

"No," she said. "I don't actually have to go anywhere."

"But I thought you—"

"It was a fib," she said. "A white lie. Just in case—" She jerked her head toward the door, to where Mother was lurking in the kitchen.

I stifled a laugh. Mother could drive anyone nuts. Then, suddenly,

I felt shy. "Will you tell me about the old Flash?" I asked her, toying with the ratty old quilt on my bed. The Shumacher twins had made that for me, a present on the day I was born.

"The *old Flash?*"

"The guy you said got shot by the East Germans."

"Oh, yes," she said. "*That* Flash."

"You don't mind me asking, do you?"

"No, I don't mind."

"Because, I was wondering…how was it you came to know someone like that?"

"You mean, someone who found himself in predicaments where getting shot by the East Germans was a real threat?"

I nodded. Elizabeth peeled off her gloves one finger at a time and dropped them into her handbag, thinking.

"Do you know what OSS stands for, dear?" she asked.

"Never heard of it," I said.

"Back during the war, which started when I was about your age, the Office of Strategic Services was much like what the CIA is today. In fact, the OSS became the CIA after the war ended. It was an intelligence service, you see, made up of America's best and brightest."

"Like you?" I asked.

She smiled again, weakly. "No, no. I was only a secretary then. In fact, at first I was only a WAC—that's the Women's Army Corps, you know. I was attached to the Eighth Army and sent to England, where I worked in an office. But then I was… *approached*, as we used to say."

"Who by?"

"*By whom.*"

"By whom?"

"By someone who wanted to know if I could be trusted with some special work. Someone with an interest in my linguistic abilities. I speak French, you know, and some German. And a little Russian."

"Wow," I said. "What kind of work? Spy work?" *This was getting good*, I thought. Elizabeth Powell in a dark cloak, dagger in hand, skulking around the shadows. Elizabeth and James Bond rocketing around in a car with built-in machine guns.

"I can tell what you're thinking, and it was nothing like that," she said. "It had to do with coded messages. They needed someone to help type them out and make sure they were delivered in a secure fashion. It wasn't very dramatic or exciting, but it was important. They had to be absolutely sure you wouldn't talk. 'Loose lips sink ships,' as they used to say. And I was flattered to be chosen, because in those days women weren't often entrusted with much that was really important."

"So you learned code?"

"Well, not exactly," she said. "It's hard to explain. There was a Nazi coding device called the Enigma machine, which the Germans used to encrypt their messages to each other. What they didn't know was that we also had an Enigma machine, which we used to decode those messages."

"And you worked on that machine?"

Elizabeth smiled. "Well, to tell the truth," she said, "I'm still not allowed to discuss that part of it. I signed an oath, you see."

"Wow," I said. "Would the OSS come after you if they knew you blabbed?"

"The OSS doesn't exist anymore, actually," she said. "After the war I went to work for the CIA. And of course I had to sign an oath for them, too. More than once, as I recall."

She sat there with a twinkle in her eye and her handbag on her lap, looking for all the world like the grandmother I wished I had instead of that crazy old biddy out in the woods.

"The CIA?" I said. "Come on. You *were* a spy!"

"I never once went undercover," she said, "so if you're hoping for tales of espionage and intrigue, I'm afraid I have to disappoint you."

"Oh," I said.

"What I *did* do, for a time, was work as a handler," she said.

"What's a handler?"

"This was after I'd been asked to stay in London, when the war ended. I saw no purpose in coming back home—after all I'd seen and done, even though I was still effectively a glorified secretary, life on the farm seemed like it would be the end of me. So I stayed in England, a choice I never regretted. Even though I lived there more than two-thirds of my life, I never grew homesick, and England never stopped fascinating me—it was so rich in history and tradition, and those are two things that have always impassioned me. And eventually, I worked my way up to more responsibility, and more sensitive material." She paused and looked up at the ceiling, like the memories she was talking about were dancing around up there. "A handler is someone who deals with spies," she said. "There aren't as many spies in the world as people seem to think there are. Very, very few people in the CIA's employ ever go under deep cover. But those that do have an extensive support network behind them—people to receive their messages, and to make sure they safely get in and out of wherever in the world they're going, and to debrief them when they get home."

"*That* was what you did?" I asked.

She smiled again. "I can't confirm or deny that I actually did that," she said. "I can only tell you that such things went on."

"Gotcha," I said. "Or they'll shoot you."

"For heaven's sake, I doubt *that* very much," she said.

"And was this Flash guy your spy? Were you his handler?"

The smile disappeared. "I can tell you we called him Flash because that wasn't his code name," she said. "It was his nickname. He had a different code name altogether. But that's actually all I can tell you about him. The rest is still classified."

"Did you even know his real name?" I asked.

"No," she said. "I worked with him for over ten years, and I never knew his real name at all."

"That's a long time to know someone and not even know what to call them."

"Yes, it is."

I saw a look of pain cross her face then, for the first time since I'd met her. It was quick, but it was there. She had cracked the tiniest bit.

"And he got shot?" I said.

"Our project was ultimately a failure, yes," she said. Her voice was hard now.

"Did you miss him?"

Elizabeth looked straight at me. After a while I realized she wasn't going to answer.

"Sorry," I said. "None of my business."

"That's quite all right," she said.

"Was your husband in the CIA too?"

Elizabeth rooted around in her purse for something, but I could tell it was the kind of rooting women do when they're not really looking for anything in particular except a distraction.

"Haley," she said. "May I tell you something?"

"Sure," I said.

"This is a secret," she said. "Not something I wish to be known. You understand?"

I nodded.

"I was never actually married," she said. "To my career, yes. But I didn't have time for a husband. I was always traveling, and the Agency didn't exactly encourage me to form emotional ties to people. So I simply didn't."

"I see," I said. "You just tell people you were married so they don't ask questions, is that it?"

"You are a bright girl, Haley," she said. "It's such a pleasure to meet a young person with your perspicacity."

"Well, thanks," I said, thinking meanwhile that the first thing I'd do when she left would be to head for the nearest dictionary. "So—then you never had any kids, I guess. And if you weren't married, you didn't have any family over there either."

"No," she said.

"So...who is there?" I asked. "I mean, who do you have?"

Too late, I realized I already knew the answer. And she could see that I knew it by looking at me, and that she didn't have to respond: The answer was no one.

Elizabeth and I sat for a good hour, just talking away, while I could hear Mother fluttering around in other parts of the house like a trapped bird.

"What, may I ask, is your interest in Flash?" she asked. "Didn't you mention another fellow by that name to me, when we first met?"

"Oh, him," I said. "That's Flash Jackson. He's not a real person. He's kind of like a...I don't know what you might call it. An idea. Or no— a philosophy. Inside me."

"An alter ego, you mean," she said. "A persona."

"I guess so. It's hard to explain. It comes out of a game me and my dad used to play, but it's gotten bigger since those days. It means more now."

She settled back in her chair.

"Tell me about it," she said.

Why the hell not? I thought. She'd told me secrets, and I felt like I could trust her. Besides, Flash wasn't really a secret. I didn't give a crap who knew about him. I *liked* talking about him. So I did just that for quite a good little while, about how when I was racing down the road on Brother, imagining that I was a stuntman, I didn't feel like chubby old Haley Bombauer, farm girl, anymore. When I started thinking like Flash Jackson I started seeing things through his eyes, and everything became an adventure. Life was suddenly dangerous, but the *good* kind of dangerous—the kind that kept you awake and on your toes every moment, waiting to see what perils lurked around the next corner. A dive in the swimming creek was a lot more interesting when the creek was full of crocodiles, after all.

But hearing myself talk about it made me realize that it sounded childish, kind of dumb—*juvenile,* to use a Miz Powell kind of word. It made it sound like the kind of game an eight-year-old kid plays to keep himself amused. And it wasn't that at all. It was way more than that. I thought of how to explain it in a way she would understand, and suddenly I hit on a good one.

"Flash Jackson is a *code*," I said.

"Do you mean a code of honor, or an encryption?" she said.

"Both, I guess. Does encryption mean all scrambled up so no one else can understand it?"

"Precisely."

"Then yes, it's that. But I like code of honor, too. Not really honor—a code of living. A promise."

"A promise?"

"A promise that life will always mean something," I said. "That I'll never let myself get trapped, or bored, or sucked under into this stupid small-town life. I mean, I *like* living here. I don't want to leave. But sometimes the people around here drive me crazy. Why can't a person live in a small town without *being* that small town? Can't I *be* New York City and still *live* in Mannville?"

"I'm not sure I understand you," said Elizabeth.

"It's just the gossiping, and the boredom, and the . . . I don't know what you call it, the *nearsightedness*."

"Myopia," she said.

"Beg pardon?"

"It means nearsightedness."

"Well, do we *have* to be that way? Can't we be higher than that?"

"A very good question," said Elizabeth. "Haley, I don't know the answer. But I do know that a girl can certainly try. She can show her spirit, so to speak."

"I guess that's what it's all about, really," I said. "Spirit. I see so many people around here just going through the motions, like. They don't care much about what goes on in other parts of the world. They don't care about anything, in fact. They just want to get through their day with nothing out of the ordinary happening. That's a good day for them—a day when everything happens exactly the way it's supposed to, and they don't have to learn anything new."

"Indeed," said Elizabeth. "That's never changed, not since I've been around."

"I'm not saying a person has to travel the world to be interesting," I said. "Although I think it's pretty neat that you've done that."

"Thank you," said Elizabeth. "I think you're pretty neat too."

I kind of blushed. Nobody had ever called me neat before.

"You sound a whole lot less English all of a sudden," I said.

Elizabeth smiled a new smile, for her—her whole face lit up, as if she was laughing with her eyes.

"What's so funny?" I asked.

"I used to know a girl just like you," she said. "When I was growing up. Her name was Letty Horgan."

"What about her?" I asked.

"She was a tomboy too," she said. "She even had a horse, as I recall. Though in those days that wasn't so unusual. And we used to say she was full of Zam."

"What's that?"

"Zam is Flash Jackson," said Elizabeth. "Same thing."

"It is?"

"Letty was a great deal like you," she said. "Same spirit, same energy. She didn't mind living the kind of life that was set out for her, but she wanted it to be fun. You see? And interesting."

"What happened to her?"

"Well, I lost touch with her when I moved to England," said Elizabeth. "I've lost touch with all my old girlfriends. It wouldn't surprise me if she'd moved, or passed away, or something. I'm no spring chicken, and that was all a very long time ago. Haley... do I really sound less English?"

"Yes, ma'am," I said.

"Strange," she said.

"Why strange?"

"Because I *feel* less English," she said. "Sitting here and talking to you has reminded me of a great many things. A great many wonderful things that I haven't thought about in years."

"Like Letty Horgan?"

"Yes," said Elizabeth. "Like Letty Horgan."

"We ought to look her up," I said.

"It would be interesting," she said. "Letty was a character. She used to have Zam ceremonies, down at the deep part of the creek. She made us wear wreaths of leaves, and we had to repeat strange chants after her. It was all in fun, of course. Pure girlish silliness. But she always called it the Zam Spot. She claimed it was magic."

"You mean ... *my* creek?"

"Haley, dear. It may shock you to learn this, but you are not the first person in the world to know about that creek. My generation was here before you, you know. And there were others before us."

"Well, I knew that," I said. "It's just weird that she would pick that very spot, because ... well ..."

Elizabeth arched an eyebrow. "Let me guess," she said. "That's where you enact your Flash Jackson rituals, whatever they may be. Am I right?"

"More or less," I said. "I don't really have any rituals, but—well, you know. It's my spot."

"It's a nice little place," said Elizabeth. "Maybe there really is some kind of magic there." She winked. "A power center. Like the Indians used to believe."

Oh, Elizabeth, I thought, remembering the sunflowers—*if only you knew what kind of magic was really afoot around here, in this very house—would you still be sitting here talking with me like this?* Of course, anyone who'd participated in Zam ceremonies as a girl, whatever they were, might be more open-minded than most. But for now I decided that some things would stay secret from her. I would have to know for sure that she could be trusted completely before I told her that I was a ... well, a witch, just like my mother and her mother before her, even if I planned on never having anything to do with Lifting the Veil again.

Two days later it was time for the Shumacher's big whizz-bang. It was one of those hot and muggy days with a haze in the air as thick as a curtain of lake water, and the smell of honeysuckle was like jam spread over the world. It would have been a perfect day to visit the creek for a swim, or barring that to float facedown in the Fireball McGinty Memorial Pond, snorkeling along and checking out the underwater life—the mosquito larvae and the tadpoles and all. Possibly some of the many goldfish I'd liberated over the years were still alive in there, too. But there would be none of that for me this summer, not with my cast.

We'd been going to the Schumachers' for the Fourth every year of my life that I could remember. Mother, who always managed to appoint herself the unofficial deputy of every cooking brigade and party setup crew in the county, went up early to help the Shumacher ladies get everything in order. Out of sheer boredom I decided to go with her, so I spent the morning and the early afternoon of our nation's two-hundred-and-somethingth birthday sitting under a tree, watching Adam and his father heave picnic tables around.

I wished, watching Adam out of the corner of my eye, that I hadn't come. He was wearing a sleeveless T-shirt, and his muscles glistened under a light slick of sweat like the hide of a young colt after running in the sun. Most people don't take kindly to horse comparisons, but coming from me that was a compliment. Yet I was downright ashamed of the way I behaved around him. Being near Adam did something to my confidence level—namely, it plummeted. He was the only person in the world who affected me like that. I knew what it meant, and it irritated me beyond all telling that I was attracted to Adam. Just the sight of him was enough to give me a fit of the grumps, and all because

I wanted him to talk to me more than anything else. I could have killed myself for going in the barn with him last year. He probably thought he could have more of me whenever he wanted now. Well, if he tried his slick moves on me this year, he was going to be learning a hard lesson.

"Ho! Haley! How's dat lek?" Mr. Shumacher called to me.

"Coming along, I guess," I said.

"Hurt much?" said Adam.

He grinned at me as a swatch of lank blond hair fell over his forehead. Used to be that the Shumachers—like many families—couldn't afford a barber, what with all the mouths they had to feed, and even though the rest of the kids were gone now and the barber in Mannville only cost three dollars (if you were a man, that is) Mrs. Shumacher was still in the habit of plopping a bowl over Adam's head and trimming around it like a pattern. (For women, the barber either charged fifteen dollars or suggested not-too-subtly that you go to the hair salon down the street, which was called Hair Today Gone Tomorrow. The Hair Today girls charged twenty, but at least they knew what they were doing when a woman sat down in the chair.)

"Some, yeah," I said, as gruffly as I could. He wouldn't get any simpering out of *me*, damn him. "Gettin' better, though."

"Dat's good," said Adam.

"Yah, dat's goot," agreed his father.

That was the Shumachers for you. Not exactly the most exciting conversationalists in the world—but they were agreeable as hell. If they disagreed with anyone, they kept it to themselves.

I kept watching him work, hating myself for it, noticing how his hair swung low over his eyes, how he grunted as he and his father carried sawhorses out of the barn and laid big planks across them. These would become the tables where all the food was set out. Mother and Mrs. Shumacher were in the kitchen, and I could hear them both talking at once, the unmarried twin—Elsa, it was—chiming in every once in a while. I just sat there, listening to the muted sounds of birds trying to sing in the heavy air.

Around one o'clock Mother and I went home again to freshen up. I didn't need any freshening, not having lifted a finger all morning, but by now I was furious at myself and I needed a dash of cold water in the face. Adam hadn't talked to me any more after asking how my leg was, and I felt like I'd been punched in the stomach. So I went back home, knowing with sick dread that I'd be back in a few hours. What drove me craziest was how *oblivious* he was—how he seemed not to care if I was there or not. I sat at the kitchen table and watched while Mother patted her face with a damp cloth and then eased herself into my dad's old chair, cucumber slices over her eyelids.

"That Adam certainly has turned into a fine young man," she said, as she leaned back and let the cucumbers work whatever magic they worked on her. I never saw that they made any difference, but I knew better than to mention it. "Think you'll get a chance to talk with him this afternoon?"

"Hell if I know," I said. "What do I care, anyway? And for that matter, what do you?"

"No need to get touchy," she said. With her eyes closed she was starting to get sleepy, and she looked kind of like an aging movie star for a moment, taking a break between scenes. "I just thought after that time you spent with him in the barn last year that you two might—well, *you* know. Talk again. More often, I mean."

Embarrassment shot like a wildfire from the tips of my toes to my forehead. I was glad she couldn't see me through the cucumbers.

"You knew about that?" I said.

Mother smiled. "Of course I knew," she said. "A mother knows everything about her children, even when she pretends not to. Which is exactly what I was doing. Pretending not to know."

"It wasn't all that serious," I said. "It was stupid. It was a mistake."

"Oh, I trust Adam. And you. I knew you wouldn't get up to anything foolish in there." She lifted the cucumbers off her eyes and looked at me. "Did you enjoy yourself, at least?"

"MOTHER!" I hollered.

"Well, Haley, excuse me for asking. But with a daughter as rambunctious and tomboyish as you, a mother can't help but wonder—"

"Wonder *what?*" I asked.

"Let's just say I was *relieved,*" she said, resettling the cucumbers and wiggling down lower in her chair.

"Let's just say this conversation never happened," I said. I got up and stumped out towards the steps. "I'll be waiting in the truck," I said over my shoulder.

To understand a Shumacher party, one has to have met a Shumacher— and since it's likely you haven't had the pleasure, allow me to describe them. Your basic Shumacher is a rare, stupendous thing, the sort of person one meets but rarely in life and wonders why there aren't more of them. As I mentioned before, they're generally large, agreeable, and strong, but that really only scrapes the Shumacher surface. Dig a little deeper and you'll find bottomless wells of geniality and decency, and also generosity—this annual party being a perfect example of all three. But dig even deeper and you'll find a creature that loves to celebrate, and needs only the slimmest of excuses to do so. All of life is a celebration when you're a Shumacher. Everything you see and hear is funny, and everything you put in your mouth is delicious.

The best thing about the annual Fourth of July party was that it started early and it went on forever, sometimes until the wee hours. Mr. Shumacher was famous for three things: homemade sausage, home-brewed beer, and party games. These included some games that everyone's heard of, like potato-sack races and pin the tail on the donkey, and other less common events, like throwing things: a huge stone, a small telephone pole, a sledgehammer. These last were usually a men-only kind of thing, although a girl *could* get in them if she wanted. I'd sort of been hoping to try out the hammer toss this year, but it looked like I would have to wait. There were also footraces, flag football, and chasing the greased pig, and after everyone was thoroughly exhausted and stuffed and overflowing with beer, there was music and dancing, and finally fireworks. But my favorite was the greased pig.

It started out with a great squealing from behind the barn, and next thing you know this little black-and-pink streak of lightning came tearing around the corner with Mr. Shumacher and Adam racing along behind it, already laughing so hard that they collided with one another and hit the ground. There was an instant uproar from the men in the crowd. Plates of half-finished food were tossed down, mugs of beer gulped in a hurry, and then about twenty men and half-grown men became a mob of howling pig chasers.

The women, who knew from experience what was about to happen, formed a barricade around the tables. This was to protect the food. The guys tore up the yard for several minutes, during which a twisted ankle, two split lips, and what might later turn out to be a concussion were sustained. First prize for catching the pig was the pig itself, so they were a pretty determined lot, but nobody ended up with it: For the third year in a row the pig got wise and promptly disappeared over the horizon, never to be seen again in this part of the world. It was a disappointment. That pig could have fed a whole family for a year, once it was fattened on kitchen scraps and slaughtered.

"Ve ought to put up a fence und try again," said Mr. Shumacher, but as this was also the third year in a row he'd said that and it hadn't happened yet, everyone ignored him.

The Schumacher party was the kind of party where you didn't need an invitation to show up. This meant it got a little bigger every year, and as the afternoon wore on, this one started looking like it was going to be the biggest party yet. Mr. Shumacher was in heaven. His chubby red-apple cheeks were glowing like a pair of headlights as he stood by the driveway and welcomed new arrivals. I saw Adam's face through the crowd, smiling, a little longer and thinner than his father's but with the same red cheeks, which he had somehow managed to adopt. He had a fair amount of beer in him by then, but it was a Schumacher trait to remain steady as a rock. After a while I realized he was smiling at *me*.

This was it—my big chance to prove how little I cared for him, and for all men in general. I could snap my fingers in his face and walk away. In fact, I was going to do just that. I would show him. I crutched over to where he was sitting, but instead of doing what I'd planned, I said, "Howdy, Adam."

Idiot.

"Hi again, Haley," he said. There was a foam mustache on his upper lip.

"Any beer left?"

He reached under his lawn chair and held up a mug, and I took a deep snort. Mr. Shumacher made beer Germanstyle, the way it was supposed to be: thick and dark and strong, and served slightly cooled, not chilled. I didn't care much for beer, but this stuff was delicious, and it went straight to my head. That was good. If I was going to be betraying my true self and giving in to whatever stupid girly impulses ruled me whenever Adam filled my vision, I figured I at least deserved a little anesthesia.

"You wanna siddown?" said Adam. He pulled up another lawn chair and patted it. I set myself down and arranged my skirt so it fell as gracefully as possible down my cast. Somewhere, I could feel Mother's eyes on me, and I knew she was out there in the crowd, watching.

"How's things?" I asked.

"Good," he said.

"What are you doing these days?"

"Ag," he said.

"Excuse me?"

"Agricultural school. Starting in the fall."

"Oh, yeah? That's nice."

He shrugged. After a while he said: "Oh, yah. And my dad got a new tractor."

"No kidding," I said. "What kind?"

"International."

"Wow."

"Yah."

We sat in silence for several minutes, taking in the spectacle of nearly one hundred fifty people growing progressively drunker. There was a lot of backslapping going on. Somewhere off in a corner of the yard a few women had raised their voices in song, that sappy one about piña coladas and getting caught in the rain.

"How much longer is dat t'ing gonna be on your lek?" Adam asked.

"Forever," I said. "I don't want to talk about it."

"Oho," he said teasingly. "What *do* you wanna talk about?"

I think the same memory hit us both at the same time: hay stuck in our hair, sweat trickling down our chests, hot salt in our mouths, heavy breathing. That stupid girly reflex took over me and I looked primly down at the ground, my ears red. I could feel heat coming from him and I knew he was looking at me. I was having the biggest shyness attack of my life.

"I don't know," I said.

"You havin' a good time?" he asked. He had the softest voice: kind and warm, with a touch of his adopted father's deep rumble.

"Yeah," I said, still not looking at him. *Damn it,* I thought. *What's happening to you?* I knew what Adam was thinking, and I know he knew what I was thinking—it was written all over my face. And as much as I hated myself for it, I knew that if he grabbed me by the hand and led me toward the barn, I would have gone.

And I do believe he was going to, but at that moment, who should appear but that little shit Frankie, breathing like he'd just run a mile.

"Hi, Haley," he said. "Hi, Adam."

"'Lo, Frankie," said Adam.

"Frank," I said sternly, but he missed it.

"Heard you were gone for a while!" Adam said.

"Yup," said Franks. "I'm back now, though. Can't tell you where I was. It's a secret."

"Frank!" I said.

"All righty," said Adam breezily. "Don't tell me, then."

"What are you up to, Franklin?" I said, gritting my teeth.

"I have to show you something," he said.

"Right now?"

"Yes. Right now."

"Good Lord," I said. "Can't you bring it over here?"

"It's too big," he said. "I can't lift it."

Adam was a pretty tolerant guy, not the sort that would make fun of Frankie—but having Frankie around was enough to kill anyone's sex drive. I could have argued with him, even ignored him, but that would have made me look desperate. So I stood up, sighing heavily, and said, "See ya, Adam."

"'Kay," he said. "Bye. Bye, Frankie." I couldn't tell what he was thinking. Absolutely no emotion showed on his face at all.

"Bye, Adam. Come on," said Franks, pulling at my arm.

"Stop that," I said. I was about to give him another tongue-lashing, but I remembered how guilty I'd felt after the last time. We made our way through the people until we came to a massive boulder that formed the centerpiece of Mrs. Shumacher's flower garden.

"Look," said Frankie, pointing at the boulder.

"You brought me over here to see this?" I said. "A fucking rock?"

Frankie looked shocked. "Haley!" he said. "That's a bad word!"

"I know," I said. "And I meant it, too."

"You shouldn't use that kind of language."

"Frankus," I said, "if you don't show me what you brought me over here to show me, I'm gonna put a hurt on you like—"

"Here," he said, bending down and pointing. "Look *here.*"

I looked. He was pointing to the outline of a fossil in the side of the rock. I gave up—I wasn't going to get rid of him until I looked. So I made a big production of lowering myself to the ground and leaning in so I could see better. It was an imprint of a little salamander or something, some kind of lizardy-looking thing, about ninety zillion years old.

"Isn't that cool?" said Frankie. He traced it with his fingers. "Isn't that the coolest thing you've ever seen?"

"Pretty cool, Frankie," I said. "Great. Wonderful."

"This salamander was around before people," he said. "It existed when the world was still a dream. When we didn't even exist yet, Haley. We were all still dreams back then, because the world hadn't thought us up yet." He looked at me, a streak of dirt smeared across his forehead. "We all existed in the world's mind, which means we existed in this *salamander's* mind," he said, "and then he died, and now here we are. He's like our grandfather or something."

"This salamander is our grandfather?"

"Well, not *exactly* our grandfather, but more like our spiritual—"

"Okay, Frankie," I said. "Whatever you say."

At that moment there was a whoop from a group of men that were starting up some new game, and simultaneously I felt a rush of air on the back of my neck. It was caused by Adam, who'd leaped over us on his way to join them. I watched him go, hair tossing as he ran.

"He shouldn't jump over people like that," said Frankie. "Not without telling them first. We could have gotten hurt."

"Adam wouldn't hurt us," I said. I watched him huddle up with a bunch of town boys and then break and form a defensive line. They were playing shirts and skins, and as luck would have it Adam was on skins. He stripped off his shirt and tucked it in his belt, and I let myself have a good long look before I forced myself to turn my eyes away. "He wouldn't hurt anybody," I said.

"Oh, man!" said Frankie, smacking his forehead.

"What?"

"I forgot I had to get my dad some potato chips," said Frankie. "I gotta go." He stood up and brushed himself off.

"Wait a minute," I said. "Help me up."

"I can't. My dad *loves* potato chips. So do I."

"Help me up, damn you," I said. But Frankie was gone. So there I was sitting by myself next to a rock, in the dirt, in the middle of Mrs. Shumacher's flower garden. Like an idiot.

"Haley?"

I turned. It was Mrs. Shumacher, wearing an ankle-length dress, her massive bosom sticking out about half a mile in front of her.

"Haley? Did you fall down?" she asked.

Here's the weird thing—she said this in German. If someone had asked me how to say that phrase in German, I couldn't have done it; in fact, I couldn't even have repeated it back. But I understood her perfectly, I guess from listening to my grandmother and my mother talk to each other all my life. It's strange what the mind remembers sometimes.

"No," I said in English. "I was just looking at this salamander here."

She reached down and held out her hand. I grabbed it and she hoisted me up, effortlessly, though if I was going to tell the truth I'd have to say that I was no petite little thing. The Shumacher women were stronger than most ordinary men, I guess because they were Shumachers. Before I knew it I was on my feet, and Mrs. Shumacher bent down and picked a carnation from her flower bed.

"Put that behind your ear," she said. "That's your flower, you know. The carnation. You look good with it."

"My flower is the sunflower," I said. But I stuck it behind my ear. "Thanks, Mrs. Shumacher," I told her.

I found myself an unoccupied lawn chair and did my best to ignore the football players. It was a short, injury-prone game, most of the contestants being already half-full of beer, and within half an hour at least four of them were sidelined. I deliberately did not look to see if Adam was all right. Then who did I see standing on the edge of the playing field but my old childhood friend, Roberta Ellsworth.

Good Lord, I thought. *What is old Robertums doing here?* I'd never seen her at a Shumacher do before. I kind of scrunched down in my seat so she wouldn't spot me—the last thing I wanted at that very moment was to have to put up with her honking and rasping in my ear.

But as it turned out, I didn't have to worry. The game was called on account of drunkenness, and what did old Roberta do but make a bee-line for Adam himself, before he even had a chance to put his shirt on.

I don't believe it, I said to myself.

The two of them stood there talking for several minutes, during which I wished all kinds of things to come out of the sky and crash into Roberta's head: pianos and anvils and anything else I could think of. Then, as I watched in disbelief, Roberta turned and ran, just took off—and what did Adam do but take off after her, laughing his head off, and before I knew it the two of them had disappeared behind the barn, a wolf chasing a very willing deer, and I knew from personal experience there was a side door that allowed you to get in and out of the barn without everyone else at the party seeing you.

That's men for you, I thought bitterly. *They are wolves—sniffing at every pair of legs that walks by, and drooling all over the ankles.*

That about tore it for me. I started looking for Mother to tell her I was ready to go home. There were still hours of the party left, but I was damned if I was going to sit there like a bump on a log any longer. But before I could find her I saw Elizabeth, talking to another lady about her age and looking happier than she ever had, since I met her anyway. She waved to me and I headed over to say hello.

"Haley!" she said. "You'll never guess who I bumped into!"

"Hi, Elizabeth," I said. "Who?"

"This is Letty Horgan!" she said. "You remember, the girl I was telling you about?"

"I haven't been a girl for more than fifty years, Lizzy," said Letty. "Hello, Haley. It's nice to meet you."

"That's a lovely carnation, dear," said Elizabeth. "Sit down, will you?"

"Don't mind if I do," I said.

"We were just talking about the old days," said Elizabeth. "And how very much has changed since then."

I noticed that Elizabeth had by now lost most of her English accent. It must have been because she was talking to someone from the old days, because even though she still used words differently than we did, her way of pronouncing them had gone back to being almost completely American.

"Lizzy hasn't celebrated the Fourth of July since the nineteen-forties," said Letty. "Not really, anyway. Can you believe that?"

"Hard to imagine," I said.

"Indeed," said Elizabeth. "We observed it formally as a holiday at the Agency, but we certainly never had any picnics."

"And we were talking about the swimming creek," said Letty. "Lizzy tells me that's a favorite haunt of yours, too."

"Sure is," I said.

"We were thinking we might take a wee stroll down that way," said Elizabeth. "It's not too far, is it?"

I was startled. It would be dark in another hour or so, and the creek was a good half mile off. A lot of the way was over soggy ground, too, which would make it hard going on my crutches. But it suddenly seemed like the greatest idea in the world. I didn't really want to go home—I just didn't want to be at the party anymore. Not with those two groping each other in the barn not fifty feet away. *Jeez*, but I was ticked.

"You serious?" I said. "You mean right now?"

"Surely," said Letty. "I feel mighty spry tonight. Must be seeing my old girlfriend like this. I think I can make it. What do you say, Lizzy?"

"I'm game," she said, "if Haley is. We ought to have a young person with us, just in case. Two old ladies wandering around the country at dusk—imagine our cheek!" She giggled then, just flat out giggled. I couldn't believe my ears.

I've read that certain holidays, such as Christmas, actually occur on former pagan holidays—as if there are certain days of the year people are just meant to party, never mind what they call it. I kind of feel that way about the Fourth, too, even though that's ridiculous. The Fourth of July is clearly not a pagan holiday, it's an American one. Yet it seems like the perfect day to have a summer celebration. It definitely struck a chord in those of us from the Greater Mannville Metropolitan Area, and not just out of patriotism either—things happened on the Fourth that would never happen at any other time of year. There was a kind of looseness in people that wasn't ordinarily there. Maybe it was just the summer heat, or Mr. Shumacher's beer—I don't know. But heading down to the creek at that hour with two old ladies seemed strange and natural at the same time. Without a word to anyone, the three of us just picked up and started walking.

The creek was in a piece of the woods that had never been touched by tractor or chainsaw or plow. There was no point in clearing it, since the land was too uneven for farming, and there weren't any houses for quite a distance—it was about as far from the Shumacher's as it was from mine, and if you drew a line between all three places it would form a perfect triangle. An *equilateral* triangle, that is. The creek was sheltered by ancient stands of birch and pine, at least the part of it where you could swim. The rest of it meandered through fields and pastures and right through the town of Mannville itself, where it was shunted into a concrete gully to prevent flooding, and then it fed into Lake Erie. In town they called it Walnut Creek, but this far out it didn't even have a name. It just was. The banks were nice and grassy and the water probably ten feet at the deepest. There was even a little waterfall at the head of it, which had worn away the creek bed little by little over the centuries until it made a nice pool there, just the right depth for diving.

By now the sun had begun to dip below the horizon. The world was covered in orange-and-gold light, and it seemed to reflect with equal intensity off every individual leaf and twig, and especially the white bark of the birches, so that the whole place seemed like some kind of spangly fairy world. The three of us sat down in the grass and dangled our toes in the chilly water. I could only dangle half my toes, of course. But Letty and Elizabeth took off their shoes and stockings and dipped their feet right in.

For the moment, we weren't talking. I lay back on the grass and looked up at the purpling sky. I had managed to sneak myself enough of that beer to feel it, and I started to drift off a little bit. The whole day and night began to feel kind of like a dream, and I watched the clouds overhead catch the last offerings of the sun and hold them in their wispy arms until it was time to let them go.

I guess I did fall asleep, for a few minutes. When I was next aware of anything, it was of two old-lady voices talking in unison, in some strange language. I didn't feel scared, and I wasn't curious enough to sit up and look. I just listened. It took me a while to realize it was Letty and Elizabeth, chanting to each other. I heard the splashing of water. They were in the creek.

Then I sat up. The two of them had taken off their clothes and were standing in the water. They were facing slightly away from me, the water coming up to their middles, and their hands were pressed in prayer position in front of their withered old breasts, eyes closed, aged bodies swaying back and forth like metronomes.

They ignored me, so I sat quiet. I was pretty sure none of what I saw was actually happening. I was sleeping, I reasoned, and this was some kind of strange dream.

Then I looked up across the creek and the dream got stranger. I saw my grandmother standing there, arms folded across her chest, staring straight at me. For the first time in my life, I looked directly into her eyes, and read not anger or hardness or mistrust of the world I lived in but something softer and kinder, almost an invitation. I didn't bother to wonder how the hell she'd gotten this far from home by herself, or how she managed to be at the creek at exactly the same time I was. We just looked at each other for what seemed like a very long time. Then I blinked, and when I opened my eyes again she was gone—nothing there but deepening shadow, playing tricks on the eyes.

I laid back down on the grass. Letty and Elizabeth had fallen quiet now, and I closed my eyes again.

Some time later I felt a hand on my shoulder.

"Haley," said Elizabeth. "Haley, dear. You've fallen asleep."

I opened my eyes. It was full dark.

"Good gravy," I said, sitting up. "How long was I out?"

"Not too long," she said. "Half an hour or so."

"We'd best be heading back," said Letty. "I wouldn't want to turn an ankle walking around in the dark."

"My goodness, no, not at our age," said Lizzy.

"I was dreaming," I said.

I grabbed my crutches and stood up. I lost my balance for a moment, and I put out one hand on Elizabeth's shoulder to steady myself. Her blouse was soaked through and I could feel her skin under it, leathery and as cold as a clam.

"Were you, dear?" said Elizabeth. "What did you dream of, if I may?"

In the darkness, all I could see of their faces were two white blurs. We were far from the party now, too far to hear it, but there were crickets and frogs singing all around us, and the night was alive with sounds.

"Zam," I said.

They didn't say anything, but I could hear their smiles.

Suddenly there was a tremendous boom in the sky. We turned to see a white mushroom of light appear out of nowhere and blossom

into brilliance, lighting up everything like lightning during a storm.
For several moments I could see both of their faces clearly. The fireworks had started.

"There," said Letty. "As long as that keeps up, we'll be able to see
our way home."

We made our way back along a tractor path through someone's field,
pausing when it was too dark to see and moving ahead when the sky lit
up again. It took us a long while to get back to the party, and none of
us spoke along the way. I was trying to remember: Did I really see my
grandmother, or was I dreaming? What were those two doing in the
water, chanting away and praying like that? And what did it all mean?

"It seems something has happened," said Elizabeth suddenly. "I see
a group of people standing around someone on the ground."

She had mighty good eyes for someone so advanced in years. I
looked during the next explosion, and sure enough there was a knot
of folks standing around the way they might after an accident. *Probably someone bashed their head in playing football*, I thought. I felt a chill
of panic—I hoped it wasn't Adam, even though he deserved it.

The fireworks had been going for a long time, but they showed
no signs of slowing. Mr. Shumacher had gone all out this year. He'd
hired pyrotechnic professionals to come in and give the folks a real
show, and the sky was filled now with fantastic eruptions of light, and
tremendous bangs of manmade thunder. It was the finale. We came to
the edge of the yard and headed directly for where the people were
standing all together. A hush had fallen over the whole gathering, and
nobody was paying any attention to the fireworks. I was pretty sure
by now something bad had happened.

As we got closer I could hear a high-pitched wail, a sick-animal
sound as though something was having its heart ripped out. I'd heard
a sound like that once before, when a stray farm dog had gotten hold
of a rabbit and was shaking it to death in its teeth. The rabbit had

sounded just like what I was hearing now. We came to the group of people and pushed our way in to see what had happened.

The noise was coming from Frankie. He was on his knees, crying, leaning over someone stretched out full-length on the ground. As the last eruptions of the finale lit up the sky, I got a good look: It was his father, craggy profile in shadow, eyes two dark recesses, as dead as the proverbial doornail.

6

Sympathy and Protection

After surviving four years of World War II, roughly five decades of marriage, and a lifetime of subsistence farming—when it seemed that he'd weathered everything life could throw at a man, including also the birth of a less-than-perfect only son whose mental development had not progressed one inch in seventeen years—Mr. James H. Grunveldt was done in by something as simple as a potato chip. These are the kinds of cruel jokes life plays on us. It was like those poor guys in that German submarine movie who almost get killed about a hundred times and finally make it all the way home, only to get blown up five minutes later. The fact seems to be that your life probably isn't going to end anything like the way you think it is, and Mr. Grunveldt was living proof of that. Or dead proof, I guess. Depends on how you want to look at it.

Mr. Grunveldt had always had a weakness for potato chips, even though the doctors had told him they were bad for him. They never could have known just how bad they would turn out to be, of course. It was one of the very chips for which Frankie had abandoned me at the fossil rock that killed him, later that night—stuck in his airway like a golf ball in a vacuum-cleaner hose, and nobody could manage to get it loose, though I heard later that Mr. Shumacher had broken a couple of ribs trying. Mr. Grunveldt's ribs, I mean, not his own.

Mr. Grunveldt never actually meant much to me. He was already old when I was born, and I didn't see him much, or know him very well at all. I was saddened by his passing, but I was more worried about how Frankie would take it.

My fears were justified. Frankie pretty much lost what marbles he had left. It took three men to carry him away from his father's body just so the attendants could lift him into the ambulance. When it pulled away, Frankie made a noise that ran through everyone there like a knife. The fireworks had stopped by then, and the only light came from a few flashlights, and a sliver of moon. It was ghostly and weird, everyone as quiet as church—almost like a murder scene, really. People acted strangely guilty, even though nobody had done anything wrong.

Those same three men later took Frankie home in the back of a pickup truck, where they had to hold him down to keep him from jumping out. He was flopping around like a fish, biting and kicking and hollering at the top of his lungs. Mrs. Grunveldt followed in Mr. Shumacher's car. *She* didn't make a sound. She was quiet and tight-lipped—*fatalistic*, as Miz Powell would say. I suppose when you get to be that age, death hardly comes as a surprise. Still, she was taking it harder than anyone knew. I heard from Mother the next day that she had to go into the hospital herself, from complications of an old illness she'd once had that everyone thought was licked; and only a few hours after that, she died, too.

It was what they call a sympathy death. You hear about them from time to time, how when one member of an old couple goes the other follows close behind. Sometimes it happens in downright spooky ways— like, they both die at the same moment but in separate rooms, or something like that. This one wasn't that spooky, but still it was the kind of thing that made everyone shake their heads in a knowing way and say to each other, *You never can tell, can you?* A thing like a sympathy death makes everyone stop and wonder if there isn't more going on underneath the surface than anyone cares to admit, whether our fates aren't all written down in some moldy old book somewhere, and whether our souls are tied to each other by real but invisible bonds.

As strange as it sounds, the whole thing was kind of a warning to me. Not about potato chips—about falling in love. It was safer never to get so close to someone that they could drag your soul along after them—this is what I decided. It seemed to me like if you gave someone that kind of power over yourself, then you didn't have control anymore, and that scared the hell out of me. I was still red-faced after my little fling with Adam that didn't take place, thanks to the foul temptress Roberta Ellsworth, and I had a new resolution: no more men, ever. I'd never leave myself open like that again.

But Adam was actually the furthest thing from my mind. I had an even bigger problem. The thing I'd feared most had come to pass not three days after I'd said it out loud: the Grunveldts were dead, and Frankie was on his own. I couldn't shake the idea that somehow I'd caused this whole thing to happen by talking about it. Even though I'd sworn off Veil Lifting, I knew it was still inside me. Just because I didn't want it didn't mean I didn't have it anymore. I was cursed. *Could I kill people just by talking about their death?* I wondered. *Should I lock myself up somewhere so I didn't hurt anybody else ever again?*

"They've had to take Frankie away," Mother told me, the afternoon of the day Mrs. Grunveldt followed her husband into the Great Beyond. "I just got off the phone with Edna Bing. She sat up with him all night, and she said he was just uncontrollable."

"Where'd they take him?"

"The psychiatric wing of Mannville General. They had to sedate him. He was so upset, they want to keep him under observation for a few days. They're afraid he might hurt himself."

I knew the place, of course—not the psychiatric wing but the hospital. It was where I'd gone after the barn roof caved in under me. For a small town, Mannville had a great hospital. It was built a long time ago by the town's founder, William Amos Mann III, whose name everyone had to learn in school because he was such an all-fired great guy, and the only hero Mannville ever had. Well, that's not quite true: His great-grandson Eddie Mann was some kind of fighter-pilot ace in Vietnam. Just about everyone around here can recite the history of old Willie by heart. There was even a statue of him on horseback near the school, which seemed to be as much a monument to the amazing shitting power of pigeons as it did to the man himself. Willie Mann found some money after the Civil War, and he used it to build all kinds of things, the hospital being one of them. The hospital was so big it looked like it belonged more in a regular city, not a small lakeside town that had never amounted to anything. I hadn't known there was a psychiatric wing, but it didn't surprise me. That place had a wing for everything you could think of.

"As long as they don't plan on keeping him any *more* than a few days," I said. "If he starts thinking he's back in Gowanda, he's gonna lose it for sure."

"He knows where he is," she said. "He knows it's not Gowanda."

"Can he have visitors?"

"No," she said. "Well—they might let you in if he tells them it's okay, but then he might not even remember you."

I was shocked. "*Not remember me?*"

"This has triggered something," said Mother. "He's having delusions, Haley. Bad ones. He doesn't seem to recognize anything or anybody right now."

We were having this conversation in my bedroom, where I was propping up the old leg again. It had been throbbing in a strange way ever since my little sojourn out to the creek with Elizabeth Powell and Letty. It didn't hurt, exactly. It was just kind of pulsing, like there was something in there trying to get out. I had it up on some pillows, hoping to drain the blood out and back up to my heart, where it could get recharged—according to my personal medical theories, that was the best way to treat it. But so far all that had happened was my leg was falling asleep. As a matter of fact, though, it hadn't really hurt much lately. It was finally starting to get better.

"I have to go see him," I said.

"Well, Haley, I—"

"I don't care if he remembers me or not," I said. "I have to see him and tell him everything will be okay. Has anyone bothered to tell him that? That things will be okay?"

"I don't know what they've told him," said Mother. "I'm sure they've tried. But—"

"He won't believe them. Not the doctors. He *hates* doctors. I have to see him myself."

"He's been given medication," Mother said. "He won't be able to talk to you."

"Jesus Christ," I said. "Those monsters."

"Haley!"

"Why can't they just talk him through it? Why do they have to dope him up?"

"Haley, now just hold on. It's for his own good."

"He has a right to be awake, at least."

"They do it so he doesn't hurt himself. That's why," she said.

"Well, he can still *listen*, can't he?" I said. "He can *hear*, right?"

"I don't know," said Mother. She was sitting on a chair next to my bed, and she was bone tired. She'd been up all night at the party and all day at the hospital, and now that it was getting on into the afternoon she looked like she was ready to keel over and take a snooze right there on the floor. But Mother was the kind of person who couldn't rest if she thought she was missing a chance to be a martyr, or in fact if any kind of drama was unfolding anywhere within her world.

"Will you take me to see him, please?" I asked.

Mother rubbed her face. "I'm so tired," she said.

"Do you want to sleep for a while first?"

She shook her head. "That's not going to happen," she said. "I won't be able to sleep. Not yet."

"Well, then, can we go?"

"Right now?"

"Yes." I gave my voice as much firmness as I could. "Right now. Please."

It wasn't the whiny me or the troublesome, willful me that was asking. It was the real me, and she saw that.

"All right," she said. "Get yourself out of bed and I'll go warm up the truck."

Turned out that calling it the psychiatric wing was a little grandiose, after all. It was only a bunch of rooms at one end of a hallway, closed off from the rest of the hospital by thick glass doors. The nurse at the desk was a tough cookie. It took some work to convince her that letting me see Frankie was the right thing to do, that hearing my voice would be a good thing for him. She said we could have five minutes, and that I couldn't be in there alone; she'd have to come in with me. Mother would have to wait in the hall.

We said that was fine. I knew right off this was not your arguing kind of nurse. This was the kind you listened to. She led us along the hall to Frankie's room. Mother sat herself down in a chair outside the door, and the nurse beckoned to me. But then she stopped me at the door.

"You're not going to like this," the nurse said.

"Excuse me," I said. I dodged around her and went in.

I wished right away I hadn't come. Poor Frankie was trussed up like a calf, his arms and legs tied to the bed with leather straps. It was all I could do to keep from screaming out loud at the sight of him. His eyes were open, and he stared at the ceiling and moaned quietly to himself, moving his head slowly from side to side. Spittle leaked from the side of his mouth. They'd taken away his clothes and put him in a dressing gown, and it had hitched up somehow over his crotch so that his private parts were plainly visible. I looked away while the nurse pulled the gown down again.

"Why is he tied up like that?" I asked.

The nurse pointed to scratches on his cheeks and arms. They were deep and ragged, as though he'd been mauled by some kind of wild animal.

"He did that to himself," she said. "We had to tranquilize him. He can probably hear you, but I'm not sure how much he'll understand. You can talk to him, if you like."

The nurse stepped back and I sidled closer to the bed.

"Frankie," I whispered. "You hear me?"

Frankie moaned. He turned to look at me, like he was moving in slow motion. Eventually his eyeballs pointed in my direction, but they weren't focused on me. They were like two soft, brown marbles, rolling independently in their sockets.

"Franks," I said. "It's Haley."

He just stared. *Jesus*, I thought, *they gave him horse pills.*

"You know where you are, buddy? It's not Gowanda. It's just the hospital."

"Mmf," said Frankie.

"You're not going to be here for long, Franks. Just a little while. Just until things calm down and get back to normal."

Now, why the hell did I go and say that? I wondered. Things were never going to be normal again. *Don't lie to him*, I cautioned myself. *Tell it like it is, but tell him he's not going to be alone.*

"I'll help look after you, Frankles," I said. "I'm on your side. And there's Miz Powell, and my mother, and everyone. Okay? So don't worry. You won't be alone."

Frankie didn't answer. His eyes just stayed pointed in my general direction, but looking at something very far away, something that possibly wasn't even there. It was creepy to see him zoned out like that. I even looked to see if something *was* there, but of course there wasn't. There was just this puke green wall that looked like it hadn't been repainted since dinosaurs were roaming New York State.

"All right," I said. "That's all I wanted you to know. I'll come see you as soon as you're out. That'll be in just a couple of days, okay? Don't be upset, Franks. Everything will work out."

Nothing. There was a strange bump from the hallway, but I ignored it.

"We can look through your binoculars together," I said. "We can spy on the whole world if you want. Whaddaya say? That sound fun?"

Nothing.

"All right," I said to the nurse. "I guess that's it."

"This way," she said. She opened the door and we went out into the hall. Mother had fallen asleep in the chair. That bump I'd heard had been her head lolling back and smacking into the wall, and it hadn't even woken her up. I jiggled her shoulder until she opened her eyes.

"What time is it?" she asked.

"I don't know," I said. "Time to go home."

"All righty," she said. She stood up, groggy, and we headed out of the hospital and back to the parking lot. "Can you drive, Haley? I'm afraid I'll fall asleep behind the wheel."

I was alarmed. "With my leg?"

"It's an automatic," she said. "You only need one leg."

"I'll try," I said. So we headed home with me at the wheel, proceeding mighty slow and hoping we wouldn't run into Madison, Mannville's police officer. I knew how to drive, but I'd never bothered to get my license. Out in the country you didn't need one—kids start driving tractors when they're around ten or eleven, or even younger sometimes, and you never see cops out in our neck of the woods. It was impossible to bend my leg, of course, and the seat wouldn't go back hardly at all because it was a pickup. So I sat at a sort of cockeyed angle and did the best I could, and I guess my guardian angels must have been watching over me, because we made it home safe and sound with Mother snoozing away in the passenger seat.

It was good that I had driving to concentrate on. I knew I'd be seeing Frankie in my mind for a long time, tied down and drugged, drool coming out of his mouth. That was a part of Frankie I'd never believed existed—and yet it was real. All the time I'd known him, there had been two sides to Frankie—the calm side when he was living at home with his parents and checking out our little corner of the universe through his binoculars, and the crazy side when he would disappear for weeks or sometimes months. I never knew what happened to him during those times, but now I'd seen it with my own eyes, and I understood that Frankie had done time in hell.

Damn it, I thought. He was like a brother, even more than I'd realized. I loved the helpless little bastard. I really did. And all I could think about was what Miz Powell had said about oracles, back in the old days in Greece. Once upon a time, according to her, we had known what to do with people like Frankie. Today, almost no one knew how to deal with him, except maybe someone like my grandmother. So he needed calming down every once in a while? Well, I was no herbalist, but one thing I did know was that for every pharmaceutical kind of medicine out there, there was a natural one that did the same thing. There were herbs you could take to relax, to clear your mind, to make your passage through the world seem a little smoother. She could help him, though I didn't think I'd ever get Frankie all the way out there to see her. Not him. He'd get too scared out there in the woods.

Now, if I knew the secrets my grandmother knew, I thought, *then I could treat him myself. He would be free to do his thing.*

It *had* been bugging me a little, the fact that Grandma was probably going to die soon without having had the chance to teach me anything. Much as she freaked me out, the old hag had some good qualities too. I felt better every time she worked me over. If I could do that myself, I could save a lot of money on doctor bills down the road. And I could help other people, too. Especially Frankie.

Maybe, I thought, *I should make the most of her while she was still around.* Like it or not, she was all I had left—besides Mother, that is, and Mother didn't seem to know a blessed thing that was worth passing on. If Grandma had ever taught her anything in her youth, she seemed to have forgotten it.

I looked at Mother, sleeping away next to me, her head bobbing against the windowpane with a gentle *tump, tump*. I had the idea in my head to visit Grandma now, but I wasn't going to tell Mother about it right away. If ideas were airplanes, she was an antiaircraft gun: *bang bang*, she popped away at them until they came crashing down in flames. She had done it to me a hundred times. I had mentioned college to her once or twice in the last year, and all she'd had to say about it was that I would be better off learning a trade a woman could really use, such as cosmetology or hairstyling. Better yet would be to marry a wealthy man and let him take care of me. That was her idea of how to live. Even though she seemed to have had a change of heart lately and thought it might be good for me to get to know Grandma, that was because it was her idea. If it had been mine, rest assured she would have thought of a dozen different arguments against it.

We pulled into the driveway and rolled to a stop. "Wake up, Mimsy," I said. "We're home."

Mother roused herself. "Oh, dear," she said, yawning. "How long was I out?"

"A hundred years," I said. "It's the future, and everyone we knew is dead. Look! There goes a rocket ship."

I pointed out the window. Mother looked in spite of herself and then smacked me on my good leg.

"You stop it," she said. "It's not funny, joking about people being dead."

"Why not?" I said. "We're all gonna die anyway. Might as well laugh about it."

We got out of the car and I reached in the back of the pickup for my crutches. She walked ahead of me as I poled my way up to the house.

"I swear, I don't know where you come up with the things you say," Mother said over her shoulder. "But you're not funny. Not funny at all."

"Not trying to be funny," I said. "Just real."

But my meaning was lost on her. She went into the kitchen without even holding open the door for me, and started directly upstairs.

"You going back to bed?" I asked her.

"Yes," she said. "I'm *exhausted.*"

"Well, what am I supposed to do with myself?"

She didn't answer. At least she didn't slam her bedroom door.

I wasn't tired. I had to talk to someone about Frankie, and about Grandma. And I still had the truck keys in my skirt pocket. So I went back outside and started up the truck, and headed up the road to the Powell house.

I found Miz Powell and Letty sitting in the parlor, chatting away, as pleased as penguins who'd come back to their home iceberg. Miz Powell looked about ten years younger than she had when I met her, and both their faces were flushed with laughter when I walked in the door.

"Look who it is, Letty," she said, after letting me in. "Isn't that a coincidence?"

"Not really," said Letty. "We were just talking about you, Haley."

"We summoned her," said Miz Powell, which was good for a burst of giggles from both of them. I couldn't believe my ears. Giggles? From these two fossils? "Come in and sit down, dear."

"Thanks," I said. I had the feeling that I'd just interrupted something, but neither seemed unhappy to see me. Miz Powell offered me a cup of her ever-ready tea, and they moved over to let me sit between them on the sofa.

"What a horrible shame about Jimmy Grunveldt," said Letty. "Ain't it, Lizzy?"

"Certainly it was," said Miz Powell. "How is Frankie, Haley? Have you been to see him?"

"Just got back," I said. "He's not doing too good."

"I was afraid of that," Miz Powell said.

"Poor boy isn't quite right, I take it?" Letty asked sympathetically.

"He'd be better off at home, if there was anyone left to take care of him," I said. "He can't really handle things as serious as this. He's too fragile. They've got him all dosed up now, and tied to the bed. He was trying to scratch his own eyes out."

"Oh, dear," said Miz Powell.

"I've been thinking a lot about what you said about oracles, Miz Powell," I said.

"You can call me Elizabeth, dear," she told me again. "What about them?"

"That's really what Frankie is," I said. "He's a visionary, isn't he? There's nothing wrong with the way he sees things. It's just that he sees them differently."

"You must keep in mind that I don't know him as well as you do," Miz Powell reminded me. "It's entirely possibly that a long time ago, you would have been right. But the modern world doesn't permit such things. It flouts our own sense of superiority to the ancients."

"You sort of know him, though," I said. "He stayed with you for a while."

Too late, I remembered that we had promised each other never to bring that up in front of other people, lest Miz Powell get in trouble. I turned beet red and looked down at my shoes. Letty looked curiously at Miz Powell.

"Isn't he the young man who was missing?" Letty asked.

"Sorry," I murmured.

"Nonsense," said Miz Powell. "I don't care what Letty knows about me. I never had any secrets from her before."

"We don't have any now, either," said Letty.

"Frankie stayed with me because he was in need, and I was pleased to be able to help him," she announced. "I would do the same again if it was required of me."

"Well, he needs something different now," I said. "He needs my help. And I don't really know how to give it to him. I have some ideas, but they're all going to take too long."

"Such as?"

"Well...never mind," I said. I was too embarrassed to bring up my grandmother in front of Letty, who was still a stranger to me. I hadn't known she was going to be there. "I'll work it out on my own, I guess. Not to change the subject any, but...the other night, when we were all down at the creek?"

I was half expecting them to be ashamed when I brought this up, but they weren't. Both of the old ladies looked straight at me, peering at me through their glasses like a pair of gophers.

"Yes?" said Miz Powell.

"You were, ah—well. Can I ask what you guys were doing?"

For a moment I could see them as they must have looked when they were fifteen years old, two girls with a million secrets between them and no desire to share them with an undeserving world. I never had a friend like that. It was like the last fifty years and more had never happened—as if a clock had stopped when they separated and started up again when they came back together. As if the two of them had their own kind of time.

"Wasn't it obvious?" said Letty.

"No," I said.

"We were Zamming you," said Elizabeth.

"Zamming me?"

"You're one of us now," said Letty.

"We thought you understood," said Elizabeth.

"I see," I said.

"It's nothing *serious*," explained Letty. "It's a fun thing."

"Well, it's *partly* serious," said Elizabeth. "We *are* the only two left, you know. Or rather we *were*, until you came along. All the rest of us are dead. It's time for us to look for new members."

"We had a club," said Letty. "We didn't really have a name for it. A Zam club, I guess you might say. There were lots of girls in it. But they're all gone now."

"Gone, indeed," said Elizabeth. "We needed fresh blood." She smiled.

"I see," I said. "You Zammed me?"

"You don't mind, do you, dear?" asked Elizabeth. "We were saying a Zammish prayer for your protection. And to help your leg get better."

Was this the same iron woman I'd met in the stable just several weeks ago? The same one who'd worked for the CIA all those years, the one who'd run spies in and out of countries all over the world? In the short time she'd been back in the Greater Mannville Metropolitan Area, Miz Powell had changed a lot, kind of slipped backward into the kind of person she must have been before she left—more carefree, open, silly. I wondered what had caused this change in her. I liked it—even though I still hardly knew her, I liked this side of her better. It was less... *formidable*, I guess.

"In what language?" I asked.

"Why, in Zammish," said Letty. "It's not hard to learn. We can teach it to you."

"Rather like pig Latin," said Elizabeth. "Hard to figure out if you don't know what it is, though. Quite useful. I actually used it once in my work, many years ago."

"You're kidding," said Letty. "You did? With the spies?"

"Oh, yes," said Elizabeth. "It was perfect for meetings on the street. Anyone who overheard us would have thought we were speaking something Slavic."

"How do you do it?" I asked. "What's the rule?"

"There's more than one, dear," said Letty. "Don't worry. We'll explain it all to you."

"It might take you a while," said Elizabeth. "But don't get discouraged."

"She won't get discouraged," said Letty. "Not this one."

"Maybe another time," I said. "I was also wondering—did you see anyone else down there?"

"Anyone else?" The two of them cocked their heads like a couple of spaniels.

"You mean—someone was spying on us?" said Letty. "A pervert?"

"No, no," I said. "I just...thought I saw someone."

"Who, dear?" asked Elizabeth.

"An old lady," I said. "My grandmother."

"She wasn't at the party, was she?" asked Letty.

"Hell, no," I said. "She doesn't believe in Fourth of July."

"I certainly didn't see anyone," said Elizabeth.

"Me neither," said Letty.

Well, that settled that. It meant either I was seeing things or they had missed seeing her, and of course I already knew the answer: Somehow, my grandmother had made herself appear to me. I'm not flat out saying magic was involved. It wasn't beyond her to walk all that way just to scare the hell out of someone. I knew it wasn't my imagination. The fact that Letty and Elizabeth hadn't seen her didn't make the slightest bit of difference to me. I just wanted to check.

"Thanks, then," I said. "I better get going."

"Good luck," said Elizabeth. "Drop in as soon as you can."

"Ta," said Letty, who seemed to be experimenting with sounding English, now that Lizzy was sounding more like her American self.

When I went home Mother was still asleep, so I made myself some dinner and then brushed and curried Brother. Poor old sad sack—he hadn't been getting much attention from me lately. He gave me the cold shoulder when I first came in, and it took me a while to warm him up to the point where he'd stick his soft mouth in my neck. But eventually he came around, and we snuggled up and chatted just like old times. The sun was going down, and a few stray rays shot in the stable door and lit up his coat like he was a model walking down a runway.

"Haley," said a voice.

I whipped around fast. It was Mother, standing in the doorway.

"Flaming frog farts, Mother!" I said. "You scared the lights out of me!"

She didn't say anything. She just stood in the doorway, leaning on it and looking down at the ground: the classic bad-news posture.

"Mother?" I said. "What's wrong?"

She had that old look on her face again, too, the same sort of look she'd had when Fireball McGinty was called to the Great Workshop in the Sky. She'd been wearing it a lot lately, what with the Grunveldts passing on like they did. It was her death look. And she had it on again.

"What is it?" I asked again.

The fact that she hadn't said anything yet told me how bad it really was.

"What happened?" I asked.

"He's dead," she said.

I knew she was talking about Frankie. Who else? You get a sense sometimes of the order in which people are going to leave you, and you know who's next on the list. My spirit floated out of me once again, just like that, without warning, and it stood off to one side watching myself have this conversation with her. I was a whole other person, one who'd just walked into the stable by chance and was witnessing this event unfold between two strangers. That was good. That way it wouldn't mean anything to me. It had nothing to do with me at all—it was these other two people, some kind of problem that was totally separate from my own. I could just walk away at any time. *What a relief*, I thought. *I don't think I could handle this type of thing right now myself. How interesting other people's problems are.*

I heard Haley ask, "How did he do it?"

Mother couldn't speak. Mother didn't want to say it. But Haley had to know.

"He killed himself," she said.

"How?" Haley pressed her.

"He...got loose, somehow," said Mother. "And he beat his head against the wall."

"Then he can't be dead," said Haley. "You can't beat yourself to death. You'd pass out first. Right?" Oh, she sounded hopeful, this Haley girl. She sounded desperate. I felt sorry for her.

"He knocked himself out," said Mother. "But then...they think he had an aneurysm. Or something."

"And he's dead?" Haley asked. "They're sure? He's not just unconscious?"

Mother nodded.

"Are they *sure?*" she pressed. Boy, did I feel bad for that girl. She looked like she was about to collapse. I got the idea she'd had strong feelings for this guy, whoever he was. I got the impression she'd wanted to marry him or something. Poor dumpy broad—she'd have a lot of trouble finding another guy. *Look at her,* I thought. *Her ass sticks out too far, and her hips are too wide, and if she wasn't wearing a skirt I bet you could see her thighs rubbing together. A girl that big ought to be big on top, too, but not this one—she is all out of proportion.*

"Okay, Mother," said Haley. "Thanks for telling me."

Mother's eyes were hollow. "I'm so tired," she said. "I'm so tired."

"Why don't you go back to bed," said Haley.

"What are you going to do?" Mother asked.

"I don't know," Haley said.

I was just standing there by an empty stall, watching this whole thing. I think the horse knew I was there. He looked at me, and I could swear he winked—but of course I could only see one of his eyes at a time, so maybe he was just blinking. Haley turned and put her arms around the horse. She buried her face in his long, warm neck and smelled him. I could tell that if that horse hadn't been there she would have fallen straight over into the muck, and that she wouldn't have cared enough to pick herself up again. And I didn't hear the woman called Mother walk away, but when I turned a moment later to see if she was still there, she was gone.

Poor people, I thought. *Poor, sad, sad people.*

⑦

Epilogue to Part One

Just like that, the entire Grunveldt family had been wiped off the face of the earth, all three of them gone in a matter of days. Their house was dark and cold, the For Sale sign that Mr. Grunveldt had never gotten around to taking out of the yard standing like a coded message telling the world what had happened. You never could tell what a For Sale sign really meant when you saw one. It might mean *We Hate It Here and We're Going Back to Where We Came From*, or possibly *There Was a Terrible Divorce*, or even, as in this case, *Everyone Here Is Dead*. It never just means For Sale.

Funerals are the worst of life, boiled down and condensed into a ceremony. I'll never forget old Fireball's service, though I've tried to many times. We cremated those bits of him we could find and put them in an urn. I was not allowed to touch the urn itself, but I put my ear close to it to listen. He was a big man, but I knew they had squeezed my father in there somehow. For years I had nightmares, imagining him trapped inside that little container, pleading to be let out and nobody listening.

A triple funeral is more than three times worse than a single one. It's three to the power of ten times worse, maybe three million to the power of ten million times. No—it's three lives ended, no more and no less, and that is plenty bad enough. So let me not dwell on the end of things but rather on the beginnings.

A few weeks after Frankie was buried, my thigh cast was taken off and replaced with one that only came up to my knee. I felt like a whole new person. My leg had gotten skinny, and hair was growing on it like I'd never seen before, but it was my leg, my old leg returned to me. It would take me a long while to get the thigh muscles back. I would have to exercise it a lot. I would have to make a point of moving around.

The good thing about the new cast was that it finally made it possible for me to ride Brother again. I saddled him up and rode out into the countryside, a knapsack on my back, a cane strapped to the saddle, and my bad foot wrapped in a plastic bag to keep the mud out. I'd given up my crutches, and the pain was considerably less now. It felt good to have all that horseflesh moving under me, indescribably good. You never realize how much you love to move until you can't do it anymore. I'd forgotten about wind in the face, about certain sounds that were accessible only when away from other humans: bird arias, for example, and the secret songs of trees, rubbing against each other in the wind.

I spent hours perusing the landscape on Brother, remembering how much I loved it in the woods. It gave me what I needed most: quiet. My mind was like a turbulent river, and I wanted it to settle down again.

It was in these moments that a plan came to me. Life, obviously, could not go on as it had been. The thing for me to do, I decided— and I had to do *something*—was to go to my grandmother's for a while, and not just for a short visit, either. I was going to stay for a while. It sounded crazy even to me, but I needed a long time in the woods. I needed to get over losing Frankie that way. I needed to figure things out.

"Are you sure that's such a good idea?" Mother asked, when I told her. "It'll be a hard life."

"I'm not planning on living there forever," I said. "Just…a while."

"Every day there is a trial," said Mother. "Believe me. I know."

"I know you know," I said. "I want to know too. That's why I'm going."

"Well, what, exactly, do you think you're going to learn from her, anyway?" said Mother. "And what about school? Are you just going to drop out?"

That was a hard one, the part of this conversation I'd been dreading. I had the brash confidence of a youth who assumes that the wisdom of the world can be parceled out and handed over on demand, if only the right person is asked. And I certainly didn't give a damn about school, which had never been kind to me. Dropping out seemed like a great idea. Also, I had reversed my original position on Grandma. I no longer cared if she smelled bad or talked funny. I no longer cared about any of the things I used to care about. All I cared about was getting away for a while. I couldn't stand it around here anymore.

"Yeah," I said. "I'm going to drop out."

Mother put her face in her hands. After she had been silent for a few moments, I realized she was crying.

"What?" I said. "It's not a national tragedy, Princess."

"You don't understand," she said into her hands. "You won't until you have children of your own."

"Don't understand what?"

Mother sat up and took her hands away from her face, revealing it to be bright red and wet. "Every mother's worst fear," she said, "is that her daughter is going to drop out of high school. Because you know what happens next?"

"What?"

"Pregnancy."

"Oh, please!" I shouted. "What do you take me for, some kind of trailer-park bimbo? How am I going to get pregnant out there when it's just me and Grandma?"

"You'll find a way," Mother said grimly. "I know the statistics. First comes the dropping out, then the drugs. Then the sex."

"I cannot even believe I'm hearing these things from you," I said. "You're worse than insane. You're—"

"Don't you dare say that to me, Haley Bombauer," said Mother. "I'm still your mother, and I'll smack that smart little mouth of yours."

"You're the one who needs a smack," I said. "When was the last time you had an original thought? One that didn't come out of a women's magazine?"

"You shut up," said Mother.

"*You* shut up," I said, and then she did it. She got up and smacked me across the face, just like she said she would. I literally saw stars for a moment, bright pinpoints of light that danced across my field of vision. I shook my head to clear it. Mother already looked like she couldn't believe she'd just done it.

"Ow," I said. "That really hurt."

"Are you going to smack me back?" she asked.

"What? I—"

"Answer me. Are you?"

"No, I just—"

"Then be quiet and listen to me," said Mother. I had never heard her sound like this before. Her voice was quiet and low, almost murderous. "Something's telling me this is my last chance with you, Haley. You're not a little girl anymore. If you're bound and determined to ruin your life by dropping out of school, there's really nothing I can do about it. But I can certainly let you know how I feel."

"Well, that's what you did, all right." My jaw felt like it had been popped out of place.

"I'm sorry," Mother said. "Sometimes, Haley, you just don't know when to close your mouth."

"I don't want to talk about it anymore," I said. Suddenly I had the feeling that I was going to really lose it, either start screaming or crying or something, and I wanted to get away from her fast. "I'm going to lay down."

"We'll talk later," said Mother. She was shaking now. "When we've both calmed down."

I didn't think I ever would want to talk to Mother again. But after I lay in bed for a while, waiting for the ache in my cheek to subside and staring angrily at the ceiling, she came into my room and sat at the foot of my bed.

"You don't know the first thing about it," said Mother. Now she sounded resigned. "You think it's some kind of holiday."

"I do not," I said.

"It's hard. *She's* hard. She's *cruel.*" As if I had already forgotten about the story of my mother as a child, left alone in the woods to fend for herself. I wondered what she had taken from that time. The more I got to know my mother the more I realized that her life was not about *experiencing* anything. It was just about getting through it. I didn't have much to say to a person like that.

"Maybe that's what I need, is all I'm saying," I told her, still looking up at the ceiling. "Something hard. Something challenging. And it can't be any crueler than *this.*" I gestured around me, not at our house or at her but at the world that encompassed us, the empty house next door and the memories of Frankie that flooded me every time I glanced absentmindedly up at his vacant cupola. It was the same world, after all, mine and Grandma's. The same sun shone on it, the same moon circumnavigated us. It was cold comfort, but it was true. I knew I wasn't running away from anything. "Besides," I said, "I thought you wanted me to get to know her better."

"Not *that* well," said Mother. "I want you to visit her once in a while. Be nicer to her when you see her. Not *become* her."

"Oh, for Christ's sake," I said, disgusted. "I'm not going to *become* her. I'm not her. I'm *me.*"

"Watch your language," said Mother, halfheartedly. "You don't know what's going to happen out there. You don't know anything about it."

I waited for her to say something else, something that might help me make some sense of things, that would make it unnecessary for me to leave home to seek wisdom and understanding elsewhere—something that would perhaps allow me to discover miraculously that I had been living in the bosom of knowledge all along. But the most unforgivable betrayal our parents commit is that they don't know everything. They can kiss away the cuts and bruises, but they can't bring back the dead, and for that we damn them, at least when we're young. And Mother was abandoning me to the world even while trying to keep me close to home. She didn't see that by her own ignorance she was pushing me further away instead of welcoming me into the same pathetic little shelter she'd been living in for years. *Just wait, it'll blow over*, she seemed to be saying. *Let enough years go by and it will be just like it never happened.* Certainly this was the philosophy that had kept her going all this time, ever since my father died. She didn't understand that if she had welcomed death, it would have made her richer. She would have been familiar with it then, and would never have been afraid again. And, more to the point, she could have taught that secret to me.

But this was not the way it was going to be with Mother, not ever.

"How does it work?" I asked, sitting up. "I mean, do you have to let her know ahead of time, or what?"

"No," Mother said. "You just go."

"I can just show up?"

"You're her blood, Haley," said Mother. "You don't need an appointment."

As if she was a doctor, or a shrink. Well, I wasn't going for an hour-long session. I was going to stay for as long as it took.

"She won't mind?" I asked.

"She's beyond minding," Mother said. "She doesn't mind anything. Your grandmother is not like ordinary people."

Well, that I already knew. That was why I was going out there in the first place. But I had to be sure that this was the right thing, and the only person who could tell me this was the person whom I least trusted in the world, yet the only person I knew who knew her.

"She's enlightened, like," I said. "Isn't that it? Holy?"

"If that's what you want to call it," said Mother. "It has other names."

"Like what?"

Silence. What else was I expecting?

"Mother?"

"You won't be the same," she said. "Ever. I just hope you're ready for that."

"Bloody hell," I said, exasperated. "Don't you see that's what I *want?*"

Mother told me there was no way she was going to mind Brother for me when I might be gone for a long time, so the next morning I took him up to the Schumachers', promising to pay them whatever I could in return for taking care of him. They had plenty of stall space, and they had boarded him for me before, so I knew it wouldn't be a problem. Mr. Shumacher looked at me kind of funny when I said I didn't know when I'd be back, but he had enough manners not to ask me any questions. I didn't tell him where I was going, either. I didn't want anyone to know. I wasn't ashamed or anything like that—it was just my business, is all. Then I had Mother take me down the county road in the truck and drop me off at the beginning of the fire trail.

"Be careful," said Mother. "And be respectful."

"All right, all right," I said.

"When will you come home?"

"For the ninetieth time, I don't know," I said. "Just let me go, will you? I'll be home when I'm ready."

I took my backpack out of the truck and turned to say good-bye to her, but she was already taking off down the road, without another word. So she'd had enough of me too. I felt a little pang when I realized that it was possible Mother was as sick of me as I was of her. Mothers weren't supposed to get like that, not where their children were concerned.

It was a week to the day after Frankie died. I hadn't been on that trail in a long, long time. I remembered things I'd seen before, like a ship-sized log, downed and rotting, and some kind of nest up in a tree—a nest so big it looked like an eagle could have lived in it, or even a pterodactyl. Things grew large out here where people never came. Everything out here was just the same as it had always been, and already I felt relieved. Still a log on its way to unbecoming a log, still a nest being a nest. Me still me, and yet not quite.

My leg was still weak and the going was slow. I came to the end of the trail after a couple of hours, and there was the shack, just like I remembered it. Grandma was sitting on a stool outside, hands on knees. Her sparse white hair was hidden by a bonnet, and the wrinkles in her face were as deep and dark as canals. You couldn't see her eyes from that distance because they were hidden in the shadow of her craggy forehead. I hadn't sent her any word—how could I?—but it looked as if she knew I was coming. She was waiting for me. I pulled up a chunk of wood, and sat down on it without saying anything. I could feel her looking at me, so I looked back at her. It was simple: We just looked. We didn't have to talk.

There was a little fire going in a ring of stones. I watched the flames dance around, almost invisible in the daylight. When we had sat long enough and it was time to eat, Grandma went into the shack and came out with an apronful of potatoes. She sat down again and started to peel them with a knife. I took the bucket down to the creek to get some water.

Funny, I'd never thought about it before—but it was the same creek that ran through the swimming hole, then wended its way through town and eventually blended in with the lake. It was way back here where Grandma lived that the creek had its beginnings, where ancient trees decomposed in peace and mysterious giant birds made their homes. I crouched down and watched the water bubbling up from the soil, at first barely noticeable as it pushed its way up from whatever dark spring gave birth to it, through the rocks and dirt and leaves that were somehow what made it pure, filtered it, gave it virgin birth. If you went down along just a hundred feet or so it ran deep enough for you to put your bucket in. So I filled my bucket up with this newborn water and carried it back up to the shack, an act I was to perform perhaps five thousand times more before I was done staying with my grandmother.

PART TWO

The Mother of the Woods

(8)

Paying Attention

Looking back on it now, years later, it's clear that the hardest thing about living with Grandma was the sheer amount of work involved in our simple day-to-day existence. That and the god-awful smell—but you can get used to that after a while, especially when you start turning pretty ripe yourself. Nevertheless, at first I could barely stand it when she got close to me, or whenever I entered the little cabin I was to share with her for the better part of the next year. The stench of unwashed old woman-flesh was like rotten skunk cabbage.

Once, early on in my sojourn in the woods, she sent me down to the creek to wash her dress for her while she sat there on her stool, buck naked, smoking a pipeful of wacky tobacky and humming a little tune. Well, I just about dropped that dress and ran. The thing was practically crawling with vermin. But within a week or so I didn't smell anything unusual, and before too much longer I was probably at about the same level as her, scentwise. So everything in life really is relative, you see. You can even get used to bugs crawling around in your clothes.

It was a shocker to realize just how much work there is to maintaining one miserable little existence when you try and do everything

for yourself. Grandma and I didn't have any money to speak of. Therefore, either we made the things we needed or we did without them.
Mostly we just did without. We had no cow—therefore, no beef. We
didn't grow wheat, so no bread. And so on. The list of things we didn't
have was so damn long it covers just about every item in existence.
It's easier to make a list of the things we did have:

> *potatoes*
> *water*
> *herbs*
> *wild greens*
> *rabbit*
> *squirrel*
> *wood*
> *knife*
> *ax*
> *mud*
> *leaves*

...and anything we could make.

Sometimes, once in a great while, Grandma broke down and
bought things, with whatever funds she'd earned from working her
cures on the odd visitor. She hoarded a few dollars in a Mason jar
under the floorboards. That would have been the first place a felo-
nious hiker or escaped convict would look for it, I told her, but she
said she'd put a spell on it so that no one could see it, and in point of
fact the couple of times I did try to seek that jar out I never could
find it, though *she* could always put her hand to it immediately. That
jar-money was where she got her clothes, for example. We had to buy
some things. I don't believe it's really possible to be completely self-
reliant—not in a place where there's winter, anyway. You have to
contrive ways to be warm, and even Thoreau used to leave his little

pond-side house and go to his aunt's place for lunch every day. Maybe if we'd been on an island in the South Pacific, we could have run around naked all year—then clothes wouldn't have made a damn bit of difference. But complete self-reliance wasn't the point, anyway. Not for me.

What the hell was I really doing there, then? That's a question I've begun to ask myself only recently. At the time, I didn't bother to analyze it, because I was too damn busy working. Work, of course, was just what I needed. It's easy for me to answer now, when I'm older and have some perspective on the matter. I can see perfectly clearly that my heart was broken in about thirty pieces, and that it wasn't ever going to be totally whole again. I needed to get away from things that reminded me of Frankie. I needed to move on, and I didn't know where else to go.

There were three big days in my life, really: the day Frankie died; the day I went into the woods; and the last—and probably most significant of them all—the day my father turned himself into a human rocket ship.

I hold that particular day up sometimes like a strange shell I might have found on the shore of the lake, and I examine it in detail, the way the light penetrates its various chambers and illuminates its colors. I have the dispassionate curiosity that the perspective of time permits. Something in me changed from that moment, even though I was just a little kid. Something hardened. I felt it happening, and I thought it was good, because it meant that the next time something bad happened it wouldn't hurt so much. But what I didn't know was, that was the day I stopped being a kid. It was too soon for me to be a teenager, and I didn't want to be a woman—*women got pushed around too much, I thought, and far too often they were the ones left holding the bag.* All I needed to do was look at my widowed mother to verify that. No, I would be a stuntman, I decided. I would carry on the tradition that Fireball McGinty and Flash Jackson had begun, and I would never let that particular torch go out, no matter what. Not only would I be safe but I would be tough and fearless. People could drop dead left and right for all I cared—it would never make any difference to me.

Except it did make a difference. Frankie's going was a sliver of glass in the heart. Time to head out to the woods, where life was stripped down to the bare essentials. Time to learn something that meant something, instead of the stupid shit they teach you in school that you're never going to use. Time to grow up. Time to become who I was.

I stopped fighting the fact that Grandma and Mother and I were all witches—or should I say, *Ladies Extremely Gifted in the Healing and Telepathic Arts:* LEGITHATA, for those of you who are fond of acronyms. It's a more accurate word than witch, and has less negative social connotations. I couldn't tell you when I started accepting the fact that I was a *legithata*, not exactly. But it started happening because Frankie and his parents passed on, and also because of that strange little interlude down at the creek with Letty and Miz Powell. There was something *legithatic*—something witchy, that is—about them too, all right—not like me and Grandma, not quite as, oh, shall we say *professional*, but like they had sort of tapped into something on their own, some kind of energy or whatever. I think I understood that I didn't have anything to be afraid of then. If those two could crawl into that creek with no clothes on and stand there holding hands and chanting in a secret language, and *still* hold their heads high the next time they saw me, well, then I didn't have anything to be ashamed about, did I?

Certainly not.

Grandma didn't seem glad to see me when I showed up, but she didn't seem annoyed either. Fact is, she never showed much emotion about anything. She just kind of took everything all in stride. Who knows what the hell was going on in her mind? She was the strangest person I've ever known. She smoked a pipe, she talked to herself, she got stoned and ate bugs (yes, bugs—extra protein, she said), she could disappear for entire days and reappear silently and suddenly, without any explanation of where she'd been. She never treated me like other grandmothers treat their granddaughters—she never gave me presents, never told me she loved me, never bragged about me at Bingo on Friday nights. She didn't even know how to play Bingo, of course. But that's what I mean. She didn't do *anything* like other people did. It wasn't that she was nasty hearted. It was like she didn't care one way or the other if I was there or not, like there were plenty of things in life more important than having me around. Not much of a boost to old Flash Jackson's ego, but then maybe that was partly what I was there to learn—that there *were* more important things in life than just me.

Part of the problem I'd always had with her was that generation gap. I didn't know exactly how old Grandma was, and whenever I asked her she merely shrugged her shoulders, as if she herself didn't know. *Entirely possible that she didn't,* I thought, *since I knew that back in the old days people weren't always careful about writing down birthdays.* Still, I figured she couldn't have been more than eighty. Even so, with her approach to ladies' dress and manners, it seemed more like she was born somewhere around 1600. She was of the sort who believed that to bathe on a regular basis was to court serious illness and death, and that a woman ought at all times to cover every part of her body except her hands and face—never mind the fact that she'd sit there naked as a jaybird while I was washed her dress, with no apparent embarrassment. She was a walking contradiction. Anyway, there was no way she was going to put up with me dancing around the place in a pair of shorts and a T-shirt. I was going to dress like a woman should. I had brought a little money with me as well, and with that she sent me back to town to get myself some fabric—the plain, dark kind. Then I had instructions to take this fabric to a certain house, way out of town, and drop it off. I wasn't supposed to knock on the door, or say hello—nothing. Just drop it off and leave and come back in two days, and whoever was inside would already know I'd been there and would have gauged with their eye what size I was, because they would have seen me long before I knew I was being watched. So I did exactly that, trying to ignore the creepy feeling of someone's eyes crawling all over me, and when I came back two days later there was a package tied up in brown paper waiting for me on the front step.

I snatched it up and stepped back from the porch to see if I could look in any of the windows. The bottom-floor ones were all curtained up, but the top ones were open.

"Hello!" I called. "Thank you!"

There was no answer. I still couldn't see anyone.

"Hey!" I shouted. "You wanna have a little chat?" Because by then I'd been with Grandma three days, and I was already going a little stir-crazy. But there still wasn't any answer. Amish, I figured. There weren't any wires going into the house, no tire marks anywhere around, no antennae, no phone lines. I opened up the package and my suspicions were confirmed—ankle-length dress, wrist-length top, and a bonnet and apron. It had Amish written all over it, just like what Grandma wore, though she wasn't even Amish, for crying out loud. She was trying to turn me into a little clone of herself. It was all a little too much.

"I'll be damned to motherfucking hell if I'm wearing this, you old Amish cunthead," I said, very quietly—whispering, in fact, because if she'd actually heard me there would have been no end to my mortification. I just had to let it out. Then I wrapped everything back up again and headed back to Grandma's. Who did she think she was, anyway?

But of course I ended up putting on the dress, because by then my own clothes were already starting to take on a bit of a peculiar odor, and the new things were clean. I put my foot down at wearing the apron and bonnet. Thankfully, Grandma didn't push it. She knew the dress was a big enough stretch. Ordinarily dresses embarrassed me, but there was no one else around to see my discomfort, and I soon realized how much cooler it was in hot weather than jeans, and how much freer it felt to move around. *This* dress wasn't designed for cool, of course—not when it was dark blue. And I would have preferred it if it wasn't quite so long. But I solved that by tying it up around my thighs in a big side knot. I could tell Grandma didn't approve, but she didn't say anything about it either. I suppose by then she'd already realized there were going to have to be some compromises made if we were going to get along for any length of time.

We didn't talk much. Grandma had probably already been toothless when King Arthur was romping around Merrie Olde England on his horsie, and that made it pretty hard to understand her. Plus, as I mentioned before, her English was never that great to begin with. I'm not even sure, to tell the truth, if she was speaking English mixed with proper High German, or Low German (which was what the Amish spoke), or if it was a language that had been taught to her by a bunch of drunken squirrels. It sounded that garbled. She taught me the names of the herbs she used, but I could never figure out if those were her words or real words. I guess it didn't matter much. I wasn't going to be presenting papers on the legithatic arts at any major universities. It didn't amount to a hill of beans whether anyone else knew what we were talking about. I just did my best to follow along, and filled in the blank spots with whatever words seemed most likely to belong.

We started our days early, before sunrise. First I carried water: buckets and buckets of it, over and over, until my arms felt like they'd been stretched about two inches longer. Then I chopped a little wood, which seemed like fun for about a day but after that was about as exciting as wiping your butt. Then we ate breakfast—usually potatoes, greens, and whatever we had managed to trap. Grandma was an expert in making squirrel traps and rabbit snares, which were her main source of meat. Needless to say, I learned how to skin and clean

a critter right away. She made me. I never have been the squeamish
type, but I have to say that at first it made me never want to eat meat
again. Take your average rabbit, for example, just a cute little bunny.
First you slice the belly open and clean it out, and then you rip the
skin off in as close to one piece as possible. Then you're left with a
steaming gutpile, a sad little empty fur hanging there like a recently
discarded coat, and a pathetic-looking creature with no skin and no
guts and two big googly eyeballs staring back at you. I started losing
weight almost immediately. Grandma's idea of cooking something was
to scorch it until it was blackened and crunchy, regardless of what it
was. I guess this was the best way of preventing disease, but what you
gained in hygiene you lost in taste. Everything we ate tasted like charcoal. Later, I would learn that even this was efficacious in preventing
upset stomach, since charcoal coats the lining of your gizzards and
absorbs acid better than anything else. Try it sometime, next time
you're camping—help yourself to a little chunk of it, no bigger than
your fingernail. Just make sure it's burned all the way through and
it's cooled down enough to put in your mouth. You think it's going to
be gritty, but it feels as smooth as silk and has no bad taste at all. You
swallow it down, and voilà—no more upset stomach.

After breakfast, which we ate straight out of the cooking pot, we
were usually off on some kind of herb-gathering expedition. Grandma
had a territory that must have covered ten square miles, and included
every variation of terrain that one could find in our neck of the woods:
soggy bottomland, dry hilltops, cool shaded areas, sun-blasted mead-
ows, acres of forest, spots where for one reason or another nothing
much grew. Every kind of land produced its own kind of plants at different times of the year, and every kind of plant was useful for something. Grandma had memorized the uses of what I would estimate to
be at least three hundred different kinds of plants, and those were
only the ones she told me about. And when you consider that each
plant had at least two and sometimes four or five uses, you can see

that's quite a bit of learning she had in her head, and all of it without the benefit of the printed page. She was a walking pharmacopoeia.

I wasn't allowed to write anything down. Well, that's stupid—I couldn't have if I'd wanted to, is what I mean, since I didn't have anything to write with. But the information came so thick and fast that I knew right away there was no chance of remembering all of it. I would have to stick to the big points, and come back to the smaller ones later. Our first few days walking the woods together were rough this way. I got bored easy, I got distracted by everything, and I wasn't used to the constant hiking. On top of that, I was having my period, and though I had thought to bring tampons from home I was cramped and grumpy. By noon I was tired and ready to go home, and I don't mean back to the shack, either. Those days a month, all I want to do is curl up on the couch with a good book and some chocolate ice cream. But my grandmother wasn't even interested in listening to me complain.

"Give this for swollen joints," said Grandma, pointing to a tender young stalk with wide, ferny-looking leaves. "But only pick it in the spring and early summer. Steep it in hot water for an hour. Then pour the water over fresh leaves and steep it again. Repeat this three times. Then give it as a tea. But if you pick it in the summer or fall, it will cause stomachache. So make sure you have it laid up beforehand. You can use it dried."

Never mind I'd never heard of anyone ever coming down with a case of swollen joints. Next time I did, I was prepared. This was my heritage. This was the sort of stuff I had come to learn.

Well, strictly speaking, not just that. There was also the looking-in-the-water stuff, that business about Lifting the Veil. That was what I was most interested in. I wasn't feeling scared of it anymore. I wasn't scared of anything anymore, in fact. I was ready to drop all the rigmarole and drama. I just wanted to know.

"I don't know what you're talking about," said Grandma, only it sounded more like "Ich k'no wa yor tagginabboud." *Of course she would say that*, I thought. It was just like her. She never gave me a straight answer about anything, at least not anything important. Grandma, I would ask, where do I take a crap? Right over there, she'd say. Grandma, where should I throw these squirrel guts? Toss them behind that tree, she'd say. Grandma, what is the meaning of life? Shrug of the shoulders, a roll of the eyes. I don't understand the question, she'd tell me. *Ich hab keine idea. Ich not k'no.* I have no idea. I don't know. And who cares? Life is not made up of such questions. Life is made of smaller things than this. Those are what is important. Those are the things you should be paying attention to.

Of course, if I'd had my eyes and ears and heart open, I would have seen that she *was* answering the question, as directly as she knew how. What she was trying to say was, there was no secret; there was no hidden meaning. There was only what was right in front of your nose. But at seventeen years old, I couldn't accept that. I could only accept that life was composed of great, unknowable things that had yet to be discovered, and that maybe I would be the first to discover them, because it certainly seemed like no one else out there had the slightest idea what was going on. But I wasn't as open as I thought, not as smart as I wished, not as ready to learn as I was going to be. Like I said, I had gone to the woods to find out how to become me. I didn't know yet that I already *was* me, that, like an acorn, I already contained all the blueprints I needed to blossom into fullness, and that the real task at hand was to wake up, slow down, and pay enough attention to realize it.

All that stuff notwithstanding, though, I knew Grandma did know secrets, that she had unseen powers at her fingertips, and that maybe she was just waiting for me to show her that I was ready enough to learn them before she would condescend to teach me. So I did my best to show her that I was ready. I didn't complain about anything, not even when the questionable quality of the water and the rough diet left me with a case of galloping diarrhea that never completely went away during my whole time with her. I didn't bitch about the clothes she wanted me to wear. I worked hard, even doing things she hadn't told me to do, trying to guess ahead of time what was needed, what had to be done. I memorized everything I could about her fantastic store of herbal lore and lay awake at night repeating recipes for various concoctions to myself, just so I could impress her with my knowledge. I learned the difference between a cold infusion and a warm one, what a poultice was and how it differed from a wrap, how to steep something just right so that you didn't kill its beneficent qualities but brought them out in their natural unharmed state, like a baby being born underwater. In my mind, I was ready. And I kept after her.

"I already did it once, you know," I said. "At home. I looked for Frankie when he was missing."

"Den varom willst Du k'no from ich?"

"Because I don't know if I did it right."

"Find 'im?"

"Yes."

"Aha." Arms crossed, eyes focused on some point beyond me, lips clamped around the pipe she'd taken to keeping in her mouth at all times, whether it was loaded or not.

"So what does that mean?" I asked. "That I already know how to do it? Mother told me it was dangerous. She said I didn't know what I was doing. She said I shouldn't mess around until I'd been taught right. And you're the only one who can teach me."

At the mention of her daughter's name, my grandmother must have remembered something. Maybe having me around had awakened her feelings of disappointment, if she was capable of something so personal, at my mother's long-ago departure. Maybe Grandma felt like she'd failed my mother; maybe she felt that my mother had failed her. Her eyes narrowed and she spat on the ground.

"She vent into die Welt," she said pointedly. She went into the world.

"She fell in love," I said. "Can you blame her for that? She met my father and she fell in love."

At that, Grandma did something she'd never done in front of me before. She laughed. She threw her head back and roared wheezily, rocking to and fro on the front leg of her stool, bracing herself with her gnarled hands on her knees.

"*Liebe!*" She howled, her bare gums shining in the sunlight. "*Ho ho ho ho! Liebe! Ach!*"

Apparently Grandma thought love was funny.

That was the end of that conversation. I got up and stomped away, my ears burning. I would have to try again later, when I'd recovered my composure. I was getting better at understanding her—not just her speech, I mean *her*—but all the same there were times when the old lady seemed like a code that not even Miz Powell herself could have cracked, not with a hundred Enigma machines working away twenty-four hours a day.

Summer was soon ending, and my leg was nearly back to its old self, though it still felt too spindly to run on. I had removed the knee cast myself within a few days of getting it. I wasn't ready yet, but I couldn't stand having it on anymore. I was none too happy to realize that I'd gained a lot more weight during my recent period of enforced inactivity—how much, I refuse to say, but Grandma never tired of poking me in the stomach as though I was a prize pig at a fair, smacking her lips in satisfaction. For a while I thought she was planning on eating me, but then I realized what was really going on: She liked me fat. She thought it meant that I was healthy. Well, maybe that's how it used to be seen back in her day, but in my eyes it only got in my way and slowed me down, and I decided it all had to go.

Luckily, there wasn't anything special I had to do to get rid of it. Eating the garbage we ate three times a day would have caused a giant to shrink down to the size of a thimble. By the time the leaves were starting to fall from the trees, that same old Amish-made dress was flopping around me like a pair of bat's wings, and I decided it was time to go home and get myself some fresh duds, ones that didn't reek of my own odor.

I expected a battle, but Grandma didn't seem to mind. I wasn't a prisoner, she reminded me—I had come of my own free will, and I could go any time I liked. She had no interest in forcing me to do anything. I told her that meant I might be gone a few days. When the words were out of my mouth I realized they were true, and my heart leaped for joy. I was getting the hell out of the woods for a while. I felt like a sailor about to go on furlough in a town full of cathouses.

Grandma, of course, merely shrugged. She didn't even say goodbye, mean old cuss. She just went about her business as though I'd never existed in the first place.

"Well, fine," I said to her back. I had gotten used to her by now and wasn't anywhere near as afraid of her as I had been. Mostly I was pretty saucy with her, but not in a disrespectful way. I couldn't bring myself to flat out abuse her. "I'll see ya when I see ya," I said, and I headed down the trail.

It was a long walk, but I got lucky. I didn't see anyone who would have wanted to stop and chat with me on the way home. I wanted to stay far downwind of everyone until I'd had a chance to take my first bath in over six weeks. I even slunk by Miz Powell's place on the sly, dying to run up the porch steps and ring her doorbell but forcing myself to think of how great it would be when I got myself all sudsed up and sank deliciously into a tub of hot water. Something told me she knew I was passing, though I didn't see her on the porch, nor in any of the windows. She had built-in radar of sorts, she did. I could feel it pinging me like I was a submarine.

Holy crap, I said to myself. *You've never felt like that before.*

And myself said right back to me, *You've never spent six weeks in the woods before with an old wit—I mean, an old legithata, either.*

Which made me think maybe Grandma was already rubbing off on me more than I knew.

Mother was glad to see me, but she refused to come near me until I'd stripped and thrown my clothes into a garbage bag, which in turn went straight out the back door. Marveling at how much weight I'd lost and at how well my leg was working, she drew me a bath and threw in plenty of the kind of bubbles I liked, chattering away like a magpie. There was all kinds of news to catch up on, none of it very interesting, of course—this couple was getting divorced, so-and-so moved to California but didn't like it, a big car manufacturer was thinking of putting a plant in about twenty miles away, which would finally mean plenty of jobs for everyone. I listened with half an ear while I let the water soak into all my crevices and loosen up the dirt. Then I bade her wait outside, if she didn't mind, while I stood up and scrubbed myself all over with one of those scratchy sponges that just about take your first layer of skin off, making you feel sort of like a peeled banana. I looked down at the water and saw that it was all brown, so I pulled the plug and turned on the shower, and stood there rinsing myself until the hot water ran out and I started to shiver. Lordy, it was good to be clean again. It made me wonder why I'd ever gone out there in the first place.

Mother had a big dinner going by the time I came downstairs. I was half-starved, but I could hardly eat any of it—not because I wasn't hungry, but because after the lean feed I'd been getting, it all just tasted too rich for me. She drowned the mashed potatoes in butter, and she'd made little hot dogs wrapped in bacon like you might serve at a Superbowl party, and so on. It was the same food I'd been eating all my life, but suddenly none of it appealed to me, and just then a flash of genius came over me—you know, one of those moments when you're able to see your own life as though it belonged to somebody else, and pick apart every little thing that's wrong with it—and I said: "You've been making me fat."

Mother hadn't shut up since I walked in the door, even yelling up to me from time to time from the kitchen while I was in the bathtub, but that quieted her down quickly, let me tell you. She stared at me with her mouth hanging open and forkful of food halfway to her mouth.

"What did you say?" she managed to reply.

"All this stuff is killing us," I said, gesturing at the laden table. "Look at it. It makes us fat, all of it. All this time you've been telling me I was big boned, but I'm not, am I?"

"Well, Haley," she said, "all big boned means is that you can't help being—"

"But I *can* help it," I said. I stood up. I was wearing my old jeans and a flannel shirt, and I had to put a belt on to keep the pants from slipping down too low around my hips. I had never worn a belt before—it was one of my dad's, and it was too big for me. I must have looked like a foundling. I took the belt off and pulled the waist of the pants out to show her how much extra room I had. "Look," I said. "I *can* help it. I'm thinner. I really am."

"Living out there like an animal would make anybody thin," she said, her dander up a little more now. "If you're accusing me of deliberately making you unattractive, then I—"

"Well, hold on now, buttercup," I said. "I have never in my life felt unattractive. If I walked naked down the street, men would practically sprain their calf muscles trying to jump me."

"*Haley Bombauer!*" said Mother, scandalized.

"All I'm talking about," I said calmly, "is that you have been killing me with food."

I wished I hadn't put it that way, because Mother started to get kind of weepy eyed. She put her napkin to her eyes and leaned her elbows on the table, and sure enough I heard the sounds that when I was younger always used to make me stop whatever I was doing and run to her side, putting an arm around her until she stopped. But I didn't feel like doing that right now. I was sorry she was upset, but I was onto something, and I didn't want to let go of it just yet. There would be time for apologies later. Besides, I wasn't going to say anything that I couldn't unsay. I wasn't mad. I was just telling the truth.

"Ma," I said, "does this have something to do with Dad?"

"What—what do you mean?" she said, sniffling.

"I mean, after he died—did we start eating more?"

"I—that's the strangest—what on earth are you talking about?"

"I don't remember these kinds of things," I said. "I was only little. You were the one doing the cooking. Did you—did you keep on cooking for three?"

Mother stared at me, leaning on her hands, as though I was some kind of oddity. Then she nodded. "Yes," she said. "I guess I did."

"Was this the kind of food he liked?" I asked her. "Like these, for example, these little hot dog bacon thingies. Were these one of his favorites?"

"He liked to eat them when he listened to football or baseball," she said. "Sports always put him in a good mood. I used to bring him a plate of these on Sundays."

"But we didn't eat them every day, right?"

She shook her head.

"Not for dinner? People normally don't eat these for dinner, right?"

"I don't know," she said. "Probably not."

"I bet they don't," I said, picking one up. "They're not very good for you."

Mother sat back in her chair and looked up at the ceiling, dreamy eyed. "Sundays always had a kind of glow to them," she said. "Your father was always cheery, always a kind man, but when he listened to sports he went into his own little world. And he took you with him. He used to set you on his lap and explain it all to you—home runs and touchdowns and everything. Remember?"

"I sure do," I said. I was starting to get kind of glimmery eyed myself, remembering the feel of his whiskers on the back of my neck, and the gentle smell of his two Sunday beers coming off him. His big hands wrapped around my middle to keep me from falling off his lap, because I was a wiggle worm. The horsey rides on his knee. Learning to yell with joy when some invisible, far-off player did something good, and imagining what it looked like when he did it. For years, "home run" meant to me that the guy just ran out of the ballpark all the way to his house. I thought everyone was happy for him because he got to go home, while the rest of them had to stay there.

"He never cared who won," she said. "He just loved sports. And he loved these little hot dogs with bacon."

"So you kept making them," I said.

Mother looked at me again. I didn't know if she knew specifically what I was getting at. I'm not sure I could have put it any more clearly, anyway. Was I accusing her of something, something beyond making me fat? Some kind of betrayal? Oh, she knew I meant something, all right—but in true Mother tradition, she sidestepped that neatly and turned it around, forming it into a question and shooting it right back at me, like a snowball caught in midair. A snowball with a hard center of guilt to it, instead of that deadly little nugget of ice you sneak in there when you really want to nail the person you're aiming at.

"Haley," she said, "I know I have my faults, but...have I been a good mother?"

I looked right back at her. *There can only really be one answer to that question*, I thought. There was no point in digging into old wounds now.

"Yes, you have," I lied. "Perfect."

She smiled.

"Thank you, sweetie," she said. "It's so good to have you home again."

"Sometimes I even wonder if she's still hitting on all four cylinders," I said to Miz Powell. "Like, maybe after my dad died she kind of lost it a little bit. And then I left. I shouldn't have gone," I said, filled suddenly with the conviction that leaving my mother alone in that house had caused her to drop the rest of her marbles. That was it—loneliness had driven her around the bend. I'd never bothered to think of her, had I? I just went and did what I wanted. Despite all my efforts at reformation over the years, I was still a selfish daughter. I was still bad.

"No, Haley," Miz Powell said firmly. "You did the right thing. The right thing for *yourself*."

"You don't think I made her lose it?"

"I'm sure she lost *something*," said Miz Powell, holding her teacup and saucer, as always, three inches above her thigh. "From what you say she loved your father dearly, and his loss must have been a terrible blow. Sometimes an emotional trauma like that can do permanent damage, Haley. It's simply more difficult to be sympathetic in those cases, because it's not the kind of damage you can see."

"You said it," I said. I tried holding the teacup and saucer like she did, but it kept rattling in my hands and I started feeling ungenteel, so I set it back down. "I just wish there was some way I could make her feel whole again."

"You are not responsible for your mother's mental health, my dear," said Miz Powell. "It's rather important that you remember that."

"Yes, ma'am," I said. I started wondering about how to help Mother, how to make her feel like she didn't have to keep plugging up the big father-shaped hole in our lives with lots of fattening things to eat, and how to help her in other ways, too. I kind of drifted off into my own little world there for a moment. Miz Powell brought me back with a gentle harrumph in her throat.

"It's really not polite to daydream when one is a guest, Haley dear," she said.

"Sorry," I said. "I was just thinking about . . . things."

"I understand," Miz Powell said, with a smile—and all was right again. Funny how much I'd changed in the short time that I'd met her. Used to be she would raise the hackles on my neck just acting the way she did, all prim and proper and making me feel like a horse apple in a bowlful of peaches without even saying a word, just in the way she looked at me. Now, though, she had the opposite effect. I found myself trying to be more like her, right down to the way I held my teacup. That was the thing about Miz Powell—that was the thing about all great leaders.

Because that was how I'd come to think of her. Miz Powell was a leader of people. Never mind that she wasn't in command of a regiment, or president of the country. She made people follow her just by lifting one eyebrow and marching along at her own rapid pace. You couldn't help but march along behind her.

"And how do you find life in the woods?" she inquired, as though we were talking about a loft in London.

"It's . . . well, it's hard to explain," I said, and I proceeded to do just that, launching into a half hour description of the more mundane details of life with Grandmother. Even though Miz Powell and I had never talked about that day at the creek, when she and Letty Horgan had done their little magic-ritual skinny-dipping thingie, and even though I had always made a point of keeping the family secret from everyone, I felt suddenly like this was the right time to unburden myself—or at least part of myself. I didn't think I would ever tell anybody the whole story. It didn't seem wise. But I said: "My grandmother has kind of a crazy reputation around here. Maybe you've heard about it. People think she's a witch."

"I see," said Miz Powell. "And is she?"

I sat looking at her, blinking and gaping.

"You are not a fish, Haley, so do stop acting like one," said Miz Powell.

"Yes, ma'am," I said. "I, uh—well. Yes. She is a witch. I can't say I care much for that particular word, but that's what she is."

"I see," said Miz Powell again. "More tea?"

I pushed my cup toward her, in a bit of a haze all of a sudden. She filled it and pushed it back.

"You seem pretty calm about it," I said.

"I am indeed," said Miz Powell. "Tell me something, dear. Is your grandmother . . . training you?"

Well, no point in hiding it now. I couldn't lie to Miz Powell. "I guess you could say that," I said.

"And what does she teach you? Don't shrug. It implies ignorance."

"I can't say precisely," I said. "I guess she's mostly teaching me how to pay attention to things."

"I see," she said. "And do you feel that you are learning well?"

"I suppose," I said.

"Good," she said.

"Miz Powell," I said. "You didn't seem very surprised just now when I said my grandmother was a witch."

"No," she replied. "That's because I'm not."

"You mean . . . you knew?"

"Of course I knew," she said. "Everyone around here knows."

"And when you asked if she's training me?"

"That's because we knew she would be choosing an apprentice soon," said Miz Powell.

"We who?"

"Just a moment, if you don't mind, dear," she said, getting up. "I need to make a phone call."

We sat in the parlor until our tea grew cold. I didn't ask Miz Powell who she had called, not wanting to be nosy. I just talked—telling her everything I knew about my grandmother, my mother, about me, about that time I lifted the Veil on my own and saw nothing but sunflowers. I didn't hold anything back this time. I told her the whole story. She listened attentively, taking in every word, nodding every so often and sometimes stopping me to ask a question, but mostly just letting me go on. About an hour after she'd made the phone call, Letty Horgan showed up, driving a tiny, ancient Pacer. She tottered to the door in her Sunday best—it occurred to me then that I didn't even know what day it was, that it had been weeks since I bothered to follow the calendar, so it very well might have been Sunday after all—and let herself in without ringing the bell. The two old biddies pecked each other on the cheek and Letty gave me a peck too, and then there we were, the three of us, sitting around with our teacups, forming what once would have been my worst nightmare—a real tea party, just us dames.

Letty got right to the point.

"Lizzy says you've been chosen as the apprentice, dear," she said to me. "That's fine news. Isn't that fine, Lizzy?"

"It certainly is," said Miz Powell, beaming.

"We were wondering how much longer it would be," said Letty.

"Indeed we were," said Miz Powell.

"I need to ask something here," I said. "Because my head is sort of spinning."

"Go ahead, dear," said Letty.

"Are . . . well, are you two witches also?"

The two ladies looked at each other and tittered.

"My goodness, no," said Miz Powell. "That's not a word one should use lightly, is it, Letty?"

"Got that right," said Letty.

"But we do have lots of things to talk to you about," said Miz Powell. "So many things to tell you. Don't we, Letty, dear?"

"We sure do, at that," said Letty. "Where do you figure we should start?"

"I hardly know myself," said Miz Powell. "But let me just say, Haley, that we've been awaiting this moment most eagerly. Most eagerly indeed."

"Oh my, yes," said Letty. "It's almost as exciting as a birthday party. I have an idea, Lizzy."

"What's that, if I may?" Miz Powell asked.

"Let's tell her about the creek," said Letty brightly. "Let's tell her all about it, from beginning to end. That would be a good place to start."

"I agree completely," said Miz Powell. She turned to me. "You see, Haley, that creek is an interesting place. It's no coincidence that your grandmother lives at its source, and it's no coincidence either that it happened to be our special place when we were young. Oh, how I missed it when I was away," she said. "It was what I longed for most when I was in England...."

...meaning, of course, that there was something special about the creek, as I'd always half known, and in fact something special about the whole area—which might have been why I never felt much of an urge to move away, as boring as things were. I was tied to the land by more than history. There was a real, palpable connection to it. I had it, Letty and Miz Powell had it. My grandmother had it. Even my mother had it, though in her case there was a problem—some kind of mental static, some kind of blockage. There was a particular kind of energy around here, one that a few people could recognize—and even fewer people could make use of. Lizzy and Letty called it Zam, but they freely admitted that it had had other names in other times, and would have yet more names sometime in the future. It was eternal, ageless, undying—as old as the land itself.

The two old ladies had always known about it, ever since they could remember. They weren't sure if they'd been told about it by someone else, or if they'd discovered it on their own. Neither of them could remember. All they knew was, from the time they were very young they used to gather at the creek, their numbers much greater in those days—at one point there were more than a dozen girls involved, all tuned in to the same frequency, in a manner of speaking. That was where their secret language came from. Back then they hadn't known exactly what they were doing. They were just playing. The creek was the source of something, they knew. The water was at the root of something wonderful. There was something there, something that had *always* been there—something a few people had always known about for as long as there were people here, from times that no one remembered, except the creek itself and one other person: my grandmother.

"You mean you knew her?" I asked. "She was living out there even way back then?"

They nodded.

"Did you know my mother?" I asked.

"Your mother wasn't there yet," said Letty.

"You mean she hadn't been born?"

"No," said Miz Powell. "We mean, she hadn't arrived."

I was puzzled by this. "I don't get it," I said. "You're a lot older than her, right? So you grew up and left before she was born."

"Not quite," said Letty. "She arrived before we grew up."

"Do you know anything about your grandfather?" asked Miz Powell. "Your mother's father?"

"Mother never talks about him," I said. "And I never thought to ask Grandma."

"Why not, dear?" asked Miz Powell.

"I have no idea," I said slowly. It seemed kind of strange that I'd never asked about him, who he was and how he and my grandmother had met, but it had never crossed my mind. The idea of Grandma having a husband was so far out that it seemed impossible.

"Ask her," said Letty. "When you think of it."

"What did she look like when she was young?" I asked. "My grandmother, I mean?"

The old ladies exchanged glances.

"She still doesn't understand," said Letty.

"No, dear, indeed she does not," said Miz Powell.

"We don't know what she looked like when she was young because she wasn't young then either," explained Letty.

"What kind of crap are you slinging?" I said, momentarily forgetting myself. The two of them appeared willing to let it slide, but I blushed nonetheless. "Sorry. What I mean is, that had to be fifty years ago at least. Are you saying she looked old even then?"

"She didn't just look old," said Miz Powell. "She *was* old."

"Well..." I trailed off, trying to do some mental arithmetic and failing miserably. There were too many unknown variables. It was like doing algebra when all the numbers were X. "I don't get it," I said. "You mean she's even older than I thought?"

The old ladies nodded.

"Well, how old? Ninety? A hundred?"

"Oh, no, my love," said Miz Powell. "Much older than that."

"*Much* older," Letty chimed in. "At least three or four times that. My own grandmother used to tell me stories about her when I was little, and she was already old then, too."

For once in my life, I could not think of a single thing to say. My first instinct, I hate to admit, was to chalk it up to senility. Clearly, the two of them were batty. But then I looked at their clear eyes, their calm, peaceful expressions, and I knew that no word of untruth had ever crossed their lips before, and that none was now. They were telling the truth. They meant every word they were saying.

"Then she's not really my grandmother?" I croaked.

"In a sense she is, if you want to call her that," said Miz Powell. "You are descended from her. You share her blood. Lucky girl."

"She is more like Mother with a capital *M*," said Letty. "My granny used to call her the Mother of the Woods. There were other names before that. She's always been there, ever since anyone can remember."

Miz Powell nudged her. "I think this is all a bit much for the poor girl," she said to Letty. "She's getting a bit glassy eyed."

"Oh dear," said Letty. "Perhaps we said too much too soon."

"Are you well, Haley?" asked Miz Powell.

"I don't know," I said. "Why... why hasn't my mother told me any of this?"

"She doesn't know," said Letty. "Or rather, she would prefer not to know. She left as soon as she started suspecting the truth. It was too much for her. She belongs in the world, the dear love. She needs it. The woods is no place for her. She's just not strong enough."

"Or not willing to see things as they are," said Miz Powell.

"And you, Haley?" said Letty. "Are you willing?"

I sat staring out the window at the fields separating Miz Powell's house from my own. I could see a single light on in my mother's bedroom, where she was sleeping off a headache. Frankie's house sat gloomy and dark, the windows boarded up, the For Sale sign canted over like a shipwreck's mast. It was full-on fall now, and with the waning of the day there were dark clouds brewing on the horizon. I had always loved a fall evening, with the scent of decaying leaves in the still-moist air, and the feeling that it was nearly time to take a long, long nap.

"Yes," I said. "I'm willing."

9

The Mother of the Woods

The next time I saw her, my grandmother was sitting by the fire as usual, tracing designs in the dirt with a burnt stick. I'd been away four days. I was in clean clothes—and had brought others with me, too, thinking ahead, for once in my life—but the earth was getting undressed, the leaves falling thick and fast and the air growing nippier with every passing day.

Grandma ignored me at first, letting me know that she was in no mood for questions. I guess she might have thought I wasn't coming back at all, and now she was trying to figure if she'd misjudged me. It wasn't an easy thing to change your mind about someone. She just sat there tracing her designs in the dirt, her knobby knees sticking out through her skirt and making her look oddly childlike. I knew better by now than to try and get her to talk—if she had something to say, she'd say it. She drew circles within circles and straight lines to either side. Then she spat into the middle of it and erased the whole mess with her feet.

A spell? I wondered. Some kind of magic ritual?

But still she didn't say anything. I was busting with questions, but I was also now more afraid of her than I'd ever been before. It had taken a lot of courage on my part to come back. If she really was who Miz Powell and Letty said she was, then she was some kind of otherworldly figure, supernatural, maybe even a spirit. I didn't want anything to do with spirits. Grandma had always weirded me out a little, but now she just plain spooked me. I wasn't going to be the first one to talk, in case she decided she was going to cast some kind of spell on me and turn me into a bug, and then eat me. I'd let her start when she was ready.

But she didn't say anything to me that day, or that evening either. We ate in silence. Night came, and I was so tuckered out from my long hike that I lay down on my nasty little bed of stinky blankets with leaves underneath, tucked away along one wall of her shanty, and fell asleep without any thought of bad smells or bugs or anything. I slept like a log and woke up as sore as a crash-test dummy, and it took me the better part of an hour to work the kinks out of my legs and back. By then Grandma had already been up for hours, and was well into the day's work.

This work seemed to consist of gathering lots of dead leaves, huge piles of them. She gathered them up in her apron and carried them to the side of the little house, dumping them along the perimeter. Since I could see full well what she was doing, though I didn't know why, I just started helping. I was still keeping my vow of silence.

This went on all day, with breaks only for meager meals, until by sunset we had scoured most of the surrounding area for fallen leaves and there was a great big heap of them running all the way up around the walls of the little house. We kept it up the next day, until most of the roof was covered too. You had to pick the right weather for this, because the slightest breeze would carry them away and you'd have to start over again. Miraculously, or maybe not so miraculously, we got lucky, though when my grandmother was involved I knew better than to think luck played a part in things. But this was not as much work as it sounds—it was a tiny house, with the roof no taller than my own head, and I had to stoop or sit whenever I was inside. All in all, it was smaller than most people's tool sheds, if you can imagine living in a space like that.

Then she started cutting saplings, fresh ones with their branches still on, and laying them on top of the leaves, all the way around the house. This took another day and a half. When that was done, we rested—and we still hadn't spoken a word.

Funny thing, when you go that long without talking. Your mind kind of goes through stages. First, you think, *Well, all right, I'll just concentrate and it won't be so hard.* So you do that for a while, and you manage to stay quiet. Then you kind of forget about it, and you catch yourself starting to say something and stop just in time. Then you start to feel like you're going to bust if you don't get to say *something*, but still you hold out, kind of like holding your breath underwater.

And then, finally, you abandon yourself to silence. And it's not so bad. Soon enough, it starts to seem normal, and you realize how much talking people do that isn't really necessary—talking for talking's sake, which never really hurt anybody but doesn't do anybody a bit of good either. That's how it is to be quiet; and frankly, I think it's a lesson more people could stand to learn.

Finally came the mud, and now I had a pretty clear idea of what Grandma was up to. She was getting ready for winter. The leaves would form insulation, and the branches would hold them down. Mud would be plastered over the whole thing, and that was how we would keep warm. We started hauling mud up from the banks of the creek by the bucketful; good, clay-filled stuff that stuck firmly to the branches and didn't fall off even when it dried. We must have carried hundreds of loads up, possibly even thousands, and smoothed it over with our hands. This took days, which were filled with a fatigue and ennui so constant that I simply stopped thinking. I just worked. It was important, after all—you could tell that winter was coming early this year, and it was going to be a bad one. We had to be ready. I already knew I was going to be spending the whole season out there with her. There was no discussion, no making of plans—I had fixed on the idea, and I knew she was going to let me do it. We were wintering in, bear style. We were going to hibernate.

And *still* we hadn't said a word.

When the house was ready, and the skies were darkening up for the first big storm of the season, I heard what sounded like a pickup truck in the distance. Alarm filled me, but when I looked at Grandma she gave no sign that she was perturbed, though I knew she must have heard it long before I did. I knew the truck wouldn't make it all the way in, so I started heading out in the direction it was coming from, sneaking up so I would see whoever it was before they saw me.

An elderly man in a tweed jacket, with a full, gray-streaked beard, had ground his truck to a halt about a quarter mile from the shack and begun unloading supplies from the back of it. There were boxes upon boxes of what looked like groceries, and he was setting them on the ground in a neat pile. He looked harmless enough—I figured I could take him if it came to it, that is, if he was a rapist or something, though I'd never heard of any rapists who went around in trucks full of groceries. So I stepped out from the trees until I stood just behind him, and when I willed him to see me he turned around as though he'd been kicked in the rear end, and his face turned the color of a frog's underbelly.

"Oh, Lord, you scairt me," he said.

"Sorry," I said, though I thought I'd made enough noise to let him know I was there. Was I getting woodsier? I wondered. Was I learning more tricks without even knowing it? The single word flopped out of my mouth like a fish, and I felt oddly embarrassed, as though my skirt had fallen down in front of him. It was the first thing I'd said in two weeks.

"You must be her granddaughter," said the man. "I heard you was staying out here with her."

"You did?" I said. "Who told you?"

"Oh, everyone knows," said the man. "Everyone who knows *her*, that is. Which there aren't many of us."

"I guess not," I said, though I had no idea what he was talking about. "What's all this stuff?" My tongue was loosening up now, and speech came a little easier.

The man unloaded the last box and leaned on the hood of his truck, out of breath. "Winter supplies," he said. "Nonperishable, o'course. Canned goods and so forth. There's enough for both of you this time. That's a first. She ain't never let anyone winter with her before, y'know. Which it seems like quite an honor. There's many who would feel privileged to spend a season out here with her."

"Is that so," I said. "Well, I *am* her granddaughter."

"Your name Haley?" he asked.

I allowed that it was, though I wondered how he knew that.

"Well, it's nice to meet you," he said, but he made no move to shake my hand. Matter of fact, he kept kind of a respectful distance from me, as though I was going to bite him. More likely it was just my personal odor, though. I hadn't been back all that long, but it was all the time that was needed for it to build up again. My smell formed a kind of personal barrier around me—just like any other animal. Sometimes I wondered what the world would be like if no one took showers. We would know people by our noses first and by our intellect second, instead of the other way around. We *were* only animals, after all.

"I'm Chester Burgess," he said. "Live over in Springville. Known her since I was a pup."

"Is that so? Then how come you keep calling her 'her'?" I asked.

Chester Burgess gave me kind of a funny look. "Do you know anything else I should call her?" he asked. "Which I mean, do you know her name? Her *real* name?"

I was about to give him a snappy answer, since I didn't much care for his tone, but when I thought about it I realized he was right. I didn't know what her name was at all. It was just Grandma—but if Miz Powell was to be believed, that wasn't right either.

"No," I said.

"Not likely anyone does," said Chester Burgess. "I got to get going. Give her my respects, would you? I always leave the winter groceries right here for her. It's a deal we made. She doesn't like folks to come much closer, unless they have a real good reason. Which I don't. She can see right through a man," he added, getting back in his truck—a little quickly, it seemed to me. I wondered if Chester Burgess was scared of us. Or of her, more likely. I guessed I wasn't the only one who found Grandma a wee bit on the frightening side.

"What deal?" I asked.

"Eh?" He started up the truck.

"What deal?" I called, over the sound of the motor.

"She saved my life, when I was just a tadpole," he shouted back. "Rheumatic fever. I been bringing her things ever since. Good day to yew."

"Right," I said. "Thanks."

Chester Burgess backed up until he got to a spot where he could turn around, and then he pulled out of there and I was left with a chest-high stack of groceries in boxes. *No need to ask whose job it'll be to carry these in*, I thought. I grabbed the top one and headed back to the shack. Grandma was sitting on her stool, puffing her pipe. She nodded in satisfaction when she saw me coming.

"Chester Burgess dropped these off," I said, forgetting my vow of silence. "Now I know how you make it through the winter out here," I added, taking the box into the shack.

Grandma still didn't say anything, but she laughed again—long, loud, and wheezy, throwing her head back and cackling at the sky, the sky that was so low it seemed like if I just climbed a tree I'd be able to poke my hand through it.

"Zo!" she said, which I think meant "so"—it was one of her favorite expressions, meaning something like, "Everything is just the way it ought to be, and kind of funny, besides."

Which, in a way, it was—if you knew how to look at things like that.

.   .   .

I was getting a weather nose. The snow came right when I thought it would, not a day after I'd finished hauling all those boxes into the shack, and after we'd gathered as much wood as we could for the fire and covered it over with a plastic tarp, also courtesy of Chester Burgess. It fell thick and wet, a couple of inches at first, then a honking big snowfall that shrouded everything in white and dampened all sound, sending every critter in the forest to sleep, or else southward.

Grandma, or whoever the hell she was, moved the fire inside when it got cold, rekindling it in a tiny iron stove that was as full of holes as an old sock and had no chimney to it, just a hole in the top. This meant I had to clear out an old preexisting hole in the roof to let all the smoke out. Snow would fall through it, but it would just hit the stove and melt, so I guessed if she wasn't worried about it I wouldn't be either. Then Grandma pulled the door shut and sat herself down on one side of the fire, and I sat down on the other, and it was suddenly gloomy and smoky in the little shack, and I had my first attack of what you might call claustrophobia when I realized that that was how it was going to be until the snow thawed and the earth woke up again. Just us two. Sitting there in the half-dark, surrounded by boxes of food and dried herbs hanging from the walls. Jesus Delano Roosevelt.

Don't get scared, I told myself. *Don't freak out. Used to be, back in the old days, folks didn't have much to do but work their tails off all year, and then come winter they'd just sit around and look at each other. That was how it always was, so you know you can make it. It's in your blood and in your genes.*

Yeah, another part of myself said, *but people used to hack each other up back then for no good reason, too. Happened all the time. Guy'd just go nuts and chop his wife and kids into flinders, and feed the pieces to the snakes.*

Just you shut up, said the other part right back. *That never happened and you know it.*

But what are we going to *do?* I wondered.

Grandma, of course, had an answer for that, even though I hadn't asked her anything out loud.

"Zo," she said again, "Du vant to learn?"

I nodded.

"You hef kvestions?"

"And how," I said.

"Tell."

I had a million "kvestions," but of course sitting there with her wrinkled, whiskery old face not two feet from mine, most of them began to seem very stupid indeed, and I kind of lost my nerve. Everything Miz Powell told me about this old lady seemed true, and I would have believed it all, except for the fact that it was all so impossible. For one thing, there was no way she could really be as old as Miz Powell said she was. Nobody was that old. So I asked her:

"How old are you?"

She snorted, gumming her pipe—which was empty for the moment.

"*Alt*," she said. Old.

"How old?"

She shrugged.

"How did you get to be zo alt? I mean, so old?"

She smiled, her leathery face wrinkling even more.

"Prektiss," she said. Practice. I stared at her uncomprehendingly until I realized that for the first time in memory she was making a joke.

"That's a good one," I said. "Here's another one. Is my mother your daughter?"

Grandma stared back at me, one arm wrapped around her middle, her other elbow resting on it as she held her pipe.

"Vat iss daughter?" she asked.

"What?"

"Vat," she repeated, "iss daughter?"

She was throwing the question back at me, asking me what I meant by "daughter." I understood. She was trying to tell me there was more to the meaning of the word than just the sense of a biological child, that there were other ways in which one could be someone's daughter. Fine. I got that. But if she hadn't given birth to my mother, then who had?

"Nicht k'no for certain," she said. "She come leetle."

Meaning she had arrived when she was very small, perhaps even still a baby.

"Did someone give her to you?" I asked.

Grandma nodded.

"Why?"

"To teach," she said. "To grow."

"They wanted you to raise her? To teach her?"

She nodded again.

"But why?"

Grandma laughed once more, a wheezy rattle.

"Because I know and they don't!" she said triumphantly, which was the longest speech I'd ever heard her make in English.

I was beginning to get a clearer picture now of what had really happened. Some parents, long ago, had decided they couldn't raise their baby girl by themselves. Maybe they were too poor, or too sick, or too something—who knew? So they left her with someone they thought would be able to give her some advantages in life. It didn't seem so strange when you considered that lots of other kids ended up in orphanages, or convents, or even stranger places. It was a shocker, though. It meant I didn't really know who my real grandmother was after all. It meant we weren't the people I thought we were. Or were we?

"Does my mother know this?" I asked. "Did you tell her when she got older?"

"I tell," she said. She began to pack her pipe, though whether with tobacco or marijuana I couldn't see. "She don't like. She make forget. Then she leef."

She pretended it wasn't true, and then she left. Was *that* why she left? Maybe she no longer felt constrained by the ties of family when she learned there were none. Maybe she no longer felt duty bound.

Maybe she'd always hated it out here, and that was the excuse she needed to leave—you're not my *real* mother, I could hear her saying. I don't have to listen to you!

But why would her parents have chosen to leave her with someone they must have known to be a witch? Because, I presumed, that was precisely why they chose Grandma in the first place. They must have wanted their daughter to learn the old ways that weren't being taught anymore. They wanted their daughter to be a legithata, too. Maybe there was nothing wrong with them at all—maybe they were perfectly healthy and capable of raising children, but they decided to sacrifice her to the Old Lady of the Woods as part of some weird deal they'd made. That thought gave me the creeps. Maybe they owed Grandma their souls! Cold chills crept over me as I sat head-to-head with this ancient and mysterious crone, and for the first time ever I was seriously afraid of her.

"Who are you?" I asked, very politely.

She smiled, as warmly as it was possibly for her to smile, sending up little thunderstorms from her pipe.

"Alt laty," she said. "Very alt laty."

"You're not really my grandmother?"

She shook her head. "More alt den dat," she said. "But—same blut." Same blood.

"So we are related?"

Nod of the head.

"So the people who gave you my mother—they were related to you too? Not strangers? Descendants of yours?"

Once more, a nod of the head.

"Grandma," I whispered. "How old are you?"

She didn't smile this time. She just kept puffing on that pipe. I knew there must have been at least a little of the green stuff in there, because I was starting to get kind of drowsy. It was a fragrant smoke, feeling almost like fingers on my face, and I felt like stretching out just for a minute while she thought of an answer. I lay down, trying hard to keep my eyes open. I could hear her start talking, sounding as though she was very far away. She was explaining things to me in a way that made complete sense, though I understood little of what she actually said... her accent, her voice blending with the smoke from her pipe and from the stove, the warm, close air of the shack all conspired to befuddle me.

She had come from far away, as a young girl, I heard her say. Yes, even she was young once! And she had been chased from her village because of the secrets she knew. They weren't her secrets—she'd learned them from her mother, and she from her mother, and so on. But people had grown uneasy about it, for some reason, although things were not always so. Once, her line had been respected. They had had a role in the daily rhythm of life. But things changed, as things always change. So she'd fled, rather than be burned at the stake—which was the fate that had befallen her mother—and had walked for many months, until she came to the ocean. It was not an easy journey, but it was made less harsh by the fact that she knew how to keep herself from being seen, and that there were all kinds of good things to eat growing all around. Once at the coast—she didn't even know where she was, only that she'd walked south and west—she waited until she met men she knew she could trust, small, dark-skinned, bright-eyed fishermen who told her of a place far out to sea where they could catch cod by the barrelful with almost no effort, and beyond that was more land.

This was the New World, they said. None of them had set foot on it, but they knew it was there. They had learned of its existence from the blond-haired giants to the north, who had already been sailing there every year in their boats with dragon's heads. The small, dark fishermen would take the girl there, they said—if she would keep them safe on the journey. For she had let them know what kind of person she was, and they knew she could help them with her magic. And she knew this New World was the place she had to go. It was calling her. Why, she didn't know—but it didn't matter. Why is not always important at the beginnings of things. It usually only becomes clear at the ends.

And so she'd landed, some weeks or months later, on a strange shore where no European had yet set foot, and continued her journey southward and westward. There were people already there, also dark, people whose skin was the color of trees, but they understood that she was in search of something and meant them no harm, so they let her alone. She'd walked west and south as though pulled in that direction like a magnet, until she found the place she was looking for—a secret place, filled with some kind of energy, some kind of power. It had drawn her like a promise. She had always dreamed of such a place. You could do wonderful things with this energy, if only you learned how. So she would learn how to use it. And it would be her job to pass that knowledge on to whoever came to her in earnest, asking to know her secrets. And she knew that, while it wouldn't make her live forever, she would be able to live a very, very long time, with the power of this place sustaining her—though she also knew this meant she could never leave.

It was an old story. Who knew how many people had heard it before me? And I wasn't the same person when I opened my eyes, and let them slowly focus on the ceiling. Something in me had changed. Had I been asleep? No, Grandma was still sitting there, smoke still spilling from the bowl of her pipe.

She kept talking. Sometime long ago, Grandma had had a child, a girl. The identity of the father didn't matter now. She didn't even remember who it was. Grandma—I would keep calling her that, though now it seemed like a woefully inadequate term—had trained that girl, and that girl had gone out in the world. Whether she was supposed to go, or whether Grandma had meant for her to stay, I don't know. I couldn't tell whether it had disappointed her or not. Then that girl had had a daughter, maybe only one, maybe many, maybe some sons too—and *that* girl had come back to the woods to be trained. Then she in turn had sent *her* daughter, and so on and so on. And this was the way it had been done, with the old lady creating a circle of slow time around her, drawing her life out as gently and slowly as possible. She was not a secret—she was only there for those who wanted her to be there, who needed her. The rest of the world need not concern themselves with what was going on in the woods. And she did not concern herself with the rest of the world, either.

The only question which remained in my mind now was this: What, exactly, was she teaching? And how did I fit into this line?

As if she had worn herself out by talking too much, Grandma once again fell silent, and remained silent for days, and then weeks. That was fine with me. I had plenty to think about, and I didn't want to distract myself with conversation. With our food already provided for us, and the weather growing steadily worse, I had nothing to do but sit and ponder and watch her. Entire days passed when I scarcely left the shack at all. Snow fell almost every day, gradually sealing us into our little mud cave. Grandma had developed the art of meditation to the point where she could remain immobile for hours, eyes shut, back stiff, hardly breathing—it was as if she put herself into a state of suspended animation, sleeping when the earth slept and waiting patiently for it to wake up one more time. I tried to do it too, but it was hard. I got better at it with time, but remaining immobile for so long hurt my back muscles, and sometimes my mind would race frantically, spinning its wheels like a car stuck in mud. At these moments I would grow almost insane with boredom. Then I would look at her again, and the sight of her would calm me—*If she can do it,* I would think, *then that means it's possible, and I can do it too.* The only sounds were the steady rhythm of Grandma's breathing, and the occasional pop as a knotty piece of wood exploded in the stove. Our appetites seemed to decrease with our level of activity, so that on some days I would take only a few mouthfuls of food, other days none at all—only a little water. Chester Burgess had brought a lot of canned goods, fruit and vegetables and so on, and we heated these up by setting them on the stove until they were warm and ate them with spoons. I ate hardly anything, and yet I was never very hungry. Something else was nourishing me, almost from the inside, as it were. Something about where I was was keeping me alive.

We really were hibernating. And even in this kind of silence and stillness, I was learning. Just by watching her be, I learned.

After more weeks passed, we developed a different rhythm. Grandma appeared to rouse herself from her constant trances, as though all that sitting still had been a preparation for something, and we fell into another routine. She would explain things to me, about this or that herb, this or that flower—more of the same things I'd learned with her that fall. Gradually, these lessons in simple botany and herbalism gave way to conversations of a much more mystical nature. Grandma knew secrets.

Here is where I have to draw the curtain—since I also made a promise that I would not teach anything to anyone who was not ready to be initiated, who had not given me clear signs that she was ready to study the natural arts. These things are none of anyone's business. What I can say about them is this: There is such a thing as magic in the world, and if you don't know that, it's because you've decided not to know, not because you haven't seen it. You have seen it—all of us have seen it. Maybe you just didn't believe it because it scared you. Entirely possible. Nobody's fault.

Yet the one thing I still didn't understand was what it was about the place that was special. Grandma never explained it to me. She freely admitted that the power of this place wasn't hers to keep—it was not something that could be transported. Maybe it was the water, she said. Maybe it was the rocks. When she had come here, the "Tree People"— whom I took to be Indians—had a ceremonial site near this very place. So they had known about it, too.

Come to think of it, she said, it probably was the trees themselves. That was why the people named themselves after the trees. If the trees were to be cut down, the place would lose its power. But she didn't worry about that happening. Grandma knew that all around her, civilization had encroached on almost every quiet spot. She knew cities had sprung up all over the place, that entire forests had disappeared, never to be replaced. But she said that this place would never be raped of its solitude. No people would ever come here except those who were seeking it out. Not even the "bad boys" who pillaged her marijuana patch from time to time were here to rob this place of its essence; they were not intentionally desecrating it. They were looking for something too, only they didn't know it, and they were too busy daring each other into acts of foolish bravery to pay attention to what their hearts already knew: that they were walking on holy ground.

"Bet boys," said Grandma, shaking her head. "Bet, bet boys. But dey look for somesink. Dey vant to learn. Someday—maybe. Maybe no. Maybe dey stay bet." She shrugged, pulling her mouth down into a frown, the line of her lips becoming indistinguishable from the crevices that ran across her face like fault lines.

Winter, usually the slowest season of all, passed purposefully along. I hardly stirred from the shack except to do my business outside and to gather snow for water. When I did exit, I stood for a long while with my eyes shut, adjusting to the glare, taking deep breaths of the clear air. It may sound strange, but I was getting better at breathing; I mean breathing like I meant it, aware of every molecule of blessed air that passed into my lungs, mixing with my blood and coursing through my body. Just this simple act could occupy my attention for an hour.

It was a long, bitter, cold winter, but it didn't bother me. I loved the silence of it, and the white.

Sometimes memories of Frankie would come galloping up to me and thrust themselves in my face, demanding to be recognized. Anything could trigger them. Now it was snow—he and I used to have fierce snowball fights. My favorite thing to do was to peg him when he was leaning out his spying window, because he was never expecting it. He would shriek with rage, come down and rub my face in it. Sometimes, when he forgot himself, he was strong—much stronger than me. But he never hurt me, or any other living thing on this planet.

Ah, poor Franks, I thought.

Because I loved him. I did.

Before I knew it most of the season had passed. We had no visitors and did not celebrate Christmas. We celebrated something else, and I had the distinct impression it was a holiday a lot older than Christmas—but that was one thing I didn't learn much about, because Grandma didn't go into detail. Mostly she chanted over an armful of evergreen branches. But none of it was explained to me, and when it was over she threw the branches on the fire, and we were nearly smoked out.

About halfway into January the weather seemed to ease up some. The cold lessened and we didn't get any more snow for a while. Not that it would have mattered by then, since we already had so much—a total of maybe five feet had fallen, and none of it had melted. Maybe in town it would have been swept up and gotten rid of by now, but out here in the woods it was settling in under its own weight, gradually acquiring the gentle inscriptions left by rodents and birds. Snow in the woods reads like a diary of every minor drama that has taken place there in preceding days. Here are the tracks of four little feet skittering along, then suddenly stopping where the creature sat up, sniffing, sensing danger—what? Everything all right? Okay then, but suddenly there's a big swoosh! where an owl's wings have stirred the surface like a helicopter's prop wash, and that's the end of one more mouse. Or rabbit. Or, hopefully, snake—but of course snakes didn't have feet. Maybe if they had, I could have related to them a bit more.

One day Grandma asked me what my intentions were as far the future was concerned. Did I want to stay with her? she asked. She still had never paid me a single compliment, never told me I was a quick study or a good student. Sometimes she tested me, asking me obscure questions about something she'd told me weeks before—and I always answered correctly, because by this time I'd opened my mind completely to her teachings, resisting nothing. But there was no sign from her that I'd done a good job. Yet one day in what must have been February she gave me the look that meant she was about to ask me a difficult question, and she from her side of the shack fixed me with her sharp eyes, and said: "Vat you do?"

Typically understated, it took me a moment to decipher what she was talking about. What was I doing? What would I do? What did I do? Grandma only had command of one tense, the present—you had to fill in the blanks yourself. I took this to be referring to the future, that is: What do you plan to do with yourself?

"When?" I asked.

"Spring," she said. "Stay? Go?"

I sat looking back at her, directly into her eyes. This no longer made me uncomfortable. Sometimes we communicated solely in this way, for minutes on end.

"Vat you want?" she asked, after a while. "Vat you neet?"

"A theater," I said.

It wasn't often I could surprise her, but I did this time. She blinked in mild astonishment and let a smile flicker briefly across the topography of her face, like a small earthquake.

"Eh?" she said.

"I want to build a theater," I said. "For people to come to. Where they can tell their stories."

"Hm," she said.

She did not speak again for some time—hours later, when dark had fallen and we were preparing to go to sleep, she said:

"Vy?"

I was lying on my back on my little bed, looking up at the ceiling. Without looking at her, I said, "I made a promise to Frankie."

"Frankie?"

"The guy who...you know, Frankie? Next door. Frankie Grunveldt."

"Boy who die?"

"That's the one," I said, though I knew I hadn't told her about Frankie's death—nor had anyone else. Things like this no longer surprised me about her. It wasn't that she was psychic, exactly. I had the impression that all the news of our part of the world was brought to her by the trees, that she could interpret the sound of the wind in the branches and know with near certainty everything that had happened nearby.

"Vell," she said, and that was all she had to say about that. We didn't discuss it again, but I had the sense that something had been decided for her. She had wanted to know if I intended to stay there for the rest of my days, studying and learning. But I didn't want to. It would have been a farce. I had needed to spend this time with her, but I didn't see myself becoming an old lady of the woods like herself. I belonged in the world. I belonged around people. I had come out here to heal myself, and now that had mostly been accomplished—the pain of Frankie's death had receded to a dull ache, then to a minor soreness. Now it hurt only if I chose to make it hurt, like a loose tooth that you prod with your tongue. I would always carry it, it would always be part of me—but that was better than me being a part of it.

"You mad at me?" I asked her at some point. "Do you want me to stay?"

She shook her head, squinting at me through her pipe smoke— plain old tobacco this time. I found myself wondering when, in the preceding centuries, she had taken up smoking, and who had taught it to her.

"You know vat you do," she said, pointing her pipe stem at me. "Not me."

Which was, when I thought about it, probably the nicest thing she'd ever said to me.

More weeks passed, and the vernal equinox was only days away—the first day of spring, the day when the earth tilts ever so slightly towards the sun again, like a jilted lover consenting to try it one more time. The sun was beginning to make regular appearances, and after months of gray and darkness let me tell you it was about the most welcome sight of my whole life. My skin had become pure white from spending all that time inside, and I was so weak from inactivity it was all I could do to traipse over to the creek through what snow remained to gather buckets of fresh running water. The good news was that my leg had been totally healed. Once I got back up to speed, I was pretty sure I could run on it again like nothing had ever happened. I couldn't wait to try.

There was another ceremony the night that spring was reborn, again one that I could sense had been repeated time out of mind, since long before Grandma herself walked the earth. Since I understood so little of it, I won't go into it here—except to say that Grandma chanted and sang in a language I'd never heard her speak before, one that sounded ancient. Maybe this was one of the advanced lessons, something she'd learned from her own mother, who had learned it in turn from the forest people back where they came from. Once, she'd told me, forest people lived everywhere.

After she'd carried on for a while she produced her special bowl, the simple clay one that she kept hidden in a corner of the shack, and made me go to the stream and fill it. This was one of the things I'd been learning about, and believe it or not most of it was pretty simple. The first step was in learning how to fill it completely full and walk back to the shack without spilling a single drop. Once I had developed the concentration necessary to pull that off, I was judged ready to learn the rest—but it had taken me days just to get to the point where I could do even that. It took forever, walking slowly, holding it level. By now I understood that the whole point of it was to teach me to focus. It took almost twenty minutes to reach the shack walking that slow, and once I made it I was already in a deep state of concentration, which was of course the whole point of making me do it.

I set the bowl in front of her, going into a low, deep bow as I did so. Then I sat down on my side of the shack and folded my legs under me. Grandma leaned over the bowl and looked down into the water, mumbling under her breath. This had become a matter of routine by now. There was no longer anything about this process that mystified me. It would be years before I was expert at it, of course. It still took me a long time to quiet my mind enough to see into the water. Grandma could do it within mere moments. Now she was doing it on my behalf—scanning the depths, as it were, to see what the future might hold. She had no need of mirrors, or any of the other accoutrements that I had used the first time I'd tried it, back at home. I would almost venture to say she didn't even need the bowl of water either.

And within another few moments she had her answer. Whatever it was, it appeared to concern her. She gave me a shrewd look and shook her finger at me.

"Pay 'tention," she said. "Und no break rules."

Most of her pronouncements were so cryptic that by the time I'd figured them out they'd already come to pass, and usually they were nothing dire or consequential. But this one had an air of gravity about it. She was seeing me in some future situation, knowing even before I did the course of action I would consider taking to remedy it, and whatever she saw me doing was making her uncomfortable. I, of course, had no idea what she was talking about. Pay attention, don't break rules—well, they teach you that in school, don't they? It's the basis of living in modern society. *Fine,* I thought. *I wouldn't break any rules. I would be a good girl once again.* Not that I hadn't been for the last few months—possibly my longest uninterrupted stretch of virtuousness ever. I hadn't had a chance to be headstrong, or willful, or any of the things that had caused me so much misery in my life. Or should I say that had caused Mother misery, which she in turn had passed on down to me in the form of hysterical headaches that were always declared to be My Fault. Don't break rules? Fine. I could live with that. Which rules exactly she was talking about would have to be determined later. I wouldn't even bother to ask.

Grandma motioned me to pick up the bowl again, and I began the same eternal process of carrying it back to the creek. The water had to be poured back in, along with a brief murmur of thanks. That was the way it was done.

.   .   .

Now the thaw was in full swing, and snow remained only in shady patches that never saw the full light of day—behind large rocks, on the north side of trees, in ravines and gullies. I began to wander around. Grandma made no attempt to stop me. She understood that I was still young and needed to stretch my legs, that sitting still for hours on end was not, after all, a natural activity for someone my age. I explored the woods, examining the changes that the weather had wrought. You can become intimate with a piece of the earth as though it was a person, and after a time you can detect minor alterations in its facade, just as you can see the signs of aging in someone you haven't bumped into for a while. That was how it was—like I was revisiting an old friend. I knew I would soon be making the long walk back home, and I rambled farther and farther afield, becoming acquainted with the world once more and building up my muscles, and my endurance. I found treasures—patches of early wildflowers, a family of fat raccoons, a small meadow where only ferns grew. One morning a robin dropped dead at my feet from the lower branches of a tree—a terrible omen if ever there was one, that is, for the uninitiated. To me, however, it meant only that the robin's spirit had flown on without its body. I carried it back to Grandma and showed it to her, but she was uninterested, so I set the bird under a tree for the first predator to come along.

The sun grew warmer. April had presented its calling card at the door, and was waiting to be admitted. The dead robin was gone the next day, presumably made quick work of by some hungry forest dweller. But that afternoon I saw a live robin near our shack, which meant the warmth was here to stay. I hoped to get home before the frequent day-long rains came. Otherwise I would be in for a long and soggy hike.

It was just two days before the day I'd determined I would leave when, during one of my perambulations, I heard sounds I hadn't heard in a while: people talking. They seemed to be chattering away so loud you could have heard them from the next solar system. I froze in my tracks, then dove behind a large sycamore. There were a bunch of them, from the sound of it—male and female, youngish, energetic, crashing through the branches like a herd of bulls, maybe just a hundred yards off. I was shocked at how bloody loud they were. Compared to them, I was as woodsy as they came. I was practically an Indian. A pack of high school kids out for a romp, maybe. One thing I knew was that it wasn't the "bet boys" who came a-raiding every so often. Those kind never brought girls with them. That, I told myself snidely, is because girls would know better than to behave like that; and I thanked God once more that I was a member of the superior sex.

Of course, if I hadn't been so busy being smug, I would have heard the footsteps behind me, and I wouldn't have been taken by surprise by the hearty male voice that boomed out from somewhere over my left shoulder, "Why, you must be Haley Bombauer!"

I just about jumped out of my skin. I shot to my feet and whipped around to see who it was. There before me stood a beefy, red-faced giant of a man in camouflage clothing and military-style hiking boots, wearing one of those Tyrolean mountain hats with a little feather sticking out of it. He looked harmless enough—I could see that right away—but nonetheless he had scared the life out of me, and it was all I could do to keep from tackling him and giving him a good pummeling. The old, irate Flash Jackson surged up in me again. You do not sneak up on the world's greatest stuntman like that, not if you value your hide.

"Who are you?" I asked. Had I not gone so long without talking, I more likely would have yelled at him, something like, *Who in blue blazes are you, you bastard son of a sewer rat?*

"Didn't mean to startle you," he said. "Aren't you Haley Bombauer?"

"I asked you first," I snarled, stepping away from him—though in fact he had asked me first. Hell with it. I wasn't in the mood for social niceties. The man looked even more alarmed. I imagine I must have looked quite a sight, and smelled quite a smell, too. I hadn't showered since last fall, and I had given up trying to change clothes, because it was pointless. My hair, I knew, was mostly dreadlocked, and I had a layer of dirt on my skin that I'd grown so comfortable with I would almost miss it when it was gone.

"Your mother sent me out this general way," the man said. "And Chester Burgess told me where I could find you, too. I'm Professor Watkins—Andrew Watkins. From the University," he added. "Sociology department."

"Chester Burgess? You're lying," I said. "He'd never do that. You followed him last fall. What are you doing out here?"

Though, if the truth be told—and the truth must always be told—I already knew what he was doing out there.

Some years ago, the county had taken an interest in the welfare of the woman whom I still chose to refer to as my grandmother. It had been a brief fling, beginning when some bored bureaucrat or do-gooding old dame had decided that Grandma didn't know as well as they did what was good for her, and that they would take her out of her miserable little house in the woods and put her into a nice, cozy old folks' home in town, where she could sit and watch television with all the other fossils and decompose in peace. Can you imagine? Needless to say, that plan got bogged down pretty quick in the endless mire of local-government red tape, compounded by the fact that when a few caseworkers toddled out this way to kidnap the poor old lady, she was nowhere to be found. They looked for days, but her little house had disappeared, and nobody had the slightest clue where it—or she—had gone.

Next step for the disappointed crusaders was to swing by Mother's and my place and ask if Grandma had moved in with us. I was just a child at the time, but I remember this. Mother was as mystified as they were, or at least pretended to be. She knew that Grandma had a few tricks up her sleeve. She hadn't seen her mother in weeks, she said, and wasn't particularly worried about it. Sometimes months went by between visits. Sometimes a year. She'd been living out in the woods all her life. It was her business if she wanted to keep on doing it.

All of it came to nothing, and eventually the county got tired of looking for her. But by then the university folks had gotten wind of what they referred to as a "living national treasure of folklore," and the afore-described Andrew Watkins, chair of sociology at the University of Buffalo, had charged out here with a pack of graduate students, all of them armed with notebooks and tape recorders and their heads filled with theories of "cultural isolationism" and all kinds of other fluff. I remembered that phrase because I remembered them, too. The little snots had actually come out to the house to interview Mother and me, seeing as how they couldn't find Grandma either, and one of them had asked Mother how it felt to grow up in "cultural isolation." I think Mother was kind of flattered at ending up as a piece of someone's dissertation, and they stuck around for hours, pumping her for information and leaving her blushing and dazzled. And when they'd gone away, we thought that was the end of that. Our fifteen minutes were over.

But they weren't. Here was Dr. Andrew Watkins, large as life and in fact several pounds heavier than I remembered him, standing right in front of me in the woods that I had come to think of as my own, poking his red nose into my family's business once again.

"You were just a little girl the last time I saw you, I believe," said Watkins, not daring to take a step closer. "Do you remember?"

"Yeah," I said. "What do you want?"

"Well, you know," he said, looking around as if an answer was going to fall out of a tree, "I've brought some, ah, students of mine with me, and we were hoping that maybe this time—"

"You won't find her," I said. "You couldn't find her last time, and you won't find her now."

"Ah, yes, I see," said Watkins. "Haley, may I ask you—why *is* that, exactly?"

Oh, how I would have loved to give him the straight truth. I would have loved to tell him it was because Grandma had the equivalent of a force field set up around her home, and she always knew when it was about to be invaded. Don't ask me how she does it, I would have said, because truthfully I didn't know. I wasn't that far along in my training. But she had a way of making herself, well, not exactly disappear, but definitely become much harder to spot—almost as good as disappearing, really. Not even I would be able to spot her, though without meaning to brag I would have liked to add that I was making middling progress on the very same trick myself.

But of course, I couldn't say that. All I said was, "Maybe you need glasses."

Watkins was about to say something back, but just then his herd of cavorting grad students found us and came trotting up, winded and eager. There were about six of them, and damned if they weren't carrying all sorts of electronic equipment with them again, a little more high tech this time: digital cameras, tiny tape recorders, et cetera. They all began babbling at once to their fearless leader, asking if I was the granddaughter they'd heard about; when Watkins announced that I was, as proud as if he'd created me himself, they turned their attention to me, pointing their tape recorders and video cameras and whatnot into my face. That was about all I could take of that. I did what I should have done in the first place: I disappeared, too.

I don't mean in a magic sense. I mean I took to my heels and ran like a gazelle on amphetamines. I dove right through their midst and out the other side, and I moved faster than a moon shadow, putting on a full burst of speed so that I knew there'd be no way they could catch me. Even if they were fast, they didn't know these woods like I did. By now I had an excellent sense of the terrain, where the high and low spots were and where the ground got soggy. I headed back for Grandma's, but I took a zigzag path to throw them off, at one point skirting a small bog in the hopes that they'd blunder in there and get stuck forever.

Then I headed at full steam for the little clearing where Grandma's house was. I was pretty well bushed by this time—I'd been running for a while, and my winter of inactivity, combined with all the time I'd been holed up with my busted gam the year before, was working against me. I still felt a little unsteady on the wonky one, and I was afraid if I kept running I would stick it in a hole or under a fallen log or something and end up having to spend another summer in a cast. So I decided I'd given them enough of a shake, and I turned towards Grandma's place.

Except when I got there, of course, it was gone.

I stopped, gasping for air, and looked around frantically. There was the creek, right where it was supposed to be; there was the remnant of a fire, a circle of charred earth and blackened stones. But that was it. She'd pulled her disappearing act again.

That could only mean one thing: One of them had stuck to me like glue, and again I hadn't known it. I turned slowly and looked behind me, and up at the top of a small rise stood one of the grad students, a fit young fellow who had dumped his equipment and kept on my tail the whole way. I hadn't even heard him. He was standing there staring at me with something like awe, probably because I looked like Medusa, my dreadlocked hair flying out like snakes—the irony!—and my face dark with dirt and streaked with sweat.

That was why she was gone—because otherwise he would have seen her. She was not a curiosity, not there to teach the uninitiated, not interested in being part of anyone's study. The things she knew were not for public consumption. They were for a select few, and they knew who they were. So did Grandma. And this yahoo from the university was not one of them.

Defeated and heartsick, I stood there catching my breath, waiting for him to go away. But of course he didn't. Gradually he snuck closer and closer, until he was maybe ten yards away. I let him come, pretending I was still out of breath. When he was too close to dodge me, I launched myself through midair and knocked him to the ground. Then I sat on his chest and let him have a couple, right in the kisser. He

screamed, I am sorry to say, like a girl. And it hurt my hands like hell—
I hadn't punched anyone in years. But that was nothing compared to
how I felt inside. I only hoped she knew that I hadn't meant to betray
her, and how much it was killing me that I hadn't been able to say good-
bye. I realized, too late, that I had started to love her, whiskers and wrinkles and all. And I knew that this was also her way of telling me that it
was time to move on. I was not going to be seeing the Mother of the
Woods again anytime soon. That much I knew for certain.

"Richard!" came a man's voice from behind. It was Watkins.
"Richard, are you all right?"

The guy under me whimpered and tried to sit up. I got off him and
sat down under a nearby tree. Watkins approached, crouching down
as though expecting another attack. Richard struggled to his feet and
looked at me in amazement, blood streaming down his chin.

"You bith!" he said. "Thee hit me!" he said to Watkins.

"Here," said Watkins, handing him a handkerchief. To me he said,
"Was that absolutely necessary?"

"Yes," I said.

"I'm thuing her!" said Richard.

"You chased me," I said. "You tried to touch me. You all ganged
up on me. I was almost raped."

Richard and Watkins stared at each other in disbelief, and then at
me.

"It was self-defense, and if you ever say any different I'll come after
you," I said to Watkins. "That's a promise."

A look of panic crossed his face. Watkins knew enough about my
grandmother to know that he was probably outmatched by me. The
other grad students had caught up with us by now, and they were
huddled in a knot, staring solemnly at us. Watkins put his arm around
Richard and helped him away.

"Watkins!" I said.

He turned.

"Never come here again," I said. "If you do, you won't like what happens."

He didn't say anything. I guess he knew I was serious. The whole lot of them turned and headed back to wherever they'd left their cars, and I was alone under the tree, left to ponder the sudden emptiness of the space that Grandma and I had called home.

10

The Tree People

Near the spot where our little house had been, looking towards the southwest, was an overhanging rock face that caught the sun's warmth from late morning throughout the afternoon, gathering heat like an upturned cat's belly under a stove, and giving it away again bit by bit in the evenings. On top of the overhang was a flat, slightly concave spot where I could sit and ponder the forest, and at night I rolled up under the rock and was almost cozy in the damp, cool gloom. It was the best seat in the house. I wasn't the only creature that knew about this place, but I was the biggest. I staked my claim by urinating around the perimeter, as a warning to the raccoons, mice, rabbits, and others who might otherwise have been tempted to burrow in the soft soil under the rock, or simply to stop awhile and rest there, availing themselves of my hospitality whether I liked it or not. The laws of the forest are generally cordial in nature—excluding the ones that allow for the consumption of one's neighbors—but they're strict where matters of personal boundaries apply, and one is within one's right to get testy if these zones are violated. I had seen it happen a thousand times before.

If you were to compare an acre of New York City—a place I admit I've never been—to an acre of virgin forest, counting each living thing in each place equally and regardless of size, the city acre would seem like an empty, desolate wasteland in comparison to the forested one. We may think of New York as crowded, and if you consider the preponderance of our species there, it is. People exist in the city in such numbers that were you to spread them out according to natural laws, tribewise, they would probably take up many tens of thousands of square miles. But there are few other creatures in that urban environment besides humans. Pigeons, cockroaches, worms, dogs and cats, squirrels—hardly a diversity of wildlife, not when compared to a forest in the temperate climate of northeastern North America. There, within that same acre, one would find an average of one hundred fifty insect species, at least fifty kinds of plants (not including mosses and lichens), roughly twenty-five kinds of birds (either permanent residents or visitors), an unknown number of snakes, a plethora of mammals ranging in size from tiny to medium (mice, voles, moles, squirrels, rabbits, chipmunks, raccoons, and muskrats, to name a few) and a handful of larger ones. Including myself.

For a human to move into this hypothetical acre, a great readjustment has to be made by the rest of the population, and, as would be the case in any other community, this is not accomplished without a great deal of grumbling and resentment. Animals are not in the habit of banding together and forming committees, but if they were I would have been visited daily by outraged woodland representatives, demanding that I unhand their resources, cease consuming their kin, and move on to bother some other sylvan municipality. Once I had become attuned to the various meanings of birdsong, I understood what the birds said to each other every time I passed by: not some glorious ode to romantic, unspoiled Nature but "There goes the neighborhood."

I couldn't bring myself to leave the forest, and I couldn't make up my mind to stay. I was alone now. It had been weeks since Grandma disappeared, and there was no hint that she might ever come back. I could sometimes sense her presence, if I searched for it, in the same way that small children can sense God. But this was always fleeting, and it brought me little comfort, just as my brief forays to church had always left me feeling vaguely unsettled and cheated of something that was just out of reach, that I was unworthy of grasping.

The animals were small help, but at least they kept my mind on the here-and-now. I was engaged in a running feud with a family of coons, notorious bandits, over my small cache of berries, pine nuts, and roots. Most of my time was occupied in thinking up ways to thwart them, and finally I went so far as to kill one of the younger ones, an adolescent. He was delicious. But this provoked such an outcry among the other members of his clan that I took to wandering in giant circles around my camp, exploring as I had never explored before, because their shrill cries of revenge had begun to haunt me even while awake. Despite the fact that the forest laws were in my favor (I was bigger, hence I was in the right) I began to suffer from a guilty conscience. This is why mankind will never again be at home in the wild; we have not left it so much physically as spiritually, and the prospect of a return journey is not a pleasant one. Conscience, when it exists, is a powerful master.

I was looking, I can see now, for a more permanent place to live. Not one that was set apart from prying eyes and curious little hands (the only thing that bothered me about eating raccoons was their hands, which have four fingers plus a thing that, if not precisely a thumb, looks enough like one to make me a possible cannibal). But such a place doesn't exist in the forest, which is the least private of anywhere. I guess I was really only looking around. Now that I had no herb-gathering errands to go on, I felt like a girl who'd been let out of school early. Mixed with my sadness at Grandma's—what? death? disappearance? evaporation?—was a sort of elation at being allowed, finally, to indulge my natural urge to move at random. I spent entire days in tracking the movements of the stream, following it to pools where the fish were large enough to eat. I developed a relationship with a fox, who enjoyed barking at me and then running when I chased him; when I'd finally give up, he would reappear, yapping delightedly at his superiority. I had known similar dogs. I passed by the same grove of ancient oaks again and again, until something about them seemed to beckon me, and when one day I stood in their center and raised my face to their canopy, I remembered Grandma telling me about the Tree People, and I realized with a shock that these were them.

The last Tree People, she'd said, believed that they were the children of the forest, descendants of trees who had gotten ambitious and yanked their own roots from the ground. Using them like feet and legs, they tried to explore the world, but they found that they were better suited for standing still than walking. When they tried to return to their natural state, however, they found it was impossible. They had succeeded in defying the laws of nature, which is never as hard as it seems, but always carries some terrible price. In this case, the price was loss of home. The newly mobile trees had to learn how to live all over again, and gradually they lost all similarities to their relatives and turned into people, with no hard feelings on either side.

For the Indians, who believed this story, living in the forest must have been like living among a host of conscious monuments to the past. For myself, who also believed this story, I understood that I had been surrounded by thinking, living beings all this time, the wise and immutable trees, whose ill-fated children were long gone but who themselves continued to exist, unperturbed.

Consider this: Me walking through that forest in that day and age, once home to many people and now empty of all but me, was as it would have been for an Indian to wander through Manhattan if everyone there had died of war or disease, and there were only empty buildings to peer at. This forest was their city; these oaks were their skyscrapers. I was existing in a ruined world. A terrible thing had happened here, and it echoed still in the living wood.

Grandma remembered everything from those days, and she told me what had happened to the Tree People with the authority of one who had seen it with her own eyes. First there had been wars with other kinds of People—Rock, Mud, Frog, Deer—but these were nothing new. Then whites had come, and brought disease. The numbers of Tree People quickly diminished. Of those who were left, a number fell victim to alcohol and went to live where they could get it more easily. Many were killed outright by men with guns. The rest of them moved on, eventually, to a reservation near the lake, where they live today, selling discount cigarettes and lottery tickets and toying with the possibility of putting in a casino.

"I'm sorry," I whispered upwards. There was some response—moaning trunks, branches rubbing together, rustling leaves. Up high, there was a breeze blowing. On the ground, it was still.

If you spend enough time in the company of a tree, you can get to know it, just like a horse or a man or a dog. Trees have personalities, moods, and opinions; their modes of expression are subtle, which means you have to pay careful attention. I made a point of visiting these oaks as often as possible. It required patience to figure out what they were about. I had deduced by then that these trees were not just alive but conscious. I wanted to learn whatever it was they had to teach me. This became my new goal. I couldn't just live in the forest and do nothing, like a nymph. I needed to continue my training.

By this time, I was going around completely unclothed. Chester Burgess had reappeared in late spring to retrieve the sacks of empty cans from Grandma and me, and to offer more supplies, but his load contained no new dresses, and for that I was extremely grateful. Had he seen me, perhaps he would have offered to return with some, but I stayed hidden the day he came and watched him from several yards off. I wasn't in the mood for conversation.

He knew I was there, of course. He was exceptionally nervous, old Chester was. Moving as quickly as he could—I could see that he was suffering from mild rheumatism—he kept looking around, waiting for me to pop out at him. Or perhaps someone else. I wondered if he knew that Andrew Watkins and his team of researchers had followed him out here last time, and that he was responsible for Grandma's

flight. I had considered confronting him with that information, perhaps even suggesting that he take a few lessons in spycraft from Miz
Powell, but I let him go on his way, unharassed. Poor old Chester. I
wondered how long he would go on paying his dues to a woman who
no longer existed. Probably until he felt that whatever debt he owed
to her was paid off. Or until he showed up one season and saw that the
previous year's offering was still untouched, at which point he would be
forced to draw his own conclusions about what had happened to us.

I wondered, too, how I would explain Grandma's absence to anyone who came looking for her. It was not unthinkable that Mother herself would traipse out here to check up on us, and when she found that
Grandma's house was gone, there was no telling how she would react.
And what would I say when she saw me? *Hello, Mother—yes, I've given
up clothes. Don't need them. And Grandma—well, she just sort of vaporized
herself, and she took the house with her. It's all the university's fault.*

I didn't even know how to think about Grandma now. I understood
the proper place of reverence one reserved for the dead, but I wasn't
sure if she fit there yet. In any case, the place she occupied in my mind
and in my imagination far exceeded the level of anyone else I'd ever
known. Was she a goddess? Was she a spirit? These questions to me
were more of degree than credibility. It would never occur to me to
dispute that goddesses and spirits existed. Of course they did. What I
didn't know was whether or not she was one of them. And really, this
was only a distinction—a formality, nothing more. If she wasn't actually a spirit, she was as close as one could get.

When Chester was gone I sorted through his boxes to see what
goodies they contained. More food, enough for two; he couldn't have
known that Grandma was gone. No one did. I buried most of it right
there, hoping the cans wouldn't rust through, intending to come back
for it in the fall, when food was scarce. A new knife, a very welcome
gift indeed. Some twine, always handy. Matches. Soap—hah! That was
a good one. A small camp shovel. Two small cooking pots. A couple of

blankets. Scissors. Various other sundry items, most of them no longer relevant to someone like me. I left most of the stuff sitting right there, knowing that the brighter items would be picked up by scavenging animals, and that the rest would be scattered by the curious bear. There was a bear, I knew, though I'd never met him, nor hoped to. I knew the laws of the forest too well.

I fashioned a sort of belt out of the twine, wrapped it around my middle, and stuck the knife in it, having first created a scabbard out of bark. This took a while, but I had nothing but time. On the other side of my waist I carried the scissors, though I had no idea what I was going to do with them. They just seemed to complete me, somehow. Then I pretended to examine myself in a full-length mirror. Hair longer now, well past the shoulders, knotted and matted. Breasts definitely smaller since I had lost all that weight. I could see my own hipbones, count my ribs. A weapon at my side for the first time in my life. Well, why not? Everyone else in the forest had one. Bear had teeth and claws. Fox, the same, plus cunning. Crow had wings. Mouse had smallness. Haley had a knife and scissors, and the gift of reason. With those things, I could do almost anything.

I guess it's not too far of a stretch to say that by now I had become more than half wild. Unlike my mother, I had been accepted by the forest. I was adept at tracking and trapping any animal I felt like eating, and I had learned to skin and cook an astonishing variety of creatures, none of which I would have considered edible in my former life. With Chester's pots, I fried and stewed and made soup, and, adding these to the variety of herbs available to me, I ate much better than I had with Grandma. When undergoing the strenuous kind of boot camp she had put me through, a sparse diet was the most conducive to clear thought. The more distanced one was from the body, the closer to the spirit one became. I sometimes think that she prepared food only to humor me, as if she had already learned to subsist on almost nothing except water and air and moonlight, and was impatiently waiting for me to do the same.

But there had been a shift in my purpose. I had mastered a certain level of whatever-it-was, witchcraft or Zam or the legithatic arts or Flash Jacksonism. I was now onto a whole new field. I intended to raise survival to a fine art, to live in the woods not as if I'd landed there by accident but had gone there on purpose. Thoreau came to mind again, and for the first time since leaving home I wished that I had brought a book; his book about pondside living, to be precise. But there was nothing to do about it. I couldn't very well place an order with Chester Burgess and hope he got around to filling in within the next nine months or so. No point. I would do without even that much human company.

Haley, I would ask myself, *are you ever going home again?*

Why? I would respond.

I never came up with a reasonable answer. I was becoming my grandmother after all. I had imbibed more knowledge from her than I'd known. I loved to walk through the woods alone now, naming every plant I saw, gauging its effectiveness in fighting this or that ailment, or as a preventative. I had graduated to a whole new level of herbal mastery. My eye was practiced. For the first time, the study of herbs began to seem like a pleasant immersion, one to which I could devote the rest of my life without ever being finished. Once this idea would have annoyed me, thinking of how far I had left to go. Now, however, it seemed like a blessing. Finally I had a purpose in life. I knew something most other people didn't.

(Note to self: When menstruating, bury used tampons very deep. Something has been digging them up lately. Something big.)

Try this, next time you find yourself alone in the woods. Plant your feet firmly on the ground, and raise your arms at imprecise angles to your body, one higher than the other. Close your eyes. Now, never move again. When a breeze comes, allow it to sway you. When something sniffs around you, let it. If that creature chooses to burrow under your skin, don't move. Eventually, your arms will drop off, and new ones will grow in their place—longer arms, and more numerous, so that at the end of your life you will have not two of them but seventy or eighty. Your skin will expand as your insides get bigger. Your heart rate will slow down, gradually, until it beats only four times a year. You will stay like that for years upon years, until you begin to die.

This is what it's like to be a tree, a millionth part of the forest. I had learned to love trees even more than before. I sat and watched them, and this is what I learned.

Your death will happen at this same slow rate, taking perhaps five years, maybe fifty. Half of you may die while the other half lives on indefinitely. Your head could be lopped off by lightning while the rest of you survives. Eventually, though, you will fall. It may take an age for you to accomplish even that simple act. Don't allow your spine to bend, not even in your penultimate moment, for a tree never gives in to death. Even after you've hit the ground, and your body begins to be consumed by thousands of insects, you are still a tree. Even after you have been carted off, molecule by molecule, you are still a tree. Even if in a hundred years, someone comes by and notices nothing where you once stood, you are still every bit as much a tree as you were when you planted yourself there, thinking tree thoughts and having tree dreams.

If we had time to make this kind of experiment, what would the world be like? But we don't have time, of course. Time is a gift that comes with size. Trees are bigger, they outlast us by far, and are superior in every respect. This is what I learned, sitting at the foot of those ancient oaks, surrounded by them on all sides. It is an honor even to be with a tree. They are infinite in patience and understanding of every process ongoing. How could they not be? This is their nature. This is the way they were made.

I loved the trees not least because they knew everything that is happening everywhere in the forest. Once I had begun to learn to pay attention to what they knew, then I knew it too. That, combined with the gifts I had taken from Grandma, were what allowed me to realize one day that someone, somewhere, had an ax, and was doing some lumbering, not a mile from where I sat.

There is a romantic notion that trees resent being cut down. They do not. They understand their role in the world, that they are there to make homes. If a human comes along, chops a few trees down, saws the wood into lumber and makes a house out of it, this is only a very elaborate version of what an owl does, or a fox, or a bird, when they construct a nest or a burrow. The fate of trees is to give up their bodies. Nothing unnatural about that.

But I had come to believe that *these* trees were different. The woman I thought of as Grandma told me repeatedly that nothing had changed in this forest since she'd come to live there, and that it was the source of her ageless power. I understood then that if the trees were cut down, that essence would go away. That's because they were, quite simply, the oldest trees around. In ordinary times, their demise would not have been significant. But these were not ordinary times. There *were* no older trees than these, at least not in this part of the world. I knew that this was not a permanent state of affairs. Trees were destined to outlast people, and someday there would once again be continents of forests, stretching so far and deep that no creature living within them would know there was any other kind of place. But that was the long view, the big picture. Today, here and now, someone was cutting down a tree, and everyone in the forest knew about it.

I, however, was the only one who could put a stop to it.

It required little forethought. I was already as dressed as I was going to be, already prepared for battle. I slipped away from my grove of oaks—not bothering to say good-bye, since they would scarcely have noticed my absence by the time I'd returned—and headed off for the epicenter of the disturbance. I wore only my twine belt, with the knife in the bark scabbard. Though I knew I was still far out of earshot of whoever it was, I moved silently, from shadow to shadow. That bear had been around again, and another forest rule is that you never make noise, unless you are trying to attract a mate. Which I was not. Silence is golden.

Moving like that, I could cover a mile in about half an hour, not counting the time I took to stop and still my breath and heart, or the moments when I heard various noises and stopped to determine what they were before continuing. Trees do not mourn their dead, but they are aware of what's happening, always talking about it. I followed the trail of gossip, that's all. In an hour, perhaps a little more, I was within a hundred yards.

For a while now I had heard the blows of the ax. I smelled diesel fuel, though I couldn't hear an engine. And I smelled a human, too. That scent, at once familiar and repulsive, cloyed in my nostrils, and I had to stifle a sneeze. Sweat. A trace of deodorant. It was, of course, a man.

I could see his outline as I crept closer, protected by underbrush and low-hanging branches. I did not make the slightest sound. There was a road near here, a seldom-used path cut out long ago by some enterprising ranger or lumberjack. It was mostly overgrown, but still serviceable for someone with a truck or a tractor. The trees here were not so old, either, but still important. They knew things that the other trees did not. I grew angry. Why, of all places, of all trees? Why did this person have to cut down these?

The man wore a baseball cap, and he swung with a calm efficiency that showed he'd done this many times before. The cap was low over his eyes, so I couldn't see his face, but his back was to me anyway. Nearby was a tractor, which he no doubt intended to use to drag home his prize. He must have been building something back at his farm.

I sat for a long time, fascinated, and thought about all the gossipy stories I'd heard about men from women. A common phrase among the women I grew up around was something along the lines of *She'll never catch herself a man.* It was something women said of other women when they wanted to feel superior, when she was following an independent course that no one could understand. A variant was, *How does she ever expect to catch a man when she goes around like that?* More than likely this had been said of me in the past. But the idea of "catching" a man had always seemed ridiculous. Men were not high-flying, unattainable creatures who resisted every attempt at domestication. Matter of fact, they were never too far off, especially when they smelled food. To me, huntress extraordinaire, catching a man seemed about as complicated as trapping a cow. No matter. None of that had anything to do with me. I was only going to scare this one off, not keep him. I had no use for a man at all.

I had, by this time, become adept at imitating a number of animal sounds. I sorted through my repertoire now, trying to find one that would be suitably threatening. Nothing came to mind except Bear, and I was afraid to throw his voice lest he hear me and think he was receiving an invitation.

What would be even more frightening to a man than a bear?

That's easy, I thought. *I'll pretend I'm another man, a bigger one.* I'll scare him off by pretending I'm human. I would say, *Get out!* in my loudest, deepest, most terrifying howl. Nothing is more frightening to people than one of their own kind, provided they believe that human is insane, violent, or possibly a returned spirit.

Just as I was clearing my throat, the man turned for a moment. He took off his cap and reached for a bottle of water under the tractor's seat, still clutching his ax, and I had a clear view of his face.

It was Adam Schumacher.

I was stunned. How long had it been since I'd seen him? At least a year. Our last meeting had been at his farm, on the Fourth of July. Embarrassment swelled in me as I remembered how I'd felt when he and Roberta disappeared into the barn, the same barn he and I had shared the year before. Blond-haired bastard. Well, I would show him.

I had completely forgotten that I was naked, of course. Without another thought, I stepped out of the brush, strode toward him—his back was to me again—and shouted: "What the hell do you think you're doing?"

It had been months since I'd said that many words, and the effect was not what I had hoped for. I did a fair amount of talking to myself, but my voice was still unused and out of shape, and instead of a stentorian lioness's roar, what came out instead was a pathetic kind of meow, the noise an irate kitten might make if you stepped on his toes.

Still, I managed to scare the daylights out of him. Adam spun around and stared at me, bug-eyed. He didn't recognize me. I had lost a lot of weight since seeing him last, and my personal hygiene left a great deal to be desired. I'm sure my face was literally invisible under the layers of dirt. It's a wonder he didn't smell me coming up behind him. And Lord only knows what raced through his mind as he stared at me.

It was only then, when I felt his eyes on me, that I remembered I wasn't wearing a stitch. Well, it was too late to do anything about that now. He'd seen me. I wasn't feeling in the least self-conscious. In fact, I was thinking that *he* looked a bit silly, wearing all those clothes when it was a perfectly beautiful day out.

Adam's eyes were huge. He couldn't move. One hand held the water bottle upside down, so that the contents trickled out, and the other held the ax. It was the ax I wanted. I intended to stop him from chopping down any more trees. These were *my* woods. So I stepped forward quickly and put my hand on his wrist, partly also to keep him from chopping me in half. I could tell that thought was running through his mind, too. I was sure now he hadn't recognized me. He thought I was Bigfoot's wife, maybe, or some kind of mutant being that was going to suck out his brain.

He didn't try to move. His nostrils widened as he took in my odor, but he must not have found it unpleasant, because there was no expression of disgust on his face. Slowly, he dropped the water bottle and moved his hand up to my breast, cupping it in his warm, callused hand.

I was completely unprepared for that, I can tell you. Nor was I any better prepared for the way it felt. No one had touched me like that before. The last fellow to put his hand there had, in fact, been Adam

himself, but that had been different. It was in the barn, and it was
sweaty and hurried and really more for fun than anything else. This
was a different story. We were both older now. Certain things were
more immediate, and more clear.

What happened next is still unbelievable, as many times as I've
gone over it in my mind. Unbelievable and exciting. Exciting and ani-
malistic. I had known all along that I was an animal, but Adam had
yet to learn that he, too, had more in common with our forest brethren
than he thought.

I think it must have been my smell that took over and made him
crazy. There was no denying that my smell was as strong as it could
be, that it proclaimed to everyone far and wide who I was. I knew Adam
had never really smelled a woman before, that I was washing over him
like a tidal wave, a force of nature. Something else took him over, some
part of himself that he didn't know he had. I had awakened the cave-
man in Adam, with predictable results.

There was no question of kissing. It was not that kind of encounter.
I watched in amazement as Adam ripped off his own clothes, tossing
his T-shirt off into the bushes, yanking his jeans down to his feet. He
was already erect. He stood there before me for several seconds, letting
me look at him, waiting to see my reaction.

I stayed. I couldn't help it. I was too fascinated. I found myself
pondering his penis, never having seen one before—not in this state,
certainly. It was shortish and thick, the soft sack of his testicles descend-
ing through a mass of blond fuzz, heavy and pendulous in the heat. I
took his cock in my hand, amazed at its rigidity, its length, the way
the blood pulsed through it with the ferocity of a river. I stepped in
closer. Large parts of me were screaming that I ought to run, but other
parts were urging me to stay, that it was all right, that it was supposed
to be this way.

I moved closer to him until I could feel his member pressing into
my belly. He rolled his eyes back and shuddered at my touch, and the

next thing I knew I was on my back, looking up at the sky, and Adam had entered me and was thrusting energetically, with simultaneous purpose and abandon.

I will not say I was raped. I may not have intended it to happen, but I certainly didn't object to it. Nor will I say it hurt. True, he was entering parts of me that had never been entered before, and the sensation was indeed painful and overwhelming, but overall not unpleasant. I had the distinct impression that he was getting more out of it than I was, that he knew what he was doing, whereas I did not. This did seem to be unfair, but I could hardly blame him for that.

Also, I hadn't the slightest idea what was expected of me.

Apparently, not much. After perhaps a minute of his pushing, I felt him explode in a great burst of moisture, and his seed trickled deep. Then he collapsed in a moaning, heaving heap on my chest. I still hadn't done anything other than lie there, my legs first hoisted up onto his shoulders, now spread out wide on the ground with him between them. I became aware that I, too, was breathing hard. A warm glow had come over me during what I would come to think of later as The Event, and I knew that this was something I could eventually enjoy, once I learned more about it.

But that wasn't going to happen just now. We were slick and overheated, and I wanted him to get up off me. I pushed on his shoulders. He stirred and mumbled something. I tried to wiggle out from under him, and only now did I feel the first faint rumblings of fear: What if he didn't let me go? What if he decided to keep me there, as his prisoner? I still had my knife and scissors in my belt, and one hand strayed down to feel the haft of the knife, just for reassurance. If he didn't get up off me, I would cut off his head. I would carry it around by those fine, blond hairs, as a warning to men everywhere.

But he got up, brushing his bowl-cut hair out of his eyes, leaving a smear of dirt on his forehead. His chest, freckled and broad, pink and nearly hairless, was wet with our mixed sweat.

"Jesus, Haley," he said. "That was amazing."

I shot to my feet. So he *did* know it was me. Well, of course he would—we'd known each other forever, and sooner or later he would have figured it out. You might even say that sooner or later, something like this was bound to happen. Him and me having sex, I mean. Him penetrating me. Us mating. I had been physically ready for some time now, after all. I was of an age.

"Why are you going around like that?" Adam asked.

He was kneeling now, naked from the ankles up, his shrinking penis dangling between his thighs, still dripping the last remnants of his essence into the dark earth. Wood chips from the tree he'd been cutting littered the ground, and a few of them had adhered to his legs. I could feel them on my back, too, stuck there by the sweat that was like glue.

I couldn't answer. Answering would have been ridiculous. I had said everything I'd had to say to him with my actions. I hadn't fought him off. I had come closer. It was as if I had urged him onto and into me, and that was as clear as anything I could ever say. What else could I possibly tell him that would be clearer than that? We were animals, and animals didn't have to explain themselves.

So I got up and ran.

I had no fear of him tracking me. His pants were down around his ankles, and he had exhausted himself with his efforts, whereas I had done almost nothing. He did call after me—"Haley, wait!"—but I was already gone by then, invisible in the protective cover of the woods. I ran the entire way, not to the grove of oaks but to the rock face, where I sat in a small pool and let the cool water soothe my bruised self, what Mother referred to as my womanly parts.

It occurred to me only then that I had never thought of my own name for my genitalia. I had always used hers. I would have to change that. A woman should have her own names for things, especially things that were uniquely hers.

Should I give it an actual name? I wondered. *Why not? Something silly,* I thought. *Vaginas were taken all too seriously.*

I know. Henrietta.

I giggled out loud at that. "Henrietta" was stupid enough that it would have to remain a private joke forever. But at least I had named it, and made it my own. That removed the image of Mother from the equation. Because I could hear her already, as if she'd been there watching me. And the things her image was saying were horrible. My womanly parts had been ruined, she was saying. I had been polluted, I hadn't saved myself for marriage. The temple had been desecrated, its doors battered down, bucketfuls of milky fluid emptied on its floors. I had been fucked but good...and I liked it.

Since becoming an animal, Mother's notions had been revealed to me for what they were: pure, ridiculous convention, nothing more. Women believed in saving themselves for marriage because it kept things orderly, a lot more so than if we were all slutting around like a bunch of Jezebels, which if you want my opinion was probably the natural state of things before we started living in cities and so forth. Already, though I had committed the act just one time in my life, I was eager to learn more, and to experiment. What if we had done it such-and-such a way, for example? These were questions that would have to be answered.

Quiet, Mother, I thought.

I spread my tender lips with my fingers and the water ran into me and cleaned me out. Then I lay there on my back, letting the stream run through my hair and into my ears, muffling all sounds except for the beating of my heart. *Good Lord,* I thought. *I only set out on a mission of mercy, and I ended up getting poked like a pincushion. Life certainly was unpredictable in the forest.*

How had it happened? There was really nothing to think over, nothing to analyze. I heard the sounds of mating animals at different times of the year, from the very small to the very large. No ceremony was involved in the act, though there was often plenty of foreplay, in the form of singing or dancing. There was nothing unnatural about two people doing it that way. I had been aware for some time before I left home that I was at an age where sex was becoming more significant, if not necessarily for myself then for those who looked at me— like Adam. Even Chester Burgess had looked at me a certain way, although he was an old man and I could hardly have been appetizing in my filthy, ankle-length dress. Fine. So I had stumbled across a male of my species, and the most natural of all things had taken place. If we had met in a museum, or a bar, the courtship ritual would have been much longer, more drawn out. Out here, away from the society that dictated such behavior, there was no need to get fancy. One simply got down to business.

Perhaps some might think it odd that I hadn't thought about sex more than I did before The Event. To them I would say that I can offer no reasonable explanation for that, except that that is the way I am. I never had an aversion to it, but I never sought it out, either, like some girls did. I rarely talked about it with anyone, especially Mother. I had a vague foreboding from the time I got my first period that someday something of significance would happen in connection with the blood that spotted my underwear, but that had more to do with motherhood than copulation. I'd always had the feeling that when it happened, that would be the proper time; and who it happened with would be the proper person. Well, it had happened now without warning, and it was over in a blink. I was no longer a virgin. And Adam had turned out to be the one.

Another thought occurred to me then, as the stream splashed between my legs and I drifted lazily, hovering scant millimeters above the streambed, barely floating: *Would it, perhaps, happen again? And with who?*

Thoughts for another day. This was more excitement than I had seen in months, and I was suddenly beyond tired. I was used up, exhausted, depleted. I roused myself from my always-running bath and stepped out of the water, letting the air dry my skin, tying my hair up with a piece of leftover twine. My mind was gradually settling. I went to my bed underneath the rock face, taking care to leave a fresh spot of urine in three or four randomly chosen spots all around— certain local residents had been getting a little too curious lately. Adam's semen dripped out of me as I peed. I wondered what the animals would make of *that*. Then, with the sun still peeking over the tops of the trees, I went to sleep, and slept more deeply than I had in a long time.

⑪

The Bad Thing

For the previous few months, since the arrival of spring, it seemed that no matter where I buried my tampons, no matter how deep, something always got them. I put them in a different place every time, and I tried to hide them better—putting a large rock over them before burying, crushing pine needles to release their fragrance and spreading them over the freshly turned earth to hide the scent. But it never worked. Something out there had an insatiable appetite for my blood. I never found the actual tampons themselves. There was only ever a clawed-open hole, the pine needles brushed carefully away, the rock tossed disdainfully aside.

This, in a word, was gross. Even in my near-animal state I was astonished at the sheer intimacy of the act. Were the tampons being swallowed, like some kind of medicinal capsule? Was my blood now coursing through the digestive tract of some wild beast, filling its nostrils as it calmly chewed the soft cotton, sucking the last drops of juice from it like a delicate morsel of meat before finally gulping it down? And who, among the endless directory of forest residents, was responsible for this outrage? Who was drinking my blood?

Once I set my mind to figuring it out, it didn't take long to realize that it was Bear. His tracks were easy to spot in the soft soil, and he left a tunnel of broken branches everywhere he went, as obvious to my eyes as a series of flashing Men at Work signs on a highway. Often as not the broken ends of these branches were festooned with tufts of his fur, snagged and torn from his thick hide as he lumbered along. Bear was big. Bear was massive. And Bear knew me better than I knew him.

That was what was most terrifying about it: With my blood in his memory, he would know my scent anywhere, and if he chose to track me down and eat me, there was little I could do about it. I was terrified that he had gained an appetite for *me* in particular, that my tampons were only an appetizer. Bears have a very large territory, and they operate methodically, always moving into a new sector before they've managed to exhaust the food supply in the old one. If I knew where he was on any given day, I could make sure not to be there. This meant being constantly on guard, always listening, turning my head upwards at every breeze to read the odors that were written on it like a telegram: Here we have angelica, borage, pine, birch, squirrels, something dead, but no Bear. Always a relief. Yet I was always on guard.

I was most on guard, of course, when I was about to menstruate. And I think that Bear had become as attuned to my cycle as I myself was. Two weeks before my encounter with Adam, when the blood was about to flow, I'd heard him not far off, too far to cause immediate flight but close enough that I did not sleep at all that night. He had stopped within smelling range—*his* smelling range, I mean. He was much better at smelling than I was. I couldn't get a whiff of him at that distance, no matter how hard I tried. Yet I knew he was there.

But he didn't come closer. The cramp-induced trickle began towards the wee hours of the morning, as I crouched in paranoia under my now-cool rock face, wrapped in one of Chester Burgess's blankets. I put in a tampon and thought about the moon, which was going to be full that night.

I was far more aware of the moon now than I had ever been before. Even though Mother and I had bled in synchronized three-day blocks— mine heavy with assured fecundity, hers already beginning to dwindle as she approached the end of her childbearing years—I had never thought that the moon was in charge of such things. Every woman knows that some secret, mysterious rule regulates this kind of tandem effusion. Women who live together bleed together. I suppose there's some kind of scientific explanation for it, but scientific explanations, with their ten-dollar words and their flashy-sounding Greek and Latin derivations, are of little use in real life, and they usually end up express- ing the same thing anyway. I checked the moon every night like someone consulting a clock on the wall, and it was a source of satis- faction to me that I could tell from its expanding shape when the blood would come.

Next morning, I trekked far away from my rock face to a spot I'd never been before and buried the evidence. I suppose it did no good that I was leaving a trail of blood scent behind me, for I knew Bear could follow it as easily as if I had been sounding a bicycle bell. I buried each tampon from that particular cycle in places far distant from one another, and when the flow was finished I went back to each place to check on them. And at each one, I found the same results: They were gone without a trace.

Bear had my number, all right.

Yet he never came after me. He haunted me, he trailed me, he sent me telepathic messages in Bear talk: *I am here.* But when the cycle was ended, he simply vanished.

I began to think of him not as an enemy but as a protector. I fan- cied that he had a fondness for me, not for my taste but for my pres- ence. Why else did he leave me unmolested? Perhaps he felt sorry for me, in some obscure, Bear-like way. Perhaps he liked having me around and wanted to make sure that nothing else got me, though in truth he was my only potential predator. I invented a new ritual: I prayed to Bear, that he be well, that he always have enough to eat. I drew a picture

of him on the rock face with the burnt end of a stick, not to summon
him but to acknowledge his existence. I understood that I was really
nothing more than his guest, and I began to leave parts of the animals I killed as offerings to him, so that he might always protect me.
I was his child. I was his girlfriend. I was his wife. I was also in his body.

Next cycle, I vowed, I wouldn't bother burying the tampons. I
would leave them all in the same place, a feast of proto-placenta and cor-
puscles for him to savor like so many candies on a coffee table. Thus we
would exist in harmony, for as long as the forest permitted us to live.

Only problem was, when the next cycle was due, it didn't come. I
watched the night sky at first with calm expectation, then with antic-
ipation, then with nervousness as the first and second nights passed.
When the third night was over and the sun had risen, and still there
was no blood, I knew what was going on.

It was predictable, of course. I had been led to Adam as directly
as though a string was attached to my belly, pulling me abdomen-first,
like a fish hooked in the gut. Before I'd even finished calculating backwards, I realized I'd been ovulating during our encounter on the forest floor. I had been thinking with my eggs. If only someone had told
me that eggs had a mind of their own, perhaps I could have outwitted
them. You heard this about men, but never about women, this business
of making decisions with the reproductive apparatus. I was learning
the truth of it too late.

Shit.

I was pregnant.

How was I supposed to have a baby in the woods, all by myself? I
became, all at once, a panicked rabbit. What would happen when I
was too big to move? How would I catch my food with no one to help
me? It was impossible. I was fond of my image of myself as alone, independent, solitary. Yet I understood at that moment why women were
doomed to be dependent on others, at least during childbirth, and that
fiercely proud image came crashing down and burst into flames before

my eyes. I watched it burn with loathing and fury. For a brief moment, and for the first time in my life, I wished I was a man.

Part of me said: *You can do it. You might die, and the baby might die, but you can try and do it. It's your right.*

Another part said: *You have every responsibility towards the baby and none towards yourself. You have to go home. There is no point in dying alone, not now.*

If there was one thing I hated, it was having decisions made for me. I would put it off a while longer, until the need for a choice became inescapable. Then I would decide what to do.

Days passed. I pretended nothing had changed. I went on with my daily routine, conscious of having broken my promise to Bear. I had wanted to offer him the tampon treats he loved, so that our relationship might continue. As a poor substitute I nicked my arm with my scissors and let the blood drip onto a tattered and muddy piece of blanket. When this was good and soaked I left it in the offering place, but the next morning it was untouched. This was inconceivable: Had *no one* wanted it? Not even Fox, not even Raccoon? It was unbelievable. Yet there it sat, the evidence of my rejection. Tears stung my eyes. My blood was not good enough.

He knows I'm going to be a mother, I thought. *He can smell it. He can tell.*

Fine, I thought. *When the baby is born, he can help me raise it. He can be his uncle. He's not getting rid of me* that *easily.*

I went to sleep that night and dreamed of a meadow a half mile to the north, a good place to gather dandelions. I dreamed I walked along and talked to the flowers, and as I passed they bowed their yellow heads in greeting. This was how simple my mind had become: At night I dreamed that I was awake, and found it every bit as pleasant as the real thing.

I awoke at sunrise the next morning filled with foreboding and fear, jerked out of sleep by some inner warning system, already alert and on guard for an attack. My first thought was that I had been discovered; somebody was watching me. That was what it felt like, at least. That, or something somewhere was happening again, this time much more serious than someone cutting down a tree. There was something strange afoot, something dangerous. Every nerve in my body knew it. *Watkins?* I thought. *Watkins and his evil band of postgraduate elfkins!* But I didn't smell him, nor did I hear his clumsy feet kicking through the leaves and snapping branches that weren't even in his way. Watkins knew nothing about silence. If ever he had to survive out here on his own, where camouflage skills determined longevity, he wouldn't last a week.

All right—so it wasn't him. But it was definitely something. In a relatively short time, my instincts had been developed—I should say dusted off and tuned up—to the point where they bypassed my brain completely, and caused my body to act at once. I didn't stop to think about what I was doing. There was no need. When you live in the woods like I did, there is only one level of danger, only one degree of warning. I wrapped my twine belt around me, making sure the knife was secure, and headed for my oak grove as quickly as I could, stopping only to take a few mouthfuls of water at the stream.

Ironically, it wasn't animals I was afraid of, not really. It was the other bipeds of the world I feared, and not for any rational reason, either. I could outrun and outhide anybody. But humans are clever and devious—I offer myself as an example—and I knew that if enough of them made up their mind to find me one day, they would do it. You couldn't beat the resourcefulness of my species.

I had never bothered to consider whether Adam would tell anyone he'd seen me, but now this suddenly seemed like a horrible oversight. *Of course he'll tell*, I thought now. *Or at the very least he's going to come back for more.*

But then I changed my mind. We'd had sex on the ground, in the woods, like a pair of animals. Would he mention that? Of course not. I knew Adam. He would be more embarrassed than proud, unlike some males. He would not brag—and you know why? Because eventually his mother would find out. Sex between animals was a daily part of life on the Shumacher farm, just like on all farms, but the family did possess a high degree of modesty about their personal lives that I had noticed more than once. And Adam wasn't very good at lying, which meant if he announced he'd discovered me and someone asked him exactly *how* he had known it was me, he wouldn't be able to keep from blushing and stammering and generally making an idiot of himself until the truth came out.

All right. So whatever it was out there wasn't Adam, or anything to do with him. That was a relief, at least. I had a soft spot in my heart for him, and I would have hated to have to kill him just to shut him up.

But I would have.

Maybe.

The branches of the oaks were too far to reach from the ground, but I had figured out a way to climb one of them: Its knots and burls provided sufficient handholds to allow me to scale it like a monkey, and to pull myself up into the lower limbs. At this point I was already fifteen feet above the ground, far enough to hurt myself badly, perhaps even die, if I fell. This thought didn't cheer me. For a wild forest woman, I spent remarkably little time in trees. I left that to those creatures who were better suited for climbing. Tree climbing had once been my trademark, it's true, but that was before my fall through the barn roof; that experience had left me paranoid, and if I fell out here I would never be discovered. The animals would eat me first, poor helpless, shattered me. Even Bear, my old buddy, wouldn't be able to resist the blood he loved so well if it was spilling out all over the ground. But an ancient, protective instinct had been awakened in me by whatever was out there, and I needed a safe place from which to view things until I had figured out what was going on. I was now the guardian of these woods. And the thing lurking in the forest this morning presented a greater danger than falling from a tree.

An hour in the oaks, and nothing. No sounds, no untoward smells. But, even so, the other animals in the forest were strangely subdued. So it wasn't just my imagination—they had noticed it too. The birds were still, and not even the squirrels had bothered to scold me for entering their leafy realm.

Slowly, ever so slowly, I let myself out of the tree, hugging the bark close at the expense of my skin. When I landed softly on my feet I could feel where the oak had scraped me along my breasts and ribs. I would have to wash myself carefully, using the bark of the elder tree, which sudsed nicely if you beat it with rocks beforehand. It was easy to get an infection out here.

But for now, I was on the hunt. I would not be able to rest until I had figured out what was up. No one was talking—the trees gave me no sign, and the animals seemed to prefer to forget whatever it was, as if it had scared them more than they were willing to admit. I crouched low and began to move, stepping carefully and deliberately but going as fast as I could. I started out moving in a broad circle, with the oaks as the center. This was the best way to commence a search.

My first clue came in the form of a whiff of some kind of fuel. Just the tiniest bit, far off. Another tractor? Another logger? No, the trees would have told me of that immediately. And it wasn't diesel fuel. Something else. Some kind of fuel I didn't recognize.

I set off in the direction of the odor. I moved warily now, like a warrior, as the Tree People had once moved through these same woods, fleeing the white pursuers who hunted them for bounty and sport. Whenever I found a spot hidden in deep shadow I entered it, waiting for as long as it took my heart to quiet and for any stray sounds to come to me. But there was nothing. I kept moving, always in the same direction. The smell of fuel became stronger, though it was still so faint that I never would have noticed it had my nose not become so keen and finely tuned in recent months. My muscles were taut and ready, like bowstrings. My breath came easily, and I knew I could keep up this pace for hours if I had to. I never felt so alive as I did in those days.

Then I came across an object partly buried in the leaves. I almost didn't see it, but its shape was out of place in the forest and my eye was drawn to it immediately. It was a small, oblong thing, the size of a man's shirt pocket, made of plastic. I picked it up and turned it over, marveling at it as Prometheus must have exclaimed over fire. Yet I wasn't pleased to see it, for it spelled trouble, and possibly an invasion.

It was a cell phone.

I stuck it in my belt and headed for cover immediately. Once safely hidden under a small pine, I took it out and opened it. A small screen greeted me, as blank as a fish's eye, and rows of tiny buttons barely big enough to press with a finger. A small antenna in the back telescoped out, and I played with that for a while. I hit a button that said PWR and the phone emitted a startling beep. I hit another one that said PRG and pressed a number, and the phone beeped several more times, as if singing to itself. It was almost beautiful. I held it to my ear and heard the sound of a phone ringing on the other end.

"You make it all right?" said a male voice in my ear.

I snapped the phone shut in a hurry. Glory, that had scared me. A voice out of nowhere had just spoken in the forest, invading my quiet. It would take days for the sound to stop echoing in my head, just as I could still hear Adam's *Why are you going around like that?* There was no way I was going to have this thing around. I had no idea how it had gotten there, but I knew it boded evil. I dug a hole in the loam and tossed the phone in. Then I covered it back up and rearranged the leaves on the surface so it didn't look disturbed.

A cell phone, out here in the middle of nowhere. Well, obviously, someone had dropped it. That much was clear. And that was even more disturbing than the phone itself. Who would bring a cell phone out in the woods? And under what circumstances would they lose it without noticing?

Who was out there?

There was still the smell of fuel to consider. It was strong and immediate, and I could tell now that whatever it was, it wasn't simply exhaust but the fuel itself—that is, it hadn't been burned but spilled. Something bad had happened in the forest once again. I was beginning to suspect that there had been an accident.

I forgot about being careful now. I started jogging towards the smell, feeling my breasts jolt painfully—it wasn't often that I flat-out ran anymore. Looking up, I could see that the trees had been parted here, like hair by a comb. The tops of them were shorn off in a line that descended gradually toward a point on the ground, as if someone had come along with a giant razor and lopped them off. I slowed to a walk, my heart pounding urgently, and stepped behind a large family of pines to stare at the spectacle that suddenly presented itself.

There, in a tiny clearing that hadn't existed a day earlier, was a small plane, or what was left of it. It had come in low and slow— obviously the pilot had been trying to land, even though he must have known it was hopeless with all the trees. I didn't know anything about planes, but this one looked like it might hold two or three or four people. The wings had broken off and the front end was badly crumpled, and the whole thing looked like a dragonfly that had been tortured by small boys and left to die. The reek of fuel now was so strong to my animal nose that I knew my sense of smell would be ruined for weeks. I nearly fainted from it, but I forced myself to stay conscious.

There was a stunned silence all around, as though none of the animals could believe this kind of catastrophe could occur here. So that was it. Word had spread, and forest creatures everywhere were still trying to cope with the immensity of it. That, and they had left the area as soon as they could. No one in their right mind would put up with that kind of odor.

I crept closer. The only really recognizable part of the plane was the tail. The rest was badly damaged, smashed in like a soda can. The eerie silence hung over all.

"Hello?" I called. My voice, rusty, sounded odd to my ears. I cleared my throat and stepped closer.

"Hello?" I said again.

Eventually I was going to have to look inside the cockpit, and though the fuel smell had blanketed everything there are some spoors that simply cannot be hidden, and the smell of death is one of them. I already knew what I was going to find. No one had survived this crash. There were people inside—dead ones.

Better get this over with, I thought.

It's funny how certain old habits will kick into gear, even in the mind of someone who considers herself more animal than human. I had been trained from early on, just as every other person is, that when one comes upon the scene of an accident one calls for help. People need you, and you cannot let them down. It's more than a custom. It's a very ancient, ingrained instinct. My two instincts were now at war with each other. One half of me was screaming *Help them!* and the other was instructing me to run far, far away.

The helping instinct won out. I edged closer to the cockpit, unwilling to look but unable to bear the suspense. I simply had to see. I put one hand on the jagged metal hole where I guessed the door had been, stepped up on one of the splayed-out wheels, and looked.

There were two of them, both men. The pilot, the one on the side farther from me, was sitting upright, in an attitude of rapt attention, as if he'd been receiving serious instructions in his last moments. In the brief second I allowed myself to look at his face I saw that one eye was bulging open, and his jaw had fallen so that his mouth gaped in surprise. I couldn't see a specific injury, but there was a lot of blood. It had all dried.

The one near me was leaning far forward, still supported by his seat belt but already in the process of sliding out of it, like the loose bag of bones and flesh that he was. He, too, was covered in blood, and one of his arms was at a funny angle, as if the impact had broken or dislocated it. I could not see his face. I didn't want to. I looked for less than three seconds, long enough to determine that they were both dead. Then I stepped back.

Jesus Hopalong Cassidy, I thought. *Tell me this isn't happening. Tell me I don't have to deal with this.*

But of course it was, and I did.

I found a rock and sat on it. This was bad, very bad. There was nothing I could do for these two—nothing. I couldn't even give them a decent burial. I wasn't about to handle their corpses, and besides, they were in the forest, which had its own way of performing funerals. If I left them alone for, say, several weeks, they would be mostly gone when I came back. There were plenty of scavengers around who would not turn up their noses at such a tasty treat. In fact, I was surprised they hadn't started work already. Must have been the smell of fuel that kept them off so far. It was everywhere.

My heart skipped a beat as I realized how lucky we were that all that fuel hadn't caught fire. There would have been a mighty conflagration then. We *all* would have had to relocate, and maybe even my beloved oaks would have been lost. The forest gods were certainly keeping their eye out for us. Maybe Grandma was spreading her hands over her forest like some kind of divine being. Or maybe it was just luck.

Shit, I thought. I already knew I couldn't pretend this hadn't happened. These men had families, no doubt. Somewhere in the world, someone was worried about them. I began to feel sorry then, not for them—they were beyond help, and I have never felt sorry for the dead, only for the dying. I felt instead what their children would feel, if they had children. I knew how hard it was to lose a father and not even be able to point to anything concrete and say, *That is what used to contain him, that is what he used to be.* They had to at least have a body to bury. It would make things much easier, at least from my perspective. And their wives, too. Their parents. Everyone had parents.

I would call someone on the cell phone I'd found. That was it. I could still hide that way. I could tell them roughly where the plane was, and then I could scurry back to my own territory, safely out of sight and out of earshot. They would come with their equipment, and do what they had to do, and then leave.

I dug up the cell phone, glad that at least I'd taken the time to make a note of where I'd left it. Obviously it had belonged to one of the men in the plane. Perhaps it had been thrown that far, though it hardly seemed possible. Perhaps it had simply fallen out when they started hitting the trees—as if the doors had been ripped open by the branches. *If I started hunting around*, I thought, *I would probably find other things that belonged to them too.* But I decided that the less I knew about them the better.

I brushed the dirt off the cell phone and blew into the mouthpiece. Then I turned it on and pressed those three magic numbers, 9-1-1. A voice answered almost immediately.

"Nine-one-one, what is your emergency?"

"Plane crash," I croaked.

"What? Hello? What did you say?"

"Plane crash. Two men dead."

"Can you identify yourself?"

"Haley," I said. Then I punched myself in the leg. Why did I tell them that?

"Where are you calling from?"

"A cell phone. In the woods."

"You say there's been a plane crash?"

I sighed. "Yes," I said.

"Is anyone hurt?"

"Two. Men. Dead."

"Okay, hold on."

There was a brief pause while this person did something, somewhere far away. Then her voice came back on the line.

"Caller—Haley—where exactly are you?"

"Ah," I said. I looked around. This would have been easy to explain to a squirrel, for example, but to some random emergency operator it

posed a formidable challenge. One mile west of the big oak grove? Half
a morning's walk from the stream?

"Take the county road east out of Mannville," I said. "Go about ten
miles, to the fire road across from a pond. Take it into the woods as
far as you can go." My voice gave out on me suddenly.

"Caller? Are you injured?"

"No," I said. "Just don't talk very much, is all."

There was a brief pause.

"I see," said the operator. "Go on."

"Plane's about another two miles from the end of the road, I'd say
northwest," I told her. "Two-seater. Both guys dead. That's all I can
tell you."

"Caller, do not leave the scene," said the operator. "Okay, Haley?"

"No," I said. "Not okay."

"Haley, do not leave the scene," she repeated.

"I have to leave. I don't belong here. I'm only calling."

"It's a crime to leave the scene of an accident. Do you understand?"

"I don't care," I said. "You'll have to find me. These are my woods."

"They'll find you," she said.

I hung up.

That is to say, I not only hung up, I clapped the phone shut again,
regarded it for a moment as it sat in my palm like some kind of artifi-
cial, space-age clam, and then threw it as far as I could. It disappeared
in the trees without a sound.

They wouldn't find me. It was impossible. I could hide better than
they could look. I could live out here forever, and no one would ever
know. So it was a crime to leave the scene of an accident? Big deal. I
didn't cause the damn plane to crash. That would be obvious even to
the thickest of sheriff's deputies.

But then I would be hiding forever, I thought glumly. They wouldn't
give up. Their official curiosity would be aroused. These people, these
law-enforcement types, took themselves even more seriously than
Andrew Watkins of the university took himself. My peace and quiet

would be ruined, and I would live in a constant state of paranoia, even more so than I did now. Oh, these bastards. Why did I make that call? Why?

I went back to the plane then, not right up to it but to a safe distance, where I could look inside and see the two men. I wanted to get a better look at the people who had ruined my life. I could just see the head of the passenger jutting out from behind a trunk.

"I hope you two are happy," I said. "Because now you're causing trouble."

Well, as Mother used to say, if you can't make up your mind about something sooner or later, you're going to get it made up for you. I hadn't been able to decide whether I belonged in the forest or not. Never mind that since having that thought I had become more comfortable here than I'd ever been anywhere in my life. I had had that time of doubt, and that had planted the seeds for this to happen. Maybe I did want to go back. That was what had led me to make that phone call. *A real forest woman,* I thought disgustedly, *would have let them sit there and rot.* Forest women do not have time for compassion. They are always on the move. But I had caved in and called the police, like a sissy. And now I was going to pay the price.

I sat back on my heels and thought. How long would it take them to get here? Hours, at least. And it would be days before they could get enough crap back here to haul the plane out. Think of the uproar *that* would cause in the neighborhood. What would happen to me when they came? Would I be arrested? What should I do with myself in the meantime? What sort of preparations should I make? What kinds of things do you do to get ready for jail?

And when, I wondered, had I stopped thinking of myself as Flash Jackson and started thinking of myself as a forest woman? It had happened so subtly I hadn't even noticed. Maybe it was when Grandma disappeared. Or no—before. When we had spent that long, cold winter staring at each other across the little patch of dirt floor that we called home, as her teachings seeped into me. Just as Adam had seeped

into me. Seeds being planted. Things growing within. Was I never
going to be anything more than a fertile field, a receptacle? When was
I going to start making things *happen*, instead of letting them happen
to me?

Umpf, said something behind me, as if to punctuate my question.

I jumped up and spun around. It was Bear.

So finally we meet, I thought.

He wasn't as large as I'd imagined he'd be, but he was large enough
to make my heart stop. I'd never been this close to a bear before. I
froze. The smell of fuel must have masked his odor as he came up
behind me, but now his smell was as massive as he was. He was about
eight feet tall, his eyes two black, intelligent beads, his nose wet like a
dog's. He was only a few short steps away. All he'd have had to do was
lunge forward and open his mouth, and I would be his.

"Oh, God," I said, unable to help myself.

At the sound of my voice, Bear cocked his head to the side, again
like a dog. He appeared to wait for me to explain myself. When I
didn't, he shambled backward a few steps and then carefully made his
way over to the plane. *The smell of death must have attracted him*, I
thought. So he wanted them, not me. Yet he must have known who
I was.

"Bear," I said, careful to keep my voice calm.

He ignored me now. He stood up and nosed the nearer of the two
bodies, prodding it gently. I had a better opportunity to admire him.
His dark, thick coat shone in the dappled sunlight coming through
the trees. His ears looked too tiny for the rest of him. Powerful muscles, strong enough to rip my head off with one swipe, moved in awe-
some waves under his fur as he poised himself on the cockpit doorframe.
I could have sworn I saw his nose wrinkle with distaste as he examined the unfortunate occupants of the plane. Bears didn't like eating
dead things—only live ones. I stayed exactly where I was, too fascinated and too afraid to run.

Bear finished his once-over of the plane and turned to the surrounding area, digging around under leaves, sniffing at the plane's tires. Every once in a while he looked up at me, as if to make sure I was still there. We locked eyes several times. I had read somewhere, long ago, that the last thing you should do with a bear is make eye contact with him. They take it as a challenge. You're supposed to drop to the ground and pretend you're dead. You let them paw you and maybe slobber on you a bit, and then they go away. But I knew that with two real dead bodies here I wouldn't fool him, and besides it was too late for that. Who knew how long he'd been following me? Maybe he was only toying with me. I didn't think so, though. I didn't think he wanted to hurt me at all.

"You better get out of here," I said to him. "People are coming."

Owf! said Bear.

"If they see you, they'll hurt you," I said. "Seriously. You better go."

Mrap! said Bear. He turned quickly and approached me again, moving at a trot. Terror overcame me once again. I felt a warmth on my thigh as urine trickled down my leg. I could only hope that he wouldn't want to eat me if I was covered in pee.

He stopped inches away, prodding my belly with his nose just as he had done to the corpse in the plane. Then he sat back on his haunches, and we locked eyes once more. His odor was so strong I nearly fainted.

Then, without another sound, he was gone. He got up and headed off at a good clip into the trees, and I knew he'd heard something.

"Bye," I whispered. I felt something had been communicated between us, though I didn't know what. I was weak in the knees, and I collapsed in a sitting position, trying to catch my breath. I became aware that I was hyperventilating. I had just escaped death, for no reason that I could put my finger on. It simply wasn't my time today. Had he known there was a baby inside me? Could he smell it, and that was why he'd left me alone?

It didn't matter. I had finally met him, and it was a meeting I would never forget for the rest of my life, especially because of what happened next.

From far away, I heard a *whump-whump-whump*, like clouds colliding, softer than thunder but no less insistent. With astonishing rapidity the sound came closer, disturbing the air far above my head. I stood up and looked around. Panic grew in me, but I forced it down. I had to face up to this. I couldn't spend the rest of my life running away from things. I had to deal.

The helicopter appeared like a vision from one of my earliest nightmares, suddenly and without any more warning than that initial soft sound, and then it was over me and I had the impression that I had been picked up and thrown into a blender. The long, dark shape hovering overhead conjured up every dark fear I'd ever had. The noise was horrific. I could only stand and stare upwards, my eyes watering from the downdraft of the massive blades. It paused overhead, and then, like a spider, it produced two long strands of rope from its belly. One of them fell just at my feet, like a portal to another world. Other shapes appeared then—men, sliding down the ropes, landing silently on the forest floor, strange and unwelcome visitors to what had once been a peaceful place. *This was how the Tree People saw the first white men,* I thought. *This is how we will feel if aliens come to Earth.* They were in dark uniforms, which posed a stark contrast to the simple twine belt I wore. First there were two, then four, then six, all in the same clothes, eyes masked with goggles, weapons strapped to their hips, frames bulky with the bulletproof vests I knew they must have been wearing underneath.

They stopped and looked at me, and then at each other, and for the first time in a long time I felt naked. I covered myself with my hands and lowered my head. I would not let them see me. Too late, I realized I had made the wrong decision. I shouldn't have stayed. I should have hidden for as long as it took for them to forget about me.

I took off as fast as I could, but I was no match for the nearest one. He tackled me neatly by diving for my ankles, and I came down softly on the bed of decayed leaves and pine needles that formed the spongy forest floor, and felt my arms being pinioned, my ankles held fast by another pair of hands.

"Stay down!" he yelled.

"Fuck you!" I screamed. I kicked as hard as I could and got one foot loose, and I felt the delicious sensation of my heelbone connecting with someone's jaw. A cry of pain reached me through the roar of the rotors. *Good*, I thought.

I heard a *pop* then, followed by several more in rapid succession. Gunfire.

They were going to kill me.

"Oh, my God!" I screamed. "Don't shoot me! I'm pregnant!"

"We're not shooting at you," said the man who was lying on top of me. He had to shout to be heard. When he heard the word "pregnant," he took his weight off.

I tried to struggle out of his grasp and look up, but he forced me down again. There came a sustained burst of automatic rifle fire, a long *brraaaapp* that seemed to tear the world in two. The sound was so loud it made me gasp. I smelled gunpowder. Then the man on top of me got up and pulled me to my feet.

"Look," he said, pointing. "That's what almost got you."

All I saw was a second man, the one I had kicked. I hadn't known that two of them were chasing me. He was writhing in pain, holding his jaw.

"Him?" I said.

"No, *look*," said the other man, and I looked farther and saw a great crumpled, dark heap laying next to a downed tree. The other four men were circling it, their weapons drawn, and when it stirred they opened fire again, pouring lead into it until it stopped moving.

"Oh, you fuckers!" I screamed.

"What is it with you?" said the man nearest me. "We just saved your life!"

"You saved your own life," I said. "He wasn't coming after *me*. He was coming after *you*. He was trying to protect me."

That crumpled heap was Bear, king of this forest and perhaps the last of his kind for dozens of miles. I knew then, in the same way I knew what trees thought, that he had come there to save me from the men in the helicopter that he knew was coming, that he had willingly given his life for me. I felt deeper shame than I ever had before, because I knew that if things had been turned around I would not have had the nobility to do the same for him. I would never know why Bear felt it was his duty to protect me, and not to eat me.

That was when I understood that I was no longer worthy of living in the forest. For that reason I didn't fight anymore when they lifted us up in the air in their machine, me and whoever was living inside me, and took us away. They gave me a blanket, which I wrapped around me to protect my naked body from their eyes. It was the first time since I'd shed my clothes that I felt like something was missing, and I knew it was because these men were looking at me. I felt hot all over, as though their eyes were exuding fire. The one I'd kicked in the face sat opposite me on the floor of the helicopter, holding his jaw with one hand and staring at me sullenly. I thought about telling him that St.-John's-wort and hyssop would help with the bruising, but I knew his kind wouldn't listen to me. He would go to a doctor and take whatever he told him to take, and that was all he deserved. He would get nothing from me.

I looked down on the waving treetops as we passed overhead, sticking my head out the door as far as they would let me. I was trying to spot familiar places, but the forest was impenetrable from this angle. All I could see was a floor of green, and soon even that was lost to sight as we came over civilization again. Within minutes I was back in the world, never as far from it as I'd thought I'd been. I had been just seconds out of reach the whole time.

12

Say Hello to Lilith

There are guidebooks for just about every kind of journey one can make through the outer world, but very few for the inner kind. I mean the journeys one makes to expand the soul, to plumb the depths of oneself and find out just how deep the well really goes. Maybe that's because so few people bother going on these kinds of excursions, and even fewer have the gift of words to express the things they find along the way. Not for the first time in my life, I found myself in need of instruction, for my return home from the woods was as significant to my spirit as it was to my body. How was I expected to adjust to life in a man-made box of tree flesh after life among the trees? From a life of rhythmic light and dark to a life where one can change the color of the air any time one feels like it, with the flick of an electrical switch? Where rain never makes you wet, where cold can't touch you, where food is stored in some miraculous, humming container that keeps it cold no matter what the outside temperature? How do you remind yourself that all these things were once familiar, that in reality you understand them perfectly, and yet only now do you see how unnatural they are? How far they have taken us from our rightful place in the world?

It was three days after my return before I would consent to being looked at by a doctor. Mother stood outside my bedroom and pleaded with me to eat, to speak, to at least unlock the door so she would know I was alive. It was my opinion that it was none of her damn business whether I was alive or not. I was going through some kind of forest withdrawal, wherein I did nothing but lie in bed—my soft bed, my warm bed, a bed that was admittedly so delicious I could hardly believe it. I was grumpy and sick, and furious with myself because secretly I was glad to be home. I did tap on the door to reassure her. That was all I had in me. She couldn't have understood—or maybe she had forgotten—how painful and harsh human speech can seem after so many months of silence, how every spoken word is a sneak attack on the senses. I needed time to get used to being in a room again, in a house, with clothes in the closet and running hot water and soap and a refrigerator with food in it. And I missed the smells of the forest, the scent of crushed leaves and pine needles and bark and soft dirt and the thousand other odors that existed there in symphonic profusion. Here, all smells were chemical—floor wax, laundry detergent, the formaldehyde in the carpets, perfume. The more she tried to push me into talking, the more I wanted to never say another word again.

I did feel a bit off, physically. There was some kind of bug living inside me—in addition to the bug that Adam had planted, I mean. I felt fluish and chilled. Whatever it was, I was sure I could take care of it myself. I knew how to handle my body. For example, I had recently shaved my head. Mother had shrieked when she looked at my locks, lying on the bathroom floor—they were crawling with lice. Of course I had noticed this earlier, but it scarcely bore mentioning until I came home. Lice had been a fact of life for the last year. Mother wouldn't touch my hair, even to throw it away. She made me throw it in the yard, and then she poured gasoline on it and set it aflame. Black clouds of greasy smoke erupted, like a signal to the rest of the world that part of my life had just ended in death and disaster...again. I sat and watched my hair burn like I was keeping vigil over a funeral pyre, and when the fire had burnt itself out—in a matter of minutes—I went upstairs and locked myself away.

When I finally gave in to Mother—more to shut her up than anything else—the doctor came to the house and looked me over gravely, making notes on a pad. He took a blood sample and made me pee in a cup. He wanted to slip on a latex glove and stick a couple of fingers inside me, but I refused because I didn't want anyone to know that I was pregnant yet, and I knew he would be able to tell immediately by feeling my cervix. He was going to find out from the urine sample anyway, but I hoped to have worked up the courage to tell Mother myself by then. Then he had the nerve to ask for a stool sample.

"I really have to have one," he said. "You might have parasites."

"If I do," I said, "I know how to get rid of them. I don't need your help."

He smirked, the smug bastard. "And how would you do that?"

Ointment of aloe, applied on the anus, I thought. *Tinctures of garlic and wormwood.* But I didn't say anything. I didn't want to give him the satisfaction.

The doctor was a youngish, earnest man with slight flecks of gray at the temples, and he stood in my room with his stethoscope around his neck and his arms folded, a pathetic figure when compared to the greatest healer this part of the world had ever known, and even more so because he seemed to take himself so seriously.

"What am I supposed to do?" I asked. "Crap in a bucket?"

He frowned. "You can leave it in the toilet," he said. "I'll take care of it."

"I don't have to go," I said.

"I can give you something for that."

"What? Rhubarb?"

He was amused, I think. I was offended. That was the remedy Grandma would have used, after all.

"No," he said. "An enema."

"Jesus," I said. "I don't need your medicine. Just leave me alone for a while. Something will happen."

I went into the bathroom, ignoring Mother in the hall except to mutter, "A little privacy, please." I can do pretty much anything when I put my mind to it, and when I had produced what I figured was a satisfactory amount I stuck my hand out the door and the good doctor handed me a plastic container. I filled it and handed it back—my offering to modern medical science.

"That will be all," I said. "Right, Doctor? You're leaving now."

I closed the door again and waited for him to be gone. I could hear him talking in low tones with Mother. Then he left. Mother knocked.

"No," I said.

"No what?"

"Just...no."

"Haley?"

What, I thought.

"If it means anything to you, I was glad you were out there so long...for your own sake, not mine."

I didn't say anything.

"I knew you were learning important things," she said. "I knew you were going through something you had to go through. I missed you, but I respected it."

I opened the door.

"If you really want to know," she said, smiling weakly, "I was kind of jealous. I never would have had the courage to stay out there by myself. That was part of why I left to be with your father. It was scary out there."

"I know," I said. "It was."

Mother had taken the news of Grandma's disappearance with a great deal more stoicism than I'd expected. I understood why; Grandma wasn't really her mother, any more than she was really my grandmother. She was whoever she was, and now that she was gone things would certainly be different. I hadn't bothered to explain to her about the death of Bear because she wouldn't have understood.

"Would you like some soup?" she asked.

Soup. Cooked on a stove, made from things I hadn't eaten in a long time. With salt. And pepper. And a piece of bread and a soda, maybe, to go with it.

"That sounds good," I said.

"You come on downstairs," she said. "I'll fix you up something nice to eat."

The big news, which had been splashed all over the front page of the Mannville *Megaphone* and the television news programs since my return, was not that a naked forest woman had been discovered living nearby in a feral state but that a small plane had gone down that was engaged in something illicit. The two men I'd found in the cockpit were not family men. They were not going to be mourned by anyone. They were drug smugglers, on their way to Canada. The entire tail section of the plane had been full of cocaine—for a couple of hours, I'd had access to five million dollars' worth of drugs, and I hadn't even known it. The authorities had known these guys would come through this way, flying low to avoid radar, which turned out to be their last mistake—they were carrying too much weight, and they had lost control over the treetops and crashed. That was why the rescue helicopter had arrived so fast, and why it had been carrying DEA agents instead of rescue personnel. They'd been waiting for the plane to appear. Now, after months of work on their part, and one lucky break, a notorious drug connection had been extinguished. Everyone in the government was happy.

This was why no one had said anything to the press about having found me. They wanted to protect me, they said, from whoever those guys were working for, because they—some mysterious Colombian drug lords or something—were the vengeful type, and if they thought I'd had something to do with their supply lines being cut they would do me in. Perhaps it wasn't very likely, but there was no reason to take chances. Of course, I think it was also that the government wanted to take the credit for having found the plane themselves. How would it look to the public if legions of men with millions of dollars' worth of equipment were outdone by a naked girl with only a knife?

"Imagine," said Mother, as I ate my soup. "You read about those kinds of people, but you never think you're going to see them. Drug people, I mean."

"If it wasn't for them, I wouldn't have come home," I said, in a way that was loaded with double meaning. I had been found out because I was acting out of compassion, but it had all been wasted on those two. I should have let them rot out there. Then Bear would still be alive, and I would still be in my own little paradise. Learning. Talking to the Tree People.

Still, I had to admit, it wasn't bad being home again. I had forgotten how comfortable simple things were, such as the easy chair in the living room that had once been a favorite of my father's. Or the sheer pleasure of letting hot water cascade over my body in limitless amounts, soaping myself over and over again, feeling it tingle on my bare scalp. I had been so dirty I'd forgotten what it was like to be clean. During my first shower, the water had run brown for twenty minutes. I was now scrubbed so pink and shiny that I practically squeaked when I walked.

"So," said Mother, watching me eat my soup—chicken noodle from a can, loaded with preservatives but not tasting too bad, all things considered. "What now?"

"I don't know," I said. "I kind of need some time to think."

We hadn't talked like this in years.

"You take all the time you need," said Mother. "Things like this take a while to settle. Homecomings. I'm just glad you're safe and sound."

"I might go visit Miz Powell, for starters," I said.

"Oh, dear," said Mother. "Oh, you don't know, do you?"

I froze with alarm. "Don't tell me," I said.

"No, Miz Powell is fine," said Mother. "It's her friend, Letty. Letty Horgan."

"What about her?"

"She passed away in her sleep, a few weeks back. Peacefully. They said she had a stroke and never woke up."

I breathed a sigh of relief. It was too bad about Letty, but it would have been too much for me to have lost Miz Powell before I'd had the chance to talk everything over with her. I wasn't done with her yet. There were lots of things I needed her opinion on. Such as: How was I going to fit into the world now? She was the only person who really seemed to understand me. Even Grandma ran only a close second— Miz Powell and I were birds of a feather, and suddenly, with the news of Letty's passing, I was seized with a strong desire to see her right away. Immediately. Now.

"Were there many people at the funeral?" I asked.

"Only a handful," Mother said. "You get to be that age, you don't have many people left. She's buried up in Springville, if you want to know."

So another piece of the circle had been broken.

"Thanks for lunch, Mom," I said. "I better go."

I cleaned the dishes at the sink. Then I changed out of my bathrobe into a pair of loose jeans, and a shirt that billowed around me like a sail. By my own and Mother's calculations, I had lost nearly fifty pounds in the last year. Nothing I owned would ever fit me again. I was going to have to go shopping. Even the maternity clothes I'd be wearing soon would be smaller than what I used to wear. With my head shaved and my cheekbones visible, I looked like a concentration-camp prisoner. Yet I could see my own face in the mirror for a change, unhidden by layers of fat, and I recognized myself as though I'd spotted an old friend passing by a store window. *There you are*, I thought. *I was wondering what happened to you.*

After much debate I struggled into a pair of sandals, because it wouldn't do to show up at Miz Powell's place barefoot. Barefoot and pregnant! That would be a laugh. The only part of me that *had* grown were my feet; all that time going around without shoes had caused them to spread. I was going to get some fierce blisters today.

I paused on my way out the door.

"You want to go shopping later, maybe?" I suggested to Mother. "When I get back? I need some new duds."

Mother had retired to the easy chair, where I knew she'd been spending the better part of her days. Maybe she'd already resigned herself to spending the rest of her life there. I hadn't told her yet about the baby, because I hadn't decided if I was keeping it. For a moment I thought maybe I should tell her, just to give her something to look forward to. But at the mention of shopping she brightened. For now, shopping would have to be enough.

"I'd love to," she said. "We can go to Kaufmann's, if you want."

"Kaufmann's it is," I said. "See you in a few hours."

Miz Powell still had the same ramrod back and steely eyes that softened when she wanted them to, and I could tell that this was still a woman who would never be trifled with, even on her deathbed. Her hair was still perfect, her makeup applied lightly but with purpose. She smiled and ushered me into the dark gloom of her house, still as neat as a hospital operating room and smelling of mint and licorice. That, at least, was reassuring. Nothing here had changed. Embracing her was like clutching a bag of twigs to my chest. I released her gently and we sat down. A fresh pot of tea was already steaming on the coffee table.

"I rather suspected you might come today," she said, lowering herself onto the sofa. Was it my imagination, or was she moving a little more gingerly? "I'd heard you were home, but I thought you might need a few days to recuperate before you ventured out into society."

"You were right. It's been quite a summer," I said. "Quite a year, all in all."

"Yes, it has," she said casually. Though the weather was warm, she was wearing a shawl that she drew close over her shoulders, warding off some imaginary chill.

"Do you have another one of those?" I asked, shivering—for in my case the chill was real.

She fetched me a plaid wrap from a closet and put it around my shoulders. "Scottish tartan," she said, "of the clan Rory. I don't quite remember how I came to own it. I don't recall knowing any Rorys. Are you unwell?"

"I have worms," I said. "Some kind of parasite."

"Oh, dear," she said, delicately. "Are you uncomfortable?"

"I felt fine until I came home," I said. "Now I feel like dog chow."

"Indeed," said Miz Powell. "I have never felt like 'dog chow' myself, but I can imagine it isn't pleasant."

She sat down next to me and the two of us huddled up under our shawls like a couple of old crones. All we needed was a cauldron to make the image complete.

"Things have happened," I told her. "Strange things. The Mother of the Woods is gone."

She waved a hand in the air as if brushing away a fly. "This was what was going to happen all along," she said. "We knew she wouldn't be around forever. Didn't we?"

"I guess so," I said.

"She had her reasons for everything," Miz Powell said.

"I guess I thought...she would stay until she found a...I don't know, a replacement or something."

Miz Powell attempted a laugh. "Replacement? Now, there's an interesting notion," she said. "Do you know of anyone who might fit that description?"

I knew what she was getting at, of course. I poured the tea out for both of us and we sipped it quietly.

"Sorry about Letty," I said. "I know she was your good friend."

"Yes," said Miz Powell. "She certainly was." But there was no sadness in her voice. The older one gets, for some people, the less frightening death becomes. It's as if the hood of the Grim Reaper gradually slips down with every passing year, and underneath one sees not a grinning skull but the face of an old and trusted friend.

"I suppose," said Miz Powell, "that you're wondering what to do with yourself next."

"Yeah," I said. "That's pretty much it."

"You haven't finished your schooling, if I remember correctly," she said. "Your more conventional schooling, I mean. What do you call it here in the States? High school."

"No," I admitted, looking down at the floor. "I skipped this last year, so I still have two years to go. But..."

"I know," she said. "You can't see yourself in that situation anymore. Not after all you've learned."

"There are other ways to get an education," I said. "More important ways."

"You are correct, my dear," she said. "The question to ask yourself now is, how might you be of service to the world? You *do* have a lot to offer, you know. The difference between the Haley I first met and the Haley of today is that today you possess unique abilities. Very few people know the things you know."

"I guess," I said.

"Don't guess unless you're being asked to guess," she said, flaring briefly into her old self. "We're not discussing theories here. We're discussing fact."

"Yes, ma'am," I said.

"What worries you most, Haley?"

"I guess I don't want to be a wife," I said. "Or a mother."

Miz Powell spluttered with laughter.

"Well, who says you have to?" she said. "Look at me!"

"It's not that I don't want to be married," I said. "I don't care, one way or the other. I mean, if it happens, it happens. But I don't want to be a *wife*. I want to be a person who's married to another person. *My own* person."

"For heaven's sake, at this age why are you even worrying about this now? Has someone asked you to marry them? Are you in love? Why?"

"Because," I said, blushing. "Something happened."

"Oho," she said. "I see." She reached over and patted me on the hand. "There may be a few generations between us, my dear, but I'm no stranger to what you're talking about," she said. "Perfectly natural, and no harm done, provided the proper precautions were taken. Which I hope they were."

I didn't say anything.

"Oh, dear," said Miz Powell. "Well, there's a different story altogether, then."

"You can say that again," I said.

"Haley, you may very well end up having some decisions made for you, then. Carelessness rarely goes unpunished."

"I know it," I said. "That's why I wanted to have this conversation in the first place." *It wasn't carelessness*, I thought. *It happened because . . . it happened.*

"Now I see what you were getting at," said Miz Powell. "You feel you might be preg—"

"I am," I said.

"Oh, dear."

"Exactly."

"You're certain?"

I nodded.

"And who was the lucky young man, may I ask?"

"Adam," I said. "Adam Schumacher."

"Tall lad, blond hair? Muscular? Lives down the road?"

"That's the one."

"Well, then, I shouldn't wonder you succumbed to his charms."

"Now, hold on there," I said. "I didn't succumb to anything. He was the one doing all the succumbing. I know a little about pheromones.

I hadn't had a bath in months. And he loved it. He was no match for me."

"I see," said Miz Powell. She appeared to be trying to hide the huge amount of enjoyment she was getting out of this conversation. "So he was your victim, and the whole thing was your idea."

"Well, no," I said. "I mean, of course not."

"So you succumbed to each other?"

"I guess you could say that."

Miz Powell chuckled. "This was your first experience with a man, I take it?"

I nodded.

"And did you take a...shall I say, an *active role* in the proceedings?"

"Well," I said, "mostly I just laid there."

"I see. And yet he succumbed to you."

I was starting to get uncomfortable. "I don't see what you're getting at," I said.

"The point is, while your presence certainly aroused him, and therefore you could be said to have initiated the...ah, event—"

"That's what I call it," I interrupted. "The Event."

"—nevertheless, that all took place on a deeper level, an underlying level. His action, on the other hand—which I take it was swift and precipitous—"

"Indeed," I said, dusting off my mental dictionary and paging through to the *P*'s.

"—was the real *action*. Correct? You did say you 'mostly just laid there.'"

"Yeah," I said. "But so what? Was that wrong?"

"Honestly, Haley," said Miz Powell. "There is no right and wrong in this situation. I am merely trying to teach you something about the dynamics between men and women. We succumb to each other, dear. We fall towards each other. It's like planets in space. When one is bigger than the other, the smaller is left to circle around it, stuck forever in orbit. And when one is falling faster or slower, or is bigger or smaller, than the other—that's when unhappiness occurs. We must always move in tandem if we are to coexist. We must be the same size. This I know."

"Miz Powell," I said, "if you know so much about men, why didn't you ever get married?"

"There's your answer right there," she said, winking. "I know *too* much about them."

"Right," I said.

"Now, enough of this romantic nonsense. Let's get down to brass tacks. Will you keep the baby?"

"I won't have an abortion," I told her. "But I maybe would give it up to someone else. I don't know. I'm still pretty young to be a mother."

She nodded. "By some standards, yes," she said.

"By my standards," I corrected her. "I don't want to be stuck at home, like most women around here are, and I don't want to have to devote all my energy to other people. Like kids. Or men. And I don't want to stop feeling like I feel right now."

"How do you feel right now?"

"Awake," I said. "Besides these damn worms, I feel great. Awake and curious, and full of energy. And power. And . . ."

She waited.

"Zam," I finished, rather lamely.

Miz Powell clapped her birdy little hands together. "Well said," she said. "Exactly what I was hoping to hear you say."

"You were?"

"Yes."

"Why's that?"

"Haley," said Miz Powell, "what I have wanted to tell you since the day we met in the stable, when you swore at me like a pirate, is . . . don't be afraid to become a woman."

I balanced my teacup on my leg and cocked my head at her, not sure if I'd heard her right.

"I didn't know I had a choice in the matter," I said.

"You don't," said Miz Powell. "Which is exactly my point."

"All right," I said. "I'm definitely not following you."

"Don't be afraid to be all the things that a woman can be," she said. "Because none of it means you can't be all the things you *want* to be. Now do you follow?"

"Sort of," I said.

"You can be a mother and still be Haley," she said. "You can cook dinner for your family and still be free. I'm not saying your life is going to be independent of the people involved in it. You have to make the right decisions. But you can have a baby and still be yourself. You can fulfill traditional roles if you want to, without letting them define you. Who you are will change when you have children, of course, but you could let it be an improvement, not a detraction."

"I don't mean to be rude, but how do you know all this?" I said. "You never did any of those things."

"No," she said. "What I have done is be a woman, with all my feminine qualities intact, in a world that was run completely by men. And you know something? They appreciated it. They didn't exactly move over and make room for me—I had to carve out my own space among them, but that was nothing different than any of them had had to do. That's something some women don't seem to understand. Nobody is accepted right away. *Everyone* has to prove themselves. The world will never make room for you—you have to make it yourself. You have to make your own place, and stick to it. And there is nothing weak whatever about those same feminine qualities, Haley. That's what I want you to recognize. They are not a liability. They are a strength."

"I sort of know that," I said.

"Deep down, you do," she said. "I know you do. But you've been fighting it. Yet there is a part of you that's been fascinated by it, also. Yes?"

I had to admit she had a point. Here at last was the guidebook I'd been looking for, the traveler's companion to the journey I was on.

"I've never known anyone like you," I said. "I wish I'd known you a lot sooner."

"You wouldn't have appreciated me if you had," she said. "The time wasn't right."

"Yeah, but how did you know it *was* right?"

"I came home for other reasons besides that of making your acquaintance, Haley," said Miz Powell, "though I must add that when I realized I could make some difference in your life, I grew rather excited. That's about the only legacy I can leave."

"What do you mean?" I asked.

"I have to show you something," she said. "Something rather difficult."

She got up from the couch with a slight effort and headed off to another part of the house. "Wait here," she commanded over her shoulder. Slowly she made her way up the stairs—I didn't dare even to consider giving her a hand—where I heard her rummaging around. A few minutes later she came back down, clutching something to her chest.

"Close your eyes," she said. I obeyed. She sat down, the weight of her scarcely depressing the springs in the couch, and put something in my lap.

"Open them," she said.

I did so and nearly screamed. There, sitting on my lap and staring up at me, was one of the most horrifying images I'd ever seen. A man and a woman, naked, stood near a tree. The woman was reaching toward the tree, as if to receive something from the creature that was wrapped around it—a woman with the body of a snake. You could see quite clearly where the woman's body stopped and the snake's started. I had never conceived of such an abomination. Worse than two-headed Siamese twins, more terrible than the most twisted Chernobyl-esque mutations. My stomach did somersaults as I stared at it. I had a hard time keeping my chicken soup down.

"Please take it away," I whimpered through clamped jaws.

"No," said Miz Powell. "It's going to stay right there on your lap."

I was being tested. I wasn't allowed to remove the picture—the old woman was doing this for a reason. All right. I closed my eyes and breathed deep.

"Open your eyes," said Miz Powell, "and look at it. Look."

"No."

"Do it."

Her hands were on my face, and gone was the trembling weakness that had been there just moments earlier. Now they were strong and hard, and one of them forced my face down while the other actually pulled my eyes open, tugging at the skin on my forehead until I had no choice but to look.

"Look and ask yourself, young woman," said Miz Powell. "What is it about this image that disturbs you so?"

"Snake," I croaked.

"Yes, indeed. A snake. And what else?"

"Woman," I said. I was suddenly reduced to monosyllables. "Woman snake."

"And there you have it," said Miz Powell. Her fingers burrowed into my forehead like drill bits. "Woman snake. But why should that bother you?" she asked. "Snakes are part of nature, are they not?"

"Please," I said.

"This bothers you," said Miz Powell, "because that woman is you, Haley Bombauer."

"No."

"Oh, yes. That woman is you, and your mother, and your grand-mother, and all of them before. And it's me. And Letty. You know us and you trust us. Yet why do you reject this simple truth? Why do you go on with this stupid stuntman fallacy, pretending you're someone else? And why do you hate snakes so much? What do they represent?"

I couldn't speak anymore. Tears had long been streaming down my cheeks, and I was choking back sobs.

"Snakes represent *you*," said Miz Powell. "They are your totem animal. They are your true self."

"Shut up!" I said.

"Say hello to Lilith, my dear, as conceived by Michelangelo on the ceiling of the Sistine Chapel," said Miz Powell. "Say hello to the oldest and most powerful demon of them all."

I grabbed the picture and threw it across the room as hard as I could, and the sound of the glass tinkling into a hundred pieces was a glorious one indeed. Then I got up and ran from the house—*we* got up, I should say, because even though I was scarcely into my first trimester, I was already cognizant of the little being growing inside me, and I knew that it was aware of me too, not as an individual but only aware of me as dimly as we ourselves are aware of the universe, and of all the strange things that exist in it, most of which we have not yet even begun to understand.

I was not a woman-snake. I was not this Lilith person. I was me, and I hated snakes. And at that moment, I hated Miz Powell.

Yet, I couldn't help asking myself as I ran along the road back home, why had something about it rung true? What about it made sense? Why did I know deep down that Miz Powell was right, just as she always was?

⑬

The Hardest Thing

Seven months later, I was out on the porch of the old Grunveldt house—now *my* house—swabbing away cobwebs with a mop. I had bought the place with my share of old Fireball's invention money, knowing that even though Mother and I seemed to be getting along better these days, I would throttle her if we lived together. I was getting too old to put up with her anymore.

When the Grunveldts were still alive and the house was for sale, there had been more than a few parties interested in buying it. But now that the family was gone, it was as if there was a force field around the place. The For Sale sign had disappeared while I was in the woods— probably stolen by vandals—and now no one wanted to come near it, except me.

The house had decomposed. Once it was a kingdom of cleanliness. Mrs. Grunveldt was of that generation of women who rarely stepped outside, who believed a woman's world was bounded to the north by her front porch and to the south by the kitchen step. Women like that took housecleaning seriously. She turned domesticity into an art form. My childhood memories of the Grunveldt house were of stepping onto wooden floors so slickly waxed that one sneeze would send you shooting backwards like a rocket. And if you happened to touch the always freshly scrubbed walls with a grubby hand, Mrs G. could identify and convict you by your fingerprints alone.

Maybe she found cleanliness cathartic. Or maybe—and this is more likely—she thought she could compensate for her abnormal child with a supernormally clean abode. These kinds of bargains are often made between mothers and the rest of the world, though the world isn't usually aware of it.

Now the house had fallen into disrepair. When I moved in, it had been just over a year since the Grunveldts died, but in that short time dust had fallen like snow over everything. Windows had been broken. Doors had warped. The forces of filth, kept at bay for so long, were dancing on Mrs. Grunveldt's grave.

Since the age of four or thereabouts, as soon as I was old enough to understand what gender I was, I had looked at women like Mrs. Grunveldt and my mother and shuddered at the fate that awaited me, a cursed girl. Housebound, driven to near madness by the confines of their existences, their only successes vicarious, through husband and male children. What of my poor mother, then? With no husband to be proud of, and no sons to beam upon, she resorted to the only form of child rearing she understood for girls: molding me in her image. Even as a tiny girl, I wasn't having any of it. And underneath the surface, beneath the still waters of that placid mind, she understood. I knew now as I had never known before that her frustrations were not at my recalcitrance but at her failure to recognize the dangers of her own life before it was too late. It would drive me mad, too, to see a daughter of mine figure out a way to be a woman *and* a person. I would probably think to myself, *Why doesn't she share the secret with me?*

Perhaps it wasn't too late for her, though. After all, it never really is too late for anything.

Cleaning the inside of the Grunveldt place had occupied a good portion of my first two trimesters, and allowed me to ignore the snow that had come early again this year. Frankie's spirit, mournful and starved for conversation, followed me through his former home as I went through the sweep-mop-dust phase, and then through the paint-everything-that-doesn't-move phase. I talked aloud to myself sometimes, to let him know I knew he was there, but I was not about to start humoring him unless he really started causing problems—throwing things around, et cetera. I didn't think he was going to be that kind of ghost. I didn't think he would turn out to be much of a ghost at all.

"Damn these spiderwebs," I said aloud, for his benefit. The mop made a gritty, ripping sound as it caught on the splinters on the underside of the porch roof.

Now, starting my third trimester, I was having to face up to the disheartening revelation that I wouldn't be able to do any more heavy work until the baby was born. For the second time in my life, I was "disabled." Not that being pregnant was turning out to be a bad thing— I was rather enjoying it. It was certainly better than having my leg in a cast. It was weird and fun and magical, in a way, and so far I hadn't suffered much. But heavy lifting or pushing could easily cause the placenta to dislodge from the wall of my uterus, and that would have been the end of the baby. And suddenly I wanted this baby more than I'd ever wanted anything in the world.

What about my theater? I heard Frankie's spirit demand. Hard to tell whether it was really him or only an echo of that old conversation that was still bouncing around the place.

"What theater, Frankie?" I asked.

The theater of the human spirit. The theater for the Indians. I want you to build it.

"Oh, Frankus," I said, "one bloody thing at a time, all right? I'm trying to accomplish something here."

Silence, though he was still there. He knew when he could push me and when he should leave me alone.

In the kitchen, hanging over the table, was a copy of the picture Miz Powell had shown me that traumatic day in her living room. I dusted this picture every day, whether it needed it or not. The snake, she'd explained, is the oldest symbol of feminine power in the world. It's not a *female* power—it's a *feminine* power. Miz Powell was very clear on this point, because men and women alike have feminine energies within them—as well as masculine ones. People were too obsessed with gender these days, she said. Really, there weren't nearly as many differences between us as we liked to pretend.

Who was this Lilith, anyway? Miz Powell, ever the walking mythological dictionary, was only too happy to explain. Lilith was an ancient figure, so old she had already been worshipped in half a dozen cultures by the time the New Testament was written. We know most about her from the ancient Hebrews—she was, in some versions of the story, Adam's first wife, before Eve.

Originally, according to Miz Powell, God had created Man and Woman as one being, an androgyne that was complete in itself. But an androgyne cannot reproduce with itself, and so they were split down the middle—one half being the man, Adam, and the other half being Lilith.

"And this, of course, led to the First Argument," Miz Powell said. "Because the two could not agree on who should dominate. Adam felt that he should be Lilith's superior, and Lilith felt quite the opposite. When he tried to force her to submit, she became angry, uttered a magic word, and flew into the air."

"What was the magic word?" I asked her.

"The true name of God," Miz Powell said.

"Which was?"

"Don't look at *me*," she said. "If I knew that, I would have flown away long ago."

"And then what happened to her?"

"According to myth, she kills human babies in their sleep," she told me. "The girls before the eighth day of life, the boys before the twentieth, which was when they used to circumcise them. Also, Hebrew parents used to warn their sons that when they masturbated, Lilith became pregnant from their seed and gave birth to demons."

"Lot more effective than the old hairy-palm rule," I said. "So you really think I'm like this...person?"

"Demon."

"Demon?"

"The *point*, my dear," said Miz Powell, "is that if the masculine and feminine halves would have accepted each other as equals, there never would have been any sort of disagreement at all, and we would be living in a world of perfect harmony. But for some reason, they couldn't do this. Later, God made Eve, and as she was made out of pure dust—Lilith being made out of filth and sediment—she was somehow more receptive to Adam's authority. When the masculine and feminine are integrated in a *person*," she said, looking directly at me, "conflict is removed, and great things can be achieved. But rare indeed is the individual who has that kind of courage. That is what I'm trying to tell you. That, and the fact that you have the same energy she has. The same spirit."

"I'm flattered," I said.

"Don't be," said Miz Powell. "Just understand. You must remember that every irrational fear has some basis in the unconscious. Perhaps it's just an ancient instinct that's more prevalent in some than in others. Or perhaps it's something else. A symbol, if you will. And snakes are positively *loaded* with metaphor and meaning."

"So Lilith was the snake in the garden of Eden?"

"Lilith has been many things, my dear," said Miz Powell. "There are goddesses similar to her in Hindu culture. The Israelites knew about her even when they were nothing more than a bunch of simple nomads, thousands of years ago. She is everywhere. She has a *job*."

"Which is?"

"She is that which does not surrender," said Miz Powell. "She is indomitable."

In other words, I thought, *she is Flash Jackson.*

.   .   .

It was directly as a result of this conversation that, several weeks later, at the end of my second trimester, I steeled myself, drove into town with Mother, and bought a snake. Just a little one, mind you—none of your Amazonian anacondas for me. I wanted my baby to live to a ripe old age, not to end up as a headline on a supermarket tabloid. He was only a milk snake, colored in brilliant reds and yellows and laced with black, no longer than my forearm when all stretched out. He was to be fed one baby mouse every other week, and he would live in an aquarium in my bedroom. This was how I was going to begin the process of overcoming my snake-o-phobia, or whatever the hell you call it.

(Note to self: Look up the name for fear of snakes. Write it on a piece of paper, chant the spell of getting rid of things. Burn it. Eat the ashes. Do this while holding the snake. That's the only sure way.)

"What are you going to name him?" Mother asked.

"Who?" I responded. "The snake or the baby?"

"The snake," she said.

"I'll have to think about it," I said. Naming something implied ownership, even more so than handing over the cash and taking it home. Sorry. Not "it." "He." Or possibly "she," since it was hard to tell with snakes.

"And as long as we're on the subject, what *are* you going to name the baby?" she asked. "There's only three months to go, you know."

"Oh really, Mother?" I said. "I had no idea."

"Don't get sarcastic. I was only asking."

"I haven't figured that out either. Furthest thing from my mind."

"Don't you think you ought to spend some time thinking about it?"

"Don't you think you ought to mind your own business?" I asked.

But I am getting ahead of myself. When I was around two months' pregnant, I had walked up the hill to the Shumachers', where Brother had been boarded. I stopped and chatted a while with Mrs. Shumacher and her daughters, but the conversation was awkward. *Did they know about Adam?* I wondered. No, it seemed that they were merely unsure of what to say to someone like me, someone who could take off and live in the woods like a mystic, someone who was, in their eyes, a witch. I was going to have to get used to this hesitation, even in people I'd known all my life. It was appropriate. A witch does not socialize readily. She must be treated with some degree of respect and standoffishness. My fuzzy scalp, which I didn't bother concealing, must also have shocked them—no sane woman would do such a thing. So, after several minutes of stilted conversation, I asked to pay up what I owed for Brother's feed and stable space, said I probably ought to get going, and asked casually, as a throwaway question, if Adam happened to be around, because there was something I wanted to ask him.

He was behind the barn. Every large dairy farm has a manure pit outside the milking area, which the droppings of the cows can be shoveled or sluiced into. It collects over the course of the year and makes excellent fertilizer, which can be sold, which is therefore as good as gold. Nothing is ever wasted on a farm. Every so often the pit has to be emptied, however, and this is not the most pleasant job in the world, as it entails standing in piles of old cow shit as deep as your hips.

This is where I found Adam now. He wore a pair of Wellingtons to protect his legs, and a handkerchief over his mouth. His shoulders and back gleamed with sweat as he shoveled it into a wheelbarrow, which he would then roll up a ramp and dump into another pile on the ground that was already chest-high. He didn't notice me. I watched him work for a while, gauging my feelings. Admiration of his strength. A warm memory of what had happened in the woods. Some sort of palpable connection, twanging between us like a rubber band, that meant he was the father of the child I was carrying.

"Adam," I said.

He stopped, turned, and looked at me. On his face I saw the same expression that had been there when I surprised him in the woods, chopping down the tree. Shock. Was I always destined to be surprising this man? Would he ever be glad to see me?

"Hello dere," he said.

"How's it going?"

He shrugged. "Pretty busy," he said.

"Yeah. I guess so."

I sat down on the edge of the pit, my legs dangling over. The smell of cow manure has never seemed unpleasant to me, though I prefer that of horses, which is sweeter. He leaned on his shovel and looked at my feet.

"You home now?" he asked.

"Yeah."

"You lost your hair?"

"I shaved it off," I said.

He nodded. He seemed to have difficulty meeting my gaze. *Is it going to be this way with everyone from now on?* I wondered. Adam looked around again, everywhere except at my eyes.

"Zo," he said. "What's new?" Without waiting for an answer, he starting filling the wheelbarrow again, the shovel rasping along the concrete floor of the pit. Farmers didn't leave much time for conversation while they worked. It interfered with the job at hand.

"Just came by to say hi," I told him.

"Yah," he said. "Everything all right?"

Now was my chance to tell him. I had already decided by then that I was going to keep the baby. I'd toyed with the notion of adoption only briefly, as a way of making the burden seem lighter. But there had never been any other reasonable course of action for me. It was the way things were supposed to be in my family. Our babies were not born just for the sake of having babies. They were born for a reason.

"I'm about nine weeks," I said.

He stopped working and looked up at me once more, this time meeting my eyes. I had shocked him again.

"Zo?" he said.

"Yeah."

He sighed. Then he threw the shovel away from him and kicked at a clod of manure.

"Shit," he said.

I didn't say anything.

"You're sure?"

"I'm sure," I said. "Of course I'm sure. I wouldn't be here if I wasn't."

Adam rolled his eyes and put one fist to his head, banging gently on his skull as if trying, belatedly, to knock some sense into himself. He climbed out of the pit and went to a hose, where he rinsed his head in cool water. Then he just stood there, hands on hips, looking out across the pastureland. In the distance, Mr. Shumacher could be seen heading toward the house, carrying a pickax.

"Adam?"

"What."

"It's okay if you don't want to talk. I really just came to get Brother," I said.

"In the barn," said Adam.

I got up and went into the barn, a knot in my stomach and another one in my throat. Brother whickered madly when he saw me, knocking at the door of his stall when his foreleg. We nosed each other for a brief moment, and then I gathered his tack and let him out, slipping a simple rope halter over his neck.

"At least *you're* glad to see me," I told him. I put his blanket and saddle on and slipped the bit in his mouth. The leather of the bridle was cracking—it hadn't been oiled in a long time. I would have to attend to that when I got home. I mounted him and we left the barn at a slow walk.

When I came out into the sunlight Adam was nowhere to be seen. I checked the manure pit again, but the shovel was still lying where he had thrown it. He was gone. Mr. Shumacher was closer now. I saw his arm rise and swoop lazily side to side. I waved back. I ought to have waited and said hello to him, but I couldn't have faced another Schumacher just then. So I pulled Brother's head around and heeled him once in the ribs, and we trotted down the driveway out to the road, where I urged him into a canter and got the hell away from there.

Miz Powell had come over to Mother's for tea that afternoon. This qualified as a Grand Event, in Mother's book; it was only the second time such a thing had happened, and so it merited the breaking out of the good china and the last of the ancient biscuits. Miz Powell had lost none of her Englishness. She still wore her white gloves and hat wherever she went, and she held her cup with pinky extended. Mother was exalted by her very presence.

When I told her what had happened—or had *not* happened— that afternoon, Miz Powell said: "What were you *hoping* he would say, dear?"

"He ought to have offered to do the decent thing," said Mother. "Marry her."

"Mother, for heaven's sake," I said. "I don't want to marry Adam. I just wanted to tell him. To be fair."

"Fair?" Mother cried. "After what he did to you? He ought to be ashamed of himself, taking advantage of a poor girl like that! It's practically rape!"

Miz Powell and I exchanged glances.

"It wasn't rape, Mother," I said. "I was as responsible as he was. I wanted it to happen."

Mother blushed from her forehead to her throat. She glared at me and tilted her head towards Miz Powell, as if to suggest that my sluttiness was a subject best not discussed in front of company. Miz Powell, of course, showed no signs of discomfort.

"It was a natural experience," she told Mother. "In every respect."

"I don't know what your father would say," Mother said. She had been told soon after my arrival that I was pregnant, and had accepted the news with only a little apprehension; in fact, she was delighted, as

I knew she would be. Mother responded rationally to almost nothing, but she was always predictable. Her reaction to my pregnancy was the least of my worries. The idea of having a baby around was exciting enough that it blotted out every other aspect of the situation. But here was a fresh opportunity for drama, and in front of Miz Powell, no less. It was too good for her to pass up. She pressed a napkin to her mouth and crinkled her eyes shut, squeezing out a few careful tears.

"Would you zip it?" I said. "Two weeks ago you were glad I was having a baby."

"He ought to do the right thing," Mother repeated into her napkin.

"The right thing," said Miz Powell, "is whatever Haley decides. Not Adam."

At that, they both looked at me, waiting. I cleared my throat.

"The hell with Adam," I said. "I'm going to buy the Grunveldt house and raise the baby on my own. With whoever's help," I added. "Whoever wants to help can help. And whoever doesn't want to help doesn't have to. It's mine. I can do it. Grandma did it. I can do it. It's our way. This is the way the women in our family do things."

"What do you think it will be, Haley?" asked Miz Powell. "Boy or girl?"

"A girl," I said. "Of course it's going to be a girl."

Mother cried anew. Miz Powell sat back and sipped her tea with satisfaction, evidently assured that all was right in the world. And I looked down at my belly, soon to be large again, and thought: *Who are you, anyway?*

"Tears of joy, my dear Mrs. Bombauer," Miz Powell said to Mother. "That's what you should be crying. Tears of joy. Your daughter has finally accepted the fact that she's a woman. And it's about bloody time, I should say."

For a witch to make it on her own in this modern world, she must go into business. And for that, she needs supplies. In my case, this meant herbs, and lots of them. While I was still able, I took off on Brother

and scoured the countryside, two big baskets hanging from the saddle. Fall had only just begun to arrive then, and plenty of herbs were
still in season. But I knew it was going to be another early winter,
and there was little time to waste.

I would have preferred to go somewhere else, but I had no choice
but to return to the general area where Grandma and I used to live,
because that was where the herbs were. Many grew here naturally, but
she had spent innumerable years quietly encouraging others to grow
which were not indigenous to our part of the world, but which did well
nonetheless. I don't know where Grandma would have gotten the first
generation of seeds—probably bartered for them with people who had
been dead several decades now, perhaps even centuries, traders who had
visited places she'd never seen. I stayed clear of the place where her
house once stood, and of the creek, and of my rock face and my oak
grove, but most of all I stayed away from the place where they had shot
Bear. Part of me couldn't stand to think of a being that immense and
powerful lying helplessly on the ground while they pumped hot lead
into him; another part was afraid I would go feral again, if given half
a chance. I had made another commitment now, another decision, and
no one was going to sway me from it—not even myself. The call of
the woods was strong in me, but the call of motherhood was stronger.

Yet the mother in me didn't trust the animal in me, not a bit—no
more than mothers in ancient times would have entrusted their children to the guardianship of wolves. I knew the woods was no place to
raise a child. The world existed for a reason, all of it, the muck and
decay and the violence and the noise and the pollution; and I existed
within it. It was no good pretending I didn't. I was needed. And my
child would be needed too.

Yet I would always come back to the forest. Grandma's garden
was the forest, and I knew it well enough to be sure of which herbs
grew best in full sunlight and well-drained areas, and which prospered
in soggy, marshy places. Lavender, parsley, basil, chives, chamomile,
garlic, St.-John's-wort, sweet flag: all these things, plus dozens of other,

lesser-known plants, I gathered in plenty and zipped up in plastic bags. With these, I could cure everything from acne to gunshot wounds. At the end of each day, I rode home and dumped the baskets on the floor of what had once been the Grunveldt living room, and was now going to be my laboratory and consulting room. After a week, I had enough material to last through winter and into spring, enough to treat a small town. The floor was ankle-deep in slippery plastic, the air fragrant with crushed leaves. I was nearly ready.

Not every herb dries well. Some must be used fresh. Others are only suitable in a tincture, and yet others are best used in poultices. There was always the problem of how to keep them in optimal condition, ready for instant use. I was lucky, because I had one thing that Grandma didn't have: a freezer. Everything that couldn't be dried or preserved in alcohol, I froze, in the hopes that they would still make a fine tea or poultice if ever they should be needed. Then I had Mother buy me three gallons of grain alcohol, and in dozens of old Mason jars I drowned the rest in booze, sealed them up, and stored them in the basement, which offered the necessary cool and dark to keep them as long as possible.

Then, with snow promised by Thanksgiving, I hung a bundle of agrimony on the porch as a sign that I was open for business. I expected it would be a while before those folks who had entrusted Grandma with their health would find their way to my door. Old habits die hard. Until they did, I wouldn't have much money. I'd spent most of what I had on the house, so I prepared myself for a lean winter.

I had no intention of depending on anyone. Mother had given me some furniture, Miz Powell a teapot and some dishes that had belonged to her late sister. I received nothing from the Schumachers. I hadn't seen them since my last visit to the farm. I didn't even know if they knew I was pregnant, and if so, by whom. That was all right—they would find out soon enough, without any assistance from me. That was the small-town telegraph, the gossip chain. It was going to be having a field day with me.

With the help of some hired men, I moved my belongings from my old bedroom to my new one next door, a hundred yards away. The Grunveldt house was large and had come cheap, but it was empty and cold; there was a rickety furnace in the basement, but I was going to resist using it for as long as I could, because of the cost of fuel. My main source of heat was a massive cast-iron stove in the kitchen— wood, after all, was free.

The stomp of my woolen-socked feet echoed oddly on the bare floors and walls. Frankie, in phantasmic form, continued to follow me from room to room, like a puppy. I could feel him just behind me, but he hadn't mastered the trick of materialization; even if I whipped around fast, I never was able to catch him.

"What is it, Franks?" I asked one day. "What's the matter, buddy?"

My theater.

"Yeah, so you said. What is it about this theater, anyway? Why is it so important?"

Voices.

"Whose voices?"

Everyone's. The Indians. Me.

"Oh yeah," I said. "That. Look, Franks, what exactly do you want me to do about it? I'm having a baby here. I'm trying to pull things together so this kid has some kind of a life. I don't have time to go building theaters. Understand?"

I know.

"But maybe later."

I had never known anyone so persistent that they couldn't give up on something even after they were dead. I wondered how on earth I would ever appease Frankie on that count. What good would a theater do out here, in the middle of nowhere? No one would ever come to it. Even if I was able to put one together, say in the Grunveldt's barn or something, it would just stagnate and rot. And I didn't know the first thing about theaters anyway. I had never even been to one, unless the high school productions in the gym counted. Which I was pretty sure they didn't.

Yet there was something about the idea that I also liked. It was pure Frank through and through, all crazy and no sense. But maybe it only seemed crazy because no one had done it yet. There was something noble about its futility. The seed of it, the core idea, was what was truly important. Frankie was right on one count—there were people in the world who needed help getting their voices back. A lot of people. Maybe it was something I could think about in the future, after the baby was born and things were a little more stable. If they ever were going to be stable, that is...which seemed to me, at the time, to be a pretty big if.

"Franks?"

Nothing.

"How much longer are you going to stick around?"

I don't know.

"Try not to spook me too much, all right?"

If spirits could smile, this one did. The old Franks was still there, though not quite as loopy. I guessed whatever had ailed him in life, his schizophrenia and his Fanex problem, was gone now; but he was still essentially Frankie, whatever that meant. That part was never going to change.

I sent away for catalogues of baby things and paged through them, disbelieving the prices. Almost everything was out of my range. My child was not going to have the Busy Hands Play Table or the Roll-n-Ride Fire Engine. Neither would it know the pleasures of the Brain Teether or Baby's First Cell Phone. It would play with the same dolls I had played with as a girl, and it would learn to love the woods as I had loved them, as soon as it could walk. That would have to be enough.

Neither, it appeared, would my baby have a father. It would have me, and my mother, and Miz Powell, for as long as she was around. That, too, would have to be enough.

.   .   .

In the first week of December, when the third storm of the season had come and gone, there came a hesitant tapping at my front door. I opened it to see Chester Burgess, hunting cap in hand, a light dusting of snow on his shoulders.

"Howdy, Chester," I said. "Come on in."

"Thanks," he said. He stepped inside and stood in the vestibule, smelling of cold, kicking the snow from his boots. I helped him out of his coat, trying to hide my excitement at having my first customer. I'd set up two chairs and a table in the consulting room, and I offered him a seat now, sitting down across from him.

"Early snow, eh?" he grumbled.

"Yeah. How's things?" I asked.

He cleared his throat, looking embarrassed, scanning the bare room meanwhile. I didn't bother apologizing for the lack of furniture.

"I just come by t'ask if there would be anything else needed of me," he said. "I was going t'drop off another box last week but the missus said I oughta check in first, see if it was still needed. Word is," he said, dropping his voice, "she ain't around anymore. Herself, I mean."

"She's, ah, moved on," I said, knowing he meant Grandma. "I don't think she'll be back."

"Right," he said. "So she don't need anymore—"

"There's nothing else you need to do, Chester," I said. "You've paid in full. I know she appreciated everything you did for her."

Chester sat back gingerly in his chair, still holding his cap, looking neither relieved nor displeased.

"Right," he said. He made no move to leave.

"Was there anything else? Anything troubling you?"

"Um," he said.

I looked him over quickly with a critical eye. There was something, all right—I could tell by the way he was sitting.

"You peeing a lot, by any chance?" I asked.

He breathed a sigh of relief, as if he was glad he didn't have to say it himself. "Lord, Haley," he said, "it's getting' so bad, I'm afeared to go to sleep at night, lest I wet the bed. Ten or fifteen times a day, seems like. And nothin' to help it."

"Painful, too?"

"Oh, is it ever!"

I nodded. "You haven't been to a doctor."

He colored. "Heck," he mumbled. "Ain't got any insurance. No way to pay for a doctor."

"Give me your hands," I said.

He stuck his reddened and callused meat-hooks over the table, and I took them in my hands and held them with eyes shut. I only needed a moment, but I took a little longer. I didn't want to appear unprofessional.

"Stick out your tongue," I commanded.

He did. I looked at it carefully.

"It's your prostate," I said. "It's enlarged, and it's pressing on your bladder. Your urethra's affected, too. Pretty common in men your age. How old are you, Chester?"

"Sixty," he said.

"I can make the swelling go down," I said. "Eventually you're going to have to get it looked at. But for now, I can give you some things to take that will help you. All right?"

Chester looked almost happy. "Right," he said.

"Wait here," I said.

I went into the basement and got some dried horsetail, enough for a few months. I added a jar of tincture of buchu, rare and almost impossible to grow in this climate—one of the few herbs that actually required attention to cultivate. I put it all in a plastic shopping bag and came back upstairs. Chester was standing by the door, his eyes wide.

"What's the matter?" I asked.

"I heard somethin'," he said. "Somethin' weird."

"It's an old house, Chester," I said. "I hear things all the time."

"Yeah, but I heard me a voice," he said.

"Your imagination," I said, knowing full well it wasn't. "Come sit down again."

Chester came, reluctantly. I emptied the shopping bag on the table and spread everything out.

"Take this stuff and make a tea out of it, three times a day," I said, indicating the horsetail. "Before you drink it, add a few drops of the stuff in this jar here. It's got alcohol in it, so be careful."

"That's it?"

"That's it."

"What do I owe ye?"

"Tell you what," I said. "I need some wood. I'm about out and this house is freezing. How would half a cord sound?"

"That's nothin'," he said. "I can have it here by tomorry."

"All right, then," I said. "One other thing, Chester."

"Yeah?"

"Tell your friends about me. Let everyone know I'm open for business."

When he was gone, I went and got a bowl from the kitchen and filled it with water. I lit a candle and set it up on the table. Then I sat down and stared into the water. Within moments I had the image I was looking for: Frankie's face.

"Now you listen to me," I said. "If you scare one more of my customers I will never, ever speak to you again. I'll trap your spirit in a jar and bury it, and you're going to be stuck there forever. Understand? I won't be pushed around like this, Frankie. Not for a second."

The Frankie in the bowl wasn't the real Frankie, or even the real Frankie's spirit. It was more of a representation, but I knew he was hearing me. The face in the water, as still as a photograph, looked back at me calmly. He seemed more relaxed now that he was dead. Passing on had done him wonders. Also, I had no idea how to trap someone's spirit in a jar, but I was hoping he didn't know that.

"Put the candle out if you can hear me," I said.

The candle sputtered out.

"Right," I said. "Just so we understand each other."

My next customer came the following day. There was that same hesitant rap on the door, and when I waddled downstairs and opened it, there was none other than Mr. Shumacher.

"Well," I said, my heart stopping at the sight of my unborn child's grandfather. "What a nice surprise."

"Haley!" he said. "I heard you was liffink here now. Can I come in?"

"Please," I said. Chester had delivered the wood early that morning, before I was even awake, but the stove hadn't had time to heat the house yet and I was wearing about three layers of clothes, which hid the size of my belly. There was no denying now that I was large. I hoped Mr. Shumacher would simply think I was still fat. Yet he made no mention of my belly, or of Adam. It was as if he had just stopped by to say hello.

"You take over from your grandmudder, yah?" he asked, merrily stomping his feet on the welcome mat and taking off his coat. "Dat's goot. Family tradition."

"That's about the size of it," I said. I sat him down at the table.

"Ve heffent seen you in a vile," he said accusingly. "You hidink?"

My God, I thought, *is it possible he doesn't know? Has the telegraph broken down?*

"I've just been busy," I said.

"Yah, efferyone's busy dese days," he said affably. "Vell, I tell you, Haley. I heff a kalt."

He didn't know. He really didn't.

"A cold, huh? How long you had it?" I asked.

"T'ree days. Most times, I get sick, I eat soup, I get better. Not dis time. I don't know what's going on. I'm neffer dis sick."

"Fever?"

"Yah."

"I don't have to ask about the runny nose. I can see that for myself. Headaches?"

"Naw," he said.

"Throwing up?"

"Naw."

"Diarrhea?"

"Aw, vell," he said, looking embarrassed.

"Give me your hands," I said.

Mr. Shumacher's hands were the largest I had ever seen—he could have held a basketball like an egg. I closed my eyes and felt the blood pulsing through him, and I thought to myself: *Oh, shit.*

"Is there ever blood in the toilet?" I asked. "After you go?"

His eyes widened, and his hearty demeanor changed. "How you know det?" he asked meekly.

I didn't answer. "You've had this cold longer than three days," I said. "Right?"

"Vell," he said, "I didn't t'ink it vas such a big—"

"Tell the truth," I said. "It's very important that you tell me everything. How long have you been sick?"

He looked down at the table.

"A mont'," he said.

"Right," I said. "Listen. I don't want to scare you, but you need to go to a doctor. Today. All right?"

"But, Haley," he said. "I come to you because—"

"Mr. Schumacher," I said gently, "I can't help you. This is beyond what I can do. You need a doctor."

It's depressing to see a man that big crumple in his chair, with the look of defeat in his face even before the battle has begun. He sagged, letting his hands fall back into his lap.

"I kent be sick," he said. "Not dat sick. I heff no time."

"You have Adam to help you," I said. "And the other boys aren't far off, in case it turns out to be something serious." The *in case* was for his benefit—it *was* serious, very serious. And it was the first time I had said Adam's name out loud since the day I told Mother and Miz Powell I was going to raise the baby on my own. It fell out of my mouth like a stone and sat there between us on the table. At least, it seemed that obvious to me. But Mr. Schumacher didn't notice it. He had heard nothing.

"Haley," he said. "Vat is it?"

"It's your colon," I said. "There's something wrong with it. It may not be all that bad. But it is important that you have a doctor check you out. It's up to you how far you let it go."

"Ach, mein Gott," he said. "Em I dyink?"

"We're all dying, Mr. Schumacher," I said. "It's the bargain we made when we agreed to be born."

His large, pale eyes watered briefly, and we looked at each other for a long time. I had known this man all my life, and I loved him as one loves a neighbor who time after time has bent over backwards to help out, often without being asked. When my father died, Mr. Schumacher had mowed our lawn every week for four years, and never accepted anything for it except a cup of his beloved coffee. The only reason he stopped was because I finally grew old enough to do it myself.

"Yah," he said. "But mebbe dis iss not de big one."

"It doesn't have to be," I said. "Not if you go into town, today, and see the doctor."

"All right," he said. "I'm goink. Vat do I owe you?"

"Nothing," I said. "I didn't do anything."

He brushed that away briskly, as if he would have none of it. "No, really," he said. "Tell me."

"Nothing, Mr. Schumacher."

He sighed. "All right," he said.

I knew that tomorrow I would wake up and find something on my porch—a frozen turkey, or a quarter of beef, or something like that. People still did things like that around here. It was one of the reasons I would never leave; I loved this kind of give-and-take of vital sustenance. But he would give me my dignity for now, and go his way as if he would give me nothing else.

Throughout that winter, Miz Powell took to coming over to Mother's for tea more and more, though she was weak and getting weaker. Pure old age, she said, and nothing more. It saddened me to see this paragon of strength slowly withering away before my eyes, but I was careful to hide it from her. The journey was too hard for her to make alone in the snow now, much to her frustration, so Mother would go and pick her up in the car. Often as not I would join them; then the three of us would sit, complicit in our various secrets, enjoying our sisterhood. Mostly, I let the two of them do the talking. I sat and contemplated my belly, awaiting the arrival of the baby.

"You never told the Schumachers I was pregnant?" I asked Mother one day.

"I haven't seen the Schumachers in ages," she said.

"Isn't that kind of unusual?"

"Why? It's not like I go over there every day."

"Yeah, but...Mr. Schumacher was over, and he didn't seem to know anything."

"I'm sure he doesn't," Mother said. Miz Powell nodded.

"Excuse me," I said, "but I find that kind of hard to believe. And I can't believe his wife doesn't know, either. You know the way people talk around here."

"Well, Haley, *I* haven't been talking," Mother said.

"Nor have I," said Miz Powell.

"It's *possible* that his wife knows and hasn't told him," said Mother. "Though I don't know why she wouldn't. And I don't know for sure. I'm guessing."

"I see," I said.

"Perhaps she's waiting to see what you're going to do," said Miz Powell.

"What *I'm* going to do? I'm going to have a baby. What does she think I'm going to do?"

"Elizabeth means," said Mother, "that Mrs. Schumacher is leaving it up to you to tell people. She's not going around doing it for you. Which I think is very good of her."

"As do I," said Miz Powell.

"So she does know," I said. "I wonder who told her?"

Both Mother and Miz Powell looked at the floor. I decided to let it go for now. For once, I was relieved someone had taken on something on my behalf. That was one scene I'd be spared.

"Adam got scared when I told him," I said. "He walked away from me. He's probably hoping the whole problem will just disappear."

"Not Adam," said Mother.

"Hard to believe anyone would be that irresponsible," said Miz Powell.

"Oh, please," I said, disgusted at their naïveté.

We celebrated Christmas together at our house, as one family. When Miz Powell tired before it was even time for dinner, she went upstairs and took a nap in one of the unused bedrooms. An hour later, I heard her calling me, and I went up to see what she wanted.

"I can't sit up," she said. She was lying flat on her back on the bed. "Can you help me?"

I put one hand under her and lifted her up with no more effort than if I was batting a balloon. "You all right, Miz Powell?" I asked.

"I'm so damned weak," she said. "I can't understand it. I've never been this weak before."

"I can help you, if you want," I said. "I can give you something to make you stronger."

She jerked her hand away from me. "Stop it," she said. "I'm not a child."

"Sorry," I said.

"I'm old, Haley," she said. "And that's all. So don't go getting any ideas."

"Ideas about what?"

"About taking care of me," she said irritably. "I don't want it and I don't need it."

But soon it became obvious that it was easier for Miz Powell to stay at Mother's than on her own, and she began to go home only occasionally, to get fresh clothes and make sure the house wasn't falling apart in her absence. She and Mother seemed to tolerate each other surprisingly well. They were the last two I would have figured to get along so nicely, but then I realized they were coming together over something common: me and the baby.

"Your mother seems to be waking up from a long slumber," Miz Powell confided in me one day. "We've had some interesting conversations about her childhood."

"I bet," I said.

"It hasn't been easy for her, you know," she told me. "But then, you know all about that."

"It's only been as difficult as she's made it," I said. "It was her idea to close down for so long. I was afraid she'd forgotten everything she learned from Grandma by now."

"I don't think she's forgotten anything," Miz Powell said. "I think it's just been a question of her willingness to use it."

"And?"

"Well, with this baby coming, she seems to have a new fire burning inside her," said Miz Powell. "We're so excited, Haley. Are you sure it's going to be a girl?"

"Of course it'll be a girl," I said. "We only have girls in this family. That's the way it's always been."

"Yes," said Miz Powell, "but then there's never been anyone quite like you in the family before, either."

"Thanks," I said. "I think."

"It *is* a compliment, Haley dear," she told me. "You've been awaited for a long time. You're going to fulfill a much-needed role."

This was not the first time she'd said that to me, but I never knew how to take it. Was I, in fact, the one to replace Grandma? Was that why she had disappeared? Words are nothing—they cease to have meaning when repeated too often. Some things it was better not to talk about. It was better just to let them happen, neither provoking nor being provoked. I was already doing things that I'd sworn earlier I would never do, womanly things—having a baby being the prime example. When I was little, I'd believed I had the choice of being a man or a woman when I grew up, and part of me still felt that way. Yet I was astonished to see myself choosing the role of a woman. Two years ago, I never would have done such a thing.

Mother hired a midwife to come and check up on me as I came closer to full term. She was a lithe, dark woman named Lydia, who wore a plain cloth wrapped around her head as she examined my cervix and pronounced it slightly dilated. It would only be a matter of days now, perhaps only hours. I insisted on being left on my own in my house until the time came, mostly because I couldn't stand them fussing over me. Yet it was nearly impossible for me to move, and so when there came a knock at the door one day in early spring, it was a struggle for me to get to the door.

When I opened it, there was Adam.

"Oh, for Christ's sake," I said. "Your timing is impeccable."

His eyes bugged out at the size of me. Gone was the willowy girl with the shaven head. I was back to my old girth, a house again—ankles and legs swollen, belly massive, my face puffed up with the water retained in my tissues.

"Hi, Haley," he said. "Can I come in?"

I stepped well aside to make room for him, but he brushed against my belly anyway as he came through the door. I felt nothing at his touch, not a twinge. There was no electricity. I didn't even offer him a seat.

"Hi," he said.

"You said that," I said.

"I, uh…came to tell you thanks for saving my fadder's life," he said. "He finally went to the doctor, and you were right. It was his colon. There was something growing in there. But they took it out, and they say he's going to be all right. You caught it in time. Zo, thanks."

"You're welcome," I said.

"Zo," he said.

I waited.

"Dere's something else," he said. "I, ah…"

I kept waiting.

"I'm not very proud of the way I've been," he said. "When that happened in the woods wid us, I didn't know what to tink about it. It chust happened, like. Den, you came and told me you were pregnant. And…I got scared. I admit it."

"Okay," I said.

"It wasn't the right thing to do," he said.

He looked around at the bare room. I could tell he was appalled at the lack of comfort there. To someone like him, who had never lived in the woods, he wouldn't have known that I didn't need a lot of extras. All I needed was me.

"Not the right thing to do," he repeated.

"Adam," I said, "what do you want?"

"I want to help," he said.

"Help how?"

"Well…" He gestured around us. "Look at this. I feel bad you don't have nottink. You shouldn't live like this."

"I'm fine," I said.

"Yeah, but…de baby should have things too. Nice things. It should be warm, for one ting. You don't run the furnace?"

"I get along well enough with the stove," I said, though in truth I'd been going over to Mother's all winter just to get warm.

"Look," he said. "I don't ask any special favors. I don't know what you think of me, but I know what I think of you. You deserve to have the things you need. I want to take responsibility."

If he'd said that with a touch of pride, with even a slight puffing of the chest—as if to say, *Look how wonderful I am for being accountable for my actions*—I would have thrown him out on his ass, then and there. But that wasn't Adam's way. He meant what he was saying.

"I guess you don't want to get married, after the way I been," he said.

"You didn't ask me to get married."

"Do you want to?"

"No."

"Okay," he said. "Me neither, not really."

"Glad that's out in the open," I said.

"But I do want to be a fadder."

"I see," I said.

"I mean, dis baby...every baby needs a fadder. I didn't have very good parents. That's why Mutti and Fatti took me in. So I tink every baby should have good parents. And not just one. Two is better."

"You saying you want to live together?"

"I'm saying," he said, "you can ask me to do anything you want, and I'll do it."

"Anything."

"Yah. Anything."

"All right," I said. "Put your hands on my belly."

Adam's eyes widened in surprise. I lifted up the three sweaters I was wearing and showed him my stomach, stretch marks and all.

"Touch it," I said.

Adam extended one finger and poked it gently.

"Come on," I said. "Like you mean it."

He rested his palm on my stomach and left it there, rough and warm. I put my hand on top of his and pressed it in deeper. The baby had been active for a while now, and at our combined touch it began to do cartwheels inside. Adam was startled. He almost jerked his hand away, but I held him there until he relaxed.

"Wow," he said. "Dat's amazink."

"That's what we made," I said. "That's you and me in there, for whatever it's worth."

A smile crept across his face.

"Don't you get smug," I said. "Don't you dare get smug, or I swear to God I'll kick your ass."

"I want to be dere," he said. "Can I?"

"When I give birth?"

He nodded.

"You haven't earned it," I said. "You know that. You have to earn something like that. I'll call you afterwards and tell you how it went."

His face fell, but he seemed to accept it. He knew I was right. But, seeing how disappointed he was, I softened. He had finally come forward, after all. He had finally accepted his role in all this.

"Tell you what," I said. "You can wait outside, and you can come in as soon as it's over. All right?"

His spirits rose again. "Yah," he said. "Dat would be great."

"Okay," I said.

"Zo," he said. "When's it going to be?"

At that moment I felt a sudden stirring inside, and something deep within me popped. A great gush of water hit the floor between my feet and spread out like a small lake.

"Looks like right now," I said calmly. "You want to walk me over to my mother's, please?"

I have done some hard things in my life. I've survived on my own in the wilderness, I've ridden bareback all day, I've communicated with the dead. But nothing could have prepared me for how difficult it was to have a baby.

It was a long labor, this being my first child—eighteen hours from start to finish. I had decided early on that I was going to have the baby at home, with Mother, Miz Powell, and Lydia to assist me. Adam was relegated to the hallway outside the bedroom, where he paced incessantly until I yelled at him to quit it because I could feel the creak of every floorboard. I didn't want drugs and I didn't want a doctor—doctors were for people like Mr. Schumacher, who was sick, but not for people like me, who was healthy. Pregnancy is not an illness. It is, in the truest sense of the word, a labor, and the final hours of those nine months are the hardest labor of all.

I pushed until every muscle burned and my throat was parched. Lydia gave me ice chips to suck on. She refused to give me water, which was right, and when I called her a fucking bitch she knew it was the pain talking, not me. I called Miz Powell a bitch too. I called Adam a faggot Nazi lover, or something equally nonsensical. I insulted the entire world's mother. I pushed until my hips felt like they were dislocated. I pushed until endorphins mercifully flooded my body, so that I didn't feel it when my perineum tore and the baby came out; I didn't feel a thing, not even when Lydia was stitching me up afterwards and Mother was toweling the baby off. I faded in and out of consciousness then, and saw faces floating before me that I knew weren't really there: Grandmother, my father, Frankie.

Grandma said nothing. She only looked on in approval.

My father was beaming. He said, or I thought I heard him say, that he was sorry he'd had to leave me so young. *It had been an accident,* he said. *It wasn't supposed to be that way.* But he was all right now, and so was I. I would not be joining him today.

And Frankie smiled too, excited because everyone else was excited.

"Franks," I muttered. "You're the only one I didn't insult. I left you out."

"What is she saying?" Mother asked Miz Powell.

"Something about trout," Miz Powell said.

"Show her the baby," said Lydia. "She's ready now."

"Here you go, darling daughter," said Mother. "I am so proud of you."

"What is it?" yelled Adam, from the hallway.

"It's a girl," I mumbled.

Mother and Miz Powell exchanged glances, amused.

"Sure about that?" said Lydia. "Look again."

I was too weak to pull back the blankets myself, so Miz Powell did it for me.

"There he is," she said. "Perfect in every way."

"What is it?" I asked, because my brain wasn't believing what my eyes were telling me

"A boy!" Mother and Miz Powell said, in unison.

I had to smile, in spite of my exhaustion. I'll say one thing about my life—it's always been full of surprises. I was so tired I was cross-eyed. Lydia helped me pull my gown aside and guided the baby to my breast. Pinched monkey face, two bootblack eyes—that was all I could make out. If the rumors were true, I had a son.

"Wow, buddy," I whispered to him. "Are you ever going to make things interesting around here."